4

HACKNEY LIBRARY SERVICES

D1513545

FEB 2014

⊖ Hackney

HELLBENT

ALSO BY CHERIE PRIEST AND AVAILABLE
FROM TITAN BOOKS:

THE CHESHIRE RED REPORTS
Bloodshot

COMING SOON:

EDEN MOORE
Four and Twenty Blackbirds
Wings to the Kingdom
Not Flesh Nor Feathers

CHERIE
PRIEST

TITAN BOOKS

Hellbent
Print edition ISBN: 9780857686466
E-book edition ISBN: 9780857689634

Published by Titan Books
A division of Titan Publishing Group
144 Southwark Street
London
SE1 0UP

First edition September 2011

1 3 5 7 9 10 8 6 4 2

Hellbent is a work of fiction. Names, characters, places, and
incidents either are the product of the author's imagination
or are used fictitiously. Any resemblance to actual persons,
living or dead, events, or locales is entirely coincidental.

This edition published by arrangement with Del Rey,
an imprint of The Random House Publishing Group,
a division of Random House, Inc., New York.

www.titanbooks.com

Book design by Susan Turner

Did you enjoy this book? We love to hear from our readers.
Please email us at readerfeedback@titanemail.com or write
to us at Reader Feedback at the above address.

To receive advance information, news, competitions,
and exclusive offers online, please sign up for the Titan
newsletter on our website: www.titanbooks.com

A CIP catalogue record for this title is available from the British Library.

Printed and bound in Great Britain by CPI Group UK Ltd.

ACKNOWLEDGMENTS

It takes a village to make a book, and this one has a whole host of people to thank for its existence. First, to the usual suspects: my outstanding editor Anne Groell, who has not yet pushed me off a cliff (a testament to her everlasting patience, to be sure); her assistant David Pomerico, who graciously fields all my dumb questions; Bantam publicist Greg Kubie, who has become legend around my household for his common-sense approach to pretty much everything; my stupendous agent, Jennifer Jackson, who brought us all together in the first place; and to my husband Aric, who is still not too sure about this whole vampire thing, but is along for the ride.

Continued thanks must flow in the direction of the folks at Subterranean Press (Bill! Yanni!) for keeping me fed during the lean times, and keeping me company when I'm in Michigan. Thanks also to all the helpful peeps in the secret digital clubhouse, for the advice and sounding board, and for not throwing me out for being a pretty-pretty princess. Likewise, a million thanks to Colleen Mondor and Paul Goat Allen, who always seem to "get" it.

Thanks to Team Seattle and all its affiliates, scattered across the country though we are these days. In particular, thanks to Kat Richardson for the fish sammiches; Ellen Milne and Suezie Hagy for the surprise snacks and the cat-sitting services; Greg

Wild-Smith for shepherding me around SF and for keeping my website alive despite my best efforts to slay it dead.

Speaking of Seattle and its support network, permanent thanks go to Duane Wilkins for managing all the signed stuff and shipping over at the University Book Store; and to Vlad and Steve over at Third Place for always throwing a hell of an event.

HELLBENT

1

It sounded like a good idea at the time, which is probably going to be on my tombstone—along with a catty footnote about poor impulse control. But when Horace Bishop called me, practically *breathless* with delight and greed, telling me he was in Portland so we should get together and have a drink or something, I said okay, even though I probably should've said "I'd sooner wear plaid."

I don't wear plaid. Ever.

I don't wear orange, either—not that there's anything inherently wrong with it. Really, it's more of a coloring thing. I'm a solid winter—blue-black hair and so fair I'm practically translucent; it comes with being undead. Orange always makes me look like I'm having liver problems, so I skip it—just like deep down I suspected I ought to skip that date with

Horace, but what was I going to do? He already knew where I lived (roughly), and he already knew my price scale (more or less), and he was practically my agent. Or my pimp.

Anyway, Horace was *vibrating*—talking so fast I could hardly understand him. And what was he doing on the West Coast? He promised to tell me in person, and since he was flying back to New York from the Seattle-Tacoma airport, it wasn't terribly far out of his way to bounce into town for a conspiratorial adult beverage.

I waited for him at a bar on Capitol Hill. I don't live in that neighborhood anymore, but that's the point. He knows I live in Seattle, but the less specific his knowledge is, the happier I am. The truth is, I *kind of* trust him. I mean, if I were wounded and bloody and practically dying in New York City and I had no place else to go, I could probably fling myself onto his couch and generally assume that he wouldn't stake me in my sleep. After all, I've earned him a metric assload of money over the years. And money has to mean something, doesn't it?

Yes, I totally laughed a little, just now.

I know good and well he might sell me out for the next best offer that presented itself, but I'd like to think he'd hesitate. Just for a second or two, if for no other reason than the fact that I'm very, very good at my job—and that I'm excessively vindictive. Even if he could reliably replace me, he couldn't assume I wouldn't track him down later and peel his toenails off.

Maybe I'd better give you some context for this contentious relationship, before you start thinking I'm completely unhinged for hanging out with this asshole.

Horace is a director of acquisitions for a prominent NYC auction house that will go unnamed here, for the sake of discretion. Basically, it's his job to scout for expensive objects for museums, private collectors, and other assorted people and institutions with more money than common sense. He deals in everything from paintings to gemstones, archaeological finds to vintage paperwork. And sometimes, his clients want a piece that is not, shall we say, strictly for sale. But for the right price, Horace will find it anyway, and he'll acquire it, and he'll pass it along. Usually, this process requires me—somewhere right in the middle, doing all the dirty work and collecting a hefty finder's fee.

So you can see where I get off calling him my agent. Or pimp.

I'm a thief, though I shine it up with an assortment of euphemisms. I'm in antiquities acquisitions. I'm a collection consultant. I'm in the security analysis business. But the bottom line is that I freelance, and if you have to ask how much I charge, you can't afford me.

Horace can afford me, and he pays up front in cash—or after the job, depending on the circumstances. He's one of the only people on earth who gets away with paying me on delivery. We've built up some trust on that front, at least. It's a sacred deal between us: I always produce, and he always pays. We have yet to let each other down, and I know of few married couples who could say the same.

So you see, it's not like we *hate* each other. It's like . . . our love is very *specific*. And limited. And confrontational.

Even so, I'll confess to feeling a tiny thrill of novelty at the prospect of setting eyes on him again. It'd been several years since we'd been in the same room, due to nothing more enormous than the physical distance between us—though it also serves to keep both of our asses covered from a plausible deniability standpoint. If something ever happens and he's caught, or (God forbid) I'm caught, there's virtually no physical evidence to tie us to each other.

This imparted a slightly illicit feel to the meeting.

And anyway, hell. He'd be more normal company than I'd been enjoying for the previous few months. If you're familiar with my previous adventure, then you already know some of my story. But in case you aren't, here are the CliffsNotes.

One: I'm a vampire. In the words of the immortal Bauhaus (you see what I did there?) *"Undead undead undead."* I don't turn into anything cool (or anything uncool either, for that matter), I don't fly, and I don't have a funny accent. I do drink blood, move really fast, look really pale, and have permanently dilated pupils— which makes me look a little like one of those creepy paintings of big-eyed kids from the seventies.

Two: I'm often mistaken for a man. Not because I'm particularly dude-like, but because international intelligence officials find it difficult to believe that a thief as accomplished and sneaky as yours truly could possibly be a woman. Far be it from me to remove any heads from asses on this point.

Three: I live in downtown Seattle, in the old quarter called Pioneer Square. Which is a fancy way of saying I live in the decrepit industrial ghetto, except that's not really fair. It's the kind of place where you can go a couple of blocks in any direction and land in a different neighborhood entirely—a tourist district waning out near Elliott Bay, the old merchant and fishing district on the port end of the coastline, or of course the blocks of decaying warehouses and factories that haven't seen any action since the Depression.

Four: I used to have a warehouse in this same quarter where I stashed all my orphaned goodies, collected over the years. It got raided by the feds. So I abandoned it and bought another one, about six blocks away because I'm a creature of habit. This new base of operations is much nicer than the old one; I renovated it from top to bottom before giving up on my condo (which was also raided—long story, see previous adventure) and moving into one of the top-floor lofts.

Five: The other two top-floor lofts are occupied by other

people. On one corner I have Pepper and Domino, last name unimportant since I don't think they've ever told me what it is. Domino is a fourteen-year-old jackass who drives me up a god-damn wall, but his little sister Pepper is about eight years old and as cute as a bunny in a sweater. They're sort of my pet people. This is to say, they squatted at my other warehouse so long, I eventually figured out that I'd inadvertently adopted them. At the other corner of the floor lives Ian Stott, who serves as a buffer between me and the kids. He's a vampire, too, and he's blind. He's also preposterously good looking, and we have a very awkward but not entirely unpleasant relationship. We're friends who make out every now and again. And now he lives with me.

I didn't plan this family-style arrangement. I didn't even *want* it, but things just happened this way and then I didn't know what to do, so I ran with it. I fear change. But it turns out that I'm not quite as good at saying no as I've always considered myself to be.

Besides, Ian used to have a ghoul who helped him find his way around—I jokingly referred to him as the "Seeing Eye ghoul"— but then he got killed, and it wasn't really my fault but I still felt responsible. Despite being blind, Ian's a total badass in his own right, as I learned the scary way. But he still needs help buying clothes, writing checks, and locating stuff.

Sometimes I pawn him off on Domino and Pepper. Domino doesn't much mind it—and Christ knows the little shithead needs to learn some responsibility before it's too damn late—but Pepper took to it like a duck to water. She loves feeling useful, and she loves helping Ian go through his clothes, sort his socks, and learn his way along the stinking, damp alleyways that make up most of our neighborhood map.

Then, of course, there's the fabulous number six thing you ought to know about: The only other member of my circle is either a first-rate ex–Navy SEAL named Adrian deJesus or a divine drag queen called Sister Rose, depending on the wardrobe and the wig.

Oh yeah. Thing number seven: I digress. A lot.

So those are the only people I see on a regular basis, and they are fairly new additions to my life, so I'm still getting used to all the socializing.

Horace Bishop, on the other hand, I've known for over a decade.

And believe it or not, he's more ordinary than all those yahoos I just listed above. I think. But like I already confessed, it's been a while since we've had a chance to sit down for a face-to-face.

I checked my watch.

He wasn't late, but also wasn't as early as I would've preferred. This is unfair, I realize. Just because I'm a crazy person who has to be twenty minutes early for everything doesn't mean other people must live by the same standard. But knowing this didn't stop me from glancing down at my watch again, then reaching for my cell phone to make sure that my watch wasn't wrong, because sometimes it *is*, okay?

But the watch wasn't wrong. Not according to my phone.

The bar was starting to fill up with the usual Cap Hill mix of gays in couples and strays, twenty-something hipsters, and homeless people who hadn't yet been pegged as such and asked to leave. When the lone waitress gave me a look that told me to place an order or get out, I asked for a cup of water I wasn't going to drink and a glass of red wine that I planned to down.

I didn't like the pressing nearness of all the people, and if I'd had any idea the joint would be so very *hopping*, I would've certainly picked someplace else—even though I'd originally chosen it precisely because I suspected Horace would hate it. Call me antagonistic, but his natural habitat is more "minimalist, with a splash of snobbery" than "Pacific Northwest logger wannabes and their strung-out beards." By "beards," of course, I mean their fake girlfriends. And also their Castro fanboy face-lawns.

But given my druthers (and what precisely does that *mean*, anyway? I've always wondered) I would've liked something equally lowbrow and gauche, but less densely populated.

Too late to change my mind.

And just when I was thinking the little scumbag was going to be late, purely to torture me—as if I ever did anything to *him*—the door opened with a digital chime that almost no one else heard over the shouted orders for beer or fruity drinks and the busker somebody'd ill-advisedly brought indoors and given a microphone.

I heard the chime. I craned my neck to look around the ass of the single serving girl, and there he was. All five-foot-six of him, impeccably dressed in a pin-striped Brooks Brothers suit and a pink tie, because yes, he is *that* secure in his masculinity.

For a long time I thought he was gay. Then gradually, over the years, I realized that he's not attracted to anything on earth except money. And maybe himself.

He saw me and his freshly threaded eyebrows lifted in a chola arch of . . . something. It wasn't surprise, obviously. And it probably wasn't delight, though it might've been amusement, or maybe curiosity. I haven't changed any since last he saw me. For that matter, I haven't changed since 1921.

The waitress slapped a glass of wine on a cocktail napkin directly under my chin, then vanished. I picked it up and lifted it in a half-assed toast in Horace's direction. He gave a weird half bow and a wave back, then grimaced as he realized the crowd he was going to have to wade through in order to join me. He immediately assumed the position of a tightrope walker shimmying above a pit of alligators and began to squeeze his way across the room, doing everything short of removing a hankie from a pocket to cover his mouth and nose—mostly, I suspect, because he didn't have a hankie.

With a laser frown and a flip of his double-jointed wrist, he whipped out the unoccupied chair across from me and said, "Honestly?" as if I'd just told him I'd bought a pair of pasties and planned to take up table dancing.

I smiled at him despite myself and said, "I swear to God, if I'd known about the busker, I would've picked someplace else." Which was perfectly true. I'm petty, but I have my limits.

"So you *say*," he accused, snapping his fingers and—like magic—summoning the waitress, whom I probably couldn't have flagged down again with a boomerang. He put in an order for a Manhattan, neat, and took a deep breath . . . then appeared to think better of it. He exhaled swiftly and, with a shake that might've been a shudder, he said, "Ray-baby!"

"Don't call me that," I told him, but not with any weight behind it. I don't really mind, usually. I especially don't mind when I can barely hear it. The busker was leaning on the lyrics of "Yellow" like each word was a hook he was pulling out of his eye. "And it's good to see you, you irascible bastard."

"Back at you, princess," he said with a grin, which squinched at the busker's manhandling of the chorus. "But really. Here?"

I shrugged, like this was no big deal. "Well, you said you wanted to talk business, and it really doesn't get much more private than a dump like this, now does it?"

"I guess not," he said, dubiousness written all over his forehead. I watched him work up to some feeble enthusiasm about slumming in utter security, and either he's better at psyching himself up than I am, or his news was good enough to overrule any environmental discomfort. "Your taste in hangouts, Christ.

Dracula's castle may have been dank and filled with homicidal hookers, but at least it was quiet. I assume."

Horace knows I'm a vampire. He figured it out years ago, which isn't such a strange thing considering his line of work. The most valuable and most wanted items in the world are those traded by immortals, after all.

"I don't have a castle. If I did, I would totally put you up and give you one of the hookers. And maybe a stake. But in lieu of a castle, this will have to suffice. *You're* the one who was dying for a powwow, so go on. Scoop. What's so important that it's worth sitting here, listening to this?"

"Almost nothing," he purred, but he leaned forward—or started to, then saw the crimson splash from where my wine had arrived and retreated, keeping his prissy, pristine elbows dry. The waitress picked this moment to deliver his Manhattan with the same messy verve she'd used to give me mine, then disappeared back into the fray. He sampled the beverage, gave a head-tossing shrug that pronounced it surprisingly drinkable, and gave in to a full swig.

"Almost nothing?" I prompted.

"Almost." And then he said what people always say, when they've got a whopper to share. "You're not going to believe this shit."

"Try me!" I said, with a mixture of both real and fake enthusiasm. Horace has been known to embellish, in order to get me on board with an uncertain gig or two, but he'd gone to real effort this time. I was curious.

Using two fingers and his cocktail napkin, he swabbed the little deck between us. "Okay, get this. Last month I was doing a gig with this assessment show."

I didn't know what he was talking about, so I said, "Can you be more specific?"

"Oh, you know," he waved his hand. "*Attic Treasures.* That PBS production where people dig out their old junk and hope it's worth money."

I tried to picture it, wee and fabulous Horace, being shown Hummel figurines by octogenarians. "Seriously? Why the hell would you take a gig like that?"

"Because sometimes"—he was purring again, which meant trouble, but maybe the good kind—"we find great stuff that way. All the big auction houses send people along on those things, you know, because usually the first thing Grandpa wants to do with his newfound Renoir is sell it. God knows most people can't afford to insure their treasures, even if they're sitting on family heirlooms—and they usually *aren't.* They're usually pieces of shit found in abandoned houses, or in dead people's basements, or estate sales, or whatever. But yeah, all the big guys, including my employers, send people along."

"And you drew the short straw?"

"Oh, shut up. It isn't *that* bad," he insisted. "Don't get me wrong—I bailed on the Bible Belt tours because, fuck me, I can't stand that folksy shit. I did an East Coast leg and a West Coast leg, figuring I might find some colonial loot or maybe some Indian stuff out this way."

"Native American," I corrected him, not because I care but because I'm contrary.

"Oh, fuck *you.* Those Eskimo toys go for a mint, and I have a buyer in Spain, of all places, who'd pay me in blood if he thought I'd take it." He gave me a meaningful look, but I waved it away.

"No way. I'm never that desperate. It's cold hard cash with me, darling, and you damn well know it."

With a harrumph he said, "It's just an expression. Anyway, when was the last time anyone gave you *cash*?" He pronounced the word with disdain. "Wire transfers are so much cleaner and easier."

"And easier to get through customs," I admitted. "So correct me if I'm wrong, but you're about to tell me something that will involve a very fat wire transfer in my immediate future. Otherwise, you wouldn't have gone to all this trouble. And"—I bobbed my head toward the busker—"you'd have never set foot in this joint. So come on. Out with it. Where's the carrot at the end of this stick?"

"Don't let me savor it or anything." He took another full drink, swallowing half the cocktail and beaming a Cheshire smile that should've been mine. "It's like this: I'm in Portland, you know. Just last week."

"Right."

"We're filming, and we're filming, and we're filming . . . you know, tedious shit. One asshole after another with a broken pot or a third-grade painting, blah-blah-blah. And then this guy—he's one of the producers, named Gary—Gary comes up to me and he's like, 'We've got something weird at the exotics table.'"

"And naturally, they call you." I used present tense because that's what Horace uses when he's telling stories about himself. Always the hero of his own ongoing show, that guy.

"The weird stuff *is* my specialty."

"Wait. What's the 'exotics' table?"

"It's where they sort out all the tricky stuff. Ivory, pelts from endangered species—or pelts that *might be* from an endangered species—anything an appraiser suspects is stolen, human remains, or the like."

"Human remains? Does that really happen?"

"All the fucking time. Usually teeth and shit, but sometimes you get Great-Great-Uncle Casper's scalp, and then we all get to have a good freak-out about it. But we never put those on the show," he said with sudden earnestness. "We don't want to encourage the freaks."

"Gotcha."

"Anyway. Over at the exotics table, Gary hands me over to Phil, who's holding a cigar box about this big." He made the motions for an object the size of a big dictionary. "And I'm getting all excited, because—"

"Because you're one of the freaks," I interjected.

"Precisely," he agreed. "I mean, you just never know with those events—they're like war. Long periods of boredom punctuated by high excitement, nay *terror*."

"You were afraid of the cigar box?"

"I was *not* afraid of the cigar box," he responded crossly. "I was *excited* about it. Now you've thrown me off. Let's see, okay—"

"What was in the cigar box?" I cued him. "I think that's probably where the point of this story lies."

"Goddamn, you're a bitch. Yes, fine. All right—so I take a look in this cigar box and it's filled with . . ." He reached for an interior jacket pocket and produced an old-fashioned Polaroid. He slid it across the slightly damp tabletop, and I picked it up.

The square picture showed the box's interior, illuminated by an overenthusiastic flash. The contents were oblong, more or less—and very white, or maybe that was just an effect of the lighting. It looked like perhaps a dozen of the objects were scattered therein, dropped like Pixy Stix.

"Definitely not cigars," I observed.

Which prompted him to muse, "Sometimes a cigar is just a cigar . . ." very softly. And then he concluded, "But sometimes it's a big fat cock."

"I'm aware," I said.

"No, no. I'm being funny. You don't get it? Don't you see what these are?"

I squinted at the photo and gave it the ol' college try.

"I . . . hmm. I don't know. There's not enough zoom. Not enough detail for me to guess. You're going to have to tell me."

He scrunched his hands into fists, and his whole body began that low-frequency hum of outrageous, joyful greed. "They're *bacula!*"

"Bacula? Like . . . Count Bacula?"

"Oh for fuck's sake, you ignorant cunt—*bacula,*" he pronounced carefully. "Plural of *baculum.*"

"Well, that clears it right up."

With a sigh that almost ruffled the curtains, he said, "Raylene, they're *penis bones.*"

Aaaaand . . . he'd finally done it. The little bastard had rendered me completely speechless. I sat there with my hand on my wineglass and my mouth hanging ever-so-slightly open, waiting for the rest of it.

He waved his hands in circles, like he was trying to diffuse a fart. "Don't you get it?"

"Apparently not," I all but stuttered.

"Honey, these aren't *ordinary* penis bones."

"Not the kind you pick up at Walgreens, with a bottle of aspirin and a scented candle?"

"Oh for the love of . . ." But he couldn't find anything holy enough to insert, so he said, "You *do* realize that some creatures have penis bones, yes?"

"Sure," I said, even though it would've been more honest of me to admit that I'd never once, in any level of seriousness, even considered the interior workings of animal sexual plumbing.

He could tell I was lying. If we'd been on the phone, I might've been able to fool him, which is why my usual preferred method of communication with Horace is phone. He said, "Okay, Biology 101: Lots of mammals have penis bones, because they lack the advanced hydraulics that keep human boners bone-free."

"Okay . . ."

"These penis bones are called bacula, or baculum in the singular."

I then asked what I thought was the most obvious question ever. "But why would anybody want them? Much less collect a whole cigar box full of them?"

He raised one finger. "Ah. The reasons are many and varied," he said, which I found extremely hard to believe. "Biological supply houses sell them for classrooms and whatnot, but only ordinary bacula—from dogs, raccoons, you know—and they aren't worth much."

"So we're talking about a box full of them because . . . ?"

"These aren't dog bones. Or raccoon bones. Or any other bones that any catalog would carry for the giggling satisfaction of high school science students. They're . . ." He lowered his voice. "From *other* creatures."

Now he had my attention. "Other creatures? Like what, like . . . like . . . ?"

He whispered, "At least one from a gryphon, and one from— I shit thee not—a unicorn. At least two werewolf bones—and I *don't even want to know* what went into acquiring *those!*"

"Bullshit," I argued. "Even if you knew what the schlongs of those creatures looked like . . . I mean . . . Let me try that again. Even if those were *real things* and not mostly *fictional things*, I am unprepared to believe that you knew, magically, what they once belonged to! For all you know they came from a horse and a wolf, and a . . . a . . ." I tried to figure out the nearest corollary to a gryphon and settled on "lion."

His pointy finger of "but wait, there's more!" was aloft again, so I knew I'd accidentally said something useful. He told me, "But that's exactly how I knew. Magic!"

"Get out of here. You don't know any *magic*."

Horace recoiled very slightly, feigning offense. "No, but I know *about* magic. And I know how to *read*. Someone had been so kind as to tag them with those—" He took the picture out of my hand and pointed at something I could barely see. "Those little tags, tied onto them like toe-tags."

"Except they're dick-tags."

"Are you finished?" he asked, sitting back and folding his arms. "Are we done with the dick jokes, just for now? Can we move along to what's important, here?"

"Most guys think their—"

"Stop it," he ordered.

"Fine, fine. No more dick jokes. For the next, I don't know. Five minutes. That's all I can promise."

"You didn't check your watch," he pointed out. He knows me well. I really *am* that precise and punctual, pretty much always.

"Let me ask you this—and in order to humor you, I will ask this in all seriousness, I swear to God. Even if they are . . . accurately labeled," I said, settling on a descriptor. "Who cares? Biologists, maybe; cryptozoologists, certainly; but it's my understanding you can't yank DNA from bones." I've heard you can get it from teeth, but I had a feeling that erection scaffolding fell outside the appropriate parameters. "Even if it's true, no one would ever believe it. Hell, I'm undead with a werewolf ex-boyfriend and *I* don't believe it." The wine must've been making me chatty; I said it loudly, and with a gesture of the glass. I made a mental note to cut myself off before I did anything truly embarrassing. My system doesn't process alcohol very well, so a little goes a long way, dammit.

"Most people wouldn't believe it," Horace agreed. "But that's fine. I'm not interested in reselling them to most people."

"Then who?"

"Oh, that's easy. Rich weirdos. The kind who are 'in' to ceremonial magic. Penis bones have their own ritual uses and whatnot, but, oh boy howdy—you give somebody one of *these* penis bones? I'm not saying the sky's the limit, but you'd be talking about some serious spell-slinging."

I said, "Huh," because he'd answered my question, but I still couldn't picture it. "People will pay money . . . lots of money? For these things?"

He leaned across the table as far as he dared, and flashed me one of his most avaricious, toothy smiles. "*Millions.* Millions *each,*" he amended. "The werewolf ones alone—and they're probably the bottom end of the cost spectrum—I could probably unload for eight or nine hundred thousand."

"Why are werewolf bones so cheap? Relatively speaking?"

"Because werewolves aren't quite so hard to come by as unicorns or gryphons. I'm not saying they're a dime a dozen, but if I desperately needed to track one down, I could probably do it in a few hours. Only because I have connections, though," he said with a lift of one golden eyebrow. "And I don't just mean *you.*"

"I would assume so," I retorted, even though I suspected he was lying. He didn't *need* any underworld contacts other than me, and he probably didn't want any. Vampires are very quietly very well organized, and very dangerous that way. They don't tend to pay for the things they want; they tend to take them. I'm only so easy to deal with because I don't have any House or family affiliates, but that's a story for another time.

I continued, "But if you honestly believed you could get me to steal you a werewolf's penis bone, it'd cost you more than eight or nine hundred. Those guys are seriously hardcore, and they are seriously attached to their body parts. Especially that one, I bet."

"Unless—" He tapped thoughtfully at the edge of his glass. "Unless you can find out where some are buried. Talk about your profitable grave robbing!"

"Maybe that's why they don't bury their dead," I mused.

"What do you mean they don't bury their dead? Everyone buries their dead!"

"Incorrect, dude. Lots of people cremate, via big stoves or pyres or whatever. Weres are big on cremation. And now, I suppose, I know why. I mean, if *my* penis bone was worth almost seven figures, and I wanted to keep it in my personal possession—even after I'm too far gone to use it—I suppose I'd put in a request for a little fire and brimstone, too."

"If you had a penis bone, I would be very confused," he said, chugging the last of his Manhattan and glancing around for the waitress, who failed to appear at his second finger-snapping summons. "Oh," he said with a sudden frown. "Well then. I was going to be a big tipper, but fuck her if—oh *hi there!*" He changed his tune as she swanned up to the table. "One more of these, please."

She nodded and took off. "You're so quick to judge," I teased.

"She'd better not spit in that," he complained.

"I doubt she heard you," I tried to assure him. We weren't listening to the tortured strains of "Yellow" anymore, but so help me God the bastard had moved on to Creed.

"That changes nothing. People spit into drinks for spite," he assured me, eyeing the glass she'd given him the first time, because she hadn't whisked it away when she'd done her drive-by.

"Stick to wine. It's easier to see gobs. I'm just sayin'."

"You're revolting."

"You have no idea. Now, let me ask you something else."

"Fire away."

"Why didn't you just buy the bones off the owner on the spot, if they're so goddamn valuable?"

"An excellent question," he said. "I picked a number out of my ass. I picked a thousand dollars because I thought it would sound like a lot of money to a poor person."

"The guy who owned them was poor?"

"Compared with me. Anyway, because I'm *so* fucking clever"—
he rolled his eyes a little, at himself, which kind of surprised
me—"I told the guy they were worth a little money, yeah—but
that he'd never be able to sell them on the open market because
they were remains of endangered species. And that's practically
true!" he pointed out, almost poking the incoming waitress in the
tit. She gave him his new drink, swiped the empty glass, and vanished. And I tell you what, that's the kind of service I like to see. I
don't know how Horace inspires it, but he's got a gift.

"More true than you could've possibly conveyed without
looking like a maniac."

"Right. So I can tell he's wishy-washy about it, and I can
tell that he doesn't have the faintest idea what these things really
are. So I add that they were probably used in Native American
ceremonial . . . you know, *whatevers* . . . and that made them an
even trickier pitch. They might be artifacts. He might need eighty
different kinds of licenses to auction the things, but oh, hey—my
auction house was imminently qualified and certified to manage
that kind of sticky situation."

"It was his lucky day!" I suggested with sarcasm.

"Damn straight! But he wasn't having it. He decided he
wanted a second opinion, because he'd inherited them from
Grandpa Somebody-Or-Another and he wasn't willing to part
with them on my word alone. I told him he was welcome to the
opinion of anyone in the auditorium—nobody knew what they
were but me, and no one else would want them—but he got all
stubborn, boxed them up, and took them home."

"And you didn't follow him into the parking lot and jump
him? You must be losing your edge."

He sighed. "He was a big fucker. Corn-fed redneck of the
large and slow variety."

"Isn't that what you took the coastal tours to avoid?"

"Yes, but my cunning plan was not one hundred percent successful. It turns out there are rednecks in every corner of this continent, to my excessive chagrin." He took a long draft of the new Manhattan, as if the very thought was so onerous that it caused him to require a drink.

"So you couldn't have taken him."

"Not without a firearm. And there were cameras in the parking lot. Believe me, I considered my options. And this is where you come in."

It was my turn to sigh, imagining the sheer embarrassment if I were to finally be caught by the feds, the feebs, or anybody else who's been following my thieving career with intense interest over a box full of penis bones. Christ, I'd never live it down. "I don't know, man."

"Look, I have the guy's address and everything! He's a mechanic, owns his own shop specializing in British cars, or something like that. Lives alone in the 'burbs. Name's Joseph Harvey. I've got everything you need, right here. It'll be the easiest case you've ever had."

See, that's foreshadowing, is what that is—or tempting fate at the bare minimum. Saying such a thing out loud is *asking* for trouble. "If it's so damn easy, why not give the gig to someone else? Someone who charges a lot less?"

"Because anyone else would want to know why I want a box full of weird old bones, and get to wondering why they're worth stealing, and so forth and so on. I trust you to bring me the goods and bring them discreetly, without a whole bunch of bargaining and demanding information."

"You trust me?" I was touched. Almost.

"I trust you to do your job and bring me what I need. And I trust you enough to have told you everything about it, because I've learned the hard way that when you pay for an expensive service, you don't want to leave out details. Success lives and dies by details, Raylene. You know that better than anybody," he said, throwing in a glare that was just short of accusatory.

He was talking obliquely about my personal . . . tics. Let's just say I'm a little OCD, and let that be the end of it. Or if you must have a follow-up to that statement, let it be this: Fine, I'm a *lot* OCD, but it keeps me alive and I don't care how weird it looks.

"Yes, yes. The details. I hear the devil's there. All right." I sighed, letting him know he had me. "Fine. I'll go get your calcified cock sticks."

"Bacula."

"Same diff. Let's talk money."

We did, and I finagled my way to a 30 percent finder's fee, up from my usual 25 percent due to the potential embarrassment factor. And also, Horace said it was worth it if I would promise to stop making dick jokes. I told him that'd be another 5 percent but he scowled me down and I took the offer. We shook hands.

Then he took off and I did the same, before the busker could inflict any more damage to my sanity or my eardrums. The aforementioned eardrums were ringing as I stumbled out into the street—swearing softly at Horace for leaving me with the tab.

"Bastard," I groused as I stuffed the receipt into my pocket.

If that little jerk thought I wouldn't tack on $51.98 to an invoice with six zeros he had another thing coming.

2

I checked my phone and saw that it was fairly early for a weekend evening. If I picked up the pace I could swing by the gay bar on my way home. Rose was working the show, or at least I thought she was. I could crash it.

The pronouns were coming easier to me, with time. I never knew precisely what the etiquette was when dealing with a burly straight man who earns a living embracing his inner goddess. So the rule of thumb is that when she's all dolled up for work, looking like a woman by design . . . she gets the feminine. When he's hanging out in my loft in full-on dude-wear glory, well then. He's a he.

It isn't perfect, and I slip up occasionally, but it seems to work for now.

"Neighbors" was only a few blocks away, and

I had to cross a loud section of the neighborhood to find it. The hill is what we like to call the "gayborhood," but that's not why it's so damn swinging; it's also the most densely occupied part of the city. The population is young, hip, queer, and moneyed . . . or made up of people trying to approximate three out of four. It's crawling with bars and clubs (gay, straight, and other), mom-and-pop restaurants that stink of grease, street-cart vendors offering vegan fare or baby seal sandwiches, high-end indie watering holes laced with neon lights, and overpriced condos towering over the lot of it.

Most of the intersections are two-way stops, which is to say, each one has four lines of pedestrian crosswalks and only two stop signs, and this leads to hilarity—especially since the pedestrians tend to wear black and the drivers tend to speed, and everyone's on a cell phone. It blows my mind that more people don't end up as road pizza around here.

It was coming up on eleven o'clock and Neighbors was ahead on the right. I followed the music, the spangles, and the long-legged ladies with the clear Lucite heels, up around a small sidewalk enclosure with a metal gate. The bouncer took my ID and stamped my hand, and the guy standing next to him took five bucks. I was glad to hand it over. Slow nights mean no cover. Busy nights mean good business and good tips for my Cuban American princess/Navy SEAL.

I'd given Rose some money about six months ago—seed money, you know. Dough to get her on her feet in the wake of me kind of completely destroying her life in Atlanta. And I didn't know what her spending habits were like, but I figured the stash must be running low by now. Seattle rents are ridiculous.

But money has a way of finding hot people, and Rose is one of those people—both under her stage name and as Adrian. He has those Latin cheekbones and thick, dark, luscious, finger-luring hair, and he also has a body to die for, regardless of which way you swing. So call it prurient interest, or call it checking up on a friend, but I was more than happy to fork over five bucks for the pleasure of seeing him prance about in a thong.

I have no idea how he does his tuck. One of these days, I'm going to get him liquored up and drag it out of him. The secret, I mean. Not the . . . um . . . tuck.

My guess at the cover was correct. The place was packed, and jumpin'. Madonna ruled the night, a remix of something that isn't one of her usual singles, but it was catchy and I could wiggle to it. I wormed my way inside and up closer to the stage, and did a little of the white-girl shuffle while waiting for the show to start.

Finally, after what felt like a forever of sweaty, unwanted pickup attempts, the DJ came on the loudspeaker and announced the evening's planned entertainment.

First up was a gorgeous queen with chocolate skin and eyes that were utter proof that if there's a God he's cruel, because those belonged on *me*. She wore a gold costume that could best be described as "slutty Pocahontas," and she got down to a dance-hall shake-up of Cher's "Half-Breed." The next queen was Asian and punk to excess, with blue-and-pink hair and a gothic Lolita thing going on. She did her routine to a song I didn't recognize, but it was entertainingly nasty, I'll tell you that much.

Then, oh wonder of wonders, Sister Rose was up. I'd been wondering what she'd be wearing; it was a game of mine, trying to predict the evening's shtick, but she always stays one step ahead of me.

Rose strolled onto the stage and grabbed the nearest pole, and I didn't even notice I had a big, stupid grin on my face until she saw me and winked. I was two seconds shy of screaming for her panties when the music got grinding and she got dancing. Tonight she was wearing a flamenco outfit, bright red. A Lady Gaga song kicked up—"Alejandro"—and she was off, this one-woman show letting it all hang out.

I mean, not *all* of it. Obviously. Just that she gave it her all, you know. Professionally. Not from a flashing standpoint. More's the pity.

Just as I was wondering how on earth a woman (who was really a man) could get her legs that far apart, the routine came to an end and she flung herself off the stage, into the audience, toward the bar. My kind of girl, right there.

I stood on tiptoe trying to see her, trying to track and follow her; she raised one hand and used it to gesture with the curled finger of "come hither."

Sometimes I wish I were taller. This was one of those times. When I was young and alive, I was considered quite tall for a woman. (I'm about five-foot-seven, maybe -eight in shoes.) These days I'm about average, and the average is slinking away from me every generation. I have some honest and deep-seated fears that in two hundred years I'm going to look like a very conspicuous midget.

Perhaps this isn't as common a piece of knowledge as I think it is, but people are getting taller.

Hey, don't laugh. I know of some old-timers in the vampire world who are looking more out of place every year. There's this one guy, Matthew Harding is his name, I think; he's at least three hundred years old, and the guy looks like a toddler in a business suit. Oh, not *literally*, no. He's absolutely covered in body hair. But he's not even five feet tall, and it's starting to look weird. Give him another hundred years and he'll spark rumors about urban hobbits.

I jostled, shoved, and shimmied my way up to the bar and a

non-spot beside Rose that became a spot when I wedged my ass into it. "Hey there, gorgeous," I greeted her.

"Hey there, yourself. Beverage?" she offered.

"Thanks, but no thanks. I've had plenty already," I said. We were both shouting. The next performer was up and things were loud again, though at least they were loud and focused. Everyone was watching a nimble redhead in a circus costume doing the funky chicken to Britney Spears.

"Oh really? Went and partied without me?"

"Just this once," I assured her. Then I said, "Naw, not really. It was a business meeting."

"Sounds joyous."

"Oh, it was. And weird, too. When do you get off, anyway?"

"Anytime after now. You feel like company?"

I said, "Yeah, yours. Mostly because you're the only person on earth who'll find this as hilarious as I do."

She replied, "Oh God," and had a brief exchange in Spanish with the bartender. When she was done, she turned to me and said, "All right, we're done here—I only did the one number to buy a bathroom coke-up for Pocahontas over there. I'm finished with my bar shift. Let's hit the road."

We escaped the club together and I guess we looked peculiar, side by side. Me, small and dark, and darkly dressed; her, tall and vibrant, and likewise attired, even though she'd grabbed a knee-length brown coat on her way out the door and had slung it over the costume with a scarf.

"So, dish," she ordered, though her voice was down half an octave and it was somewhat less, shall we say, *dramatic*. I hate it when she does that. I'd rather she stays in character, so my pronouns stay easy. Why the world won't accommodate my every whim, I just don't know.

"I will. Hey, where are we headed?"

"I don't know. Where do you want to go?"

"You want to go back to the flat? The usual suspects may or may not be hanging around, but there's free booze."

"Free booze? Shit, honey. That's all you had to say."

I knew that, so I smiled. "Okay. Now for the dishing."

I filled her in on everything from Horace's wardrobe to the magical penis bones, and I was right—she found it precisely as hilarious as I did. Together we wandered down until we caught a bus—which is usually not my thing, but I didn't want to go rooftop-to-rooftop with Rose while she was in stripper heels. When she was a he, and in his old special-ops outfits, it was a different story entirely. I'm not saying he can keep up with me—I mean, shit, I know *other vampires* who can't keep up with me—but he's no slouch. Underneath that feather dress and bumpit hides one hardcore, badass dude.

Once I'd wrapped up the bulk of the story, she asked, "Are you going to take the case?"

"Sure, I'm going to take the case. Why wouldn't I?"

"Because it sounds too easy."

I shrugged. "Sometimes things sound easy because they *are* easy."

"And sometimes things that sound easy only sound that way because you're completely fucking delusional," she retorted. "Didn't you say the same thing about—" She stopped herself. *"You know."*

"Of course I know." And I knew why she didn't want to say anything. We were on a bus, surrounded by hipsters in head-phones with earpads the size of coffee mugs, muttering crazies, and a couple of bitches hollering into their cell phones.

Some topics aren't meant for public consumption, and the story of our first meeting is one of them. But we both knew I took that case because it looked easy as pie . . . and maybe also because I liked the look of Ian Stott, my eldest boarder.

We reached Pioneer Square via the number ten (or is it twelve? It changes at some point during the route) and walked the rest of the way to my digs, about eight blocks off the last stop, in the oldest part of town. Seattle burned down to its foundations in 1889, and I live in the stuff that was built right after the smoke cleared. But if you're hunting for ancient history or even antebellum lore, you should probably look elsewhere.

I think my building was originally put up in 1899; I remember that loose fact from the Realtor who sold it to me, because that date—that one span of less-than-twelve-months before the turn of the century—meant that the building was "worth" more than it would've been otherwise. I thought this was completely preposterous, considering the condition of the thing, but something about the façade warmed the burly cockles of my heart (if they are still warmable) and I bought the place anyway. It's not like I didn't have the money.

Without going into enough detail for random interested strangers to find me, my home turf is a four-story stone-and-brick jobbie with some scrollwork down by the main entrance, and some bizarre little gargoyle-y things hanging around on the roof corners. It also has owls all-freaking-over it. I am told that the owls (mostly made of stone or concrete) are intended to scare off pigeons, but I've seen pigeon nests mounted on the heads of those owls, so I'm thinking it's possibly the dumbest affectation on earth. At this point, I think we can safely quit calling them "pigeon prevention devices" and move on to "decorative superstition."

We arrived home by one AM and there were lights on upstairs, though all the blinds and curtains were drawn—so all was as it should be. The bottom three floors are pretty much dedicated to my stash of stuff, and by God I did not want to see anybody poking around in there.

Yes, I still have a stash of stuff. During the raid that prompted my initial relocation, I nearly lost it all—but I've been gradually stealing it back or replacing it. It's mostly left over from cases that went all wonky. Sometimes I get left holding the bag after a client goes to jail, sometimes a client can't pay up, and every now and again a client dies before the final transaction can be made. I'm not going to say I work for dangerous people, but every single person who's kicked the bucket mid-assignment has been murdered, so make of that what you will.

And, okay, I won't lie. Every blue moon I spy something I want for myself. Even—and don't tell anybody—sometimes I see something I want and I (*gasp*) *buy it.*

Just think of the building as a house with an enormous attic in reverse. We live on the top floor, and all the cool stuff is stuck in the big space underneath us.

For a while I tried to con Rose/Adrian into moving into the top floor, too, out of some sense of . . . I don't know. He was integral to me solving my last assignment-slash-case, and so was Ian Stott—and even, in their own strange little ways, the two formerly homeless children who live there, too. Maybe I was just trying to collect the whole set.

Irrational, yes. But if you stick around awhile, you'll learn that irrational is my specialty. I ought to teach a master class.

I keyed the code into the security pad downstairs and then unlocked the dead bolts because yes, I really *am* that paranoid. And then some. If you had a household half as valuable as mine, you'd keep a close eye on it, too. Or that's what I like to tell myself, in order to feel less crazy . . . even though the fact is that I'd probably behave similarly if I lived in a cardboard box and didn't own enough stuff to fill a sock.

There's an old-fashioned freight elevator at the end of the entry hall; it's not one of the posh fancy gated ones, but it's a very large industrial gated one that is still kind of cool to operate. I do it with a lever and some buttons. It took some getting used to. The first time I gave it a whirl, I wound up stuck between the second and third floors and had to climb out like a monkey.

I was careful to keep that from happening this time, though. I wouldn't want Rose to have to hike over the floor hump in those shoes.

I was getting better at it. The elevator stopped dead right where I wanted it to. I drew back the grate and we stepped inside to a different world, or so I liked to think.

Sure, the bottom three floors were essentially hundred-year-old architecture with exposed wiring and brick, but the fourth floor had money poured into it. Believe me, I know. It was my money.

The interior feels a little cavernous, with each unit having an open floorplan—and the elevator opens into a lobby that could be another unit if I wanted to make it one. It's maybe a thousand square feet of space, with lovely hardwoods and a few long running rugs. The windows have dark maroon curtains that are drawn over venetian blinds—and bulletproof glass.

Yeah, I sprang for it.

"Hey!" hollered Pepper, a little close to Ian's ear for his personal comfort. They were seated together on a love seat in this lobby—this common area, for lack of a better way of putting it—and he'd quite clearly been urging her to read to him. It's one of his tricks to educate the little monster. She won't go to school and I'm not in a position to make her (and neither is he, obviously), so in order to ensure that her brain doesn't rot, he's making sure she can read and write with some expertise.

It's a good idea. She's almost nine. One of these days, she won't be as cute as she is now, though I find that hard to imagine. Someday, she might need a job. Or more obviously and certainly, someday she'll need to be able to navigate the real world of civilized adults who are not undead.

If I have to, I can buy her forged paperwork to show she has a diploma for anything, from almost anywhere she wants. And I'll probably be willing to do that one of these days. But first she'll have to prove to me she can handle the basics.

Her brother's another story. He's not as stupid as I've (repeatedly) accused him of being, but he's got a lot less discipline— which is saying something, because an eight-year-old girl doesn't exactly have the world's reservoirs of the stuff. But he wasn't there right then when Rose and I came back from Neighbors. It was just the little girl and the blind vampire.

"Hey, you," I said back to her.

She stood up like it'd almost crossed her mind to come give me a hug, but she wouldn't do that. I wouldn't know what to do if she did. She's a great kid, don't get me wrong, but I don't get hugged very often. It would throw me for a loop. I'd be exactly as startled as she would be if I picked her up and gave her a big honkin' smooch on the cheek.

The precocious little stinker said, "And hi . . . um . . . Rose!" She seized the name and blurted it, dodging the pronoun issue altogether.

"Hey kid," my companion greeted her back. Then she asked me, "Do I still have that drawer?"

"Yeah."

"Time for the ol' switcheroo," she said, striding off toward my room.

The bottom drawer of one of my dressers is dedicated to men's clothing, and these days it's mostly Adrian's. If this sounds strange, allow me to remind you that several international agencies believe I'm a man. So every now and again, I masquerade as one, but only when I'm up to no good and I suspect I might get caught on camera.

Adrian and I are nowhere near the same size, but somehow his stray shirts, pants, socks, and the like have made their way into my dude-wear collection over the last few months. I know it sounds promisingly dirty, but it's as simple as this: I have a washer and dryer down on the third floor, and my favorite drag queen likes to keep her quarters to herself. She comes over to do laundry.

As she wandered off, I joined Ian and Pepper, who wanted to show me what they'd been reading. It was Mark Twain, *A Connecticut Yankee in King Arthur's Court*. Ian told me, "She's doing very well."

"I should hope so," I said.

To which she informed me, "Ray*lene*, of course I'm doing very well—I can *totally* read," in that kid voice that carries the subtext of, "Clearly I am speaking to the dumbest person alive. Or dead." But she was being friendly and not actually accusing me of being a moron, I was pretty sure.

"I'm *glad* you can read. At this point, I'd be concerned if you couldn't."

Ian smiled up at both of us, his icy-white eyes fixed on neither. "She's a quick study. I'm not the world's best judge of such things, but her reading level is easily above her . . ." He hesitated. "Estimated grade level."

As far as we knew, she'd never seen the inside of a classroom.

"Ian's a good teacher," she told me. "But I could already read. Domino taught me."

I wasn't sure I believed that, but I didn't feel like arguing with her. And maybe he'd taught her the ABCs at some point while they were on their own, before I met them. I was prepared to concede that it might be tricky, learning how to read from a blind man. I jumped topics. "Speaking of your brother, where is he?"

"He went to get groceries."

"Awesome," I said, not meaning a single consonant of it. I'm no expert on children's nutrition, but I'm pretty sure Ho Hos and Pringles ought to feature less prominently in anybody's diet. "Maybe he'll bring back some fruit or something. One of these days."

"I don't like fruit."

"You should eat fruit anyway. And vegetables."

"*You* don't," she pointed out. She and Domino both know what Ian and I are. I'm not sure when they figured it out exactly, but one day they just acted like they'd known all along, so I quit pretending.

I told her, "*I'm* not a growing girl anymore. If you eat nothing but junk food, it'll stunt your growth."

"But it's not hurting my brain," she insisted, holding up the book and waving it at me. "My *brain* is working fine."

"Well, if you're content to be short and enlightened, I guess that's no problem of mine."

"Have you read this?" she asked me. "It's a really good book."

"I've read some of that guy's other stuff, but not that one. He's pretty funny."

"You should read it," she said firmly, in precisely the same tone she'd told me I ought to have more video games—with the absolute confidence of a kid who's found something she likes and is convinced you will too, if you only try it.

"Maybe I will, one of these days." Then I asked Ian, "What's next on the educational agenda?"

"I was hoping you could offer some suggestions. We're burning through the *suitable* items in your personal library," he said, meaning they'd raided my bedroom and the boxes of loose paperbacks I keep under the bed. I've been meaning to put up bookshelves, but you know how it goes.

"Who's Anaïs Nin?" Pepper asked, pronouncing it *Ann-iss*.

"Someone you're going to *love* in another twenty years."

Ian would've done a facepalm if he hadn't been too dignified, so instead he gazed toward us indulgently and told her, "She's an author who wrote many books, none of which I expect you'd like particularly well right now. But perhaps, Monday evening, we ought to see about getting you a library card."

"I can have a library card?" she asked, her eyes wide with wonder.

I said, "I don't see why not. If you and Ian want to find your way down there and fill out the paperwork, I bet you could con someone into hooking you up."

In truth, I wasn't so sure. Ian has no legal relation to Pepper, and obviously neither do I. If she and Domino have any parents anywhere, they've never cared enough to report them missing. I know. I've checked the listings. It was kind of like scanning the classified ads, looking to see if anyone's missing a puppy you've found. I struck out. No one wanted them, so I was stuck with them.

Before long, Adrian deJesus emerged from my bedroom looking all-man . . . except for a smudge of silver cream shadow glittering at the corner of one eye. I pointed it out and he wiped it off on the back of his hand.

The liquor cabinet, such as it is, is also in the big common area—along with a television that has a screen the size of a twin mattress, and a couch next to the love seat where Ian had been instructing Pepper. I ordered Adrian to bring me a glass of wine and help himself to whatever he wanted, and I plopped down on the couch, bogarting the TV remote because I'll be damned if I'll let these kids have it while they're living under *my* roof.

I don't lock the cabinet because I'm not stupid. If Domino wants wine, he'll find a way to get it regardless, and I'd rather he doesn't break the thing. It's an antique. Besides, I'm reasonably certain that Pepper doesn't have any real interest in it yet, and if she ever develops any, I'll cross that bridge when I come to it. God knows I'm not their mother. It's not really my job to look after them.

Don't you dare say a word about how I feed them, clothe them, and now am in the process of educating them. (Or one of them, anyway.) I know I'm an idiot, so let me delude myself, will you?

Behind us, we heard the old freight elevator creak, groan, and rumble back down to the first floor, and soon Domino joined us with a big box of Twinkies and two 2-liters of Coke. Nutritious.

Yeah, I should really do something about that, I know.

But since everybody was there, and since the night was still young for the likes of us, we all settled in to watch whatever was fresh off Netflix. It turned out to be the third *Underworld* movie. We laughed, shut up, and drank.

3

When I woke up the next night, I was virtually alone. Ian was sleeping in and by the sounds of things, the kids were out doing . . . whatever the hell they did every time they left the place. Out in the main living area, the large love seat was rumpled and the throw that usually went across its back was wadded up on the right seat cushion, but it was otherwise empty, meaning Adrian had pulled himself together and gone home at some point during the day.

I want to say that the silence was kind of refreshing.

Before the adventures that had brought us together, I'd spent virtually all my time alone. I got accustomed to it. I came to enjoy it. But these days, it was funny. The gang drove me nuts when they were around, but when they were gone, I kind of missed them.

If I wasn't completely insane before, I must take this as a sure sign that I'm headed that way now.

I retreated to my room again, took a shower (because I like them, not because I sweat much or get very manky on my own these days), and once I got myself dressed again, I began to pack for Portland.

Because packing while naked is weird, that's why.

I could've flown, but it's only about three hours from Seattle by car, and nobody is going to x-ray my stuff before I put it in my car. I don't go into these situations unarmed and/or unprepared. That's just the nature of the business. Every time I leave on a business excursion—even an excursion that I am assured will be the world's easiest walk in the park—I bring a full roll of keys, picks, cards, knives, and a whole lot of other stuff that a lesser thief might leave behind.

Say it with me, kids: *There is no such thing as overprepared.*

In addition to the expected arsenal, I also bring small motion detectors, tiny cameras, a wee bottle of baby powder (you never know when someone will have lasers), some knockout powder I get from a very discreet source (you never know when there will be dogs), zip-ties that will hold my weight if they have to, a cigarette lighter, two cell phones (you never know when one will have a bum battery), and a nine-millimeter. Look, I can run fast, but not faster than a speeding bullet. And sometimes someone will run away from me. I don't always feel like giving chase.

If this sounds sinister, it's supposed to. I am, quite frankly, not very nice.

Maybe that's why I put up with the gang's shenanigans. Because the gang is willing to put up with mine, which makes them damn near unique. Another batch of lunatics like these may never come along again. I may as well take advantage of the company while it's dumb enough to stick around.

I double-checked my ammo, packed everything in an obsessively orderly fashion, and slung the one bag over my shoulder. The telescoping handle on the roller bag came out with a *snikt* like Wolverine's claws. I love that sound. That sound means *money*.

Beside the television is a pad of Post-it notes. I took one and scrawled a hasty message to Ian, then stuck it smack in the middle of the screen. That little yellow note said I'd be back within a couple of days, and to call if anything blew up, caught fire, or fell down.

As if there was anything I could do about it from Portland, if it did.

But I like to pretend that I'm covering my tracks, bracing for any contingency. Ready for the worst, and all that jazz. I always feel better if there's a plan in place. And in this case, the plan was, "Leave the blind guy in charge of the juvenile delinquents and everything will be just fine. Probably."

I exited quietly, or as quietly as I could, given the clanking gate on the old elevator.

Outside, Seattle was in rare form.

It was raining just barely hard enough to say "it's raining" not "it's drizzling"—and the wind off Puget Sound was blowing in sideways, drilling all those nasty little drops right into the cracks of everything I was wearing. I understand the whole idea of spring showers and I can even get behind them with a little cheer, but I could live without the wind, and I could also live with a little lightening of the chill, seeing as it's April and all. I'd be dumbfounded and delighted to see it crest sixty degrees.

Goddamn, I mean *seriously*.

My car was parked in a private garage two blocks away. I hiked toward it with a glum sort of resignation, all my glee from the *snikt* of the luggage drained right out of me by the weather. I don't usually mind it, so I'm not sure what my problem was that particular evening. Maybe I took it as a sign—a sign that this was not going to be easy or pleasant after all. A sign that I was in for a good soaking.

Or I was just pissy about being wet.

After snagging the right wheel of my roller in a metal gutter grate and generally getting soaked right to the bone, I reached the parking garage and crammed all my stuff into the trunk. I let myself inside the silver Taurus and pulled out of the garage, into the street. Then I began the roundabout route to the interstate.

Yes, the Princess of the Night drives a Taurus. At the moment.

I don't go for flashy cars because I don't want anyone to look at me. Usually I drive something five or ten years old and as utterly bland as I can arrange. *Voilà,* Taurus. And to clarify the other half of that whiny paragraph about getting out of the city, let me be clear: At no point, anywhere in Seattle, is there a clear and obvious route to an interstate. And, if you find yourself magically right beside an interstate on-ramp, you can safely assume that it's leading the wrong direction. You might say to yourself, "Self, if I've found the on-ramp going *this* direction, surely the on-ramp going the *other* direction must be right nearby!" But you'd be wrong. This place was designed by crack addicts, I'm convinced of it.

Eventually I made it onto the main drag and out down I-5, headed south. It's not a particularly pleasant or unpleasant drive to Portland—not at night, anyway. You can't see Mount Ranier or any of the other mountains, and mostly you spend all your time squinting at headlights as they glare up at you from the darkness. But the path is straight even if the road is potholed and crooked. It's an easy shot, all in a row: Tacoma, Olympia, Vancouver (the Washington one, not the one in Canada), Longview.

Portland.

You cross a big bridge on the way into town, driving over the Willamette River and down into a sprawling, industrial sort of place that was once called "Stumptown" because they'd cut down all the trees as far as the eye could see.

Once I'd made it into town, it was first things first. I got myself a hotel room down by the river, which put me a little outside the city center, but was worth it for the nicer accommodations. Then I hunkered down, unpacked my stuff, made myself comfortable, and commandeered the television remote because it was MINE ALL MINE and no one was going to fight me for it.

I also took a few minutes shortly before dawn to fool around online and get a better feel for the address I was about to breach.

Using Google Maps and other assorted search-engine explorations, I examined Joseph Harvey's house, his neighborhood, his nearest restaurants, gas stations, and easiest routes of exit from that little shred of sparsely built semi-suburbia. If I'd had a printer handy I would've printed everything I found, but I didn't, and I kicked myself. It's always the one thing you forget to pack, you know?

Realistically speaking, I could find my way over there without any real trouble. I memorized the streets and counted the number of houses in every direction. But I love having paper backups, if only because of the joy I get from shredding or burning them when I'm finished. It's like crossing something off a list in a violent, warm fashion.

Paper backups are psychological bread-crumb trails, or that's how I like to think of it. But I didn't have them, so I was on my own with only my neuroses to keep me company. Just like the good old days!

I went to sleep sometime around dawn and woke up roughly

when the moon began to rise, which meant I was out of bed around nine o'clock and out of the hotel about half an hour later—when it was good and dark, and I was good and ready.

Harvey's house was eighteen point two miles south from my present position, outside the main chunk of town, and outside most of the better-planned 'burbs. It took me over half an hour to find the general location, and another five minutes to pinpoint my target. This is partly because I'd misjudged the satellite photos, thinking that Harvey lived in some kind of neighborhood. He didn't, not really. He lived in the woods, with next-door neighbors who were half a city block's length away from him on either side and across the street.

I chalked this up in the "win" column. Distant neighbors meant no one would be listening for trouble at his place. Then I wondered if there would be dogs. Horace had called Harvey a red-neck, and rednecks—in my limited experience—were like dogs.

I don't like dogs, and dogs don't like me, but that's what the knockout powder was for, wasn't it? I saw no sense in killing some-body's pets in the course of robbing his house. That would be bad form. And it would also be risky. Dogs are shifty fuckers—faster than they look, louder than hell, and all kinds of nosy. Dogs also smell me, right away—which is to say, they smell that something is wrong with me. Some instinctive bit of their wee, primitive brains tells them that I'm trouble. Wee, primitive brains have their uses, but I'd rather not be called out by a Doberman, if at all possible.

On my first drive-by, I suspected someone was home at the Harvey residence. None of the lights closest to the front of the house was on, but a glow from deeper within suggested some-one watching television, or possibly sitting up reading. By now it was coming up on ten thirty, so it wasn't atrociously late for your average law-abiding mortal, and this was fine. I was patient.

I'd just wait for everyone to turn in for the night, then let myself inside for a look around.

After doing some initial scouting, I parked my car at the bottom of the hill upon which Mr. Harvey's neighborhood sat. As far as I could tell, it was really just one long road running the length of a ridge, with houses plopped along it and not much else worth noting. I made sure the car was inconspicuously stashed (it was, behind a closed and abandoned gas station), and started to hike toward my goal.

It was a nicer night in Portland than Seattle. Not quite as windy, and not quite as cold. I'm led to understand that this is typical, and I'm sure it has something to do with complicated jet streams and weather patterns, but I don't really give a shit about any of it. The point is, the night was cold, but not cold enough to be brittle. And it was breezy, just breezy enough for the rustle of trees and bushes to hide the sound of my footsteps.

I spent fifteen minutes poking through the woods, squinting to catch every splinter of moonlight and praying I wouldn't encounter any raccoons or anything.

I don't like raccoons. They look . . . *shifty*, with their little burglar masks and everything. Also, they carry rabies. Can I catch rabies? Probably not. All the same, it sounds gruesome—and I think we all know that cute, fuzzy woodland creatures are not to be trusted on general principle.

I crunched through the dark in my boots that were frankly too expensive for this sort of thing, and I counted the backyards I passed until I knew for a fact—even before I made my way around to the front of the house—that I'd found Joseph Harvey's place.

Uninspiring from all angles, the Harvey place was a fifties ranch house too mundane to achieve the descriptor of "midcentury." It was in relatively good repair, but it was also accessorized with an aboveground swimming pool full of slimy leaves, an ATV up on cement blocks, and a long front porch that had a motorcycle parked on it.

Ugh. The things some people spend their money on.

The interior glow I'd witnessed during my drive-by was still the only sign of life within, but something was bugging me. I couldn't put my finger on it. I just had a weird, intense feeling that something was wrong, and I haven't survived this long by ignoring those feelings.

I stood still, up against a side wall of the house, hoping I blended into the shadows and listening for all I was worth. I detected a steady drip, like water off a rain gutter. I heard canned applause, and what was either a baby crying a long way away, or a kitten crying much closer. Hard to tell, but I was leaning toward a kitten.

I didn't smell any dogs, and I didn't see any sign of dogs, either—no water bowls, leashes, or coiled piles of crap to be avoided.

From this train of thought came another: the idea that I shouldn't be listening. I should be *smelling*. My nose isn't as good as a dog's, but it's better than a person's—and it was working overtime to tell me to be on guard. All around me was a prickly, sharp, electrical odor like the smell of cooked air right after a lightning strike. It insinuated itself slowly, but once I'd noticed it I couldn't un-notice it.

I couldn't tell where it was coming from, but the skies were clear above and I could count the stars, so it wasn't the smell of a storm. Something else, then.

The kitten (yes, I was sure now, a kitten) upped its caliber of wailing, hitting that pitch animals make when something is very truly wrong and they're in no position to do anything about it. This kitten was inside the fifties ranch home of Joseph

Harvey who, if my ears could be believed, was inside watching television.

Or was he?

The longer I stood there, feeling my shoulder blades go numb from being pressed up against the chilly bricks, the more I thought this couldn't be right. No one sits and watches television with a yowling animal—at least, not without telling it to shut up, or throwing a pillow at it or something. And I heard no signs of a serious deep sleeper. No snoring, no sounds of apnea horking through the bedroom or living room, or wherever the TV was located.

Of course, I told myself, if this guy can sleep through Mr. Bigglesworth's serenade, he can sleep through a gentle home invasion.

Did I believe this? Only halfway. But the other half of me believed that no one was inside, and no one was asleep, and the smell was getting stronger, and I was getting tense, just hanging around outside like some common felon.

I couldn't stand it anymore. This wasn't a jewelry heist, or *Ocean's Eleven* out in bumblefuck. This was some dude's house, and he didn't even have a cheesy THIS PROPERTY PROTECTED BY . . . sign on any of his windows. He'd probably never considered the possibility than anyone would break in, not in a million years. This was most likely a guy who left his car unlocked.

I shimmied around to the back door—it was built into a screened-in porch—and gave it a tug. It opened with a soft squeak, stuck slightly, and the handle came off in my fingers. Ah. Not a door that saw a lot of action. I breached it, stepped lightly to the door that would actually let me into the house, and tried it. The knob swiveled without so much as a click of protest.

The kitten had stopped meowing. It'd heard me and was coming to investigate.

Before I could even get the door open enough to let myself inside, there it was, paws grasping out through the crack. I nudged it back inside with my foot and shut the door behind me, holding a finger up to my mouth as if any eight-week-old critter in the world knows what the universal gesture for "shush!" means. The kitten was gangly and gray, with a white smudge on its nose and murder in its eyes. Or it might've been peevishness. Hard to tell with those things.

It sat down at my feet and let out a silent meow that I would've mistaken for a yawn if it hadn't been so insistent about it.

Believe it or not, I knew what it was trying to tell me. I'd have known even if I hadn't seen that the creature's paws were dipped in something red and delicious, and I'm not talking ketchup. I smelled blood. And I could tell, when I gave my rudimentary psychic senses a little stretch, that (the kitten notwithstanding) I was the only living person inside the house.

Throwing caution and quiet to the wind, I dashed away from the back door and toward the blood. It was easy to follow. The house wasn't very big and there was a whole lot of it.

I found Joseph Harvey (I assume) lying facedown on a keyboard in front of a big, flat-screen monitor. The screen saver refused to yield what he might've been watching, but the rows upon rows of video game boxes told me this was a playroom, not a workroom.

Horace had been right. Joseph was a big son of a gun. His forehead had crushed the keyboard, sending keys flying all over the place, and his slashed throat had ruined everything within about six feet of the place where he still sat, having run out of extra lives for the final time.

Poetic, really.

Behind me the kitten squeaked. Trails of red paw-prints criss-crossed the room, and when the little bugger sat down, it left a bloody butt-print, too. The poor thing had been climbing all over the dead guy, trying to wake him up. Or eat him, for all I know.

"Yeah, yeah," I told it. "I see what you were hollering about. Um. Sorry about your owner."

It narrowed its eyes and meowed again, with more vigor this time.

"What?" I asked it. "What do you want me to do? He's already getting cold." Then I muttered, "My advice is to pray that your next owner is richer."

This reminded me I wasn't just sightseeing. I was looking for a dusty old humidor filled to the brim with magical penis bones.

My unease had not exactly lifted upon finding the bled-out corpse, and now to add to my discomfort I had the nasty suspicion that I was not going to find a dusty old humidor—and if by some amazing chance I *did* locate such an item, it was likely to be empty. The briefest glance around the premises told me that this guy didn't own anything else worth stealing.

And this was all kinds of problematic. I made a mental note to ask Horace who else knew about the penis bones, and began a systematic-but-speedy search of the place, top to bottom.

I still couldn't shake that *other* smell, the one I'd picked up outside, before the blood.

Ozone, that's what it was. The stink of electricity gathering, collecting, and . . . and . . . that's when I noticed that the hairs on the back of my arm were standing up. A fast glance in the bathroom mirror revealed that the stuff on top of my head was likewise coming to attention, creating a fluffy black halo that was neither flattering nor comforting.

Outside, I heard an incongruous rumble. I say it was incongruous because, as I already mentioned, the weather outside was clear as a bell not ten minutes previously. But I know thunder when I hear it, and it wasn't a car backfiring, or the television—which, yes, was still playing in the living room. What a fucking waste. Turn off your TV if you're going to hole up in the "office" and shoot zombies.

I found the remote and turned the TV off to make doubly sure that the ambient noise wasn't coming from the boob tube. No sooner had the last pixels imploded into a tiny blip of light than the thunder came again. And this time it was much, much closer.

Storms weren't supposed to move that fast, were they?

In the kitchen, I opened all the cabinets and dumped their contents onto the floor. In the closets, I yanked all the coats and shirts and painfully tacky shoes out into the light and abandoned them. In the master bedroom, I fished under the bed and turned up absolutely nothing I wanted to touch, including a small wet hairball that the kitten had deposited with disgusting recentness.

Nothing, nothing, and nothing.

The humidor wasn't hiding behind the rows of video games, and there weren't any bookshelves upon which it might've been stashed. Not in the storage closet, not in the garage, which was virtually empty except for the stink of gasoline, paint thinner, and a lawn mower that hadn't cut anything since Clinton was in office. A few tools were hung up on a pegboard; rusting containers of the previously noted smelly, flammable liquids were lined on un-finished wood shelves; and a washer and dryer were strewn with dirty laundry.

More nothing.

And although it was utterly irrational, at that point I knew a few things—none of them good. Call it that rudimentary psychic sense, call it woman's intuition, call it a lifetime of bad luck and hard-earned learning experiences . . . but I knew that not only were the bones absolutely missing, but that whoever had taken them had killed Joseph Harvey.

Okay, so that wasn't such a leap of logic. But the next part was.

I knew that I needed to get the ever-living fuck out of that house or I was going to die. I was pretty sure I was going to go up in flames, but that's probably just my subconscious running the numbers: electricity plus flammable liquids, multiplied by the hypothetical possibility of lightning.

I'm no good at math, but I know a very nasty word problem when I see it.

Outside, the night was changing colors—deepening and darkening, and the rumbling from the clouds rolling in was less a crack of thunder than a constant, rolling rumble, increasing incrementally with every second I stood there considering my next course of action.

Was it madness to assume that a freak thunderstorm was homing in on me? Oh yes, of course it was. But I'll be the first to admit I'm more than a little crazy, and I'll bet being crazy has saved my ass more times than I can count.

So my next course of action was obvious: Get the hell out of that house.

The kitten sat on the floor eyeing me with unsettling intensity. It was making a request—or trying to burn its little face into my memory, in the event I left it all alone in a house that was mere seconds from going up in a fireball.

"Fuck it," I declared to the house, the storm, and the kitten.

I grabbed the animal under its belly and whipped it up inside my jacket as I ran.

For something whose life was getting saved, the kitten wasn't super-grateful. It wriggled and writhed against my left breast, leaving unsightly scratches that itched ferociously. But what was I going to do, leave it there? Not unless I wanted kitten flambé to haunt my nightmares.

I could feel its wet little paws kicking, shoving, and pushing against my shirt. Good thing I was wearing black, though I still felt like this was an unfair coincidence. If I was going to ruin a shirt with blood, I ought to at least get a meal out of it.

For a split second I considered sucking the blood off the kitten's feet, and that's when I realized it'd been a while since I'd eaten, and that sometimes I am honestly too gross for words when I'm hungry.

Even a sense of imminent mortal peril cannot override my stomach, I swear.

But the imminent mortal peril was making me paranoid and light-headed. I stumbled through the house, which was now almost entirely dark—since I'd turned off the television—and slipped in a trailing tributary of blood that had oozed out into the hall.

I'd told the kitten that the body was getting cold, but that'd been an exaggeration, and I suppose we both knew it. The guy hadn't been dead more than a few minutes. I had just barely missed something violent, by the skin of my teeth. I wanted to ask the small cat, "What happened here, anyway?" but my psychic powers don't extend to animal ken. It's not like it would've mattered.

Finally I located the front door and fumbled with it until I had the dead bolt turned. I yanked the door open, except that there was one of those stupid dinky chains—so I ripped the door halfway off its hinges instead, breaking that dinky chain and flinging myself outside at a dead run.

Above, the sky had sunk down low and close, and the death-black clouds weren't just rolling, they were boiling. And the ozone . . . if that's what it was . . . had grown so thick I could hardly breathe. It felt something like getting a hearty, inadvertent whiff of champagne bubbles, but without the happy promise of alcohol to follow. The air was sharp and hot, and heavy, as if the atmosphere itself were fighting me—trying to keep me inside, or keep me from running.

I ran anyway, and when I'd barely reached the end of the driveway where the mailbox leaned at a rakish angle, a blinding column of jagged white heat snapped down from those boiling clouds and struck the satellite dish on the roof. The ensuing crack sent shrapnel of metal, plastic, and roofing tiles flying in every direction, and it made my ears ring all the way to my brain. I staggered and caught myself on the mailbox. I used it to right myself, and then to launch myself forward again—away from the sizzling aroma of tar and metal.

The second strike took the garage, and the fireball that went up when the lightning met the paint thinners and the gasoline shoved me face-forward into a ditch beside the road—literally lifting me off my feet and throwing me. I landed on the other side, in the ditch, in a fetal-crouch roll, beside somebody else's mailbox. I couldn't hear much, but I could hear windows breaking and fire coughing. I hate that noise, that whooshing gasp fire makes when it's so big it takes all the oxygen and turns it into a brilliant plume.

Don't tell *me* lightning never strikes twice.

No longer dark and sleepy, the hill and its sparse neighborhood were lit up like lunch hour in the glowing red-and-gold strobe. The explosion was distilling itself down to an ordinary house fire—not that it mattered to all the blast-sheared trees within fifty yards. But hey, the fire probably wouldn't spread since there was nothing close to feed it.

My knees were shaking as I hauled myself up, using the across-the-street neighbor's mailbox as a temporary crutch. I could see the fire licking up the walls, chewing on the roof, and gnawing into the interior of Joseph Harvey's house, but I couldn't hear any of it. I couldn't hear anything but a high-pitched hum, and the dull, faraway chimes that I finally recognized as sirens.

They sounded unreal and muffled, like toy police cars held underwater.

I shook my head, which didn't help. It only made everything hurt, in addition to the ringing and humming. Well, if I hadn't tried it, I wouldn't have known, now would I? And if nothing else, the action got me moving again.

Sticking to the road would've been a bad idea. Emergency vehicles were on their way. I didn't want to be spotted or, heaven forbid, assisted. I just wanted out of there, and back to my car, so I could flee for Seattle before anyone could stop me and ask what I was up to.

I'm not sure what I was so afraid of. It's not like anyone could've reasonably accused me of blowing up a house by striking it with lightning. Twice. I'm awesome, don't get me wrong, but weather manipulation is altogether outside my sphere of influence. My roommate Ian can do it a little, but not (so far as I know) with the kind of laser precision that I'd just seen demonstrated.

And no. Not for one brief, sparkling moment did I honestly think I'd just witnessed some colossal coincidence.

I went looking for magical items. The items weren't there, and the owner had been freshly murdered. Mere minutes later, his house blew up. None of this—not in any arrangement whatsoever—added up to a coincidence. I wasn't sure what it *did* add up to, but my gut told me it couldn't be good.

I took off at a brisk lope behind the neighbor's house and in the general direction of my car, and it wasn't until I was leaning against that car, fishing around for my keys, that I remembered I hadn't escaped the Harvey household alone.

The kitten, not being completely stupid, had crawled down inside the interior pocket of my jacket—a pocket I'd been only dimly aware the jacket possessed, presumably intended to stash a cell phone or a pack of cigarettes. Well, it stashed a four-footed hitchhiker almost as easily. The poor thing had curled itself up tighter than a snail. It made a whimpering noise when I poked at the lump of its rear end.

"Still alive, huh?" I asked it, and my voice sounded funny to my stopped-up ears. "That's good, I guess. Wouldn't want to explain a mashed kitten to the dry cleaner, anyway."

It whimpered again.

I let myself into my car and shut the doors, cracking the window just enough to listen for sirens. I wanted to know when they arrived so I could sneak out past them. Two fire trucks, a cop car, and an ambulance all went speeding by, scooting around the turnoff and trundling up the hill.

I yawned to pop my ears, in case that would work.

It did, but not very well.

Satisfied that no more emergency vehicles were immediately forthcoming, I rolled up the window and reached into my pocket. I extracted the kitten and held it up so it was facing me. It was small enough to use my palm for a recliner, and its bloody paws hung over the edge of my thumbs.

"Okay . . . *you*," I said to it.

It blinked slowly.

I briefly and temporarily held it by one hand while I reached up with the other, turning on the car's dome light. Then I up-ended the kitten, got a good look at its undercarriage, and finally had a pronoun.

"You're a boy," I informed him. "Congratulations."

He squeaked a meow at me. It was a tired meow, and maybe a hungry one. Definitely a nervous one.

I agreed with the sentiment, whatever it was. "You and me both, kid. Christ, you're filthy. You smell . . . delicious. But don't worry, we won't go there. Instead," I informed him, setting him down on the passenger's seat and randomly trusting that he wouldn't take off, "we're going to go back to the hotel. And you're going to get a bath. If you want to survive the night, you're going to have to smell a little bit less like a snack."

He gave me the closest thing to a shrug I've ever seen an animal attempt, and curled up in a ball right there on the seat. But I noted that he dug his claws in, so as not to slide off during the car ride. Good kitty. Or at least, somewhat intelligent kitty.

Back at the hotel, I made a point to let myself in via a rear entrance—away from any pesky reception desks, where employees might want to know why the hell I looked like I'd just survived a Patriot missile strike . . . and oh yeah, why I was carrying a bloody kitten. Sure, I could protest that the blood on the kitten belonged to someone else, but I doubted that'd do much to ease anybody's mind.

It wasn't until I was halfway down the hall that I saw the blood on my boots, along with enough mud to build a hut. I removed the boots and held them with one hand, and the kitten with the other, and I made it back to my room with a giant sigh of relief—and the sudden realization that the kitten had peed inside my jacket.

No good deed goes unpunished, et cetera.

This also reminded me that I didn't have anyplace within the hotel room that a kitten might use as a toilet, but since he'd already peed, I figured that a few kitten turds wouldn't be the end of the world. They'd be more like the shit frosting on a crap cupcake of a day, really, and I couldn't bring myself to care.

I was tired, and my head hurt, and I wished I had some blood—human or otherwise—but there wasn't any handy except a few drops floating around in a skinny kitten, and I didn't actually need it. I don't drink very often in my old age, but sometimes it's comforting and it's just what I want.

But we can't always get what we want.

Instead we get to turn the bathroom sink into a kitten spa,

much to the indignation of the animal in question. When I was finished with him, the water looked like bloody tea, and I came this close to giving it a sip, but that would be pathetic—and I wasn't quite desperate enough to be pathetic.

I towel-dried the kitten, used one of the hotel coffee mugs as a water bowl for him, then I took a long, hot bath.

Because I deserved it.

I also deserved to turn in for the morning and sleep until I damn well felt like waking up, but that's hard to do when something with four sets of very sharp claws is climbing all over you and yowling like it's the end of the world. I picked up the kitten by the scruff and asked him, "Why did I bring you with me again? Why?"

He meowed.

"Not good enough," I replied. "You should be doing cute kitten things, or at least sleeping quietly. That's how you thank a nice lady for saving you from becoming a fritter. Not this bullshit."

But he wouldn't shut up, and I knew he was hungry, and maybe scared, and certainly confused. I couldn't do anything about the last two things, but there was a twenty-four-hour drugstore down the street and they had kitten food, God be praised. I snuck some back to the hotel just in time for the sun to start peeking up, and when I finally crashed for the day, leaving the DO NOT DISTURB sign firmly on the door knob, the last thing I remember hearing was the *munch, munch, munch* of the kitten burying his face in kibble.

4

The next night I awakened to a whiff of cat shit, and I was almost pissed about it—but then I realized the little bastard had done his business in the potted plant on the table beside the front door. The plant was fake, but the soil was close enough to sand, or gravel, or whatever, that the kitten had climbed in and made himself at home. Three cheers for instinctual behavior, eh? After all, it wasn't his fault I hadn't sprung for any kitty litter.

I congratulated him with a head pat, then began my evening routine of readiness. What was I readying myself for?

Frankly, I wasn't sure.

How should I proceed? I had an assignment and lots of directions, and oodles of bio information . . . all of it leading me back to a smoking crater a few miles outside Portland.

Like the kitten, I had nothing to go on.

So I did the only thing I could think of. I called Horace.

"Darling!" he answered the phone before I could squeeze out a "hello." "I'm so glad to hear from you. I was just now sitting here, wondering if a big box of penis bones was in my future—and wanting nothing more on this whole earth than a big box of penis bones, or rather, the money those penis bones will bring me—and here your number pops up in my phone like magic!"

"Are you going to say 'penis bones' again? Because I think you could work it in another couple of times for good measure, if you really tried."

"Penis bones penis bones penis bones."

"You're deranged," I told him.

"And rich. When can I expect a delivery? Should I come in person? Maybe we should do this exchange the old-fashioned way. This is probably the most expensive thing I've ever asked you to get. I'm not sure UPS can be trusted on this one."

"I'm not sure UPS can be trusted to scoop my litter box."

"Your . . . your what? Oh my. I'm not sure which joke to reach for," he mused.

I helped him out. "You could make a crack about the state of my bathroom, or you could simply be aware that I've picked up a kitten and find some pun to work into the situation."

"Why the fuck do you have a kitten?"

"Nightmares of charbroiled baby cat."

"Gross."

"Agreed." The tiny monster climbed up beside me on the bed where I was sitting, and put in a yowl for good measure.

"I heard that," Horace said. "And you have a kitten. I'm having a hard time picturing it. What's its name?"

I had no idea. On the spot, I decided, "PITA."

"Pita? Like the tasty bread-type substance?"

"PITA—like short for 'pain in the ass.' I don't know what I'm going to do with him, I just couldn't let him go up in smoke. Speaking of going up in smoke . . . um . . . I don't have your penis bones."

Silence.

"Horace? Did you hear me?"

"Oh, I heard you," he said. "I just don't *believe* you."

"Well, believe it. And I'm starting to get the feeling you haven't told me everything I need to know about those dick sticks."

"Dick sticks. That's a new one."

"It just now came to me. You should be proud of me, keeping my sense of humor intact, even though I nearly got blasted into the Great Beyond."

I filled him in on what had happened, how it'd gone down, and the depths of my surprise—with the added bonus of explaining how I'd ended up with Pita sitting beside my knee, chewing on his toenails.

Horace was silent again, which made twice in one phone call—and surely a personal best. He's hard to shut up.

I prompted him. "All right, now it's *your* turn to talk. There's more to the case than a corn-fed redneck with a box of valuable baubles, and if you want those baubles, you're going to have to tell me something useful."

"I have to admit," he finally said, "I'm not one hundred percent shocked to hear of your difficulty. I'm *surprised*," he added quickly, lest I start yelling at him, "but not shocked. I swear to you, Ray—I thought you were way ahead of the competition on this one. I had no idea anyone would beat you to the score."

"You might've informed me that I was in a race," I grumbled. "I would've made it more of a hurry."

"This kind of money wasn't enough to spur you on? Jesus, woman. I don't understand you at *all*."

I rubbed at my eyes with one hand, then almost set it down by accident atop Pita, who gave me the ol' stink-eye. "It's not like I paused to do a sudoku before taking the gig. It's barely been seventy-two hours since you told me about it, and in that time I've made it all the way to Portland, scoped the location, found a corpse, almost got struck by lightning—*twice*—and adopted a kitten. So it's been an eventful couple of nights, utterly free of dilly-dallying. Regardless, if you'd told me that someone else was looking for the stash, I would've made an effort to speed it up— but no such mention was made. And now, if you still want your cock blocks, you're going to have to give me a hint."

"You want a hint?"

"I want a hint. Tell me who else knew about them, and who else wanted them."

He sighed, and for once it wasn't the dramatic kind. It was the kind of sigh people make when they aren't sure how to answer. "Shit, honey. For starters, everyone else at the curiosities table saw the bones and knew I was interested. I might not have been as completely discreet as I should've been, but rest assured, I didn't tell a goddamn soul what they really *were*."

"But?" I knew there was a but. There's always a but.

"A couple of years ago, I got a phone call—the quiet kind— from someone looking for, shall we say, 'endangered' bacula. I think the caller wanted something from a werewolf, but she made it clear that other offerings might well be considered. Anyway, I didn't have anything at the time—and I didn't know where to go and grab any, either. It's not the sort of thing that comes up for sale very often."

"Hard to believe," I muttered. Pita had moved on to cleaning his crotch, which I watched with grossed-out fascination.

"Yeah, well. I forgot about the conversation until I was at that stupid road show, and then it all came rushing back to me, covered in dollar signs . . . and I was just wondering if I'd saved that phone number when things got weird."

"Dude, you're dealing in *penis bones*. It *begins* weird, and it can only get weirder from there."

He pretended he hadn't heard me. "It didn't take me long to chase down the number; I never forget a wallet, and this was a potential customer with some pretty specific needs. But when I called her back last night, implying rather strongly that I'd gotten a lead on some objects she might want . . . she turned up her nose at me. Said she didn't need my services, because she'd gotten a lead on some bones herself."

"I find it hard to believe she would've come across such things without any outside assistance."

"Yeah, me either. Then she said the magic words that made me hang up on her. She said she couldn't afford to pay me anyway."

"No wonder you hung up."

"Well, I mean, come *on*. She had a lot of nerve, asking me for a product and then telling me she didn't plan to buy it. That's just sneaky—and not in a good way. It's practically fraud, is what it is."

"Or shopping," I noted. "Do you think this woman went after your bones? Do you think she jumped them?"

"Now is not the time for jokes!" he practically yelled at me.

I pulled the phone away from my ear, and even Pita stopped his craw-gnawing to look up and wonder what the fuss was about. "Geez, sorry. Get a grip, would you?"

"Right now I'd like to grip that bitch's neck!"

"So you think she beat me to it? But how would she have known about the stash?"

He grumbled. "She dropped a name. She said somebody named 'Bill' had hooked her up."

"Awesome. I'll just start with all the Bills in Washington State, and we'll see if we get anywhere."

"I don't think that'll be necessary." He lowered his voice, suddenly all craftiness and vengeance. "I think I know which Bill gave her the tip-off. I think it was one of the road-show guys, one of the grunts who hefts the furniture around so us civilized chaps don't get our suits all sweat-stained."

"You're such a fucking snob."

"A clean fucking snob, with a dry-cleaning bill that's exorbitant enough as it is."

I shook my head. "But why would a furniture-hefting grunt know a box of penis bones when he sees it?"

"I haven't the foggiest. Maybe he's a secret cock enthusiast, maybe he's got a relative with a fetish, or maybe he's an amateur magician himself. All I'm saying is, he showed an inordinate degree of interest in that box. He tried to argue with me while I was doing my assessment—"

"You mean, trying to pass off your bullshit?"

"Yes, yes, bullshit was being deployed. It's like I told you, I was trying to push it as Indian artifacts or endangered species parts, but Harvey wasn't having it. And while I was talking, this fucker Bill leans over and starts in like he has a differing opinion."

"I assume you shot him down."

He sniffed. "You can assume I got him fired, and you can bet your sweet ass I had him booted out of the building. Still, it would've been easy for him to see Harvey's contact information—and share it, if anyone wanted it."

I gave this some consideration, and for about half a minute neither of us spoke. I broke the meditation by saying the obvious out loud. "That's a stretch, man. One annoying man named Bill, and one annoying non-client who has a friend named Bill. It's thin."

"It's a hunch. A strong one."

"No," I said. "It's not enough. I'm sorry, but if that's all you've got, I'm cutting my losses now. And since you're already so pissy about losing the bones, I won't even bill you for my time or travel expenses."

"Oh, you're a real *peach*," he told me, in a voice that could've blistered the paint on a Porsche. "Do you just . . . do you simply *fail* to understand how much money we're talking about?"

Off the top of my head, I guessed, "A few million? Something like that? But I don't need it, and honestly, neither do you. You only want it."

"A few million *apiece* on some of those things! And who the hell *doesn't* want a few million extra dollars? You say that like I'm some kind of lunatic!"

"You *are* a lunatic, but it's not your greed. That's normal. What's not normal, and what *is* lunacy, is expecting me to track down this semi-fictitious Bill and chase him down for your penis bones. It's impossible, Horace, and I won't waste my time trying to prove otherwise."

"What if I up your finder's fee?" All the way from New York City, I smelled his desperation.

"Baby, you could up it to thirty or forty million and I still wouldn't do it. Because unlike whoever wants those bones, I'm not a magician. I don't have the power to spontaneously know the identity and address of one miscellaneous Bill or one mysterious— and as yet unnamed—potential client, and I'm not going to waste my time or yours over this."

"But Raylene—"

"But nothing, Horace." Then, out of the kindness of my kitten-softened heart, or something, I threw him a bone. "Look, if you can find out anything else—anything useful—I'll take another stab at it. But it'll have to be more than 'some woman' and 'some guy, allegedly named Bill.' Bring me more to work with, and I'll give it another shot."

"You promise?"

Ooh. Promising things to Horace was like signing a contract with Rumpelstiltskin. However, I won't lie—it was an awful lot of money to walk away from, and all my relocation in the previous six months had left me less flush than usual. Therefore, against my better judgment I said, "I promise. And I'm not asking you to draw me a map with an X on it. I'm asking for a solid lead. A name, or an address. Or a building. Something."

"Yeah, yeah. I heard you." He swore, but his mouth was away from the receiver and I didn't quite catch the full spectrum of nuance, though I heard "bitch" and "cunt" feature prominently. "I'm on it," he declared, then the connection went dead.

I felt a huge and overwhelming sense of relief, only slightly tempered by disappointment at the revenue loss. If it hadn't been so much money, I probably would've just stuck with the relief.

Don't get me wrong. I wasn't about to lose any of my holdings, or go hungry in any figurative sense. But my cushion had taken a big hit, and now I had this whole household of people to support. Granted, Ian wasn't exactly running up a grocery bill, and at least Adrian had a job to support himself—and his own apartment, even. Thank God somebody was capable of independence, even if sometimes it honestly felt like he *did* live under my roof. Now if I could just get the almost-fifteen-year-old and his almost-nine-year-old sister into some gainful employment, I'd be back in the black.

Or I could take a really big case and clean up on the finder's fee.

Even so, the prospect of yet another hideously protracted, convoluted, endlessly complicated case of "fetch" just wasn't at the top of my priority list. Maybe I was being a princess. Maybe I was only being reasonable. Either way, there was another bubble bath in my future before the night was out.

There was also another stop by Walgreens, where I picked up an aluminum roasting pan (they didn't have any bona fide kitty trays) and a ten-pound bag of litter for the kitten to shit in. Then I threw him and all his supplies into the car and began the long drive back to Seattle.

I arrived home around one in the morning.

As I got off the elevator, I was greeted by the sound of Pepper hollering something obscene at Ian, which didn't surprise me as much as it should have. Ian was being his usual unflappable self in return, which only appeared to enrage her further.

I walked into this little hurricane saying, "Hey now, what the hell is this about? Settle down, pipsqueak."

"I don't have to settle down!" she yelled at me, but she immediately had the good grace to look embarrassed by it. She composed herself quickly and, I don't mind adding, mercenarily. The kid knows what side of her bread is buttered, that's for damn sure. "Oh. Raylene, it's you. I didn't know."

"What's going on?"

"He's trying to make me do algebra," she accused. "I'll read, because I like to read. But I will *not* do algebra!"

"Algebra?" I asked. "Is that all? Christ, it's not—" I was going to say "anal sex" but I restrained myself. Don't ever say I don't know when to rein it in, because buddy, I nearly bit off my tongue holding back that particular gem.

"It's not algebra," Ian argued. "It's basic arithmetic."

"I can already count!" she shouted.

I held out my hands in surrender. "I know you can, babe. Stop shouting, please?"

"He's trying to make me learn stuff and none of it is useful at all, and I'm not very good at it, and if I wanted homework, I'd go to school!"

The last half of that sentence had come out shouted, and

I very seriously needed to make her stop shouting, or so help me God I would not be held accountable for my behavior. I cannot *stand* the sound of children shouting. It's like nails on a chalkboard to me, and this was particularly grating because the number one reason I liked Pepper was that she was usually so mellow and reserved.

I couldn't handle it, and I was about to start shouting above all of them, offering eviction notices effective immediately.

Then I remembered I had an ace up my sleeve.

Quite literally. Pita had wormed down my left jacket sleeve. (Different jacket—like I'd wear one smelling of cat piss.) I wrestled him out into the air with all the grace of a dinner-theater magician on meth, and displayed him like a trophy.

With the world's lamest, most inexpert subject change, I announced, "Hey, check it out. I found a kitten."

Well, it shut down the yelling.

Ian and Pepper were both stunned speechless. Ian sat alone on the big love seat, and Pepper stood in front of me, both of them with their mouths hanging open.

Ian found his voice first. "You found a . . . what?"

"A kitten. His name is Pita."

Pita became impatient with the way I was holding him and began to writhe, fighting to find a way down, even though I was holding him four or five feet off the floor. Stupid cat. I withdrew him to my chest where he Velcroed himself to my collarbone.

Pepper cocked her head at him. "You brought home a kitten . . . named Pita? Who named it Pita?"

"I did," I said defensively. "It's short for 'pain in the ass.' The nickname would suit you and your brother just as well," I complained. "So if you want to fight the kitten for it, you're welcome to. Or . . . or rename him. I don't care. I needed something on the fly, and that's all I could think of."

"You're weird," Pepper observed crossly. But she approached me anyway, not reaching to take the cat, but squinting at him to get a better, closer look. "He's cute."

"Yeah, he's pretty cute. It's a good thing, too. That's why I grabbed him on the way out."

Ian asked, "On the way out of what?"

"A building that was about to blow up."

"You saved him because he was *cute*?" Pepper asked.

"He was sitting there, making this *accusing* face at me, and the place was about to go up in smoke . . . and I don't know. I freaked out and grabbed him. Then he ruined my good black jacket, and now my car smells like cat ass." He'd taken a dump on the way up from Portland. I had to roll down all the windows and gulp for fresh air for half an hour. It was un–fucking–*real*.

But something I'd said bothered Pepper, and she retreated a few steps—still thinking about Christ-knew-what.

Domino poked his head around the corner where the back stairway dumped into the main living area. This place is an old warehouse. It has some quirks.

The boy asked, "What's this about a kitten?"

"I've got one," I announced. "No one seems very psyched about it, though."

He sauntered up to me with what could only be described as "somewhat more enthusiasm" than his sister and actually poked at Pita, very gently. "He's cute," he observed.

"Yes," I said drily. "It's his only defense. Here. You want him?"

"Do I . . . do I *want* him?"

Both the kitten and the teenager looked at me as if I'd suggested they shave and set up a webcam. "Yeah. Do you want him?" Pita gave me a glare as I picked him off my shirt and dropped him into Domino's unexpectedly offered hands, and I couldn't blame the critter. If the shoe were on the other foot, I'd be feeling dubious, myself.

"I don't want him," the boy said. He used one finger to pat the white spot between Pita's eyes. "Hey Pepper," he tried. "You want a kitten?"

She just backed away, eyeing the both of us. "I don't know. Do *you* want him?"

Ah, I saw what she was doing. She thought this might be some kind of trick or trap—a suddenly introduced gift, and one that might require some responsibility on her part.

"Okay, forget it. Domino, he's your problem for now. Are you good with that?"

Pita put his nose out, and Domino touched it with his own. "Sure. But—" He frowned. "I don't know how to take care of . . . anything."

"You've done all right with your sister all these years," Ian pointed out. Everyone turned to look at him, having almost forgotten he was there. He shrugged. "I think a pet is a fine idea. And cats aren't much trouble, really."

"I have some kibble and some kitty litter downstairs in the car." In a gesture that showed more trust than he truly deserved, I tossed him my keys. "Go grab it, and the little dude is all yours."

Pepper, still suspicious, asked, "If you didn't want to take care of him, why'd you bring him home?"

"I told you, he was *cute*. And I would've felt bad if I'd let him get blown up. He probably would've haunted me. I don't need that kind of stress," I grumbled, reminded of my out-of-town adventure and its failure. "Just look after him, would you? I'm going to change clothes. Or take a shower, or something."

I left them all in the living area. I'm sure they were collectively wondering either what I was up to, or if I'd lost my marbles—but let 'em wonder, that's what I figured as I tossed my overnight bag onto my bed. I took a long shower in the big bathroom that's connected to my bedroom, then threw on a towel and exited the steam-filled nook to find Ian sitting on the bed.

"Oh. Um. Hello," I said.

"I'm sorry to intrude, but the kitten is making himself at home out there—and despite her earlier reservations, Pepper seems to be taking to him a bit. While they're distracted, I was hoping you and I could have a private chat."

Out in the main living area, something crashed, and Pepper laughed. It struck me as strange only because she laughed so rarely, and this one seemed both real and ordinary.

Ian corrected himself. "Or as private as is reasonable to expect."

"Yeah, it's a madhouse around here," I agreed, still clutching the towel to my chest.

After a pause, Ian asked, "Are you standing there in a towel?"

"Yes."

"You know I can't see you."

I nodded, and he couldn't see *that*, either. "I know. Old habit, I guess. Residual modesty, or whatever. Anyway, I feel dumb about it, and now I'm going to stroll around the room buck-ass-naked while hunting for some clothes to put on."

He smiled without showing his teeth—the same smile he gave me when we'd first met. Cautious but pleased, and a little sneaky. "If you're going to narrate, I suppose I'll sit here and enjoy it."

"I wasn't planning on giving you a play-by-play," I groused, but I was grinning, too. "But if you're really dying for one, I'll see what I can scare up." I went to the top dresser drawer and said, "First, underpants. I'm reaching for the yellow polka dots because I'm feeling kind of kicky." This was a lie. All my underpants are black, white, or nude. I'm not very creative in the underpants department.

"Excellent," he said. "A playful side you don't often show."

"And now I'm . . ." I opened another drawer and as I fished through it with one hand, I used the other to yank my underwear up over my ass. "Hunting for a pair of jeans. Something comfortable. The dark wash, with the skinny cut."

"A classic color. Goes with anything. Easy to dress up, or down."

"I didn't know you were such a clothes horse," I said almost under my breath, but added, "But you always look good, particularly for a man who can't tell if his socks match."

"Ah, well. These days I have the children to thank for that. It's nice to hear they aren't leading me too far astray, or using my evening routine as a chance to play tricks."

"They're getting a little old for pranks. But the other day you were running around in a green waistcoat, and I had to wonder."

He lifted an eyebrow. "It was green? Very green? I was led to understand it was more of a moss-colored affair."

"Leprechaun green, I'm sorry to say." By now I was inside the jeans and fighting with the button at the top. I threw on a T-shirt and grabbed a light sweater to throw over it.

"No bra?" Ian asked—and drat his powers of deduction or hearing.

"None. I'm off duty tonight, and anyway, I've never had much that required a lot of structural support, if you know what I'm saying."

"I'll use my imagination."

"I bet you will. Now what's up?" I shut all my drawers, stayed barefoot, and came over to sit down on an old steamer trunk I keep beside the bed. It let me face him, and it felt less weird than sitting on the bed with him, even though "weird" does not necessarily equal "bad." I was tired, that's all. It'd been a busy couple of days, and I wasn't feeling up to any of the really hard conversations. Not yet.

"What's up," he mused an echo, and I only then noticed that he was fidgeting with a piece of paper. He must've just taken it out of a pocket or something; otherwise I would've seen it sooner. "I'm not completely certain, but I have an idea, and I have some concerns about it."

I sat back on the trunk. It creaked, but held. I leaned my shoulders against the wall and folded my arms in a subconsciously defensive position. Call me nuts, but I had a feeling I wasn't going to like this. Usually, he was much more direct—though letting himself into my bedroom was, I had to grant, pretty direct. "What are you getting at? Just let it fly. You're starting to worry me."

"Oh no." He shook his head and held up the paper like it was worthless, absolutely nothing to be concerned about. Just a pizza order someone scratched down beside the phone. "It's not any-thing . . . *alarming.* Merely worrisome. *Mildly* worrisome, even. I didn't mean to worry you. Not at all."

"With every word you are worrying me more. I think you need to get to the point before I take a jump off the high dive." The expression was a private one, a joke between us that we'd never bothered to explain to anyone else. It meant that I was going to have a neurotic meltdown of the spiraling variety. And since he didn't want that to happen because it drives him crazy, he needed to work himself around to what he really wanted to say.

"All right, yes. You're right, and I'm stalling. I apologize, but I'm . . . I'm not sure how much I can ask of you."

Oh. He needed a favor. How bad could it be? I wondered, and then hated myself for wondering. It's always worse than you expect. "Try me," I suggested. "Let's get this over with."

He pressed his lips together, frowned gently—like he wanted

to blurt out the word "fuck" but had no intention of doing so—
and finally he told me what he didn't want to tell me. "Earlier this
evening, Domino took a message from someone who'd called my
phone. I didn't hear it ring; I suppose I was outside. But he heard
it, and answered it."

"Is he supposed to do that?"

"I don't mind if he does. What could he possibly learn that
would be to his detriment? Almost no one ever calls but you, and
sometimes Adrian—and him only if he's looking for you."

I'd heard the disclaimer, and I pounced on it. "*Almost* no
one?"

He went on, but not without pausing so dramatically I thought
I'd have to prompt him. "I've had this phone for several years. Cal
set it up for me. The number is untraceable so far as we know,
and it's been an easy way for me to keep tabs on things in San
Francisco—if I really feel the need. I still have friendly contacts
there, though I could count them on one hand. And tonight, one
of them called."

"With a message about your old stomping grounds?"

"My old House, yes. Something has . . . happened."

"Something?"

"The House's judge has died. That's all I know—that's all the
message said." He held it up, and I saw that Domino's barely com-
petent handwriting had in fact recorded nothing more detailed
about whatever had been said.

House judge died. Call San Francisco.

"Shit," I said.

"Maybe, maybe not," he replied, but he sounded like a man
desperate to make the most of a bad situation. "It could be an
opportunity for me to withdraw from them for good."

"Bullshit. If you thought anything useful could come of this,
you wouldn't be weaseling around. This is bad news, isn't it? Did

Dom tell you anything else? Offer any details beyond what he scrawled on the back of . . . what is that, a Starbucks coupon?"

"Yes, it's probably bad news. No, he didn't tell me anything else. I don't know if it's a Starbucks coupon; it's whatever Domino found to be the handiest bit of scratch paper."

"Well, you just answered three questions in a row with direct yes-or-nos, so I'll consider that progress and press my luck for one more: They still don't know you're blind, do they? At your San Fran house?"

"No." He said it softly.

We both knew what it meant. It meant that he wasn't in as much danger as he could be. Yet.

And now for one of those digressions I warned you about. I'll try to keep it short and sweet.

Vampire Houses are Machiavellian to the core, and Ian used to be a major power player in San Francisco. Then he was captured, experimented upon, and blinded. To date, the blinding has proved permanent—though we hold out hope that one day, it might be improved.

If word of his disability made it back to San Francisco, Ian's shelf life would shrink considerably because, as I understood it, he's one of the legal heirs to the House's seat. Merely wandering away doesn't undo that legitimate claim to power, but that's what Ian had done, or that was his cover, anyway. After his blinding, he'd announced his intention to withdraw and hand the reins over to his brother, and then he'd relocated to New York for a while. Then Mexico. Then . . . I don't know where else, but obviously he'd ended up in Seattle.

Unfortunately, all this did was buy him time. Houses don't let vampires "retire." It's just not allowed, and for good reason. Once or twice before someone has wandered away from the gig, only to return years—even decades or centuries—later, wreaking havoc on whatever organizational structure rose up in that vampire's absence.

It's far better to make sure deserters have deserted on a permanent basis. It lets everyone sleep better at night.

Everyone except the deserters, and those of us who care about them.

"So," I said, and the word sounded loud in the near-darkness of my bedroom, illuminated only by the bathroom light behind the half-closed door. "What are you going to do about this?" I asked. "Is there any way anyone could track you here?"

"I don't know—to both of your questions. If I remain here long enough, someone will find me. They always do, don't they? I've deserted, and that's bad enough. Now they'll need me to come home as a matter of House life or death; they need to sort out the succession, and I'm in line."

"You can't go," I said flatly.

He started to say something, but changed his mind and closed his mouth. He reached out for my hand, and I gave it to him. While he spoke, he toyed with my fingers—and his were warm, meaning he'd recently fed. That must've been what he'd been up to when Domino took the message.

"Raylene, you've been so wonderfully kind to me these last few months," he began, which sounded like the start of a breakup conversation, and I didn't like it one bit. "You've given me a House again, which is something I hadn't had in years. You've given me a home."

"I'm pretty sure it was at least partly my fault that you lost your last home."

"Not at all. It would've come crashing down around my ears one way or another, and this way I was lucky enough to have help picking up the pieces. I'm very glad I hired you last year, and I'm glad you took the case. I'm glad that you're my friend," he added, hesitating just a hitch at the last word. He stopped playing with my fingers and just held them. "But you can't protect me forever. I don't even want you to try."

I pulled my hand away. "Stop talking like that."

"Like what?"

"Like you're *dying*—or like you're gearing yourself up to go wandering into the sunrise."

"Raylene—"

"No, it's bullshit!" I declared far more loudly than I should have. I stood up and walked away from him, then came back like a tetherball. "First of all, I'm not keeping you here like some goddamn pet. You're part of this . . ." Of this what? This family? Is that what we were? "Household," I concluded, because it was safer. "And sure, you have some . . . some special needs, but so do I. So do those kids out there. We're a commune of gimps here, Ian. And we look after each other, because nobody else will!"

"Raylene . . ."

"No, don't you use that Mr. Calm-and-Reasonable voice. It won't work!" I announced, which sounded like something a twelve-year-old would say, and I loathed myself for it. "You're trying to do something noble and stupid; you're going to tell me that you're leaving, for my own good. Aren't you?" When he didn't answer right away, I pushed harder. "Tell me I'm wrong."

He sighed. "You aren't wrong, but I'm still right. I *do* need to leave. If I don't, I'll put the whole . . . household"—he used my word—"in danger. You know it as well as I do."

"Fuck that. We're all in danger all the time, anyway. Those kids are one loitering offense away from being yanked off to a foster home. I'm one satellite snapshot away from being picked up by that psycho ghoul in Silicon Valley. Adrian is one drunk SEAL's glimpse of recognition away from a court-martial."

"This is more concrete than that. More pressing," he argued.

"Really? If anyone in California had any means of chasing you this far, someone would've nabbed you months ago. It would've happened when you were hiding in Ballard on a boat, or it would've happened while Adrian and I were tying up loose ends last winter. It would've happened by *now*."

"What can I say to make you understand?"

"Say you'll drop this. Say we can pretend you never said anything, and this conversation never happened. Everything will go back to being fine and you're not going anywhere; *that's* what you should say."

He insisted, quietly but firmly, "I have an obligation to them. It is a matter of personal honor that I return now that they've summoned me."

"But that's bullshit!" I shouted, and somewhere in the back of my brain I was aware that things had gone quiet in the living area, but that didn't slow me down. "You've been running and hiding from these fuckers for years. Now you're telling me that all they had to do was run your name up a flagpole and you'd salute?"

"This isn't like that. This is a power vacuum, one that I am obligated to address whether I like it or not. I accepted my position in that House, and with that position I accepted certain responsibilities. Those responsibilities didn't end when I left. When I was taken."

Sounded like a load of baloney to me, but I'd already said as much. I tried another tactic. "Let me ask you, do you even know for a fact that the judge has died? What if it isn't true, Ian? What if this is just another ploy to lure you back—to call you out?"

"Why would they lie?" he asked, but he didn't ask it with much conviction. I'd actually given him something to think about, which was a minor victory if only paltry relief.

"Because they're crooked, power-hungry, and fucked-up. Go on and tell me I'm wrong."

"You aren't wrong. Not in that particular assessment."

"Thank you for that one ounce of credit," I fumed.

"Listen, it's true that I haven't personally touched the corpse of William Renner; you've got me there. But the House has always been contentious, and he was never very well liked. It was only a matter of time and opportunity before he was ousted—and now that day of reckoning has arrived. Or so I assume."

"You assume. You'd walk right into a trap over an assumption?"

He was getting frustrated with me, and that was fine. I was well beyond frustrated with him, so if he wanted to be bitchy, I didn't give a damn. "If Renner is dead, then the House is vulnerable until it elects a new judge. And I was the next in line, so they can't very well elect me when I'm living here, now can they?"

"And what do you care?" I asked, which was a bigger question than I'd realized until it came out of my mouth. Because he *did* care, that much was obvious. And he *shouldn't* care; that much was equally obvious.

There was something he wasn't telling me.

"Familial duty?" He had the good sense to add a question mark.

"Who?"

"What?"

"*Who*, Ian. Who are you trying to protect down there?"

"You're reading too far—"

"Oh, knock it off. It's the only thing that makes sense—you wanting to protect someone. And I want to know who. I *deserve* to know who, if you're going to walk out over this."

He turned his face away, unwilling to even pretend he was looking at me. "A son," he breathed. He said it so gently, I barely heard it.

"What kind of son? Vampire son, or bio-son?"

Still barely speaking in a whisper, he replied, "Vampire son. His name is Brendan. He's next in line after me and my brother, and Maximilian will take his frustration out on him if I don't return."

Hm. A blood-son. Ian had never mentioned such a person before, but obviously he was rather deeply invested in protecting him, so I tried not to let it hurt my feelings that this was the first I was hearing of it.

I asked, "Could Brendan run the House? Or is he weak?"

"He's . . . not *weak*. And if anything, I think he'd be a very good judge. But I don't think he's strong enough to seize the position, whether or not he's savvy enough to hold it. Maximilian is certainly more determined to fill the seat—and it sounds like he's planning to do so, one way or another. I need to make contact with Brendan," he said, pleading now. Begging me, or negotiating with me—even though there was no chance in hell of me holding him against his will, or even stopping him if he'd made up his mind. I should've been flattered, but I was horrified. "I might be able to help him, to counsel him. I may be able to give him the boost he needs to take the leadership position or, I should hope, keep him from getting killed. He doesn't know Maximilian like I do. He doesn't know what he's capable of."

"You've been gone now, how long—ten years or so? You think in all that time, this son of yours hasn't climbed the learning curve enough to stand on his own two feet? You don't give him much credit."

A look of pure anger flashed across his face and was gone in an instant. But whether it'd appeared because I was right, or because I was insensitive, I couldn't say. Both, maybe. He replied, "I give him all the credit in the world, for a young man I abandoned to his own devices in the middle of that treacherous family."

"I was pretty sure you were kidnapped."

"But I could've returned. I could've been there for him, at a distance if not in person. I could have . . . could have . . ." And finally we'd reached the crux of the matter: Ian's unholy capacity for guilt. I was about to comment on it when he continued, "I should've contacted him privately, once I'd escaped. I should've sent for him, removed him from that snare of a House. But I was ashamed, and I was frightened that he might be intercepted somehow. I was afraid that I'd put us both in jeopardy if I reached out to him for help."

"You think he would've come?"

"I *know* he would have come. I stayed away for his own protection, you see."

Yes, I did see. It wasn't just that Ian felt an obligation; it was that he felt an opportunity to reconnect without putting his "son" in any deeper danger than the kid was already in. I am embarrassed to admit that the jealousy felt like heartburn, clawing up my chest.

"All right," I said, calming myself down by force. Nobody wins by being the jealous bitch. I know that the hard way. "All right. But let's not get ahead of ourselves, okay?"

"How is this—"

"You're talking about walking out of here on the basis of a rumor, and I'm talking about taking a deep breath and giving this some investigatory attention before you do anything rash."

"Investigatory attention?"

"Yes." The idea had sprung into my head fully formed— a reverse-Athena, ready to raise hell. "I want you to go unpack your suitcase"—I was pretty sure he'd already packed a suitcase, don't ask me why—"and then come back and tell me everything you know about this House—even the stuff that might be out of date. You're also going to tell me everything about this Brendan guy, and your brother."

"I don't think I like what you're getting at."

"You can't possibly dislike it more than I dislike the idea of you dashing off into California like the fucking cavalry." *When you can't even see,* I wanted to add, but didn't. No sense in pointing out the obvious. "Here's what I'm thinking . . ." And this is the part where I started winging it. "For starters, I'll go down to California and check things out."

"What?"

"I'm not trying to cramp your style or anything, but in all objective reality, I can get down there and back faster and with greater ease than you can."

"Raylene—"

"Just give me a few days," I pleaded. "Time to go down there and poke around. There's no real risk—hell, I could even go about it all formal-like, and it shouldn't be a problem."

He said, "But you don't have a House. You're unaffiliated, and there's no one to vouch for you."

"So? San Francisco and my old House in Chicago aren't exactly best friends. I could probably show up and tell San Fran the truth, and make up some excuse for my presence. Nobody would bother me, I bet." I didn't have any intention of actually doing this, of course, but it was the kind of thing that might make him feel better.

"It's a bad idea."

"Not as bad as you marching down there and stampeding into harm's way. And alone, too. You were going to go alone, weren't you?"

"I was planning on it, yes."

"No ghoul or anything?"

He folded his arms. "I told you, I still have friends. I could acquire a helper or a ghoul quickly, upon arrival." This meant he'd been making plans and phone calls behind my back. For how long?

I had no clue, and he probably wouldn't tell me, no matter how hard I badgered him. Call that a hunch.

"Good for you. But I still hate it, won't stand for it, and will attempt to actively impede you for your own good."

Pepper and Domino nudged the bedroom door, and it opened far enough to show both of their faces. They gazed at us worriedly, the veritable picture of, "Mom, Dad, stop fighting!"

I cleared my throat. "Hey, um, you two."

Domino was holding Pita, who squirmed until he was allowed to sit on the boy's shoulder. Pepper leaned into the room and asked, "Ian? Are you leaving us?"

She couldn't have possibly calculated a question more likely to inspire guilt and self-hatred in the pair of us. And it might've been calculated, for all I knew. The kid has always been a master manipulator. Or maybe she was only a little girl who'd found some semblance of stability for the first time in her short life, and she was watching its foundations crack beneath her feet.

In short, that kid did in five words what I'd attempted in ten minutes of hollering. She drove him to silence, and to something like contrition.

His only defense was to say, "I . . . well, I was thinking about taking a trip, that's all. To California. I was going to visit someone." It was a chickenshit way of spinning the truth. "I'd think you'd be thrilled with the idea—having no one around to bother you about your math skills for a few days."

Oh no he *didn't*. He wasn't getting off the hook that easy.

I said, "He was going to take a very dangerous trip to California, yes. But I think I've convinced him to stay home with you guys while I go check things out."

He glared at me with his silver, unseeing eyes. Actually he glared at a spot just to the left of my head, but hey. I give him an

E for Effort. He set his jaw and said, "Raylene has offered to do this, yes. But it's not a smart idea."

Domino grasped the situation, and was kind enough to be on my side. "It's a better idea than you going down there, ain't it? Were you going to go by yourself? I'd go too, if you needed me. But you didn't even ask."

This was possibly the sweetest thing I'd ever heard the boy say, but now was not the time to pat his head over it. I didn't even look at him. I made sure we were all three ganging up on the blind guy, who lived with the world's guiltiest conscience.

And a few secrets, obviously.

Deeply buried secrets, and therefore dangerous ones. I filed this information away and resolved to consult it later, in the event that I began assuming I knew everything about everyone under my roof.

"Thank you, Domino," Ian said. "That's a very kind and generous offer, but I did not ask for your help because I did not want to invite you into any danger. Raylene is right. It's a risky trip. And I suppose she's furthermore right that it would be smart for someone else to investigate the situation before I enter it. But this is a time-sensitive matter," he said directly to me. "I have a . . . someone I care about, in San Francisco, and I need to make sure that he's safe."

"Your son?" Pepper asked. Of course she asked. She has ears like a fennec fox.

"Yes, dear. He's not my child, exactly. I'm a different kind of father to him."

Either the sensitivity of the topic eluded her or she ignored it. "You made him a vampire?"

"Yes, that's what happened. He is in danger."

I was quick to note, "But Ian will be in *worse* danger if he gets too heroic. So it's settled then!" I clapped my hands in a gesture of, "Hurrah, we all agree!"

"Settled?" He frowned. Hard.

"Yes, *settled*. I'm fresh off a case that didn't pan out, and nothing else is on deck. I can take some time to bop around San Francisco, no problem. I'll head down there tomorrow night and sort the whole thing out. Ian can hang around here and look after you two for a few days by himself, I assume." After all, he'd been alone with them for the past twenty-four hours.

I stood up and walked to the kids, plucking Pita off Domino's shoulder and giving him a squeeze. "Great. Then I'll open a bottle of wine, we'll all settle in for the night, and Ian, you can fill me in. Don't leave anything out," I admonished as I strolled into the living area. Over my shoulder I called, "I want to know *everything*."

And I did. Kind of.

5

I asked Adrian if he wanted to come with me, which was probably dumb, but at the last minute I started having second thoughts about going it alone. I didn't tell Ian. I didn't want to worry him, or to give him one more thing to gripe at me about.

Ian was a giant tight-lipped douche during my interrogation—I mean, during my attempts to learn more about the situation into which I was about to walk. But by the time we were done, I had what amounted to a dossier on the Renner family and all their known associates. Sure, it was almost a decade out of date—updated in bits and pieces, as he'd cobbled pieces of gossip over the years. I marked these pieces of gossip with an asterisk when I wrote them down. I needed to remind myself they weren't set in stone.

Adrian was gung-ho to accompany me on the expedition until he remembered he'd have to take a week off work. Then he talked me into paying him for his time. I'd just write it off on my taxes as bodyguard work. If I paid taxes. Which I tend not to.

He wouldn't be *guarding* anyone, anyway, but he was one of the only mortals I knew who was tough enough to come close to keeping up with me. For that matter, he was one of the only people I knew, period. And I didn't feel like doing too much self-analysis with regard to why I wanted his company.

I'd spent a full human lifetime working alone. What had changed? I didn't get it.

Maybe I was just as pathetic as Pepper, suddenly feeling my sense of security threatened. It was fragile enough, and new enough, without the impending threat of Ian leaving us to stress us all further. We'd only had our weird little collective for about six months; before that, everything had been utterly upended. Building a cocoon of safety is a lengthy and terrible process. I hate doing it, and I didn't want to do it again anytime soon.

Like I said, I fear change. I fear it more than pain or death. And I fight it with every weapon at my disposal, every time it happens.

Adrian was one of my weapons now: a fist of inertia, helping me hold things together. He was also a potential liability, and I knew that, and I decided I didn't care. He was a big boy; he could make his own decisions. I wasn't forcing him to tag along. He was doing this of his own free will.

I picked him up from work on my way out of town. He'd already changed into dude-wear, which meant he was already fending off the guys from Cuffs, down the street.

Cuffs is a leather bar. Let us say no more about it.

Adrian is always good-natured about rejecting the advances;

he earns most of his living as a drag queen, and he knows how to fend off a grip. He's straight—or so I gradually deduced, over the last few months of knowing him—and he always *does* decline. So far as I know.

But when I pulled up to the curb in the Taurus of the Damned, as he liked to call my car, he was up against a wall with a motorcycle leather-daddy leaning in for the kill.

I honked. The off-duty queen waved, excused himself, flung open the car door, then tossed himself inside. He chucked a duffel bag over the seat; it landed on the floor behind me with a very heavy thud, and I smiled to consider what useful stuff he might've brought along.

"Everything but the kitchen sink?" I asked as I pulled back out into traffic, nearly smacking a cyclist who didn't think the rules of the road applied to him. Mr. Cyclist flipped me off, and I honked while gunning the engine to make sure he got the idea that he needed to get the fuck out of my way.

You have to be firm with the cyclists in Seattle. When it comes to smug self-entitlement, they're worse than the pigeons.

Adrian unclenched his hand from the *Oh-Shit* bar and said, "What? I'm sorry, I thought we were going to die, so I wasn't listening."

"If you're going to start this adventure by picking fights about my driving, I can pull over and let you out on the next corner."

"Who's picking fights? I'm just making observations," he said, his faint Spanish accent buffing the words to a shine. He sounds a little like Antonio Banderas crossed with Tommy Lee Jones. It's hard to explain, but easy on the ears.

"If you're hinting that you'd like to take the wheel, you can forget it. And I was simply noting that you've got a whole lot of gear."

"Of course I do."

"You don't have to pack like you're going to war, you know. I've got that covered."

"Sure," he agreed. "But sometimes you forget things."

"No, I don't."

"And when you forget things, it's up to me to pick up the slack."

I said, "You're full of shit." Because we both know I am the most ludicrously overprepared woman in the world. I have a stack of neuroses that a toddler could use for a booster seat, and those neuroses keep me braced for every possible contingency.

He asked, "Did you remember the duct tape?"

"In three colors."

"How about the handcuff master keys?"

"Two different kinds," I said.

"And an extra shooter? With ammo?"

"I brought four, and if you want something small enough to stash, you can take your pick." I'd seen his tuck-job when he's dressed in full lady-wear and working a room. I had every confidence that he could hide a small firearm with such efficiency that it would go unnoticed by any casual searcher. It might not be comfortable, but it'd be successful.

We played that game all the way to the interstate.

I could've shut him up by pulling over and showing him what was in the trunk—an arsenal of emergency and self-defense preparedness—but I let him guess. Our grown-up version of "I'm thinking of something red" was more entertaining than calling out license plates from other states, or slugging each other in the arm every time we spotted a Volkswagen, that was for damn sure.

We stopped for the night in Medford, Oregon, to break up the trip. The drive from Seattle to San Francisco is about a thousand miles long, so it's not like we were going to make it in a straight shot—and we'd decided not to fly.

For all the previously mentioned ravings about packing lots of contraband, it's easier to hop in the car and drive down the westernmost slice of the nation, even though Oregon has that weird thing where they won't let you pump your own gas—"For your own safety" or some other bullshit. I hate filling up there, and the next night my hatred of this intrusive practice almost led to us running out of gas before crossing the California state line and finding a gas station where I could service myself. I mean the car. You know what I mean.

But we didn't end up walking along the shoulder with an empty gas can and a scowl, despite Adrian's dire predictions, and fully ninety minutes before dawn we were checked in to a nicely restored turn-of-the-century hotel in downtown San Francisco. It was a little close to the tourist district for my liking, but the room was quiet and clean, and it had two big queen-sized beds—which I joked about rather endlessly, at Adrian's expense.

I tell you all that in order to tell you this: Within three nights, I was right where I'd promised I'd go, and doing exactly what I'd promised to do.

If Adrian were reading this over my shoulder, he'd take this opportunity to insert some snark about how I must've promised to sit in the hotel room and drink while surfing the Internet, but he's a bitch sometimes, and there were moments when I wished I'd left him at home.

I've already mentioned that I'm not sure why I dragged him along, other than a whiny, obsessive need for comfort-company at a difficult time in my personal life. But it's probably worth examining why *he* agreed to come along, when nobody in his right mind would have done so.

The answer, I suspect, is pretty simple: He adores me, and will do whatever I ask.

Ha! Yes, I'm kidding.

Don't get me wrong, I think he likes me well enough— I mean, he's the closest thing to a girlfriend I've had in ages—but that's not the *real* reason he's along for the ride. The real reason is sneakier and more sinister, and if he thought I didn't know about it, he was deluding himself.

Adrian came to San Francisco on a vampire fact-finding mission because he wants to know more about vampires and how their Houses work. The underlying basis for this near-suicidal desire has to do with his sister, Isabelle—who was turned into one of us night-stalkers when she was a teenager. She was also experimented on by the government, but that's another story. Come to think of it, that's also the story of why Adrian is now a drag queen, and not a Navy SEAL. But I don't like to repeat myself, so I'll make this rehash quick.

Suffice it to say, Isabelle ran away from home—or was taken; that's still up for debate—and ended up running with the House in Atlanta. Atlanta's House is run by the Barrington family, and those sons of bitches are about fifty different kinds of trouble.

My own House in Chicago, back when I had one, was trouble, too, so I suppose I should qualify that statement by saying *all* vampire Houses are trouble. All of them.

But some Houses are more stable than others, and some are better run than others. The Barringtons aren't just numerous, they're psychotic—or at least their judge and her immediate family members are. They're beyond capricious and well past understated. They're the kind of vampires who dress like goths every chance they get, and probably have entire DVD collections dedicated to old movies about the undead.

They are very, *very* excited to be vampires. I would say

"comically so" if it weren't so fucking frightening. It absolutely says something about the House that it's so violent—and it creates such a preposterously high body count—but the mortal authorities are prepared to look the other way.

Obviously they know about it. They *have* to know about it.

But worst of all, the authorities probably aren't even in the Barrington family's pockets. They're probably too scared to do anything about them, or maybe they just buy in to that old line the Mafia dons used to throw around—"We only kill each other." But it was bullshit when the mob said it, and it's bullshit when vampire Houses say it.

For the Atlanta House to be so unapologetically badass that it's been operating this way for nearly a century . . . you *know* that means they've got power.

Why?

See, here's the dark, terrible secret that every vampire secretly knows, but refuses to admit out loud: Houses can be huge and intimidating, and immensely dangerous to vampires and those who cross them, unwittingly or otherwise. But generally speaking, they can be brought down by ordinary mortals with very little effort and pressure.

There, I said it. Call me an iconoclast.

Maybe it sounds strange, but it's true. And it's true because, for all our heightened senses, our speed, and our occasional psychic abilities . . . we're fragile. We're freaky little hothouse orchids, is what we are, and all it takes is sunlight to wipe us off the map. All you have to do to demolish a vampire House is show up during the day and burn some buildings down. You can effectively unseat an entire community that way. Simple. Brutal. Effective.

And rarely attempted.

The drawbacks are obvious. Anyone ambitious enough to try to burn out a House would have to get through an army of intermediary ghouls (or not, if he or she were crafty enough); and there's always the chance of collateral damage if mere mortals are employed or otherwise present. And most important, vampires tend not to let that kind of thing slide—so if an arsonist were to undertake such a plot, he or she would have to cover his or her tracks very, very well. Retaliation is a bitch with fangs.

I'm not sure why I just now used all that "his or her" bullshit. The truth is, *I've* thought about it before. A lot. Fantasized many a time about taking Chicago's House by a cleansing, fiery storm.

But I've always chickened out. Or, if I were to treat myself more charitably, I'd argue that I came to my senses and walked away instead.

It was easier for me than for Ian. Ian was a power player, someone high up in the hierarchy. I was a total nobody. Bottom of the pack, and bottom of the barrel. I suspect that no one at all gave a shit when I left, except perhaps my "mother," who was angry that I didn't stick around and take the fall for her indiscretions.

To this day, I'm not sure if I escaped her because of my outstanding brains, wit, and paranoia . . . or if she only concluded that I wasn't worth the effort. Either way, it doesn't keep me up at night or anything. Not anymore. I stopped wondering about why she did the things she did a long time ago.

What was I saying to begin with? Oh yeah. Adrian.

So Adrian's little sister became a vampire, then became a government subject in the same weird experiment (Project Blood-shot) that had blinded Ian. No, this wasn't a matter of ludicrous coincidence, that three friends found out we had this weird connection; it's this weird connection that brought us together.

For a long time, Adrian assumed that his sister was dead. After all, that's what Uncle Sam told him—and he had no evidence to the contrary. But now we had reason to believe that she might well have survived, and that perhaps she was roaming around as a loner.

As a favor to Adrian, I'd done a little bit of reconnaissance through the gossip grapevine, and I'd learned that Isabelle had most definitely *not* rejoined the Barrington House, which surprised me not at all. I'd also learned that there are rumors of a deaf vampire matching her description lurking around North Georgia, and Vegas odds suggest it's her. Whatever she's up to, she's keeping a low profile like a smart girl. Any vampire on the outs with the Atlanta House would be wise to vanish (begging the question of why she's still in Georgia, or back in Georgia, as the case may be), and any vampire with a significant physical disadvantage (see also: Ian) would be likewise smart to keep that under wraps.

There are no civil rights groups out there lobbying for fair treatment of the disabled undead. Disabilities make vampires targets. And nobody anywhere is going to do anything about that.

Adrian isn't a vampire, though.

And in case it isn't abundantly clear by now, I'm not the kind of vampire who runs around knocking off denizens of the night who are weaker in some fashion than myself. So if I could help Adrian find his sister, awesome. He'd owe me a favor, and he'd be happy, and I'd be two vampires into collecting the whole Bloodshot play set.

(No, we don't know exactly how many vampires—or other creatures—were carved up by that project. I won't know that for certain until I get my hands around the neck of a guy named Jeffery Sykes, and he's proving rather difficult to locate. But I'm working on it.)

Come to think of it, I probably shouldn't have brought Adrian along.

I was only putting him in mortal danger, and whether or not

he was excited about the prospect was rather beside the point. I didn't think he could learn anything in San Francisco that I, personally, couldn't have told him . . . but hadn't yet. I've been trying to protect him by pretending that all my information is fiercely difficult to come by, and impossible for a living human to acquire.

It isn't.

But it *is* true that if he went sticking his nose into vampire lairs, asking questions about a deaf undead girl tootling around Fulton County, he'd be calling dangerous, unwanted attention to them both. So far, I've been utterly unable to convince him of how bad this is, or how badly he should not attempt it.

He'd been sticking his neck out, which is literally the stupidest thing I can imagine anyone doing when it comes to vampires. That ought to be Rule Number One For Dealing With Vampires, right there. Don't stick your neck out!

So I guess that's why I invited him, if I have to offer a less selfish reason than "so I don't have to do this alone." I'd rather have him dive headlong into that danger while I'm standing around, available and willing to dive in after him and pull him out.

Adrian stole the television remote from me, and clicked through all the usual cable channels while I surfed the Web. "What are you looking for, anyway?" he asked. "When do we get out of this room?"

"As soon as I figure out where we need to go when we *leave* this room," I said, answering his second question first. "You want to run downstairs and find a latte? Go ahead. This might take a few minutes."

"Why?"

"Because dens don't advertise. Or, okay, they *do* advertise—but not in any way that's immediately obvious or helpful."

He seized on the niblet of information I'd let slide. "Dens? What's a den?"

"Sort of like a lobby," I muttered, sticking a pen in my mouth and reaching for the pad of paper that sits beside every phone in every hotel room everywhere around the country. "Or . . . think of it more as a foyer, I guess. The foyer of a vampire House. It's where they receive visitors, out-of-towners, and the like."

"Is it a public place?" he asked.

"The storefront is usually public, yes. But the real action goes on somewhere else. Downstairs, more often than not."

"So you're looking for a storefront . . ." He dropped himself onto the bed beside me and narrowed his eyes at my screen.

"Not a *literal* storefront. Well, okay." I chattered with a lisp as my mouth moved around the pen. "*Maybe* a literal storefront. Probably not."

"You're being obtuse."

I removed the pen so I could reprimand him without sounding like a third-grader with a mouthful of paste. "I'm *trying* to answer your questions, but the answers aren't so much *direct*. It's like this," I explained. "Dens are hidden in plain sight, but they aren't marked with a big neon arrow pointing down, declaring VAMPIRES HERE! That would be stupid. Instead, the dens come with little telltale clues about them."

"What kind of clues?"

"Subtle clues. The kind only another vampire would pick up on. They'll have funny names—something with a double meaning, or sometimes an anagram of the House's family name."

He nodded thoughtfully. "All right. Then what's the SF House's family name?"

"Renner. Not super-inspiring, I know." I jotted it down on the paper pad beside my thigh. "Or in case it broadens the

possibilities, the judge who just died . . . his name was William." I
scratched that down, too, and tried to imagine the letters in different configurations. "I'm not saying for absolute certain that we're
hunting an anagram, but it's a place to start."

"And probably not an actual storefront, but maybe."

"Yeah. I mean, no. I mean . . . shit, Adrian. Look at the clock.
It's ten PM on a weeknight. We're looking for an establishment that
might reasonably be open, routinely, at ten PM on a weeknight—
and much later than that. And nothing too quiet. Something noisy,
like a bar or a club."

"So a late-night coffeehouse is out."

"Correct." I scrolled through the listings, demonstrating that
yes, I was checking the names and addresses of bars, clubs, theat-
ers, and pool halls. There were, to my best estimate, approximately
a bajillion of them.

"How are we going to narrow it down?" he wanted to know,
and I didn't know what to tell him.

"This isn't my town, dude. If I were local, or if I had local
ties, I could ask somebody and that would be faster. But I'm not
local, I don't know anybody local, and—"

"Why don't you just ask Ian?"

I sighed heavily. "I *did* ask Ian. The last den he knew about
closed down three years ago. And nothing has reopened in its place."

"What was it called?"

"Claret Drip. It was an anagram of someone else's name—
whoever had been judge or family before the Renners came into
the picture. Sometimes the new guys change all the signs right
away; sometimes they let the old things ride awhile."

"I get it. I think." He flopped down on his stomach and
propped his face up on his hands. "Wine is kind of a code for
blood, and it was an anagram, too. Double the meaning, double

the chance someone would twig to the fact it was hiding a den. But probably not someone who didn't need to find it."

"Smart cookie. And now that you grok the generality of how this works, keep your eyes open for something similar. I'll scroll slowly."

"Scroll faster," he suggested with an imperious swish of his finger. "I'm a fast reader."

"I'm a fast reader, too, but I'm trying to give my subconscious a moment to absorb all this crap," I complained.

He wriggled to make himself more comfortable, and the bed rolled like the wave pool at a theme park. I smacked him on the shoulder and told him to settle down, and he smacked me back, and told me to hurry the fuck up or we were never getting out of here. I told him it was his own damn fault for not bringing a laptop, and he replied that it was my fault for not telling him to toss one into his go-bag.

And after another couple of hours populated by similarly childish bickering, he jabbed at the screen almost hard enough to crack it. "Wait!"

"What?"

"This one, there. Look at it."

I read aloud, "Ill Manner," and clicked through to the listing. "Looks like a goth bar. But that doesn't mean real vampires hang out there."

"Ill Manner . . . the place's name, though. Check it out—lots of the same letters as *William Renner*." He took my pen and wiped off the end as if I were germy or something, and started fiddling with the letters on the hotel's letterhead.

I observed, "It's close, but not quite. Still . . ." I wondered if he wasn't on to something. There was the double meaning of *manner/manor*, and vampires love a good entendre. "Hang on.

Maybe we've got this. What letters are you missing to make the anagram complete?"

"*R, I, W,* and *E.*"

"Hot damn," I declared with a smile. "Ill Manner is on Wire Street. I do believe we've found it."

"Great!" He hopped up, swung his legs over the side of the bed, and stretched so hard that his back cracked. "Let's throw on some eyeliner and hit the dance floor. Or whatever the protocol is, in situations like these."

"I think we're a little old to . . ." I almost said "hit the dance floor" but then I remembered who I was talking to. "Never mind. Do you have any kohl? I don't usually wear eye makeup, myself, but I think I could use some tonight."

"Do I have any? Woman, I could write a book with it. And come to think of it, that's true, isn't it? I never do see you made up." He gazed at me with a critical eye and his hands on his hips. "You'd better let me put it on you."

"What? No. I may not be Rembrandt with a stick of liner, but I'm not a monkey at the obelisk, either."

"My makeup, my rules."

"I can't believe you even *brought* makeup."

"I'm sorry, have we met? Of *course* I brought makeup."

"To a reconnaissance operation?"

He shut me up with, "In San Francisco? Hell yes, I brought makeup. And oh, look—it's an emergency supply that *you* failed to pack."

"Oh, shut up."

"No. Now hold still . . ."

"This is ridiculous," I griped, but in ten minutes he had me looking like a supermodel. A very pale, sulky, raccoon-eyed supermodel, but a supermodel nonetheless. I was impressed, but I didn't tell him so. Didn't want him to get a big head about it.

In ten more minutes, he'd given himself a good swath of guyliner, which I qualify as guyliner because he wasn't in drag. He was wearing black head-to-toe, just like me, but he was sporting a black fitted stretchy sweater and black cargo pants—and I was in a black blouse (not too frilly, but just a smidge girlie) and black cigarette pants. And boots. Always the boots. It's hard to kick anybody's ass in sandals.

By half past midnight, we were down in the lobby hailing a cab, and on the ride over we got our story straight.

"We need a story?"

"Absolutely. Neither one of us can or should walk in there cold, with nothing but a smile and a handshake to recommend us. First of all, you're going to be my ghoul, get it?"

"Your *what*?"

"You heard me."

"Do I *look* like a ghoul to you?" he asked.

"Ghouls are like serial killers, they look just like everybody else. At least, they do unless they've been ghouls so long they start the slow-change, but that doesn't happen very often. You'll pass for one, don't worry about it."

"What do I have to do to pass?"

"Everything I say. Down to the letter. And you have to be nice to me. You have to pretend you respect me, and you don't want to kill me where I stand."

"Oh for fuck's sake. You're making this up."

"I'm not, and you'll see that for yourself when we get there."

He gestured toward the driver with a jerk of his chin. "Maybe we should have this chat . . . later? In private? There must be a coffee shop or bar nearby."

"Don't worry about it," I said, waving his concerns away. "He barely speaks English, and he's not paying attention anyway." I could feel the driver's apathy. It radiated off him—or oozed off him, really. My psychic sense didn't even need to flex its metaphoric muscles to read him.

The cab hit a pothole and nearly followed that up with a pedestrian. Swearing and honking ensued, and I continued, "Your job as a ghoul is to serve and assist. Ostensibly, you're kissing ass because you want to be a vampire someday. Got it?"

"Got it." He said it like he was already plotting my death. I was in for a humiliating demise, I could tell. Probably something involving autoerotic asphyxiation and small rodents.

"Just play along, would you?" I implored. "Do it right, and we'll probably survive this visit. Do it *well*, and we might actually learn something useful."

We pulled up to Ill Manner after twenty minutes of further pedestrian abuse. I paid the cabbie and stood on the sidewalk next to Adrian, who was staring up at the big red sign with silver and black accents. It looked like a custom artisan job, wired for lights. A regular work of art, it was.

Outside on the sidewalk, the air was choked with cigarette smoke and accented with the tang of cloves. I think they're illegal to buy and sell now, as a result of some ridiculous "protect the children!" big brother campaign gone ludicrously awry. But that doesn't stop people from getting them, and it sure as hell doesn't stop goths from smoking them.

Most of the smokers were wearing black (shocker, I know) and too much makeup, and a whole lot of silver. I also saw goggles here and there, and the occasional Technicolor dye job, so all was pretty much *de rigueur* for the scene.

Disaffected young people? **Check.**

Stupid accessories? Check.

Flavored cancer sticks? Check.

Adrian looked like the oldest guy there, but that was sort of a tricky thing to quantify. It would be more accurate to say that he stood out as a potential drug dealer or narc, but I'm baby-faced enough that I didn't earn many second glances. I think it annoyed Adrian. It pleased the hell out of *me*.

He reached the door first, and the door-guy didn't card him, but asked him for an eight-dollar cover. Adrian covered us both, and then I got carded—ha ha *ha*—and we squeezed inside.

The dance floor spun with moving lights in dark, bloody shades of purple and red, and there was a stage but it wasn't occupied. The bar was lit up like a shrine, as it damn well ought to be, and it was crowded—but I was pretty sure I could sneak up and get the information I needed without too much fuss.

"Madness," Adrian said, just loudly enough for me to hear him over the thudding drone of some old Combichrist song.

"What's madness?"

"These . . . these . . ." He gestured at himself, and at the ceiling. "Black lights. Terrible idea."

I shrugged. "I thought black lights were pretty . . . um . . . goth, or whatever."

"No way. No self-respecting, black-wearing goth wants to be anywhere near a black light."

"Why's that?" I asked.

"Look at all this lint!" He picked a piece off his sweater, held it high, and flicked it onto the floor.

"Damn." And now that he'd said something, I couldn't *not* notice it.

"Pathetic," he sniffed. "A good red light works better, it's more atmospheric, and is easier on your night vision."

"Spoken like a SEAL."

"What did you expect?" he asked.

"Everything else you've said, pretty much all night, has been spoken like a drag queen. I'm glad to see you can jump back and forth so easily. A SEAL will be of more use to me downstairs."

"So you *think*."

I let it go, and said, "Hang out here, or near the stage. I'm going to go bother the bartender."

"Why?"

"Because she's a ghoul. And she knows where the action is."

He started to ask me how I knew that, but I was already out of his reach and he didn't want to shout it in a crowded room, Combichrist or no.

As for me, I wormed among the dancers and pushed when I had to, slinking sideways when it was doable and elbowing a few people out of the way when it was necessary. It took a minute to get to the bar, but that was fine—because it gave the bartender plenty of time to see me, notice me, and probably push the silent alarm that told the folks downstairs that one of their own had arrived.

I used my shoulders to make room between two girls sucking down cherry-flavored somethings, and the bartender was right there waiting for me.

She was gorgeous, with slick, short green hair and a nose ring that hung down from her septum like a bull's more utilitarian jewelry. I suspected she made a goddamn fortune in tips. "Can I help you with something?" she asked.

"I think you can." I could "hear" her, sort of—she was communicating with her boss, somewhere else in the building. I couldn't trace her psychic signal or follow it, but I knew what she was doing. That's how I'd pegged her for the ghoul in charge—that thin stream of psychic vibration, pulling back and forth between ghoul and master. It's a soft sound, but a distinctive one.

The beautiful bartender said, "I could make you a drink. What strikes your fancy?"

I played along. "Nothing from the front room, but I've got the money and taste for the vintage stuff. Do you have anything in the back?"

"We might. I'll have to ask."

"By all means."

She was looking past me, over my head—since the bar was lifted off the main floor by a couple of steps. "You brought a friend."

"Yeah." I shrugged. "He's with me. I keep him close."

"He's pretty."

"But he's not any trouble. He knows how to do what he's told."

All of this was silly, and necessary.

To share it on another level—she was asking me if Adrian was my ghoul, and if I had him on a tight enough leash to bring him to the vampire party; and I was telling her that of course he was fine, he was with me, and he'd behave. I presented this as if it were gospel fact, though let's be real: I had no idea what Adrian would or wouldn't do if things got tight and he started to chafe in his role as underling. Didn't matter. We were too far deep to back out now, and I'd promised him he'd stay with me, so that's how I pitched it.

The phone behind the bar rang. It lit up in time to the ringing, so the staff would notice it above the social din. The bartender picked it up and turned away from me to talk. I couldn't read her lips and there was too much background buzz to pick out the details, but she was telling someone that I checked out—or at least I knew the lingo—and I wanted to chat in the den.

She hung up and returned her attention to me. "Someone will be with you in a moment." Then she nodded toward Adrian as if I should fetch him, or join him—but what she really wanted me to do was call him over without a sound.

I can do that, sometimes. Not because Adrian is my ghoul, but because I have that pitiful rudimentary psychic sense, and sometimes it works better than others. It's not common to all vampires; only a relative few of us have it, and no one knows why (or why not) it ever appears. Mostly it's just a heightened sense of

awareness with regard to what people are feeling, and it's kind of
crap as a communication tool.

But it's worked in the past, and I hoped to God that it'd work
now.

I concentrated hard, but tried equally hard not to make
any kind of straining, squinty face that would betray the effort.
Brain-chatter between ghouls and masters is as easy as a whisper.
If it looked like I was fighting for the connection, the pretty lady
with all the booze would know something was up.

With all my might, I "said," *Adrian, look at me.*

He did, though whether it was a case of my powers at work
or his natural curiosity over where I'd gone off to, I can't say and
don't care. I added, *Get over here,* with a casual crook of my head
to underscore it—in case my psychic powers were experiencing
an off day.

He ducked his chin in return and began working his way
across the floor to meet me. In order to do this, he had to perform a
wacky, forward-moving, martial-arts-style dancing due to the fact
that it wasn't Combichrist playing anymore—it was Lady Gaga,
which frankly surprised me. What had been a half-empty dance
floor five minutes previously was now crowded with clusters of
spinning, bobbing, weaving dancers.

Goths. Who can fathom, am I right?

Almost as soon as Adrian managed to join me, we were both
joined by a thin, pierced, mohawked kid whose attitude implied he
was the servant of someone important, but he probably wasn't. He
was probably your average teenager with a part-time job, only his
part-time job involved getting the occasional infusion of bodily
fluids from someone important.

"I'm Gabe." Even though he shouted it, it sounded disaffected and very, very bored.

"I'm Raylene, and he's with me." Visitors don't introduce

their ghouls except to the bigwig. They don't need names. They aren't important.

Adrian's scowl said he wanted to object to this already. My return scowl told him where to stick it. To his credit, he swallowed his pride, shut up, and walked behind me as I followed Gabe through the bar-area crowd and to the back of the club. We maneuvered past a pool table that was being used as a shot-glass buffet, a pair of restrooms that were each marked as unisex, and a small kitchen off to the right—on the other side of some swinging doors.

And then we hit the stairs.

There are always stairs. Vampires are creatures of tradition and habit, despite any insistence to the contrary. When we want to feel safe, we head underground.

Two floors down—into a sub-basement—we were led through a large mahogany door and through (I shit thee not) an arch with a beaded curtain. The beads looked like obsidian, or heavy glass. Something expensive that tinkled prettily as it announced our passage.

On the other side of this curtain, five people were scattered—sitting, standing, and leaning around a large open room with one of those seventies-tastic sunken seating areas. Inside this retro depression in the floor, a curved red couch ate up two-thirds of the circle, and seated alone upon it was an ethnically ambiguous brunet who'd probably been about thirty when he'd died. He was expensively dressed in a navy wool suit and purple tie, and his wavy, dark hair was allowed to hang tastefully free just above his shoulders. If I had to check a box or two, I'd have guessed him for Latino with a North African influence, but it was hard to say. He was good-looking in a distinctive way, with strong features, good bone structure, and a lean build. At a glance, I could both (a) imagine him on a United Colors of Benetton ad from the eighties, and (b) ascertain that he'd never be so gauche as to shop there.

You didn't have to be a vampire to see that this was obviously the Guy in Charge.

The other four people in the room were less of a problem. Two ghouls, a man and a woman in adult gothwear (all black clothes and hair, but less makeup and bling); two vampires, one by casual appearance an elderly woman, and the other a teenage boy who looked enough like Gabe to be his brother—or maybe not. It's hard to tell when everyone's in Halloween mode.

The Guy in Charge smiled at me, showing enough tooth to be a little impolite, but hey. When you're the Guy in Charge, you get to do that. He said, "Hello there, and welcome to San Francisco."

I stopped at the edge of the sunken couch pit and said, "Thanks." This is the part where, under ordinary circumstances, I'd make some blah-blah-blah about bringing greetings from whichever House I hailed from. "My true name is Raylene Pendle, and this is my ghoul—but I am here on behalf of no House, and I claim no affiliation."

He lifted an eyebrow. "No . . . House?"

"None, but don't let that bother you. I'm no ostracist, and if I meant any trouble, I would've made it in a more roundabout way. I wouldn't present myself."

"Then what *does* bring you here?" he asked smoothly. He didn't offer us a seat or anything, but that's typical. The man (or woman) in the power position always wants to preserve the appearance of control.

"Information. I might have some that can be of use to you."

He brought the eyebrow back into its original position. "And you've come to volunteer it? How kind."

"I've come with an offer to pursue it. I understand you're looking for Ian Stott."

I hadn't told Adrian about this part, and I had to trust him to trust me. I wasn't about to sell Ian out, but I needed to share a bit of the truth if I was going to get anywhere with these guys. My statement was met with silence and stares, but it wasn't an innocent silence and they weren't disinterested stares. Eventually Dude in Charge gave a little laugh.

"Perhaps we should speak privately, you and I." Then he clapped his hands and said sharply, "Out."

I glanced over my shoulder to see Adrian looking iffy about this, and uncertain about where he was supposed to go. So I said to the Dude in Charge, "He stays with me."

"No, he leaves with *mine*. Annabelle, please make our visitor feel at home." Ah. Then she was the ghoul-in-chief. The female half of the tasteful mortal goth pair nodded and gestured for Adrian to come with her as the room emptied. "Get him a drink, or a bite to eat." And he added to me, "They aren't going far."

I didn't like watching Adrian leave, even though he put on a good show of not giving a shit one way or another. I hoped maybe he'd learn something from the other ghouls; they're like the "help" anywhere. They know things . . . the kinds of things they're expected to keep to themselves, but don't always. If they believed Adrian was a ghoul, they might talk to him like one of their own. He knew to keep an ear out for info regarding Brendan, and he knew how to keep his mouth shut if he needed to.

I'd just have to trust him to think on his feet. It was all I could do, short of raising a stink that might get us both killed. The mere absence of copious vampires in my immediate presence did not mean they weren't nearby. Or watching. Or sharpening their teeth and eagerly anticipating some kind of trouble.

When even the other two vampires had exited the premises, slinking out through the glass beads and toward the stairs, I was finally invited to sit down.

"Join me, won't you? Raylene, wasn't it?"

"That's right."

"House-less, at the moment, but you know the manners of a House. So you've either left one, or been evicted from one."

"Those aren't the only two possibilities," I said, leaving him in the dark and not offering to clarify. "And that's not what I'm here to discuss. I'm sorry, but I don't believe I caught your name."

If he withheld it any longer, he ran the risk of being rude. He didn't want to be rude, not if he was smart—and he didn't strike me as a dummy.

Lone vampires who aren't afraid to approach a den are likely to be powerful enough to survive by themselves. Quite obviously, this is true when it comes to yours truly. I may be neurotic as hell, paranoid, control-freaky, and prone to hissy fits, but I'm no pansy.

"I'm Maximilian Renner," he said, which I knew already— but it still made me want to blurt out, "And I'm your mother!" because nobody really comes born with that kind of name. He'd probably adopted it along the way. Lots of vamps do that; it helps cement their integration into a House by making a public, more or less permanent declaration of loyalty.

"Nice to meet you, Max," I said as I stepped down the four steps that would put me onto the pimp-couch with the Guy in Charge. It really *was* pimp-a-riffic. Straight out of a vintage porno, I swear to God.

We didn't shake hands or anything, but I slipped into a seat near him—far enough away on the curve that I could make eye contact without getting a cramp in my neck.

"Now," he began, leaning forward and crossing one leg over the other in a show of body language that was meant to convey that I was in his space, at his discretion. "You want to talk about Ian. Is he a friend of yours? Do you people without Houses have little conventions or something?"

"We're acquainted. I don't know where he is at this precise moment, but I could find out."

"And what would it cost us?"

"We aren't up to that part of the conversation yet, Max. You're obviously"—I almost said, "the Guy in Charge" but I didn't—"an authority figure here in San Francisco. It's a nice den you've got. Nice front, too." There was no telling how far flattery would get me, but it's usually worth a shot.

"Thank you and yes, we're rather happy with it. Of course, this is only one of several dens," he said almost curtly, like I was wasting his time—or he was afraid that I was about to.

"I would assume. So here's my question, if you'll pardon the bluntness: Are you the top of the food chain? Or is there someone else I should speak with, if I want to talk to the people in charge?"

He forced himself to relax—loosening the tight crossing of his legs and leaning to rest one arm on the back of the curvy couch. But the sharp line of his mouth didn't soften, and I knew better than to take this show at face value. "Bluntness is preferred above outdated niceties. At the moment, I'm the man on top."

"You say that as if it could change at any time."

He glared at me big time, and without fanfare he said, "Three weeks ago, my father died."

"William Renner?"

The glare deepened. "That's him, yes. He'd been the judge in this city for decades, and his passing has left a tremendous vacuum."

"You seem to be filling it ably," I pushed the flattery a little farther, hoping to soften him up—maybe take the edge off his sourpuss demeanor.

It didn't really work, except that it earned me a civil reply. "It's kind of you to say so. Have you been in the city long?"

"I only arrived tonight." It was pretty much true. And you really, *really* don't want to hang out in a city with a powerful House without introducing yourself. It can be bad for your health.

He said, "I see. And you wish to talk about Ian."

"How do you know him?" I wanted to get him back in the habit of answering my questions, and not vice versa.

"He's my brother." He unveiled this piece of information with the clear intent of surprising me, which it clearly didn't. "We spent many years side by side in this House, working together for its continued survival and improvement."

Christ. He sounded like a sales brochure. "And what of Brendan?" I asked with all the innocence I could muster.

Maximilian hesitated, balking as he considered whether or not to lie. In the end, I think he went with the truth—albeit a careful, no-doubt vigorously spun version of it. "He left the House two weeks ago. No one has seen any sign of him since."

"How . . . convenient," I said. "For him." And me, too. I wasn't sensing any deception, only caution—and if Brendan was out of the House (on vacation, furlough, or running for his life), he wasn't being menaced by Maximilian. Regardless of what the wannabe-judge was telling my beloved roommate.

"I suppose. I thought he might've tried running home to Ian . . . ?" He hinted strongly, pointing an eyebrow at me like a weapon.

"Not to my knowledge, he didn't. But I could be wrong."

Max smiled, keeping his jaw clenched and his mouth shut. It looked mean. "Well. I'm sure he's fine, wherever he's gone, though no one is clamoring to have him back. It's *Ian* we need. I was never meant to be left in charge. It was never my destiny, or my goal."

He was right about it not being his destiny. Ian had told me that Max was the youngest, and last in line. Unless the judge changes the rules, Houses run like royalty that way, oldest to youngest. At any time, a judge can change up the mix—it happens with a fair degree of frequency—but if those arrangements aren't specified before he dies, vampires default to the old-fashioned birth-order school of thought on inheritance.

I said, "Maybe not, but looks like things are running smoothly." I tried to sound friendly, and no doubt did a terrible job.

"Is that what it looks like?" He sneered. "I suppose that's good to hear, that the illusion is holding up." Maximilian made a face like he wanted to bite the head off something, maybe me. His lifted nostril raised one corner of his lip, exposing another impolite flash of fang. "And it *is* an illusion. Perhaps a temporary one, because my father picked one of the worst possible places to die, damn him."

"And that would be . . . ?"

"Atlanta."

I produced a low, unhappy whistle. I couldn't help it. "Atlanta? He was with the Barringtons? Jesus Christ."

"Tell me about it." He uncrossed his legs, then changed his mind and draped them one upon the other once more.

"What happened?"

"I'm not sure that's any of your concern," he said tightly.

"It's not my concern, no. But I'm curious, and I'm not accusing you of anything. What was he doing in Georgia? It might matter to Ian," I tried. Maybe his brother's name would haul him back around to feeling cooperative. Or somewhat cooperative. Or whatever "cooperative" looked like to Max on an ordinary night. "I'll need details, facts. Particulars. If I want to lure him out, I mean. He's already gotten the message that the judge is dead. But it'll take more than that to bring him home."

Max chewed on this, eyeing me the whole time without blinking, and without even the faintest hint of friendliness. What had begun as a civil meeting was devolving into hints, tricks, and political confrontation, and I didn't like it . . . mostly because I only had the one card to play—Ian—and if I didn't play it right, there was an excellent chance I was asking for trouble. Real trouble. The kind that would end up with me staked to a roof and waiting for dawn.

I eyed Max back, keeping pace with his stare.

Oh yeah. He'd do it. He was just the type. After all, he was already hunting down his brother with extreme prejudice. God only knew what he'd do to a new acquaintance.

His nostril lowered, once again concealing the irksome fang. He'd made up his mind about something. It was hard not to worry about *what*. I steeled myself.

But he said, his voice as tight as a guitar string, "Last month we came upon a newspaper clipping with a photograph of Theresa Barrington and Robert Croft, dressed to the nines, exchanging handshakes and smiles. And I can tell by your expression that you already understand our concern."

I was pretty sure I wasn't doing a full on horror-face, but I was definitely thrown by the mention of Croft. Oh yes, I knew him. Or I'd been acquainted with him, a long, long time ago.

I cleared my throat and asked, "Robert Croft? One of the favored sons of the Chicago House, isn't he?"

"You say that like you aren't certain."

"I'm not. It's been quite some time since I've had anything to do with the Great Lakes region. Let's leave it at that, shall we?"

"All right, we shall. And if anything, your ignorance of that situation raises your standing—so far as I'm concerned. Robert is now the judge of the Windy City, and has been since 1998. In the intervening years, Chicago has been no great friend to San Francisco."

I supplemented the sentiment with a guess. "Or to Atlanta, either. What were the two of them up to?" The northern and southern Houses typically view one another with contempt. It's like that whole Civil War thing happened last week or something, and it's stupid as hell. You'd think maybe Chicago and Atlanta would make friends, since they have so much in common. They both burned down, didn't they? That's totally something in common.

"We didn't know, but if some . . . *alliance* was in the works, it was worth finding out the details. According to the newspaper blurb with the photo, they were donating money to each other's pet charities."

"Bullshit."

"You said it. But laundering money in public is easier than doing so in private, as often as not. The Crofts and the Barringtons had struck some business deal, I assume, or that was my father's guess. So he packed up and headed out there to see what he could learn. And he never came back."

I frowned. "Very bad form. On Atlanta's part, I mean. Then again, bad form is Atlanta's favorite kind."

"So you're familiar with them."

"I'm afraid so. I've had a run-in or two with them in the past, and nothing good has ever come of it."

Something about my honesty warmed him. Slightly. Let's just say he went from ice cubes to margarita slush, so you don't get the wrong idea. He didn't leap up and give me a hug or anything, but his gaze gleamed upon recognizing his enemy's enemy.

"I'm sorry to hear that they've given you trouble, though it puts you in good company. And as you might expect, I was concerned when my father ventured that way—but he insisted on the usual arrangements despite the recent unpleasantness there."

"There's been recent unpleasantness? I thought the unpleasantness was basically ongoing."

He laughed, briefly and too loudly. More like a seal's bark than a tinkle of amusement. It was the guffaw of a nervous, angry man who wasn't sure exactly what he was dealing with—but whether he was worried about me or the Atlanta lunatics, I couldn't tell.

After giving me a hard appraisal with those pretty, dark eyes of his, he said, "You know what I'm up against. The judge of one of the largest Houses in America left town to be sheltered by the influence of another . . . only to die in less than forty-eight hours. They only returned his remains yesterday."

"Remains? Not a body?" I asked. I'm good at reading between lines.

"A box of ashes. A very nice box," he added wryly. "Mahogany with ebony overlay. I'm sure it was expensive."

"How thoughtful of them."

"An explanation would've been more thoughtful. A phone call would've done wonders, really. The email seemed somehow insufficient."

I said, "Wow," because it was all that sprang to mind. Yet it was quite in keeping with what I knew of them already. Inconsistent, the whole lot of them. A beautiful, valuable mortuary box and an email. Neither one was out of place in that wacked-out household. "What's the correct response to such a . . . oh, let's call a spade a spade—a breach in diplomacy?"

"I'm fairly certain there's no protocol. To date, I've sent them a card thanking them for my father's return, his state notwithstanding, and requesting a full report as to what became of him."

"I hope you cc'd that message to whatever email address they used."

"That too. I'm not going to obey tradition to the point of idiocy. If they want to talk by email, that's fine," he said, but his grouchy emphasis suggested that it was not, in fact, very fine at all.

"Wow," I said again. "It's kind of a pickle you're in—father dead, brother missing. Must make it hard to move forward with a clean start."

"Never mind Atlanta's interference."

"They killed your father . . . don't tell me they're going out of their way to be even bigger assholes?"

"Would it surprise you?" he asked.

"Well, no. What's their angle?"

He sighed, and it was the bitterest sound I'd ever heard. It was noise that cut. It was a knife in search of a back. "As a *gesture*"—he poisoned the word so that it sounded like a curse, "Chicago has called a convocation a week from today, inviting the big Houses to attend and assist."

"Assist what, exactly?"

"Themselves. They want to establish an interim judge here in San Francisco, since we appear unable to sort out the matter for ourselves."

"Can they do that?"

"They can try. We can deny any verdict they declare, and I can insist on the position till I'm blue in the face." He sighed again, razor-sharp and full of hatred. "But the only way to shut down their power grab is to show up to this convocation in person, with the official title and full support of my House. And I can't do that until my brother is accounted for. Which brings us back around to Ian," he concluded, turning the conversation on a dime. "You say you might help me locate him."

Holy shit. No pressure or anything. If Max weren't such a mean-looking devil, I might've felt sorry for him, seeing how he was between a rock and a hard place. Or two or three of them.

Still, I had my own problems to manage. So I played my card and crossed my fingers. "That's because I can."

He leaned forward, eager now that we were getting down to brass tacks. "You've been in contact with him?"

"Yes."

"In what capacity?" he wanted to know. "Is he living with some other House? Has he run away to join the circus, or some ostracists, or something like that? One day he just *vanished*."

I opted to stick with a streamlined version of the truth, sanitized for Ian's protection. "He hired me last year."

"He . . . he hired you? For what?"

There was no time like the present to deploy my Cheshire cat smile. No teeth. Smooth line. Slightly predatory. Not reaching my eyes. I said, "I'm something of an acquisitions specialist. My expertise leans toward antiques, jewels, and other assorted valuables, but I can sometimes be persuaded to seek out other quarry."

As it turned out, Max was good at reading between lines, too. "You're a thief."

"Yes, and an expensive one. But he had an open checkbook, and I had a free slot in my schedule, so I took the gig. He wanted me to retrieve some long-lost records from the government."

His eyes went wide before he had time to keep them narrow and cool. Still, they reverted to narrow and cool in a fraction of a second. "Really?"

"Really. About ten years ago there was this military project, and to make a long story short, they were swiping vampires and weres for experimentation. Ian was looking for information about a vampire who had disappeared into the program—a man named Bruner—and that's pretty much all I can say without delving too far past the boundaries of client privilege." I'd made up the part about Bruner on the spot. If he were still alive, it might've annoyed him. I liked the thought of that.

"You'll sell him out to me, but you won't tiptoe over the line of client privilege?"

"This is how I earn my living. Without a House to back me

up, all I have is my reputation as a professional—and my own personal capacity for self-defense, which is not at all negligible."

Just then the potential overlap between my interests and Adrian's interests and Maximilian's interests occurred to me in kaleidoscope form, in such a fashion that I wasn't sure, for a moment, how to proceed. If I wasn't careful, things could get sticky. Coincidence or divine design would see to that. If I was *too* careful, I'd look even more suspicious than I already did.

"Raylene?" Max asked.

I hate it when I get lost in thought and it's that fucking obvious to whoever I'm sitting with. "Yeah, sorry. Listen, here's the thing. Ian's case tied in with another case I'm working on. The funny thing is, I think it ties in with yours, too, and that throws a monkey wrench into my proposal."

For just an instant, he looked uncertain. "How's that?"

I went on, winging it, winging it, winging it. "It's like this: I was going to offer to put you in touch with Ian . . . if I could get your permission to proceed on my other case with the weight of your House's support."

"It might be a fair trade—I'm not sure yet. But you're asking us to put our family name and resources on the line."

"I know," I said quickly. "And I was hoping that you wanted Ian badly enough to reach such an arrangement."

"But now you're not certain?"

I shook my head. "No, I'm certain that you'd *let* me ride under your banner. But now I'm not sure that I *want* to."

"What's that supposed to mean?" he nearly growled.

I realized the perceived insult shortly after it flew out of my mouth, so I hastened to correct myself. "Please don't misunderstand me. The failing is not with you, or your city. But the House I hoped to investigate was . . . Well, you see, I need to poke around the Atlanta House."

Maximilian exhaled and leaned back into the plush stuffing of his curved couch. "Ah. Thus your concern, yes. Though I must ask, what do you want with the Barringtons?"

Again I stuck to the truth. I was more likely to learn something useful that way. "A young vampire of theirs, a girl by the name of Isabelle, disappeared years ago—and the circumstances are approximately as straightforward as those surrounding your father's death. Isabelle's brother is looking for her, and it's my job to help him find her."

"Diversifying your business into people-finding, eh?"

"Whatever pays the bills. But surely you can see where I'm coming from, and why I was interested in a mutually beneficial arrangement. I have something you want—or I can very likely get it. And you have something I want—the authority and protection of a House. Call me nuts, but I wasn't interested in showing up on the Barrington doorstep as a loner."

"No, it makes perfect sense. It's the kind of thing I might do, were I in your situation."

He tapped his fingers against the top of his thigh. They made a soft thumping noise against the wool/cashmere-blend suit in which he'd sheathed himself. "Obviously, I would not ask you to part with such valuable information as Ian's whereabouts for nothing," he lied.

I had a feeling that he would've been more than happy to pound matchsticks under my fingernails until I talked, but everyone knows that's not always the most direct and efficient way of getting correct information.

"Let's not talk money," I said as an opener. "I don't need yours, and you don't want to give me any."

"Information," he said.

"Authority," I countered. "If I go to Atlanta now, under the auspices of the San Francisco House, they're going to assume

I'm investigating your father's death. They'll be on the defensive before I get in the front door. Your House's protection can only get me inside; it can't get me results. But if you designate me as a temporary seneschal, I might get somewhere. If nothing else, they'll think twice about murdering me on the spot for minor indiscretions."

"But only twice," he correctly pointed out. "The third thought will see you cast out at sunrise."

"Let *me* worry about that. You just worry about signing off on my passport, and I'll worry about getting Ian in touch with you before the week is out. See? Not a dime exchanging hands. And we can both get something we want."

"You're very persuasive, but I have some concerns. How do you plan to reach my brother?"

"He used to keep a pair of ghouls. As far as anyone knew, he mostly allowed a guy name Calvin Kelly to run his affairs. But Cal died last year, and since then, his secondary has been in charge. I have an 'in' with this pinch hitter."

Maximilian nodded. He'd probably been at least tangentially aware of Cal, and by name-dropping him, I was planting the seeds of sincerity. "Keeping a spare—good idea. That Ian, always thinking ahead. Why would his backup be willing to make contact with you?"

"Because I did this kid a favor, on the side. And on the house," I added. "His sister was homeless. I found her a place to live and set her up. He'll give me the time of day, and more if I push him for it."

His fingers stopped tapping. "Before the convocation?"

"I might have to freshen up some of my contact information, and it may take me a night or two to get Domino on the line. But I know it can be done."

"That'll be . . . fine. And if you can make such contact

happen—so that we can follow up, and establish a firmer connection . . ." He spread the euphemisms thicker than peanut butter.
"I'll get you your seneschal pass. On one more condition."

"Name it."

"While you're there, you find out what really happened to my
father. I want a full report when you return, and if I'm not satisfied
that you've done your best—or that you're telling the truth—then
I will be very, very displeased."

I swallowed, discreetly enough that I hoped he hadn't seen it.
"Absolutely. I'll find out whatever I can, and I'll pass everything
along to you when I return. Assuming I return."

"Your death, dismemberment, or otherwise running afoul of
the Barringtons would absolutely be considered a fair excuse for
not reporting back to me. But anything else is grounds to find
your name listed beside my brother's. Deal?"

"Deal," I said, though the syllable nearly choked me.

He leaned forward, extended his hand, and I shook it—
because that's how we civilized undead murderers do business.

6

Adrian returned with the rest of the ghouls, looking relieved to see me and thrilled to be leaving—even though he'd been the one who wanted to come in the first place. But he played it cool, and he looked unharmed. I couldn't wait to grill him about what he'd learned. I've never been comfortable with ghouls myself, but I'd be the last vampire on earth to suggest they don't have their uses.

All was looking well, I'd successfully winged my way into a productive conversation, and we were just about ready to take off . . . when Maximilian decided to get a little old school. I'm sure he thought he was being gallant—or maybe he was just showing off how well he knew the routines that no one practiced very often anymore—but when he walked to the liquor cabinet and withdrew a couple of crystal brandy glasses, I had the sneaking suspicion that we were in for trouble.

Not huge trouble. Not life-altering trouble, or violently dying trouble. Merely some awkwardness the likes of which I would've preferred to avoid.

No such luck.

"Before you go," he said as he set the glasses on a silver tray, "let's settle the matter with a toast." Then he pulled out a slim silver knife that would've passed for a letter opener at twenty paces, but was as sharp as a razor.

Adrian noticed immediately that Max didn't pull out a decanter of brandy, or any other container of anything else. He was trying not to look worried. He's a sharp lad, that Adrian.

"Annabelle," Max summoned his ghoul-in-chief, the pretty woman with the black hair and dress. Particularly favored ghouls are often included in these things, as a nod to the fact that they will likely be involved somehow in whatever business dealing is being sealed. This meant that Adrian was going to be called upon for involvement, and I hadn't told him about it.

In my defense, that's because I didn't think in a million years that Max would whip out the old tradition.

Oops.

"Raylene," Adrian said softly, halfway between a begging and a warning.

"Don't be silly," I replied with more stiffness than I meant to. "You've done this before." Then I said to Maximilian, "But it's been a while. The Exchange isn't often practiced in other cities, not anymore."

"Nor here, either."

"And what was that you were saying earlier, about outdated niceties?"

Without looking at me, he said, "But my father liked it, and

I'm hoping to see it make a comeback. It's so delightfully *personal,* don't you think?" He picked up the knife and offered it to me with one of the glasses. It's polite to let the guest go first.

I took it and shrugged, like this is something I do every damn day with Adrian, whom I assumed would sooner drink turpentine than anything that came out of my veins. I turned the knife's sharp little tip down, and with a flick of my wrist, I opened a small slash—then upturned my wrist to catch whatever fell before the incision healed itself. Usually this means filling about half a small-form brandy glass, which is exactly how it went. Then I passed the knife back to Max, and he did the same.

"In collaboration," he murmured as he passed his glass to Annabelle, who held it up to her mouth.

She paused, waiting for Adrian to do likewise. This was supposed to be a synchronized event.

I turned my head so that—it was to be hoped—no one but Adrian could see the look I gave him. It was a casserole look, layered with threats, pleas, insistence, and bribery. I had no idea if it would work, but I was pretty sure that if I'd broached the subject earlier in the evening, he would've told me where I could stick my pretty glass of vampire goo.

For a fraction of a moment, I wished to God that he *were* my ghoul—and I could tell him things one brain to another, so I could reassure him that this was mostly normal, and not sinister, and I didn't plan it, and if he wanted us to get out of here without heaping great stinking piles of suspicion and possibly violent death down upon our heads, then he needed to play along. If he were really my ghoul I would've told him the one thing that would've had him line up with a salute: *Drink this, and these yahoos will fund and support a trip to Atlanta, where I might find out what happened to your sister.*

But I couldn't tell him any of that. I had to trust that he

trusted me, which was a precarious thing to balance a con job upon.

Following a slight hesitation that ran *almost* long enough to rouse curiosity in our hosts, Adrian took the glass and held it to his lips. He watched Annabelle, taking his cues from her, which was smart. I couldn't give him any cues because I'm not a ghoul.

To my unending astonishment (which I did my best to mask), he began to drink.

Not a lot. Only a bit. A few seconds' worth of sipping, and a slight lowering of the blood level in the glass.

When Annabelle stopped, Adrian stopped. When she handed her glass back to Maximilian, Adrian handed his back to me.

I could've whooped for joy at how smoothly this was going; I wanted to do a jig and slap Adrian on the back, because God knows I didn't think he'd go that far to keep a cover—and hot damn, he pulled it off. We were almost home free.

Maximilian and I then exchanged glasses and downed the remains of each other's blood, kind of like sorority girls doing shots off a bar. One quick chug, swallow, and then back onto the tray the glasses went. The tray was sent off with Annabelle, and then our host showed us back through the beaded curtain.

"I trust you can find your way out?" he said, holding the fringe so it didn't drop back and tickle us, or tangle up in our hair, or whatever it is that sinister beaded curtains do to inconvenience the unwitting masses.

"Sure. And we'll be in touch. If things go according to plan, I'll have you on the phone with your brother within a couple of nights."

"Excellent. Upon such a call, I'll draw up your paperwork. And I'll anxiously await your report from Atlanta. Deliver it to me before convocation, and we'll consider the deal settled."

"When did you say the convocation was, again?"

"Next week. You have six nights to get Ian on the phone, and get yourself in and out of the Barrington House."

"Great," I said without enthusiasm. I knew he was hoping I'd find something in Atlanta to help him undermine their power grab, but making too many promises could get me killed. So I stuck with what was already on the table and promised to do my best.

I meant it, too. Now I wasn't just headed south for Adrian's vengeful satisfaction. Cutting the Barringtons down to size was a tall order, but I figured you never know. I might find something so shocking or helpful that Max could seize power without ever having to worry about offing his wayward elder sibling.

Pure fantasy, yes. And deep down, I knew it.

We shook hands again and slipped up the stairs, into the front of the club, through the crowd, and back out the front door where we spilled onto the sidewalk with the smokers and drunks who always collect like a scab outside such places. Adrian and I didn't speak until we were once more ensconced in a cab and on our way back to the hotel.

I wasn't sure what to say. I wondered how he was feeling—if those few sips of my blood had done anything to him. Would he want more? Would it not affect him in the slightest? It could go either way. Maybe he didn't know, and was trying to sort it out for himself.

About halfway to our destination he asked, "Why did you promise to have Ian call him? A phone call won't bring him back to San Francisco."

Happy to land on a subject other than the elephant in the cab, I replied, "Max wants to get Ian on the phone because he knows him, and he knows that Ian is a man made of guilt. Max is pretty sure he can manipulate him into coming home if he can only speak to him in person—and not through ghouls, or whatever intermediary they've been using so far."

"Is he right?"

"Yes. No. Maybe."

He shook his head. "You have no idea, do you?"

"I have an idea, but not much more than that. Hey, did you hear anything useful about Brendan while you were hanging with the nearly-deads?"

"Only that he's not around, and they don't know where he went. If Max is lording Brendan's safety over Ian, it's probably bullshit."

"That's what I'd gathered, but it's nice to hear independent confirmation." Unless, of course, they were all lying to us. Which was not outside the realm of hypothetical possibility.

"Do you think he's dead?"

"He might be. Or he might have just made the strategic decision to lie low and let Uncle Max have his way for a while. If he's smart, he's staying out of the way until the power balance settles. Regardless, Ian obviously thinks he's still alive and somewhere near the Renners, and Max will use that to his advantage."

"At least until you tell Ian the truth."

"Right. *I* am a good manipulator, too, and I will con Ian into staying put."

"You sound confident. But what if he's already made up his mind? What if he lies to you?" Adrian raised two very valid concerns.

I took a deep breath, let it out slowly, and leaned my head against the cold, vaguely damp and icky-smelling window. "I don't know. He's a grown man. A civilized adult. I can't tie him down and force him to stay." The truth of it sank in and weighed on my stomach like a brick. It made me feel queasy. "When all is said and done, I can't save him unless he wants me to."

Adrian leaned against his own window, mirroring my pose and staring at me. The city lights drew colors and streaks across his face, both illuminating him and hiding whatever he was feeling. Finally he said, "I know from experience, when it comes to the people you love—there's only so much you can do to help them, without their consent."

"Yeah. I guess you *do* know what it feels like."

We rode on in silence a few minutes more, eventually reaching the hotel and letting ourselves out of the car. I paid the driver and sent him on his way; and when I turned around, Adrian was looking at me funny.

"What?" I asked him.

I'd like to accuse him of blindsiding me, but that wouldn't be fair. He wanted to know, "Why didn't you tell me about that *thing*?" Rather than clarify, since we were standing on a public sidewalk like rocks in a stream, he said, "You know which thing I mean. You could've warned me."

I focused my earnestness and honesty into a laser. "I didn't know," I swore. "That thing—it's an old tradition, the kind of thing nobody does anymore, like a gentleman dropping his coat on a puddle so a lady can keep her feet dry. I swear to you, Adrian, it's damn near *that* obscure."

He considered this. "If I hadn't done it, they would've known you were lying, and I wasn't a ghoul like you'd told them."

"Yes."

"They could've thrown us out or killed us."

I countered, "They could've *tried*."

"No," he shook his head. "There were more of them than you saw."

"Doesn't surprise me. But yeah, they would've known we were full of shit. I'm sorry," I added.

He turned to head inside, and stopped to hold the revolving door for me. As I joined him, we slipped into the lobby and he asked, "Why?"

"Why what?"

"Why are you sorry? It's not going to fuck me up for life or anything, is it?" He broached this right as we were crossing the lobby, heading toward the elevators.

"What? No, no it won't," I assured him, but I also smacked him on the arm in a "Shush, you fool! People are listening" gesture that may have undone some of the sincerity.

Once we were back in the room, he made it clear that he hadn't believed me—not completely. "No, it won't fuck me up for *life?*" he revived the subject. "How about in the short term? Will it fuck me up for a week?"

I threw my bag down on my bed, and he sat down on his bed.

I told him, "No, it won't fuck you up, period." And because I was too crazy and dumb to let it lie there, in case I was wrong I added, "As far as I know."

"What's that supposed to mean?" he demanded, but he was peeling his shoes off while he was demanding it—and people who are peeling off shoes in a leisurely fashion aren't typically the kind who fear for their lives. Not in my experience.

"It means . . . I don't know. Did you . . . feel anything?"

Finishing with the shoes, he moved on to the socks and flung them one at a time with a snap against the TV cabinet. "Feel anything? Hard to say. I felt disgusted, but in a vague way, like other people's bodily fluids aren't my cup of tea. And I was nervous, because I know that's how you make ghouls—by getting them to drink some of your blood. Isn't that right? You let them drink from you?"

"Yeah, that's right. But listen." I sat on my bed so we faced each other. I drew my feet up until I had an Indian-style pose going on, and I concluded, "That wasn't enough for you to . . . um . . . become one of them. Or anything like that. I'm pretty sure."

He frowned. "You're pretty sure? That's all? Not even very sure, or totally sure—just *pretty* sure?"

"What do you want me to say, Adrian? I've never had much ghoul interaction before, much less made one myself. I don't know what the proportions are. There must be some formula, something to do with height and weight, I assume—something that lets people drink without crossing that line, but I don't know what it is. Regardless, I'm virtually totally confident that the few sips you took from a wee tiny brandy glass weren't enough to make any real changes in your body."

"Virtually totally confident. I guess I can live with that," he said, but I knew he was putting on a show. It'd unsettled him—as it damn well should have.

I wished there'd been another way to gracefully escape the House, but there hadn't been, and there was no undoing it now. I'd let him drink from me. Now we had a connection—a paranormal one, whether either of us wanted to admit it or not—and only time would tell how deep it went, if it went anywhere at all.

"What . . . um . . ." He faltered his way to the question, "What's different about ghouls, anyway? How are they ghouls, and not just . . . plasma enthusiasts?"

"It varies from person to person, but generally ghouls end up psychically bonded—like it's a substance addiction—and the vampire is able to control the ghoul that way."

"Hang on. *Control* the ghoul?"

"Sure. They use their mind-powers, and the link between them. Not all of them, obviously. Not everyone comes from the better-to-be-feared-than-loved school of co-dependency. I mean, I don't think Ian was shuttling Cal around like a puppet or anything."

"But he *could* have, if he'd wanted to."

"I don't know. You'd have to ask him." I didn't like where this was going, but it was going there anyway, so I braced myself for it.

"Does that mean you can control me now, since I drank a little of your blood?"

I threw up my hands. "No? I don't think so? It was only a little blood, and you were a very good sport about it. I very strongly doubt I could make you do anything, okay? And keep in mind why we kept up the charade in there."

"Hey, I like Ian just fine, but I didn't plan to set myself up for programming!"

"Dude, I think we both know you didn't come along on this wild carpet ride for the sake of Ian. You're on board because you want to know what happened to your sister, and I'll have you know, we might have gotten ourselves a lead out of this mess."

"Wait. What?" Ah. Now I had his attention.

"You heard me. I think I might've scored a pass to the Atlanta House. And believe me, it wasn't easy."

"What does that mean? You're going to Atlanta? You're going to find my sister?"

"I'm going to try. And I'm also going to solve the mystery of what precisely happened to William Renner, upon pain of death. Or that was the subtext of Max's offer."

Then Adrian asked the thing I was most afraid he'd ask. "What about me? I'm coming with you, right?" I didn't answer fast enough. He asked again, *"Right?"*

"Adrian, I don't know."

"What do you mean you don't know? She was *my* sister—and I have a right to know."

"Absolutely you do," I agreed. "And I'll see what I can do. But frankly, those people are crazy and I can't guarantee your safety. Hell, I can't guarantee my *own* safety."

"I can take care of myself," he reminded me in a too-loud voice that told me he'd be happy to demonstrate, perhaps on my battered corpse, if necessary.

I shot back, "I know you can, you idiot! If I thought you were a pretty-pretty princess who couldn't do anything but wink and giggle, I'd have left you at home!"

By now, we were both shouting. "So why would you try to keep me out of Atlanta? It's the one House I really want to visit, and *now* you want to protect me? *Now* you want to lock me out of this?"

"Yes, *now,* you asshole." I flung one of my own shoes at him, and nearly clocked him in the ear. "There's a better-than-fair chance that Ian's quietly planning to run out and get himself killed, and in case you hadn't noticed, my life isn't exactly crawling with friends." By the last word, I wasn't even yelling.

I kind of felt like crying.

The only one more surprised than me was Adrian, who stared at me with my shoe in his left hand, which he'd caught before it broke the window and sailed out into the street. He opened his mouth to say something, and I opened mine to say something, too—but neither one of us had any words on deck and then, thank God, my cell phone rang.

I grabbed it like a lifeline, glared down at the display, and said "Horace" as much to myself as to Adrian.

"Who? That art guy, in New York?"

"I'm taking this," I said as I snapped the thing open, relieved for the excuse to change topics. I turned my back to Adrian. "What?" I said into the phone.

"You told me to call you back when I had any leads. Well, I have some leads, and I still want you to go get my penis bones."

"Awesome, because it's not like I'm doing anything else right now," I muttered sarcastically. I gave Adrian a wave and headed for the door. I didn't know where I planned to wander while I talked, but I had to get out of that room.

"It *is* awesome, I'll have you to know. Those things are worth—"

"A fortune, yes, you've mentioned." I shut the door behind myself and stood in the hall. I picked a direction and wandered out to the lobby by the elevators, figuring that if I was quiet enough, I probably wouldn't bother anybody.

He was quiet for a few seconds, then he asked, "Did I interrupt something?"

"No."

"You're lying."

I sighed. "You didn't interrupt anything *interesting.* I was in the middle of a conversation with a friend, but he's an understanding friend when it comes to money."

"I like him already."

"Great. Now what have you got for me?" I prompted. I was still calming down from what had not, precisely, been a conversation but more like a fight. I needed something to distract me, something that was all business—because my friends were nothing but fucking trouble right now.

"I've got a woman. A crazy woman."

"Sounds like the start of a country song to me," I said. "Did she total your truck or shoot your dog?"

"No, but she stole my box of penis bones."

"Even worse!" I declared with mock drama. "Give me the deets."

"The *details*"—he emphasized the word to be contrary, I

assume—"are as follows: Her name is Elizabeth Creed and she's crazy. Not just rhetorically crazy, but actually crazy."

"I believe the correct term is *mentally ill* these days, Horace."

"To hell with you and your correctness," said the man who had just fleshed out my abbreviation for "details" with a neurotic's flair. "But you can call her mentally ill if you like. She qualifies. She even has papers certifying it."

"Was she committed or something?"

"Actually, yes," he said. "That's partly how I found her out, the sneaky bitch. She was in attendance at the antiques show. I've got her in the footage, in several places."

"Footage? Like, she made it onto TV?"

"Briefly, in a crowd shot or two. More important, she was hovering over the exotics table, and paying an inordinate amount of attention while I was lying to Joseph Harvey. She's practically *looming* behind him. Very sinister stuff. I'll email it to you sometime. Anyway, we got her on film, and I noticed her while I was going over the Portland footage. I have access to all the extra shit—the shit we don't bother to show, or the shit that gets cut. So I watched it. Obsessively."

"I bet." He was fully capable of being as obsessive as me, if he felt like it. And there was nothing like a few hundred million dollars to make him truly dedicated to a cause.

"And it wasn't long before we singled this broad out. She even *looks* crazy, my God. And the cameras caught her talking to Bill, the ousted volunteer grip—badgering Harvey's contact info out of him, I can only assume. Anyway, I have a friend at the FBI," he said, which meant he was bribing someone at the FBI. "I got him to run the footage through some facial recognition software, and boom. We got a hit."

"What are the odds?" I asked flippantly.

"Pretty good, when you used to work for the government but

had a big nervous breakdown that led to your involuntary incarceration in a mental hospital. That kind of shit goes down, and people will draw up *all kinds* of paperwork on your ass."

"Oh, wow. So you're not just hyperbolizing?"

"Is that even a word?"

"It is if I say so."

He went on. "Then I wasn't hyperbolizing, no. She's a full-blown paranoid schizophrenic who was once a brilliant astrophysicist working at NASA's installation in Florida."

"That's . . . Actually, that's kind of sad."

"It's very sad, if you give a shit about crazy scientists, which I don't. I give a shit about my penis bones, which are in that woman's hands even as we speak."

I didn't giggle, even though I wanted to. "All right, fine. You've got a name and a psychiatric report. I don't guess you're going to make this easy for me, and give me a location?"

His response startled me. "How fast can you get to California?"

I hedged my bets. "Depends on where in California. It's a big state."

"Okay, I need you in a state park."

"Kindly be more precise," I urged.

"The San Juan Bautista State Park."

"What makes you think she's there?"

He said, "Credit card activity. She arrived last night, and has been eating gas station food or Carl's Jr. ever since. And if that doesn't speak to her depravity, I just don't know what *does*."

"Jesus, you're a snob."

"What of it? Listen, this park is about a hundred miles from San Francisco. You can fly into SF and hit the road. But do it fast. I don't know how long she plans to stay, and I don't know where she's going next."

"But you can track her via credit cards? That's very helpful and convenient, I must admit." It was exactly the kind of thing I might've thought of, if I'd had any idea how to go about it. Unfortunately, I didn't have a friend at the FBI.

"Yes, I can keep an eye on her that way. But I need you to pin this bitch down fast, Ray. She's up to something." The ensuing silence was suspicious.

"Horace?" I pushed. "What do you mean, she's up to something? How do you know that?"

"It's . . . let's say *hypothetically* possible . . . that she's trying to *use* the bones."

"Wait. What? Using them for magic, or for purposes inconsistent with their labeling? Because if she's having *too* much fun with them, I'm not sure you want them back."

"Stop making light of this!" he said, suddenly all sharpness and reproach. I'm not accustomed to seriousness from him, so it startled me. I was about to ask him what the big deal was when he continued. "I read about the fire that destroyed Harvey's house—"

"After I told you about it. Nice detective work."

"But what you *didn't* tell me, I looked up. It was all over the local news—and it even made it to the conspiracy nuts on the Internet."

"Lots of things make it to the conspiracy nuts."

He said, "Yes, and *some* of those things are true. Come on—a freak storm, coming out of nowhere; lightning striking twice just to make sure the house went up in smoke . . . ?"

"Could've been a coincidence," I said. But even I didn't believe me.

"It wasn't a coincidence. It was *her*, covering her tracks. She's using the bones to *bend*."

"Bend? Are you trying to draw more penis jokes out of me? Because if you give me a few minutes, I'll think of some. You just wait."

"She's *bending*, Ray. Bending natural forces to her nefarious whims."

"With the bones?"

"I *told* you they were intended for ceremonial magic. Weren't you listening?"

I dropped myself into a seat by the wall. It was mostly decorative, and therefore not very comfortable, but I felt the need to sit down. "I was listening, but I didn't know how serious you were. For that matter, I had no idea you actually knew a damn thing about ceremonial magic. Because before, you acted like you didn't." And really, the thought stopped just short of horrifying me.

"I don't practice it, but I know something about it—otherwise I wouldn't have pegged the bones, and don't you dare turn that into another dick joke."

The more I thought about it, the less it would've surprised me to find out that he was lying, and that he had a basement shrine with wands, powders, formulas, and the occasional pentagram. Horace is all about money and power, and ceremonial magic is all about power, if not money.

I didn't call him out on it. Instead I said, "Fine, I won't turn that one into a joke, even though you totally set me up with that straight line. But I was under the impression that magic is an inefficient, troublesome, and mostly pointless way to be greedy. From everything I ever heard, it seems like it'd take your entire life just to learn how to levitate an egg, much less do anything really important."

"You're not altogether wrong, but that's why the bones are such a big, expensive deal. In a basic sense, they're amplifiers—they take little magic and make it into big magic. All the bang for a fraction of the effort. Practitioners euphemistically refer to it as 'bending.' Because you can't break the laws of nature . . ."

I finished the sentiment for him. "You can only bend them."

"Atta girl. I think she blew through one of the bones making that storm, or whatever you want to call it. Lightning struck twice because she was still getting the hang of it, not because the bones aren't powerful enough to give her the necessary mojo. We need to get those things back, Raylene."

"Because she's going to destroy the world? Oh my God, Horace. Please tell me we're not dealing with a supervillain here, because that kind of thing is so far outside my field of expertise that I'm getting a headache just thinking about it!"

He snorted. "No, Ray-baby. No one's trying to save the world. I'm trying to save those bones! The more of them she burns up playing magic games, the fewer of them I have to sell . . . once you steal them back for me."

Ah. That was more in character. "Right. Silly me, thinking there was an ounce of humanitarian spirit lurking anywhere within that black little heart of yours."

"Silly indeed. Now get out to that park as soon as you can, and *get me those fucking cock rocks.*"

7

I don't know if Horace knew where I was when he'd called, or if he just assumed I'd picked up teleporting as a special skill somewhere in my travels. Maybe he honestly thought this Elizabeth Creed would hang around these particular stomping grounds for a few days yet—though that was an assumption fraught with peril. I didn't know what she wanted, but I didn't really think this poor woman was out to destroy the world. You have to be crazier than just schizophrenic to have an interest in that kind of thing. Usually you have to be a religious nut, too.

I hoped she wasn't a religious nut.

And I hoped this park was close enough for me to get this out of the way tonight, because I'd just made plans to bolt for Atlanta, hadn't I? And when all was said and done, Ian was the greater priority. Or that's what I told myself, as I tried to keep the needling thought of *hundreds of millions of dollars* out of my head.

I could use the money. *We* could use the money. It could make us more secure. It could keep us safe. Or as safe as any of us could reasonably expect to be.

With roundabout thinking like this, I convinced myself that the quest for Creed and the penis bones was a case that would benefit Ian as much as it'd benefit me. Call it trickle-down economics, if you must. But money in my bank account is good for all of us—blind, beautiful, beloved companions included.

Back in the hotel room, Adrian was lying on his bed and wrestling with the remote, which also worked by arcane ritual magic, or so it appeared. He could only get the channel to turn over when he aimed it from just the right angle, to just the right spot.

"Problems?" I asked, letting the door drag slowly shut behind me.

"I think it needs new batteries." He smacked it against the nightstand. "Oh hey, *MythBusters*," he declared upon getting the channel to move another notch. "I can lie around and watch this."

"Clearly."

"So what was that about?"

"My case," I told him. "The one that doesn't involve Ian or your sister."

"I thought you didn't have a case."

"Remember that penis bone thing I told you about? It might be back on. Hey, what time is it?" I asked.

"Going on one in the morning. Why? You got a hot date?"

"Hardy har *har*. No. And I don't have a lot of time, either—not if I want to scratch this off the list tonight." I dragged out my laptop and plugged it in, since the battery was getting low. "You ever hear of a place called the San Juan Bautista State Park?"

"No," he admitted. "Why? You thinking about taking a tourist detour?"

"Yeah. Horace said it's about a hundred miles from here."

"And you'll find your rod nuggets there?"

"I don't know. But he gave me a lead on the woman who stole them. She's a paranoid schizophrenic who used to work for NASA. Horace basically caught her on tape. And he's been watching her credit cards—don't ask me how; I don't know the details. Give me a minute to boot up, and I'll look it up. All knowledge is contained within the Internet, after all."

Within two more minutes I had the park's website on the screen and Adrian sitting on the bed beside me, as if we were naughty teenagers sharing a monitor full of porn. I clicked around a little and discovered that the park was a pretty place like most old missions, but I didn't quite see the significance.

What did Elizabeth Creed want there?

Adrian asked it, just as I was thinking it. "What does this woman want from this place?" It surprised me, how his question had come right on the heels of my wondering. It was an obvious question, one any intelligent person might have spontaneously generated; but again I thought of the sips he'd taken, and I worried that maybe great minds don't necessarily think alike . . . that maybe sometimes they're artificially linked by a bloody cocktail.

I swallowed and answered as if there was nothing weird about it—since there might not be, for all I knew. "Horace didn't say."

"He might not know."

"He *must* not. Otherwise, he would've told me. Anyway, this is the place, and she's been hanging around it." I glanced over at the big digital numbers on the hotel clock, confirmed what I already knew, and said, "If we want to head over there tonight, we'll need a hotel waiting for us."

"Us? Will I get a cut of this gig if I keep you company?"

"Maybe if you make yourself useful," I retorted, but it brought up a good point. "I'm not in the habit of doing these 'retrieval' gigs with a partner, so if you want to head out in the morning without me, there'd be no hard feelings. But since I'm already here, it'd be a little dumb for *me* to drive back to Seattle without checking it out."

"Sure, I hear what you're saying." He shrugged. "But it's not like I'm doing anything important at home until Friday night. I already put in for the time off in order to come down here with you."

"And if you can talk me out of a cut, so much the better, eh?"

"Right."

"But dude, not twenty minutes ago we were having a . . . discussion about me trying to keep you out of harm's way. It'd be awfully damn inconsistent of me to say, 'Hop in my car, baby—let's hit the road.'"

"Naw, not inconsistent. Logical!" he insisted, reaching for his suitcase. "There's a world of difference between keeping me out of a vampire den and keeping me away from one lone crazy lady with a box of mystical peen."

"Okay, I can see that. But she's not just one lone crazy lady with a box of mystical peen. She's one lone crazy lady who successfully murdered a man and blew up his house with a box of powerful relics. And when I frame it that way, now that I think about it . . . no, I'm *not* super-comfortable with the idea of you joining me."

"You're not my mother," he groused as he began to pack. "And I'm not Domino. Think of it this way: I'm far less likely to get into trouble because the crazy-lady gig isn't personal to me. You can grant me that much, can't you? Even when we went after

Bruner—which was *completely* fucking personal—I didn't do anything to endanger either one of us. You're not the only badass on the block, you know."

He had me there.

Adrian and I had worked together just fine on a personal mission the previous year—I mean, we'd hunted down a guy and killed him together, so I knew I could trust him to pull his own weight. But this was different. This was my real job, and I'd never invited anyone to ride shotgun before.

I had a feeling it didn't matter. And although I could easily leave him behind . . . I didn't want to. Maybe he was right, and it'd be okay. After all, this woman didn't know anyone knew about what she'd done, much less that anyone was after her. We'd catch her off guard, steal the box of goodies, and be back home before forty-eight hours were out.

"Fine. If you promise to stay out of the way."

"People who stay out of the way don't get cuts of the profit."

"You never know," I said. "In this case, I might well pay you to keep clear of the trouble. Call it personal peace-of-mind insurance."

He said, "Whatever," but he was smiling.

While the *MythBusters* rerun played itself out, I called around the park's general vicinity until I found a hotel room—since we wouldn't have time to drive back before morning. We loaded up quickly, checked out, and hit the road.

The drive to the park took almost two hours, so by the time we pulled up, the place wasn't just dark—it was utterly deserted, and closer to dawn than sundown. We left the Taurus outside the park's more sensitive boundaries, since we didn't feel like forcing past the gate or busting through any of the feeble barriers that kept cars off the historic roads after hours.

It was both good and bad that the *mission* San Juan Bautista is really the historic district of a *town* called San Juan Bautista. It's not much of a town, and they rolled up the sidewalks at twilight except for a couple of tourist hotels and a bar or two, but it meant there was an off chance we were blocking someone's private drive, and there was also an off chance we'd be spotted as the kind of people who "aren't from around here."

I didn't expect any trouble, though. For that matter, I didn't really expect to find Elizabeth Creed. She might be spending her days lurking around the park, but I assumed she must be spending the night elsewhere. More than anything, the point of this trip was to see if we could get an idea of what precisely the crazy lady wanted with the place. Since we were in the neighborhood, and all.

I'd given Adrian the rundown on keeping his head down on the way over, lecturing him (or so he accused) on things he already knew, and generally driving him nuts, I'm sure. But the closer we'd gotten to the site in question, the harder I began to second-guess bringing him along.

And now that we'd quietly stalked past the San Juan city hall, and were working our way toward the plaza in the dark . . . it felt a bit *real*. I had actually teamed up with somebody for a case—a for-profit event that was in no way personal. This made it a first, and I couldn't tell if that was a good thing or a bad thing.

But it was too late to do anything about it now.

He slinked along beside me, or behind me in my wake, and together we snuck around the mostly empty, sprawling place. Gray wood fences offset the private homes and businesses—most of them in a similar adobe or stucco style with only one or two stories—and the streets had that gritty feel that implies they aren't fully paved, even though they are. Everything was sandy and dusty underfoot, and overhead the sky was dark and clear and speckled with stars but not much moon.

At least if Creed tried to raise another storm, we'd have plenty of warning. I vowed to keep an eye on the sky, just in case. On a night like this, any cloud was cause for suspicion.

It occurred to me that it was a shame we hadn't thought to bring along night-vision goggles for Adrian.

"Damn," he said. "I wish I'd thought to bring my night-vision goggles."

I almost stopped in my tracks, but only stumbled. There he went again, reading my thoughts. Or not? Yet again, this was an example of an obvious thing, spoken aloud. It probably meant nothing.

"If I'd known about this in time, we could've brought them," I murmured softly. "But this is the price we pay for the coincidence of timing. We're not as prepared as we'd like to be."

"You're never as prepared as you'd like to be. And this place is a goddamn graveyard," he whispered back.

He was right. It felt deserted, and unnaturally so. "*Shh*, I'm listening. In case it *isn't* a graveyard and we run into company."

He made a grumpy noise but he shut up, which was all I wanted from him anyway. Nothing about the place felt right, from the utter silence to the too-bright stars and the long, flat buildings with their shutters drawn. Some of the structures appeared to be in states of restoration; some hadn't made it there yet, and were boarded or offset with chain-link fences. It looked like a ghost town under construction, which is exactly as weird as it sounds.

I stopped with my back flat against the wall of a store that had been closed for decades. The stucco prickled at my shoulders, and the stored warmth of the place leached out into my back. Adrian drew up beside me, a shadow in black—silent as hell when he wasn't talking, though he outweighed me by probably fifty pounds of muscle.

"There it is." I gestured with a nod of my head. "Across the plaza. That must be the mission itself."

It was a low, long building like so many of the others, and graced with a series of arches. A steeple or a bell tower or something pointed up from the far end, though I couldn't see it well enough to tell at such a distance. The plaza was pretty freaking big, and wide open, without a shred of cover.

Adrian made another vague "hm" noise, and this time I asked, "What?"

"It looks familiar."

"Yeah," I agreed. "Wikipedia said that one of Hitchcock's films was shot here." As I made this feeble observation, I watched the mission as if it were going to do a trick. I was trying to talk myself out of the necessity of investigating it.

"You're probably right. Do you think we should check it out? That's a lot of open ground around it. I haven't seen anybody, or any cameras. Have you?"

"No." I hadn't smelled any, either. Usually there's a faint electric whiff to them, and a high-pitched hum. You know that sound when you've got the television on, but the volume is turned all the way down? It's like that. It hangs out in the back of your head, not doing anything but taking up a fraction of your attention, making you aware that it's *there*.

That's what all electronic equipment sounds like to me, but my hearing is a whole lot better than the average mortal's.

Still keeping my voice low, I confessed, "We ought to take a look around it, but maybe we should save it for last. It's the centerpiece of the park, so it'd be stupid to skip it. We should check out everything, everywhere, since we have no idea what we're looking for."

"Gotcha. Time to split up?"

I almost grabbed his arm, but I caught myself in time and kept my eyes on the mission. Christ, I was clingy as of late. Undignified, that's what it was.

I took a deep breath and said, "Yeah, let's split up. I'll take the east blocks over here, you take the west blocks over there, and we'll meet up at the mission when we're done. Stick to the shadows, and if anyone spots you, lose them however you can. Run if you have to, but if you have to take the car, send me a text message or something so I know not to hang around—and I can find a place to hide before dawn. You got that?"

I turned to look at him, and was both annoyed and impressed to realize that he'd jaunted off in the middle of my dissertation without me hearing him. I didn't know how much of it he'd caught, but I'd front-loaded the bit about east blocks and west blocks, so I grumbled my frustration (quietly) and breathed "Motherfucker" as I vacated my position against the shop, or house, or whatever it'd been back in 17-when-the-hell-ever.

I went through the blocks and dodged only three people, two of them teenagers who didn't want to be spotted any more than I did, and one older woman who was taking out the trash behind a restaurant.

Except for the occasional scurry of rats and cats, and the intermittent yowl of a coyote somewhere too close for civilization's comfort, I heard nothing but the soft swish of my own steps.

There was nobody here. Just me and Adrian and the desert, and the small things that crawl in the sand, and the owls that swoop about more silently even than me at my sneakiest.

Except that I didn't believe it.

I could *feel* that I was wrong, even though I had nothing concrete to base it on.

When I'd completed my rounds, discovering nothing except that this must be one boring-ass place to live, I found myself at the edge of the plaza again—this time in front of it. I crouched in the shadow of a beautiful old hacienda's second-story wraparound porch and squinted as far as I could.

I can't see in perfect darkness, so thank God it wasn't perfectly dark. It was only mostly dark, which meant I couldn't make out much detail, but I could see the huge expanse of grass sprawling out before me, and the pale, skeletal-looking frame of the old mission at the far end of it. To my left was a white building that was closed and fenced off; it could've been an old-fashioned saloon made out of clapboard, but it was hard to tell at this distance.

No hint of light peeked around its windows. No noises emanated from within. It was a shell of a place, and when I stretched out my feeble psychic senses, I was quite confident that it was as empty as it appeared. The closer building, the one I hunkered beside, was occupied—but not by anyone who was up to anything. Two children were resisting bedtime upstairs someplace, and downstairs someone was cleaning a kitchen while watching television.

Where was Adrian? I stretched the sensation, closing my eyes. Does closing my eyes help? I don't know. I'm not sure why I do it. I'm not sure why I leave my mouth hanging open when I put mascara on, either, but it feels like two sides of the same phenomenon. You do little things like that in order to concentrate.

So I concentrated. And I didn't pick him up, so either he was out of range, or my waves were failing me, either of which was fully possible. Rather than dwell on these things, I dwelled on how the hell I was going to approach the mission. If I wanted to take the long way around, there were some scraggly trees off to my right that I could hide behind. But when I judged how little cover versus how much added inconvenience that entailed, I split the difference and decided to run along the inner perimeter, and fast.

No one would see me, even if anyone knew to look for me. At a good sprint, I can run faster than most people can detect, and faster even than many recording devices can catch. Usually I turn up as a vague streak, and only then if the frame rate is good enough.

So I ran.

It took a couple of seconds to cross the vast expanse, and in those couple of seconds my rudimentary psychic sense told me two things that almost slowed me down, but didn't.

Thing #1: Adrian was over there, someplace on the back side of the building. Or maybe it was the front side—the architecture didn't broadcast the difference, and it looked similar from all angles. At any rate, he was on the side farthest from me, and sneaking slowly along the wall. This was excellent, for it meant that I was running right toward him, and I wouldn't have to go hunting for him after I checked out this one last thing.

Thing #2: Adrian wasn't alone. Someone else was over there, inside the mission someplace—not at my partner's side, and not stalking him or anything . . . but definitely within a stone's throw of his position.

Slightly distracted by these two revelations, I almost ran smack into the mission's adobe exterior, but caught myself in time to keep from plowing into the wall and leaving a Raylene-shaped dent in the side. Just barely, mind you.

I flattened myself against the wall I had so narrowly avoided puncturing with my face and scooted around the nearest corner. This put me along the short side of the building, and facing what was left of the trees that surrounded the place in that weird living fence that served as a boundary to the property. As I stood there, listening with every sense I had available to me, the little hairs on the back of my neck stood up.

Never a good sign, that.

I peered up at the sky, checking for sudden and improbable clouds, but saw nothing but stars—more of them than you ever see in a city, much less a city like Seattle, where the sky is so often overcast. A plane was sweeping past overhead, its red and white blinky lights revealing its southern trajectory.

And nothing else stood out against the black.

It didn't mean that nothing was wrong. *Something* was wrong, but it wasn't coming from above.

In case it would work, I sent out a silent call to Adrian. *Dude. Where are you?*

No one was more shocked than I was when he responded. *Around back. There's someone inside.* It wasn't a strong response— not like a shout in the ear. More like a muffled murmur. But I heard it, and I understood it.

Hang tight. I'm on my way.

"And you're not my ghoul, not my ghoul, not my ghoul," I mumbled as I hastily trucked around to Adrian's side of the building.

I could sense him, but I couldn't see him. The far façade of the mission was as pale as the front, all of it the color of desert-bleached bones in the heavy darkness. The archways appeared to go on forever, extending back to some distant vanishing point. An absurd impression, I know, but that's how it felt. It felt like a fever dream, a hallucination, a dizzy moment brought on by a sudden feeding or too much wine.

My ankles felt loose, like they'd rattle if I shook my feet. I looked down at them, thinking my whole body was betraying me in this weird moment, and then I realized that it wasn't my ankles . . . it was the ground.

A shock of grass and a dusting of pebbles beside my boots quavered and bounced, very slightly, as if they were set atop a speaker playing something that was heavy on the bass.

An earthquake?

I'd been in an earthquake or two. Nothing serious, nothing

big. Seattle gets them every once in a while, being on the Pacific Rim and all, but not with much frequency or damage.

But this didn't feel like an earthquake.

It wasn't a shake. It was a vibration, coming up from a spot down deep, like the earth was humming. It set my teeth on edge. I gritted them and continued my hunt for Adrian.

I ducked inside the nearest arch, which placed me beneath a corridor that ran the length of the place. From inside this over-hang, the mission felt even more infinite, or maybe it was only the disorientation from that deep, low-level buzz. I couldn't hear it, exactly, but I could feel it with every inch of my skin. The tiny bones in my ear jostled together, and my eyelashes itched. I wanted to scratch at myself—scratch everything, all over.

I tamped down the urge and felt along the wall, stopping at the occasional window or doorway, all of them shut.

I struggled to recall the rough layout. I hadn't planned to come inside; I'd assumed it'd be shut and locked, since I was head-ing out here after hours. And it was, wasn't it?

I tried a door.

Of course it was locked. But this did not prevent someone from being inside, any more than it was going to prevent me from *getting* inside, just as soon as I found Adrian and could get a better grip on the situation. I didn't need a perfect layout of the interior in order to get cracking. I'd worked under worse circumstances.

Adrian?

Over here. I see you.

An arm waved up ahead. I couldn't really see that it was an arm. I could only detect the loose shape of a swaying appendage and, given the height of it, I assumed it was an arm and not a leg, or a tentacle, or whatever.

I approached the arm, and yes, found it attached to Adrian, who had crushed himself up against a shuttered window. The shutter had a crack in it, where something had busted a couple of slats. Air breathed gently out through this crack, slightly warmer than what was outside around us.

"Someone's inside," he said, and pointed at the hole.

"I know. But I don't think she got in *this* way."

"Very funny," he said. "I don't know *how* she got in, but I saw her for a second." He pointed inside again. I didn't see anything but a room with a desk and some chairs that looked like they belonged in a doctor's office circa 1970. But as I stared a little longer, letting my eyes fine-tune to the dim interior, I detected a doorway without a door to block it, and in the hall beyond it, a glow so faint I might've been imagining it.

"She has a light," Adrian told me. "She was walking that way." He indicated an imprecise direction off to our mutual left.

"I just came from that way, and I didn't notice anything open. She must've gotten inside farther down. Did you see any point of entry?"

"No, but it's fucking *dark*."

"Thank you, Captain Obvious."

"You're welcome. We could break in, couldn't we? Just pop one of these doors or, or whatever it is you do?"

Our voices stayed very, very low. I didn't think anyone could hear us, least of all someone inside. "It's noisy," I said. "If these windows weren't all shuttered, I'd cut the glass out and let us in that way. But breaking the shutters open is just as loud as breaching a door."

"Raylene?" he asked, the one-word question a tiny bit loud. His eyes went big, and he was getting that glazed, disoriented look that I'm sure I'd been displaying a few seconds before. "Do you feel that?"

I nodded. "Yeah, I feel it. I've been feeling it."

"What's she doing?"

"I have no idea. Fuck it," I declared, and I reached for the nearest door. It was doubled, and its planks were held together old-fashioned-style with big iron bands. It had a new-fashioned lock, though. A dead bolt built unobtrusively into the wood, destroying the authenticity but offering modern security.

Well, not perfect security. I jostled it open with less finesse and more noise than I wanted, but I didn't exactly kick over an air raid siren, either.

"Come on," I told my companion, who almost tripped over me in his eagerness to get inside. I understood. I was feeling it too, that urgent sense that shelter should be sought, even if shelter meant a building some two hundred years old and probably, God help us, not built to meet earthquake codes.

Inside it was even bleaker than the overhang with the arches, which seemed impossible but apparently wasn't. We staggered toward the open doorway and into a hall. By then I could see again, a little, but Adrian couldn't—so he grabbed the back of my shirt and I led him in the direction he said she'd gone.

"It has to be her, doesn't it?" he asked me, so close I could feel his breath on the back of my head.

"If it isn't, we're going to feel real silly in a minute," I told him. Then, more to myself, "I wonder where she's going."

Up ahead I could hear something; it hovered on the edge of the buzzing hum, a staccato noise . . . or not quite. Footsteps, yes. Off in the distance, deeper in the mission. I kept heading toward the footsteps, and Adrian kept his death-grip on my shirt, and the hum grew harder—not louder—beneath our feet.

Adrian all but sighed, "Earthquake?"

"I don't know," I sighed back. At least it wasn't lightning. Aggravating hum notwithstanding, there was no undercurrent stink of ozone—and as of a few seconds previously, the sky had been utterly clear. I knew, because I'd been checking it. A good

lightning strike or two within fifty feet of you will make you paranoid that way.

So yes, this had to be some kind of earthquake.

It made sense, from a warped, crazy-person angle. In the
Pacific Northwest, she'd reached for a storm—and in California,
she was reaching for the ground.

Adrian stumbled behind me, yanking my shirt so hard that
the neckline jabbed me in the throat. Our feet were going numb
from the vibrations, and we were both getting clumsy, so I didn't
smack him. I'm just charitable that way.

Besides, my obsessive compulsions and neuroses were distracting me. Should we get outside after all? Isn't that what you're
supposed to do, in case of a quake? Override that instinct to find
shelter, and find a place that won't fall on top of your head?

But no, this wasn't something so normal or simple. Adrian
and I both knew that.

Christ, that mission was an interminable building. Again I
had that sense that the interior was warped, that it was larger than
it looked from the outside—larger than it could possibly be—and
we were only pushing dream-like forward, skulking in place without making any progress.

Until finally, up ahead, the timbre of the footsteps changed
and their location began to rise.

I stopped, and Adrian ran into my back.

"What?"

"Can you hear that?" I wanted to know.

"No."

"She's going upstairs. I didn't know this place even *had* a
second floor."

"It doesn't," he whispered. "But there's a bell tower, remember? You can see it from outside."

Bell tower? Oh yeah. *"Vertigo,"* I said.

"What?"

"*Vertigo.* I just now remembered. That's what movie was filmed here. There was . . . there was a big scene," I muttered. "In the bell tower. Jimmy Stewart."

"If you say so."

"Come on. Let's go imitate some art."

He said, *"Yikes,"* but he tagged gamely behind me.

She was using a light, yes. A gas-powered lantern, a Coleman or something like it. I could smell it as we gained on her, that small, burning scent of fossil fuel and a cotton sock wick. And up ahead, somewhere around a corner, the glow it left behind was calling to me—drawing me moth-like onward.

We passed through several rooms, mostly decked out like museums with glass cases, informative plaques, and long benches for tired tourists to rest upon. And then we spotted the gate that usually blocked off the tower. It hung open, its padlock cut by something big, maybe bolt cutters. I ran my hands over the jagged edge left by the snipping and I knew the feel of it. I've cut plenty of locks in my time. It's not the most elegant way to breach a barrier, but it'll do in a pinch.

I had a feeling that Elizabeth Creed didn't expect anyone to find out what she'd done, and she didn't care about leaving a trail. As the low-key hum underfoot grew to a more distinct tremor, I started to run.

Adrian kept up with me fairly well. I couldn't do my usual blinding speed, since we were indoors and it was almost too dark to see, and the stairs weren't the kind of perfectly even steps people produce in modern times, so I had to be careful. But there was a light up ahead and I chased it, and he was hot on my heels.

When finally I burst out into the open air, the whole place was shaking and I realized in that instant that part of the hum I'd heard, and felt with my whole body, had come from the bells.

They were big and solid and utterly black in the shadowed night of the tower. They were bell-shaped failings in reality, heavier than anything had a right to be.

They were bells, and not bells at the same time, and I was entranced by them.

She'd done something to them—or she was *doing* something to them, I couldn't say. But they weren't here, not anymore. They weren't part of my universe. Or maybe (and this might be closer to correct) they were in two places at once—our world, and some other world, too.

I tore my eyes off them with difficulty. They were black holes, these bells, and their gravity stole everything.

"Elizabeth Creed," I called. It wasn't a question. If not her, who else could it be?

I was answered by a croaking bark. It was a cry of dismay and irritation, tempered by blind hatred. I didn't like it, this certainty that someone wanted to blow me to smithereens on general principle.

I spun on my heels, again resisting the pull of those bells, and I saw her.

She was out on the roof, standing on the curved clay tiles that baked themselves brittle under the California sun. Her feet were steady and she was not moving—not fidgeting, not humming, not vibrating like everything else. She was the one stable speck in this warped old mission, which reassured me not in the slightest. I already knew how unstable she was on the inside.

In her hands she held a box—the kind children use to keep their pens and pencils together. It didn't look like a humidor to me, but maybe she'd swapped it out for something of her own. She wasn't quite the wild-eyed mad scientist I expected; her hair was graying in rivulets and it was contained in a tidy ponytail. The jeans and T-shirt she wore wouldn't have looked out of place on . . . well, on *me*, or anyone else.

She asked, "Who are you?"

Suddenly I didn't know what to say. I was being called upon to account for my presence there, and my future actions, and what could I tell her? I'm not ordinarily put in the position of defending myself to my victims. Most of the people from whom I steal have no idea who robbed them, and *none* of them ever catch me in the act. Then again, I never have to chase them down and physically take things away from them, either.

I made a mental note to consider it a deal-breaker on future assignments.

I had to tell her something, though. Or at least I *thought* I did, despite the fact that, in retrospect, I could've just barreled into her, swiped the box, and moved on with my life. I'm not sure why I didn't. Maybe it was the hum, or the bells. Maybe it was the way she met my eyes without blinking, and made me feel like a naughty schoolchild who's been caught eating crayons.

Regardless, I said, "I'm here to take back what you stole." Because that sounded better than, "I'm going to steal your stuff for my own nefarious purposes," yet it did not fully spell out my intentions.

"Why?" she asked.

"Because I'm being paid to. Put down the bones, Ms. Creed." She said, "No."

Her eyes hardened and mine probably went wide. I don't know; I couldn't see them. But I could feel myself starting to freak out—my hair was standing up on end again, like before the lightning in Portland, even though the sky was still as clear as a bell (but not the bells behind me).

"What are you doing?" I shrieked at her. "Put down the god-damn bones and get out of here now unless you want to die!"

She snorted. "You didn't answer my first question, so I won't answer yours. That's fair, isn't it?" Then she stuck the box into a bag she was wearing cross-body style, the strap slung across her chest. I hadn't seen it before because it was resting on her ass. "And I'm not going to die."

We faced each other down, both of us increasingly convinced that the other one was being ridiculous, and possibly about to breathe her last.

I have no idea what kept me from launching myself at her, knocking her off the roof and smashing her onto the ground below, but it might've had something to do with her right hand, which was clutching something thin, pale, and just long enough to stick out both ends of her fist.

"Last chance," she told me. "This whole place is going down."

"While you're standing on it?"

She smiled, and her knuckles were so white they gleamed like teeth. "Did you know this mission, this whole town . . . sits on the San Andreas?"

"I did not," I admitted, sticking to the facts because, holy shit, I only just then noticed that she was not actually standing on anything. She was hovering a few inches above the tiles, which accounted for why she was able to hold herself so steady while the rest of the world quivered.

"It has to go. All of it."

"Why?" I asked.

"Mistakes need to be unmade," she declared.

Her eyes rolled back into her head. Her hand crushed harder around the brittle white bone, and I could see even from these few yards away that it was beginning to bend, creeping toward some shattering point.

The harder she held it, the louder the hum buzzed—and the harder the ground moved. Her lips moved too, but I couldn't understand what she was saying, muttering in that weird, dark rhythm. What had started as an odd vibration blossomed into a lurch, a heave, and a shudder—accompanied by the crack of trees and the tinkling crash of clay roofing tiles falling to the sidewalk.

Something moved behind me; I saw it out of the corner of my eye.

Adrian. I'd forgotten he was there, behind me—still on the stairs, or near them.

Elizabeth Creed hadn't seen him. That much was apparent from the surprise on her face when he struck her in the chest. He'd flung himself at her, shoulder-first with his head down, and hit her square and with his full weight—perhaps 180 pounds of off-duty drag queen catching a fifty-something engineer like a ton of glitter.

As they dropped to the banging, jostling roof, tiles went scattering and more than the wind got knocked out of Creed.

At a distance and in slow motion, I watched her fingers unclench and the bone slip away from her palm. It scooted down the roof and rolled awkwardly toward the edge, ambling toward the rim, over which it would tip in a matter of moments.

For no logical reason, I knew in the bottom of my stomach that I *had* to catch that bone. I knew that it couldn't break, that I had to pick it up and take *very good care* of it until this spell, or enchantment, or whatever it was . . . had either dissipated or been undone.

The world heaved beneath me, or maybe only the roof did, I couldn't tell. I tried to jump toward the escaping bone as it loped downward, but my next step dislodged a tile—sending it shooting off the roof and over into space. Forward I flopped, skidded, and flailed. Down I scooted, and the sound of clay grating against my pants, knees, and elbows was a pottery symphony . . . and although it felt (and surely looked) like I'd lost all semblance of control, at the last second I stretched and lashed out—and grabbed the bone right as it toppled off the edge.

I toppled off the edge behind it, or rather underneath it. I shifted midair to put my body between that precious penis nub and the hard ground below, and I did a good job.

Flat on my back, I landed with a smack that cracked my skull and left me seeing stars before I saw nothing at all.

As I blacked out, a muddy procession of half-formed images and thoughts went sliding through my mind. The sky above, speckled and domed. A cheer of relief that the mission was only one story, and I hadn't fallen any farther. The taste of powdered clay and sidewalk dust flavored with rubber sandal soles. And the brittle, unbroken bone cradled against my belly.

The world stopped moving, but if it was the whole world or just me, I couldn't tell.

8

Adrian wanted something, but he could wait. It was dark and pleasant where I was lying, and nothing hurt. Except the back of my head. And my spine. And my ribs. On second thought, pretty much everything fucking hurt.

What the hell?

I opened my eyes and he was there above me, shaking me like a British nanny.

"Get up! Up, goddammit! We have to get out of here!"

"We have to . . . what?"

"Out of here, *now*," he added for emphasis—and then he yanked me up off the ground in one smooth move that underscored how badly I had gotten hurt when I'd thrown myself from the roof.

I yelped, and he yanked again. "This is no time

for you to require babying," he said and I tripped behind him in the dark, trying to get my thoughts together and my body upright of its own accord. Both tasks at once were more than I could swing with any real grace.

My legs alternately buckled beneath me and wobbled forward behind Adrian, who towed me through the darkness with considerably more confidence and determination than I, personally, possessed. But he hadn't taken a header off a roof as recently as I had.

"Dude," I gasped as my knee stuck in the "straight" position and pain went cavorting through my nervous system. "Slow down!"

"No way. We're getting the fuck out of here," he wheezed, "before this gets any worse!"

"This what?" I asked like an idiot.

This was the earthquake that was getting a good shudder going, and *this* didn't even remotely help my feeble ability to put one foot in front of the other right at that moment.

"I don't know. The Big One?"

I couldn't see where we were going. It was like I was wearing sunglasses in the middle of the night. Man, I'd really knocked myself good. "The Big One? Like LA falling into the ocean?"

"I don't know. I'm a southern man, and I don't do earthquakes."

"I don't think this one is very bad," I told him.

He didn't believe me. "Get a move on, Ray. The car's still another few blocks that way."

"We're not going to . . . we won't . . . we can't . . . out*drive* an earthquake."

"We're going to give it a shot."

"What about . . . ," I stammered. "The bones? Did you get them?"

"No. She went off the other side of the roof and took the bones with her."

"But I caught one. I have one," I mumbled, even though my fingers were spread wide, and wiggling like bait.

"She took it away from you."

Because I was staring at my hands like an idiot, I tripped over a rock or something, did the stupid trying-to-find-my-balance dance, and found it in time to ask, "She took it away from me?"

"Yes."

"If she went off the roof, we could go back and catch her." I looked back over my shoulder, seeking some sign of another woman loping in the other direction.

He said, "I doubt it."

"Why?"

"She didn't casually *leave* the roof. She *flew* off it, swooped down and took the bone, and left you there. And you weren't looking so good."

The texture beneath our feet changed, and we were over a curb, onto a sidewalk, and running between two buildings. "Aw . . ." I burbled. "And you came to check up on me?"

"It was either that or chase the flying crazy lady, and I thought you'd be less trouble. It might've been a judgment error on my part, but there you go."

My bearings were gradually returning to me as I healed on the run, but the process wasn't swift or comfortable. I should've just been grateful to heal up from such a crash with so little downtime, sure, but it was hard to feel any gratitude when my head was spinning like a dryer and my semi-ghoul was dragging me toward a car I couldn't remember having parked. I sure hoped he knew where it was. And I hoped he had the keys, too, because I had no idea where they were.

"Slow down!"

"No, we're almost there!" He was right. I hit the car with a smack as he tossed me up against it and spun me around by my shoulders. "Keys?" he asked as he patted me down like a convict. "Where did you put them?"

"Pocket?" I guessed.

Yes, I could feel the lump of them as he swatted at them. "Got 'em."

Rifling around in my pants in a rather personal fashion produced these keys, and he abandoned me to let himself into the driver's side. Momentarily, I heard the power locks click and I floundered for the door latch—but not fast enough to get the thing open before he opened it from the inside.

"Get in!" he commanded.

"Working on it," I groused, climbing into the passenger's seat—one of my least favorite places ever, might I add—and I reached back behind my shoulder for the seat belt. I don't always worry about buckling up, but if there was one thing I didn't need tonight, it was another set of life-threatening injuries. Or injuries that would have been life-threatening if I'd been alive in any proper sense.

As it was, everything throbbed when Adrian threw the car into gear and pulled out onto the road. If I closed my eyes, I could feel the tiny spider cracks in my skull knitting back together; it tingled and tickled, but not in a good way. It felt like a very strong man giving me a very deep tattoo. On my cranium.

But like Daddy always said, the sting means it's working. Or that's what I told myself as we peeled out of our improvised parking spot and headed back through town. We couldn't peel out through town, though Adrian gave it a good effort: The quake had drawn all the sensible people out of their homes—and some of the less sensible of those sensible people were loitering in the street, or perilously close to it.

Riding along while the road was shaking was peculiar, but not altogether different from driving around in a car with terrible shocks. And before long, right as we got outside the town's city limits, things smoothed back down to usual and the stars quit buzzing up above.

Adrian was visibly shaken, if you'll pardon the expression. I guess he wasn't kidding about being a southern man, and ill prepared to feel the earth move. He looked as bad as I felt.

"You okay?" I asked him.

He didn't take his eyes off the road. "I'll live. How about you?"

"My head hurts." I left out the bit about my shoulders, spine, and pelvis. All of it had been rattled, but the head was the worst.

"How long will it take you to heal?"

I said, "I don't know," which was true. Depending on my injuries, a couple of nights. Or a couple of hours if I could score a snack. I wasn't sure how probable this was, and I didn't feel like bringing it up, so I fibbed. "I'll be fine by the end of the night. Tomorrow's dusk, at latest." It wasn't a huge fib. Not my worst by far, considering that, within this time frame, I'd undoubtedly be able to fake it.

"Ray?"

"Yeah, Adrian?"

"That was some fucked-up shit."

"Tell me about it. She really . . . she *flew* off the building?"

He nodded. "Not like Superman flying. More like Magneto. She drifted, and then soared. I couldn't have caught her if I tried." Then he paused before asking, "What happened back there? That was . . . it was magic, wasn't it?"

"Either magic, or that woman is so crazy she can *fly*."

"*Ray* . . ."

"Magic, yes. It's magic. Wizards, magicians, sorcerers . . . all those guys use it. And gals. But I've never been inclined to associate with them."

"You don't like people who fling magic around?"

"It'd be more accurate to say that there just aren't very many of them. And yes, I'm uncomfortable with it. I don't like hanging out with people who can do things I can't." I rubbed at the back of my head and felt little plates of bone crinkle beneath my fingers. Wincing, I leaned forward so I didn't knock against the headrest or the window. I put my face in my hands. They were the only cushion I had.

"That's good. That there aren't too many of them, I mean."

"Usually, it's neither here nor there. From everything I know about it, magic isn't much better than useless. It takes a lifetime to master the basics, and longer than that to learn anything more complicated than levitating quarters. I don't know how this woman got so good, so fast . . ."

"Was she helped by the bones?"

I pondered this. "Horace says they work like amplifiers, and I've never heard of a magician who could blow up houses with lightning, much less start The Big One on a whim. But she has some *serious* skill, even without them. If I had to guess, I'd say she's been studying for decades. She was what, maybe in her fifties? If she got started as a teenager, and if she had some natural ability . . ." The prospect wasn't helping my headache.

Adrian pondered my pondering. "So what about vampires?"

"What about them?" I asked, because I'm stupid.

"Vampires have decades and decades. Centuries, some of them. Are there any vampire magicians?"

"Christ, no. And thank God. Something about being dead makes magic a no-go for vampires. Only the living can practice it. Don't ask me why," I said quickly, since that was the next thing on the verge of shooting out of his mouth. "I have no idea. But that's why I'm not an expert on magical mysteries: I've never performed any, and I don't know anyone who *has*. However . . ."

"However . . . what?"

"However, I have a sneaking suspicion that Horace is a dabbler. It might be time to call him up and quiz the shit out of him. This woman is dangerous."

"Dangerous enough to leave alone from here on out?"

I shook my head, slowly. "Nah. If there's time I'll take another stab at her, once Horace gets a good lead on her credit cards again. Maybe when we get back from Atlanta."

"Are you *insane?*"

"Clinically so, I'm rather certain of it."

"How droll."

"Honey." I was too tired and achy to baby him, any more than he'd been able to baby me a few minutes earlier. "It's a *lot* of money. And this is my job. Besides, next time I'll know what to expect."

"Oh really? Are we going by the process of elimination, here? First time you meet, she tries to kill you with a lightning bolt, and then the second time she tries to create the island nation of Los Angeles. Next up, what do you see happening, eh? A hurricane?"

"Look, I don't know for certain what she's going to do, no. But I've seen her. I've met her. I've watched her work. She caught me off guard this time, but it won't happen again."

"Here's hoping."

"You're such a fucking optimist," I accused. "Just get us to the hotel."

We fumed in silence for another few miles, until finally he asked, "How bad are you hurt, anyway? I've never seen you get hurt."

"Bad enough to complain. Not bad enough to worry."

"I thought you were invincible or something."

"Think again," I told him. "I take damage as easily as you do. I'm just better at avoiding it, and I recover faster. Earlier this evening I did a back-flop off a roof, onto a sidewalk. I've got some cracks, okay? But it'll be all right."

"When?"

"*Soon,*" I promised.

We dragged ourselves to the hotel room and crashed. Maybe *crashed* isn't exactly the best verb I could use. I'd done plenty of crashing already. At least this round was pleasant.

When I awoke the next evening, Adrian wasn't there.

He'd left a note on the television saying he'd gone out to find food and he'd be back soon, which left me with some alone time. I removed the note and turned on the television for company— settling on a Discovery Channel documentary, something about great engineering disasters of the seventies.

I needed something interesting enough that it didn't annoy me, but not so interesting that it was distracting.

I ran myself a hot bath and came out of it feeling a lot better, if not great. So I'd hardly lied after all, which was nice, I suppose. But when I stood naked before the full-length mirror on the closet door . . . ugh. It wasn't pretty. When I twisted my neck to get the full view, I could see my shoulder blades, hips, and lower spine showing through my skin in a shadow play of conspicuous bruising.

I looked like an X-ray in reverse.

I prodded myself gently, even the back of my tender noggin. Nothing was broken anymore, and the painful smashed spot had filled itself out while I slept. As far as hangovers went, I'd had worse.

From the back of the bathroom door, I grabbed a robe and put it on. I didn't want to look at myself, if for no other reason than that it reminded me how I was getting hungry from all this healing, and looking at those bruises got me thinking about how a good meal would fix them up right quick.

I flopped down on the bed with the television remote and my laptop, and reached into my go-bag for my primary cell phone.

Horace didn't answer when I dialed him up, but I left him a message that was cryptic enough to make him call me back. If he thought I had the bones, he'd go have himself a celebratory drink and get back to me when he felt like it; if he thought I didn't have them, he'd stew about it awhile just to punish me.

I know this guy. He's easy to handle if you figure out where his buttons are.

As I waited for him to call, I settled in with my laptop and the semi-crappy wireless Internet provided by the hotel.

I struggled with the spotty coverage until I'd retrieved my email and discovered a query from Ian, wondering how things were going. It was so very *like* him to email. Silly man. Never wanting to intrude with something so gauche as a phone call. A warm fuzzy ran up my bruised spine as I typed out a quick reply, swearing that all was well and we'd be home soon—and I'd tell him everything.

I also had an email from Horace, including a PDF of the odds and ends he'd been able to gather on Elizabeth Creed, and since I was still vegging out in my borrowed bathrobe, and since Adrian wasn't back yet from his hunting and gathering (I stifled a pang of envy because it was silly, and I could go hunting, too, if I really wanted to) . . . I settled back against the pillows to read.

The better I could get to know my enemy, the more effectively I'd confront her next time.

Also, having encountered her face-to-face, I was curious.

How does somebody go from being a respected aerospace engineer to . . . to . . . whatever she was now? A schizophrenic sorceress with world-destroying ambitions? It was strange to me, how someone who built a career looking into outer space could show such rage toward her home planet. Or maybe it would make perfect sense, if I could see it from another angle.

I opened the PDF, and from time to time I followed up with the Internet. Over the course of an hour, I teased out bits and pieces of information about Elizabeth Creed until I had an uncomfortably clear picture of her psyche to go along with the image of her face, which was burned into my brain. Her face, after all, was the last thing I'd seen before grabbing that bone and going off the roof.

When I say that the picture was uncomfortably clear, I mean it.

Elizabeth Creed was born in 1953, in Houston, Texas. Her mother died when she was young; her father was a chemist working for the Dow chemical plant in Freeport. She first began to display psychological problems in grade school, and was briefly institutionalized as a teenager, but she was released with a high school diploma and very high test scores in math and science. She went to the University of San Francisco, which partly explained what she was doing in the region. She was married in 1974 to a guy named Harold Hopkins, which explained the rest of it.

Their wedding had been held on the mission's grounds.

Her words came back to haunt me. *Mistakes need to be unmade.*

Did she honestly think she could . . . what? Turn back time? Reverse her marriage—make it so it'd never happened? I kept reading, and learned for certain what I could've guessed: Her marriage ended badly three years later, when Harold left her for another woman. In 1978, she was institutionalized for a second time, and formally diagnosed with schizophrenia.

But she was very, very smart. Upon her release, she changed her name, taking on the identity of Rachel Olsen and getting a second degree, this one from MIT. She went to work for NASA, which meant the woman had some *major* identity theft skills—but I knew what that was like, didn't I? I'd done it before, myself.

My imagination could fill in some of the holes. She had taken her medicine in secret, visiting psychologists under other assumed identities. She'd struggled in the dark, battling her own mind as it turned on her.

My own mental health issues had come and gone the same way, diagnosed nearly a hundred years ago as simple "hysteria," which only meant that I was a woman and really, who gave a shit what was actually wrong with me? Or that's how I took it at the time. I was fortunate that my father hadn't sent me away, even though he could have, and even though he was urged to do so more than once.

It wasn't until the eighties that I finally figured out what was wrong with me. Severe obsessive-compulsive disorder with a touch of the old manic swing.

For added irony, OCD is something that defines vampires in a number of traditions around the globe. Have you heard the old stories? All you have to do to get rid of us is throw a handful of rice, and we'll have to stop and count every grain before pursuing you . . . or you can do the same with sand, or running water, or crossed lines. Some people have argued that the running water and the cross are religious wards, water being the element of baptism and the cross as the sign of Christ. But people like me—and maybe people like Elizabeth Creed—we know better than that. We know how it feels to hesitate before something that's moving, unwilling to put a toe in, and unwilling to step across it for no logical reason whatsoever. And step on a crack, break your mother's back. The more lines, the more prohibited things to step on—and things to avoid.

In the years since figuring out my problem, I've often

wondered why it wasn't fixed when I died and became what I am now. How come my mental malfunctions weren't repaired like my asthma, my allergies, and my nearsightedness when the supernatural blood went coursing through my veins? Why did I get stuck with the one truly bad thing—the thing that kept me from a normal life, and now keeps me from a normal afterlife?

I looked at my go-bag, loaded with a thousand and one things I would never need in a hundred jobs, in a thousand years. I considered my army of cell phones, my elaborate precautions, my grasping nature that never finds enough to hold *just in case* tomorrow everything implodes and I have to start over . . . so I won't start over with nothing.

And when I looked at Elizabeth Creed's life story, something in my stomach constricted with sympathy. Such a mind, such potential. Did the magic make her mad, or was she born that way, same as me?

I suspected a congenital problem. Magic isn't like hat-making; there's no mercury in it to create a wild-eyed stereotype. Wizards, magicians, sorcerers—whatever they call themselves—they're usually a controlled, calculating lot.

I'd like to say "You'd have to be," though Elizabeth Creed was pulling it off with full-blown schizophrenia, so I might be wrong. It definitely takes a mind that's comfortable with vast catalogs of data, and a firm memory, and a serious attention to detail. Either Creed had all these things lurking beneath her illness, or she'd found a way to work around them.

In 1996 Elizabeth Creed had been discharged from NASA and arrested for her identity theft, but by all appearances she'd only impersonated the dead and hadn't screwed up anybody's credit score or given anyone a criminal record. Back then it wasn't all digital, like it is now. One number couldn't unhinge an entire lifetime. She hadn't hurt anyone, she'd only lied, and she'd lied in order to survive as a free woman. It was hard to hate her for it.

Well, it was hard for *me* to hate her for it, even though my back cracked as I sat up and adjusted myself on the bed. As I'd been reading, I'd sunk lower and lower into the bedspread and deeper into the feather pillows. I hate feather pillows. Nobody gets any decent support from those things. They're worthless.

As I was extricating myself from this downy quicksand, I heard a keycard in the lock and Adrian came slinking in—peeking around the door before letting himself inside.

He said, "Hey."

I said "Hey" back. "How was supper?"

"Fine. I found a TacoTime and went to town. I was starving when I woke up this afternoon." Nice, how easily he was adjusting to vampire time. Or maybe it was only that he was already adjusted to drag-queen time. Come to think of it, they were probably similar. "Sorry I was gone so long, but I assumed you'd call if you got worried."

"No problem. It gave me time to catch up on my reading."

"And take a bath? God, the windows are still fogged in here. How hot did you run it?"

"As hot as it would go. It felt great."

"I bet." He came to sit down on his bed, and he held out a brown paper bag that'd been rolled up like an oversized school lunch. "I . . . um. I brought you something."

"A present? For me?" I joked. But when I took it from him, it was heavy. And it sloshed.

"It took me some time to track down a place that would give it to me, and I used your credit card. Sorry."

I unrolled the brown-paper top and stared down into three pints of human blood, sealed in the usual plastic pouches and labeled thusly. I was absolutely dumbfounded. I gazed up at him with abject adoration and asked, "Adrian . . . where did you get this?"

He shrugged and began to kick off his shoes. "There's a plasma donation center at the other end of town. It's not the world's cleanest joint; most of the donors are paid, and they obviously need the money. But there's blood banking on the premises, too. You uh . . . you don't want to know what it cost."

"I couldn't care less what it cost," I assured him, lifting the pouches out one by one as if they were filled with nitroglycerin. They were still cool from refrigeration, but not cold. I didn't care how fresh they were, or if they were fresh at all. Nothing mattered except that I had acquired a snack—a snack via my not-a-ghoul, who had justified his existence like never before. "Thank you. Thank you, thank you, *thank you.*"

I heaved my bruised little self out of the bed and went pushing through the coffeemaker supplies.

"What are you doing?"

"Coffee mugs. You don't want any coffee, do you?" I asked, holding up both of the provided containers.

"No, why?"

"These cups are microwavable. And if you don't want one, I'm going to use them both so I can two-fist this stuff. They won't hold it all at once, but they'll hold enough to get me started."

"Ah," he nodded. "I don't guess it tastes very good cold."

"In fact, it does not. It's better than nothing when it's cold, but since I have a microwave right here . . ." I bit the corner of the first blood bubble and squeezed its contents into the mugs. Then I propped the baggie up against the counter and chucked the mugs into the microwave. "I'm prepared to delay gratification a few minutes for the sake of a warm meal."

He grinned at me. "You're more human than you think."

I licked the edge of the tooth that'd punctured the bag. Blood, yes. Tasty, tasty blood—albeit cold blood. As the microwave counted down, I tapped my fingers impatiently on its door. "I never said I wasn't human. I started out human, didn't I?"

"Fine, that's true. You've never said it, but sometimes you act like you're more different than you really are."

"Dude, I'm dead."

"I know," he said, still giving me that grin. I wasn't sure I liked the grin; it said that he knew something about me—something I didn't know. I thought he was wrong. He and I were plenty different, and if he believed otherwise, it was only because I'd never showed him the extent of how different I could be.

Maybe watching me down a few mugs of O-positive would give him a hint.

I opened the microwave door before the final *ding* and pulled out both mugs. I stirred the contents with the plastic coffee stirrers (hey, nobody likes a scalding spot in a chilly drink), licked the stirrer clean, then pounded the mugs like a frat boy at a kegger.

Adrian watched with only the mildest interest, and I'm not sure what that says about either one of us, except that he must've been getting more comfortable with me by the day. Perhaps having a sip or two of my bodily fluids had acclimated him to the idea faster than anything else possibly could.

I guzzled every drop. It was laced with preservatives, not quite the right temperature, and it'd been sitting in a fridge for a couple of days. Regardless, it was the best blood I'd ever tasted and I couldn't get enough. I squeezed the last bit out of bag number one, mashing its edges like it was a toothpaste tube and I was a cheapskate, and then I moved on to bag number two. Two more minutes in the microwave and another moment of stirring to get the temperature even, and I was back in hog heaven.

In this way, I killed off all three bags—despite the fact that I almost never drank that much, and I was full by the end of the second bag. Didn't care. Couldn't let it go to waste, and if I didn't down it then and there, it'd go bad overnight in the dinky dorm-room fridge with which our room was stocked.

Besides, after a meal like that, I could go for weeks without taking another one. I liked the idea of being all full up before undertaking any further adventures, even adventures so mild as "trying to get a good day's sleep on those fucking feather pillows."

When I was finished, I collapsed back on the bed and closed my eyes. "Adrian?" I said softly.

"Yes?"

"That was the most awesome thing you have ever done. And I want you to know, I'll make it up to you, one of these days."

"Oh, I know you will," he said, and I couldn't see the nefarious grin, but I could hear it. "You're going to take me to Atlanta to see about my sister."

I frowned but didn't open my eyes. "We didn't agree to that. Not yet."

"You have to admit, I'm wearing you down."

"I only have to admit that you've made yourself inordinately useful. Which you have. And which I appreciate."

"Isn't that a ghoul's job?" He asked it with a faux innocence that jolted me out of my near-catatonia.

"Hold up now. We didn't agree to that, either. And when we talked about it last, you didn't like the idea." I sat up, determined to square this away once and for all. "You're not my ghoul. That little swap of blood wasn't enough to do it—"

"Or so you *think*."

"So I'm sure. You know why I don't like ghouls, and I don't want a ghoul. I think that whole nonsense with Jeffery Sykes ought to be enough to explain why," I reminded him. Sykes had been a ghoul once, and now he was something much, much worse—and much more dangerous. To vampires, to humans, and to everything else. He'd been mutilated after betraying his master. They'd left him deaf, blind, and mute. And piece by piece, Sykes was attempting to repair himself—at the expense of the rest of us. Wherever he was, and whatever he was doing, I intended to put a stop to it one of these days.

But first, I had Adrian playing mind games.

He said to me, "I can hear you better than I used to, and now when you concentrate I can almost hear you perfectly. It used to be you could only send me a vague idea of what you wanted or what you meant. Now I knew, even though you hadn't told me, that you were dying for some blood."

"You could've known that just from hanging around me for the last half year. You know how it goes when I get hurt. You know the blood makes it easier to heal."

"Sure, but I never cared before. Or . . . well, *care* isn't exactly right. This afternoon, when I left to go find food for myself, it was almost like I could hear you being hungry. Does that make sense?"

"No."

He gave me one of those lovely, fluid shrugs that he always delivered with the grace of a martial artist. "It doesn't have to make sense to be true. Shit, I just watched an old lady fly off a two-hundred-year-old church with a box full of penis bones. That's true, and that doesn't make a damn bit of sense."

"She's not that old," I corrected him. "She's fifty-eight."

"All right. But the rest of it—"

"You've got me on the rest of it. But let me get this straight." I rubbed at my temples, which were faintly throbbing. But only faintly. "Last night you were utterly freaked out by the prospect that you'd downed enough vampire juice to bind you; and tonight you're . . . what? Auditioning for the role of Raylene's ghoul?"

"I'll audition for it if it'll get me into the Atlanta House, sure. You've already made the arguments against it"—he interrupted me before I could repeat myself—"and I understand them. But I also understand that if I go there as your ghoul, I can walk in through the front door—and I won't have to break into the place in the middle of the day. I'd rather deal with a whole horde of petty, politicking vampires than a bunch of idiot people and their daytime security systems."

"Then maybe you're the idiot," I accused.

"Maybe, but I'm getting into that House one way or another. And if I have to pretend to be your lackey to do it, that's fine."

"I'll remember you said that."

"Just remember who brought you blood. Hey look—you're already looking better," he noted.

"How can you tell? All the bruising was on my back."

"Your eyes looked weird. Like you'd been punched, or had a nose job, or something."

"Awesome."

He insisted, "It wasn't *bad*. It was just something I saw, when you were standing in the light. Anyway, you look more like yourself already."

"Good." I pulled a pillow over my face, and learned that the downy contents were easier on top of my head than under it. I liked the darkness, and the softness, and I liked how they didn't really smell like anything but the cotton pillowcase. They weren't entirely useless after all. "But just so you know," I said, enjoying the muffled sound of my voice, "we aren't going to Atlanta yet."

"I know. You have to go to Seattle and get Ian to talk to his brother." He vacated his own bed and sat down on the edge of mine, right beside me. He smelled like lettuce, sour cream, and Mexican beef with a whiff of Dr Pepper. The weight of his body made mine roll toward him, just enough to be uncomfortable. He said, "It won't be long before Max figures out Ian isn't coming back, and you can't make him."

"Max is bad news. I have to stay between him and Ian, and I don't want to throw you into that mix." I was going to fall asleep again, I could feel it. My body was delighted by the fresh infusion, and it was sucking every last platelet into my system, making me drowsy despite the early hour.

Adrian pulled the pillow off my face. "But you *will*. If I'm a good ghoul."

I squinted up at him. "I'm too tired and beat up to argue with you right now. Let's save it for later. Hey, you want to boost your odds?"

"Yes."

"Then book us a hotel room, back wherever we stayed on the way down here. We start back for home tonight. I think you know where my credit card is," I said, waggling an eyebrow at his crotch—though I meant to waggle it at his pocket. It was hard to differentiate when he was sitting so close.

He didn't get up right away. Instead he said, "You're going to keep doing this, aren't you?"

"Doing what?"

"Bribing me into helpful little favors."

"Yup," I confirmed. "Hey, you want to be like a ghoul? Act like a ghoul. Look at it this way, I'm prepping you for the hypothetical possibility of a Georgia adventure. You were rusty at Max's place. You'll have to be smoother with your duties if you want to breach the Barrington House."

"So you *say*," he replied suspiciously.

I sighed and put a hand on his leg. I tried to make it friendly, warm. Motherly, almost. But it's hard to feel motherly about someone with a thigh that could crack a horse's ribs. "If I honestly thought you wouldn't get yourself killed within an hour, I'd tell you to check it out for yourself."

"I'm not helpless, you know."

"I *do* know. But you don't know the Barringtons like I do, Adrian. Please trust me on this."

"I'll trust you if you agree to take me with you."

"We're not having this conversation right now."

"Sure we are."

"No," I said. "Go get us a hotel room. We'll hash it out when we get back home, and when we know how Ian's going to take what I've learned. You never know. He might freak out on us, and blow the whole thing. Our free pass to Atlanta depends on his cooperation, so really, you should direct some of this charm offensive at him."

"When we get home?"

"Yes, when we get home."

9

We arrived home Sunday which was good—since that's roughly when I'd told Max he'd hear from Ian. Adrian and I had discussed my strategy in the car on the way up, and together we decided I'd drop him off at home and I'd work on Ian alone first. I could always summon Adrian as backup emotional blackmail, if such became necessary.

I hoped it wouldn't. And the truth was, I was afraid Adrian would push too hard. His eagerness at the prospect of infiltrating his sister's old House . . . I'm not saying it made him sloppy, but it worried me. I didn't think he'd stay put if I ordered him to, and I'd been absolutely honest with him when I'd warned of his one-hour life expectancy there.

Adrian is a badass. Let the record reflect. But let the record also reflect that the Atlanta House is considered a badass house among badass houses—tempered with a good measure of insanity and very bad behavior, both in public and behind closed doors.

I told myself that if I *had* to, I could drug Adrian and leave him locked up in the penthouse flat with Ian and the kids to look after him for a few days, but that was an idle threat. My not-a-ghoul was full of surprises, and even if I could keep him home for a few days, I couldn't keep him there indefinitely. He'd find a way to get loose, find a way to Atlanta, and get himself killed if he tried to get inside without me.

No matter how I approached the problem, the same conclusion always worked its way to the top: I would almost certainly have to bring him along. And if he could present himself as a plausible ghoul, so much the better. He'd be safer, for a feeble value of "safe." If something were to happen to me, they might not kill him. They might just absorb him into the House—a nightmare scenario if ever I heard one, though I didn't think he'd see it that way. Adrian would look at it as a silver lining in case of my death—an opportunity to get even closer, even more quietly.

I hated all those goddamn variables. It made it tough to plan, and if I can't plan, I start getting crazy. Not that I'm always a very *good* planner. I think this ought to be apparent by now.

So. One thing at a time.

First: Ian.

I entered my compound via the old service elevator and found the place in cheerful havoc, with Pita tearing around and Pepper tearing around after him—and Domino ignoring both of them while playing a video game in the common area. Whenever the kitten felt cornered, he'd rush to Domino and try to hide in his lap, as if the boy were "base" and it meant Pepper couldn't grab him and . . . I don't know. Tickle him, or whatever torture she was inflicting. I could tell by watching the cat that he wasn't really afraid and that Pepper wasn't really out to hurt him, so I didn't worry about it.

"Hey," I announced myself.

Domino paused his game, looked over at me, and replied, "Hey."

"Hey!" Pepper shrieked as Pita ran across my feet, and she followed close behind.

The kitten doubled back, climbed my pants like a ladder, and snuggled up on my shoulder, panting happily into my ear. Pepper drew up short in front of me, likewise panting, and she was smiling, too.

"I'm glad everyone's been having a great time," I said, scanning the room for Ian. I could sense him back in his room, and within a few seconds he emerged to join us.

Pepper composed herself, clearing her throat and adjusting her posture so that she stood up straight and appeared fully calm. "It's been okay," she informed me.

"Okay?" Ian said from his doorway. "I've been listening to you shriek for the last hour." It sounded like a complaint, but it didn't look like one. He wasn't angry. However, he was tense—that much was apparent, despite the show of pleasantness.

Domino leaned forward and pressed a button to end his game, or turn it off, or whatever. He unfolded himself from a cross-legged position and stretched, then stepped immediately to Ian's side.

Ian didn't need any assistance; he knew the layout of our flat well enough that if you didn't know he was blind, you wouldn't be able to tell it from watching him navigate the place. It was a nice gesture all the same. Domino had been such a total, complete little shit when I'd first found myself taking care of him . . . it was nice to see him attempting responsibility for a change.

Mind you, I didn't trust it. I casually suspected that he was up to no good, regardless of his good behavior. But I'd like to think I was doing a decent job of keeping that opinion to myself. Most of the time.

"Ian, *darling*," I said in an exaggerated fashion. I even smooched his cheek, which made him smile. "I believe we have some things to talk about."

"You're not leaving us," Pepper declared. Like she was informing him that this had been decided without him.

I told her, "Mind your own business, you nosy kid." But I tried to keep my tone light enough that it wouldn't worry her. "I have some things to run past your favorite babysitter, and I think it's all going to work out fine."

"Are you sure?" Domino wanted to know.

"Pretty sure. Ian, how about you and I head outside for coffee or something? The twenty-four-hour place around the corner," I added upon checking my watch. We were barely too early for the very early breakfast crowd, so we'd have to keep it short and sweet. That drive through California is a killer, even for lead-footed souls like me and Adrian.

"That sounds fine to me." He sounded relieved, though not entirely. He'd been waiting for word for days, keeping up his end of the bargain—and now it was time for me to come through on my end. I'd been doing a lot of thinking about how to spin the situation, and I was reasonably confident I could keep him in our weird little court.

"Okay. Let me drop this stuff off in my room." I wanted to unload my jacket which, in true Seattle fashion, was suddenly too warm to wear, and I didn't intend to bring the week's luggage along for the faux coffee break. So I dumped everything on my bed without bothering to sort it, shut the bedroom door (as if that'd keep anybody out), and rejoined Ian in the common area.

"We'll be back in a while, kids," I told them, then I drew

the gate across the service elevator's entry and set the thing into motion.

When we were down a floor or two, and out of the kids' hearing range, he asked, "How did it go?" Because we were saving the specific questions until we got outside, apparently.

"It went well, all things considered."

"I'll know if you're lying," he warned, which may or may not have been true, but I didn't intend to do any serious lying anyway.

"I know. And I won't. Hey, I got out of there and home without incident, didn't I? It couldn't have gone *that* badly. Wait, well. Okay, there *was* an incident, but it didn't have anything to do with Max or the San Francisco guys."

On the rest of the way down, and out on the street, and all the way to the café I filled him in on the saga of Elizabeth Creed and her powers of flight, distracting him with someone else's drama for once. By the time we reached the coffeehouse, I'd laid out most of the story, and he was shaking his head while we waited in line.

"Unbelievable," he observed.

"If I didn't still have the sore neck, I'd be inclined to agree with you. And thank God I had Adrian there with me for backup. For one thing, he may well have saved my ass by leaping on Creed, up there on the roof. And for another, he gives me someone to corroborate the story. Otherwise, no one would ever believe it."

I'd left out the part about Max doing the old toast ritual, and all the stuff about Adrian worrying over—or perhaps sneakily encouraging—potential ghoul-dom. That's why Ian was able to say, "Except for the swan dive off the roof, it sounds like you two had a good time on your road trip."

"It was more of a back-flop than a swan dive, but sure. We had a pretty decent time. I even got a new lead on Adrian's sister, sort of."

"Really? How's that?"

By now we'd received our steaming mugs of something we had no intention of drinking, and were homing in on a small table, conveniently located in a back corner without too many ears to overhear us. It wasn't a huge concern, anyway. We were practically experts at speaking in public without being self-incriminating, and the place was half empty, courtesy of the hour.

As we lowered ourselves into the wood slat seats, taking care to keep from spilling our almost-overflowing mugs, I went ahead and let the subject shift.

"Not a lead on her, personally, though I remain convinced that she's still loitering about, somewhere in the area. But I got a lead on the Atlanta House, and a way inside it. Courtesy of your brother Max."

"Ah" was all he said. He drew the mug up to his face and breathed in the aroma as if he were about to sip it.

"I don't know how much you've gathered through the grapevine about how your father died—"

"Virtually nothing. No one would tell me anything unless I agreed to return home and hear it in person."

"Okay, well. Your father went to Atlanta to check out a potential alliance between—"

"He went to the Barrington House?" he interjected, which amused me because he so rarely interrupts anyone.

"Yes, the Barringtons—who are cozying up to the Crofts in Chicago, which makes exactly no one in any other city very happy."

"The world's a safer place without those two courts in cahoots."

I agreed wholeheartedly. "Someone found a picture of Robert and Theresa hobnobbing, and your father went to insert himself into the gossip grapevine, as far as I can tell. He wasn't there long before he died, and no one wants to talk about what went down."

"None of the Barringtons, you mean."

"Yes, that's what I mean. Your old House is trying very hard not to get up in arms about the whole thing, because, well, the Barringtons are being difficult. It's hard to say whether or not they're being difficult at a usual level, or if this is something unique to your father's situation. But Max is now in the crappy position of trying to assert himself as judge, and get them to recognize his position before the other Houses hold a convocation. Atlanta and Chicago see a chance to gang up on San Francisco, and they're going for it."

"They're trying to insert a judge?"

"Basically. Since Max can't prove he has the job free and clear, due to you being out there, aggravatingly alive. It's an assault on his pride from all angles: They won't recognize his authority, and they refuse to answer to him with regard to his father's death. Convocation aside—he's entitled to answers, and if he doesn't get them, he's entitled to seek recompense."

"He can seek it all day from the Barringtons, for whatever that'll get him."

"I know. Thus my description of this as a crappy position. I call 'em like I see 'em. For what it's worth, your son is out of the picture. He took off a couple of weeks ago, and it doesn't look like anyone's looking for him very hard. If Brendan has any sense, he'll keep his head down and let this blow over."

Ian lowered the mug. He'd been all but resting it against his chin, and now he held it cupped in his palms. "So you didn't see him? Brendan, I mean?"

I thought about lying, then didn't. "No. But Max hasn't, either. Whatever threats he's made to you regarding Brendan . . . ignore them. He's talking out of his ass. So let's just worry about you, for now, okay?"

"If you insist."

"Thank you. You're the one in the crosshairs, here. Max needs to shore up the idea that he's in charge, and the Barringtons need to know that they can't keep pulling this kind of shit. It's entirely possible that this time, the Atlanta House has bitten off more than it can chew. Barely."

"Barely," he echoed. Then he ticked off the pros and cons. "San Francisco has the population, the resources, and the moral imperative to call Atlanta's bluff. But Atlanta has a long-standing tradition of refusing to play by the rules, and it *might* have Chicago on its side. It could be disastrous for everyone."

"And down on Peachtree, the crazy goes all the way to the groundwater. They've gotten away with murder for so long—if you'll pardon the expression—that now they simply assume they're entitled to do so. They could stand to be taught a lesson, and if anyone is in a position to teach it . . . it's San Francisco."

"An open war would cost both Houses so much," he mused unhappily. "But Max has always been wily."

"That's a pretty good word to describe the guy I met, yeah. I didn't come away a fan, but I can tell you this much—he's no dummy, and he's got a good grip on the situation, except that he needs you dead. You're a loose end to be tied off. He'll kill you if he can catch you."

"Of course he will. I could come down and challenge them, disrupting everything. I could challenge *him*."

Something about the way he put it made me wary. It didn't sound like he wanted to go take over the whole show, but it sounded like he'd thought about it, and he'd concluded that if push came to shove, he could do it. "Ian . . . ," I broached.

He set the cup down on the table and waved one hand. "No, I'm not making any plans. But I'd be an idiot not to have weighed the possibilities. Max doesn't know about . . . my infirmity. He would assume that I'm considering these things."

"True, and you're right. But since we know something he *doesn't* know, let's just take that right off the list of options."

"Done. For now." He folded his hands together, elbows planted on the table. It reminded me of how he'd been sitting when we'd first met, at the wine bar downtown near the water. "Good God, what is Max going to do? He can't let it go, but he can't launch an assault, either."

"Not with you in the way. But that's where *I* come in."

"I beg your pardon?"

I cleared my throat and spit everything out fast. "I got Max to agree to loan me out as his seneschal on a fact-finding mission to the Atlanta House, on the condition that I have to find out what really happened to your father when I get there."

He didn't blink. I think maybe he *couldn't*.

I continued. "Look at it from my point of view: One of these days, Adrian is going to get himself killed poking the Barringtons with a stick, and if I can solve this mystery for Max without starting World War Three, then that's great for everybody, especially *you*."

"Why especially me?"

"Because if I can sort out the Atlanta mess, I can buy you time."

"Time for what?" he asked.

"Time to figure out how the hell we're going to get Max off your case for good."

He shook his head slowly. "You may as well give up on that. I genuinely fear that one of these days . . ." He lowered his voice, and his gaze. "One of these days, he'll find me here. He'll wreak havoc on you, on the kids. On everything you've built, Ray."

"Don't you turn this around on me. I'm the one protecting *you* here."

"But don't you see? This is the only way I can return the favor.

I can take myself away from here. Start over somewhere else, find a new ghoul. Begin a new life. I've done it before."

"So have I. It's not any fun, it isn't easy, and I don't want you to go. And I don't need your protection," I added. "I just need some time to figure out how we can . . . I don't know what, just yet. But I'm unwilling to roll over and give up."

"Admirable," he said drily, "but *I'm* unwilling to see you wander off to Atlanta . . . with Adrian? I assume he's made a bid to accompany you."

"Of course he has, the dumb motherfucker."

"You don't mean that for a moment, and we both know it. What will you do, pass him off as your ghoul?"

"That's the obvious answer, isn't it? I don't like the idea, but he won't let me go without him."

"And what do you hope to learn? What does *he* hope to learn?"

"*I* hope to learn what happened to your father. And Adrian hopes the same thing he always hopes—that someone, somewhere, knows something about his sister. If he infiltrates her old House as part of the servant class, he might learn something. The ghouls know all and see all. If she's still in Georgia, they'll know about it."

"True." Ian drummed his fingernails on the table. "But I still don't understand how you got Max to agree to the seneschal position. What did you promise him? He doesn't know you well enough to assume you're Nancy Drew with fangs."

"Right. Yes. I was getting to that." Slowly. Carefully. With not an ounce of pleasure, but a whole lot of optimism. "That's the one place where a small measure of trickery enters the picture."

"I would assume."

"The truth is, I promised him *you*." Before he could butt in again, wondering if I'd lost my mind in the last year or if I'd always been this inconsistent, I continued hastily, "I didn't tell him you were *living* with me. I made up a song and dance—a good one, I'll have you know—about having a distant but credible connection to you. He wants proof that I know where you are, and that I have the capacity to reach you."

"So that you can hand me over."

"Yes. I mean, that's the trickery. I needed something to leverage the seneschal position in Atlanta, and you're the only thing I have that he wants. I'll need you to make a phone call, put on a show, and put up with some posturing from your brother— ostensibly at my behest. You'll play dumb, like you know who I am if the subject comes up, but you had no idea that I've spoken with the San Fran boys. You'll tell him that you're calling him because I told you about the strange circumstances surrounding your father's death, and that the House is on the lookout for you. Max doesn't need to know that you'd already heard about it; the less he knows about how well you're still plugged in, the better."

"But how does this lead to him assuming you can bring me in? Or lead him to me?"

"I've been thinking about that," I told him slyly. "And all you have to do is hesitate. Hedge your bets. Tell him you want to talk to me first. Tell him you and I will arrange a meeting—that way he'll hear it from your own lips that I'm about to be in direct, physical contact with you."

"You really have given this a lot of thought."

"Oodles. All the way back from San Francisco. You have to be flexible in this business, Ian. And I excel at flexibility," I lied out my ass.

He called me on it. "Utterly untrue. But you're excellent at preparing to be flexible, I'll give you that much."

"I'll take it. Now what do you say?" I asked, disappointed that he couldn't see the puppy-dog eyes I was making in his direction. "Will you play along and call him? Let me work some magic, or let me try—before you gallop away from Seattle."

He closed his eyes and rubbed at his temples. "I don't know, Raylene. This sounds . . . messy."

"Please trust me," I begged, reaching across the table to take one of his hands. "I will take care of everything. I will fix everything. I will make everything okay."

"Even if it kills you?"

"It won't kill me. It might fuck me up a little, but I've survived worse."

We spent a conversational beat in silence, during which time I held his hand and wished I really did know some magic, for all I talked about how useless it was. I sure could've used some then and there, to convince this stubborn old vampire that I could save us all by the seat of my pants.

For that matter, I could've used a little magical help saving us all by the seat of my pants, but there's no sense in wishing too big. Every now and again, the little wishes do come true.

Eventually, he broke the awkward quiet with an awkward question. "Ray, when you've started over, how have *you* done it?"

"Oh, there's a knack to it—a few steps you always have to take. It gets trickier every decade, now that there's so much information out there, but—"

"But," he stopped me, "you've never had to fake your way out of a House obligation, have you?"

And therein lay the rub. "No, I haven't. When I left my House, they let me go because I wasn't worth chasing down. If it ever occurs to anyone to wonder, they surely know I'm still out here someplace."

"It wouldn't be so easy for me," he said quietly.

I was forced to agree. "No. Not unless you know a couple of Houses willing to sign off on your passing."

"You know I don't."

"And neither do I."

You see, there's actually a formal loophole to vampire deaths—not a formality that's always observed, but one that *can* be, in a pinch. A good sunbath will reduce our kind to ashes, given enough time, and ashes are tough to identify. Therefore, if a vampire has died—by his or her own hand, or otherwise—the sworn statement of two other vampires can function as a death certificate of sorts.

Basically, you get two vampires from two different Houses to sign a document saying, "I saw him/her go up in flames, and he/she isn't coming back." Then you present it to the House of the deceased, and that House is forced to accept it . . . even if everybody knows it's a crock. If the House wants to argue about it, that House has to essentially call the two signing vampires liars. And that is a good way to pick a fight that starts out stacked against you, two Houses to one.

I'm not sure who set up that system, but you can bet it was someone who (a) had a lot of friends, and (b) planned to fake his death someday.

But alas, it wasn't too helpful in our situation. I doubted we could find anybody in one House, much less two, who'd risk reputation and recompense on Ian's behalf. He'd been out of the game for years—an isolation deliberately intended to keep people from knowing he was blind. His secret was safe, but he had no allies to speak of . . . apart from yours truly, and I barely counted. Seattle didn't have a House, and that's one reason I liked it there so well. No protective structure, but nobody's rules to follow, either. The world is built on trade-offs like these.

I squeezed Ian's hand, then picked it up and kissed it. "We'll think of something. Will you trust me? For now? I'm begging you, because I know I can't *make* you do anything—and I wouldn't want to, besides. Give me time to pull some strings, call in some favors, and wreak some havoc back in Atlanta. If I can give your brother his father's murderer, you never know. It might be enough to satisfy him."

"It won't."

"But it won't *hurt,* either. And if Atlanta had a hand in his death, and I can prove it . . . it'll gum up their plans to take San Francisco by genteel force."

He relented with a sigh, and put his other hand on the table so I could hold that one, too.

"All right. You have a phone number for him?"

I reclaimed my hand and dug around in my bag. "Yes, I do. And I picked out a cell phone just for the occasion." It was a disposable jobbie, acquired at a gas station somewhere between Medford and Grants Pass, Oregon. Effectively untraceable, pay-as-you-go. I handed over the phone and said, "The den operates out of a club called Ill Manner. The ghouls there can pass the phone around until they find Max. If he isn't there, he'll be there soon, so just keep trying."

"Ill Manner? That's not quite—"

"It's on Wire Street."

"Oh," he said, drawing out the vowel. "Clever." Ian took the phone and lightly ran his hands over the buttons. "I'll call tonight." Then, to change the subject, "Has your coffee gone as cold as mine?"

"At least."

"Then let's bus our table and go home. I want to give this some thought before I actually get Max on the phone."

"Gotta psych yourself up for it?"

"Something like that," he said, meaning he'd take a bottle of wine and go sit up on the roof by himself for a while, and I sure as hell wasn't going to stop him.

If he wanted company, he'd ask.

For some reason, the kids were out when we returned. God

only knew what they did on their own time, and since it was pretty much all their own time when they were out of my sight, I suppose I should say instead that I have no idea what their lives were like when I wasn't present. Probably they were out getting ice cream at the IHOP, or for all I knew they hit the town to beat up hookers. As long as they weren't in my hair or in jail, I didn't worry about it.

The place seemed weirdly quiet with them gone, and with Ian upstairs on the roof, keeping to himself for this last hour before dawn. Pita was curled up underneath the television, in the cabinet next to the Wii—which apparently kept him warm, or at least mushed up in the preferred fashion of kittens everywhere.

I should've copied Ian and taken a bottle of booze and a bubble bath or something, but I wasn't sure what to do with myself. Crazy, right? I lived alone for eighty years, more often than not, and now having ten minutes of silence made me want to wander around looking for someone to talk to.

How quickly routines can be upended.

I thought about pestering Adrian, just to see if he wanted to go out and do something, but then I remembered he was probably at work—and even if he wasn't, he'd no doubt had his fill of my company for a while. Besides, he was making a stink about coming to Atlanta with me, so we'd be traveling together again soon enough.

Horace, then.

Before I dialed, I potted around in the kitchen long enough to grab a wineglass and the bottle of whatever Ian hadn't taken with him to the roof. It was white, and bubbly. Why did I buy it again? Damned if I can remember. But it was better than nothing, so I toted it over to the couch in the main living area, kicked off my shoes, sipped at the bubbles, and called Horace.

The phone rang once. Horace picked it up, and before I could say "hello" he began, "There you are, woman. I was just thinking about you. But goddamn—do you know what time it is?"

"Yes. But I'm tired of playing phone tag, and I thought I might catch you now."

"That's fine, and I'm glad. I know where Creed's going."

I reclined and sipped, obnoxiously pleased to have landed in a familiar sort of conversation. "Are you sure?"

"Of course I'm sure. She's headed back to her old stomping grounds."

"Which ones?" I asked.

"Houston. As in, 'Houston, you're about to have a problem. Her name is Creed.'"

"I see. Is this a guess on your part, or—"

"It's an *educated* guess," he insisted. "I've been tracking her west to east, and she's on a beeline for the Johnson Space Center. And as if her general trajectory isn't evidence enough, NASA is holding some big fat event there tomorrow night."

"Wait a minute. I thought she worked in Florida, at the Kennedy Space Center?"

"She *did*," he confirmed. "But she also worked out of Houston for a few months here and there. More to the point, her old boss—a guy named, or at least *called* Buck Penny—is getting some big service medal as part of a banquet event. Black tie and everything. I bet you a million dollars she's planning to crash it."

"Wait another minute. The guy's name is Buck Penny?"

"Really? That's what you're hung up on—some asshole's wacky name, not the million-dollar bet?"

I laughed into the phone. "Buck Penny? You're shitting me."

"*Ray—*"

"Okay, okay." I calmed myself, wiped my nose with the back

of my hand, because a few bubbles had shot up it when I laughed, and continued. "The majestic Buck Penny is getting honored in Houston and you think Creed is going to make a scene."

"I'm almost positive of it."

"Is he the guy who fired her?" I asked.

"What an excellent guesser you are. Yes, he's the one who signed off on her paperwork, basically throwing her out without the pension or the safety nets."

"Harsh."

"She knowingly lied, and he caught her. She forged documents, impersonated someone else, and hid her potentially dangerous mental illness from her bosses. He was well within his rights to eighty-six her."

I knew Horace was correct, but it still felt wrong. Or more likely, I was still feeling an uncomfortable measure of kinship with this fellow fucked-up bitch. "Sure, I get it," I told him. "And if I were her, I'd be pissed off at Mr. Penny, too."

"Excellent. I'll arrange to get you a pass for the banquet."

"Are you serious?"

"Yes I'm serious!" he blustered. "You always ask me that, and I'm always serious! I'll get you inside, and you'll get me my bacula with no excuses this time. I'm putting you in the same room with her, not sending you out to a town and asking you to look around. This should be a *slam dunk*, Raylene."

"You are jinxing the mission with every word out of your mouth. And anyway, I'm sort of tied up in . . . some other work right now. Did you say it's tomorrow night? I don't know if I'll be able to squeeze it in."

"Oh, shut the fuck up. This is easy money, and I want it. And I am even willing to share it with *you*!"

"How generous, considering you're asking me to do all the work of collecting it."

"You know what I mean."

"If it were that easy, you'd go and get it yourself, so let's not kid each other." I rubbed at the spot between my eyebrows, like it could make this headache go away. "I don't know, Horace. It'll be tight. I'm supposed to go to Atlanta." Assuming that Max and Ian were having a productive phone call right now, upstairs on the roof.

"Go to Houston first. Come on, it's practically on the way!"

"Your grasp of geography is appalling."

"So's my love of money, and this is more money than you can refuse, woman. This is set-you-up-for-life money, even on commission. And you've been burning through a lot of dough in the last year."

"My finances aren't any business of yours."

"Go get it, Ray. She won't be in Houston forever, and with every stunt she pulls, she burns up part of your commission. Does that light a fire under your ass?"

It didn't. Not when stupid vampire politics were threatening to kill my Ian. I simply could not muster any enthusiasm, even as I recognized how helpful the money would be. I might need money like that, if all this blew up in my face. Nothing covers tracks better than cash.

I took a deep breath, did the math, and cringed at the thought of how close this was going to be. But I said, "Fine. I'll go to Houston. I'll go intercept Creed at the black-tie event. But I need one more thing from you first."

"And that would be . . . ?"

"Get me two passes for the banquet. I'm bringing a date."

"What?"

I didn't give him the whole scoop, but I told him enough to get him off my case. "Get me two passes for the banquet, because I'm bringing the drag queen with me. It's like I told you, we have business in Atlanta. There's no sense in doubling back to Seattle once I'm halfway there."

"Fine. All right. Two passes. I can get you digital invites, but you'll have to print them out and bring them with you."

"Works for me," I said.

"You're always so fucking difficult."

"I know. Just keep thinking about those petrified peens and all the money they'll bring you. That'll keep your mind off my difficultness."

"Whatever," he concluded, and hung up.

I hung up, too, a shit-eating grin on my face. Yes, he's *that* much fun to rile up.

I chewed on my lip for a minute, and made a decision. I called Adrian's cell, and when he didn't answer I left him a voice mail that was short, sweet, and to the point.

"Hey, sexy thing, you and me are flying to Houston, and then on to Atlanta once I wrap up this thing for Horace. Be here at sunset and bring a black-tie-appropriate suit, or eat my dust."

10

Adrian was already hanging out in my living room when I got up the next night, on the very razor's edge of sunset. At his side, he had a small rolling suitcase that was packed to bursting; a zip-up garment bag was slung over one arm. He was tapping one foot impatiently as I emerged from my bedroom.

"Are we doing this, or what? When does our plane leave?" he asked, beginning the trip with demands—and that didn't bode well, but I wasn't awake enough yet to start messing with him.

I squinted at the DVD player's digital clock. "It leaves in another couple of hours. Hold your horses; we have plenty of time." We had plenty of time to make the plane, anyway. I wasn't half so confident about our arrival in Texas, but we'd have to cross that bridge when we got to it.

Ian had spent the rest of yesterday's evening upstairs, on the phone or whatever—and I still didn't know what he and Max had talked about, or even if he'd actually, successfully reached his "brother." We hadn't had a chance to regroup and share. I was just looking around for him when I realized that he was already there in the living area, only I hadn't seen him at first. The big loud Cuban dude had commanded all my attention, drat him.

My roommate and fellow vampire said, "I don't know how you always find flights so quickly."

"You can get anything on the Internet. There are a couple of websites devoted to last-minute and standby stuff. It's usually not a problem."

"We're going first class, aren't we?"

"Don't be ridiculous. Of course we are," I told Adrian. "I don't do coach, and neither does my date."

Ian's ears perked, and his face set into a carefully neutral mask. "Your what?"

"My date. Adrian and I are hitting up a black-tie gala, something over at the Johnson Space Center, before we dash off to Atlanta. Which we are totally doing as soon as possible, don't worry."

"I didn't worry until you told me not to. The space center . . . is this regarding the magician with the bacula?"

"Look at you, using the right word and everything." I went back into my bedroom to withdraw one roller case that was almost too big to count as carry-on. "And all this time, I've been trying to come up with new puns."

"A waste of energy, when the proper term is odd enough."

"Fine, you pedantic old fart, you," I teased. Then I told Adrian, "Make yourself at home. I'll take a quick shower and get dressed." I could've cornered Ian and asked for a recap, but now didn't feel like the time—or maybe I was stalling, because I was afraid maybe he'd struck some bargain behind my back.

But surely, if he'd done something like that, he'd stop me before I had a chance to go charging into Atlanta, wouldn't he? He wouldn't let me fling myself headlong into that kind of danger, not when all his protestations about leaving had been presented under the guise of keeping me out of danger.

This is what I told myself as I avoided him, while making loud declarations about my plans. If I didn't give him the opportunity to stop me from heading to Georgia, he wouldn't sneak out in the middle of the night to get himself killed in California.

A roundabout set of conclusions, I'll grant you. But sticking my head in the sand was all I could do, so I stuck to it and made a show of busily readying myself to scoot out the door. I'd already packed—even a nice red Chanel dress that now officially qualified as "vintage," though I'd bought it new ages before—so after my shower, all I really had to do was throw on the nearest, easiest clothes. And slip-on boots, because fuck airport security, that's why.

I was ready to go in fifteen minutes, during which time Adrian had called a cab and it was waiting for us downstairs. We could've driven and left the car at the airport—but if he wanted a cab, that was fine with me. Besides, parking at SeaTac is nothing short of extortion. So in retrospect, good on Adrian for thinking of it, especially since we expected to be gone for several days at the very least.

I told Ian good-bye. He gave me a quick kiss that was sweet and warm, and it made me want to stay. But I burbled something about Atlanta again—drilling that point home. "Don't you go anywhere until I get back," I added. "You promise?"

"Ray—"

"Promise me, or I will freak out."

"Don't do this."

"Promise. Say you'll stay put, and say it now or so help me God—"

"All right, all right. I promise."

Quickly, without giving him time to go into any detail, I asked, "Did you talk to Max?"

"I talked to Max, yes. Your seneschal papers ought to be in your inbox, if his bargains can be trusted."

"Thank you, and please—be patient. Just for another couple of nights. If I can't fix everything by then, we can talk some more. But first, be patient."

"I already promised, Ray."

He kissed me again, and it was a little faster—a good-bye kiss, the kind you give someone you're trying to shove out the door. But I was glad to have it anyway, because I'd take any reassurance I could get.

Adrian watched all this with an eyebrow up and a still-tapping foot, but he could fucking wait, that was my thought on the matter.

I grabbed my case and jerked it toward my "date," who rolled his eyes and clearly was thinking something about me being weird and pathetic. And I didn't have to exercise any psychic powers to figure that out.

As for me and Adrian, our trip to the airport and subsequent flight to Houston were uneventful except for some truly god-awful turbulence that had my companion seeing green and excusing himself for the tin can of a restroom as soon as the seat-belt light flicked off, the poor dear.

I tried to stay cool despite the fact that the flight was a long one, and I always find long flights troublesome. Long flights, especially long flights that begin at ten in the evening, mean a somewhat narrow window of opportunity when it comes to getting indoors before sunrise. Usually this leads to a world of nervous fretting on my part, but something about having Adrian present calmed me down. I'm not sure why. It's not as if I could fillet him and use him for a sleeping bag.

I'll admit, by the time we were cabbing our way to the hotel, I was getting antsy. The sky was pinking, just a rosy fraction, over in the east—and that's closer than I like to call it. I drew a pair of sunglasses out of my go-bag (which of course, I had brought with me as my second piece of "personal item" carry-on—bereft of its usual knives and weaponry) and pulled them on. It took the edge off the stinging my eyes began to feel as we waited in traffic, and the pinking spread like a puddle.

"Ow," Adrian said quietly—a message to me, not a declaration of any distress.

It was then that I realized I'd been squeezing his leg. Hard. I'd left half-moon impressions of my fingernails along his almost-inner thigh, so really, I think he ought to receive some award for patience and trust. He should've said something sooner, but I guess my agitation was apparent enough that he hadn't bothered.

By the time we were checked in and racing for the elevator, I was relieved to the point of feeling ill. I jammed my fingers against the buttons to close the doors, and when they finally did shut, I felt my first relief in hours.

"Told you we'd make it," he said, leaning into the mirrored corner as we rose the fifteen floors to the honeymoon suite. Hey, it was all they had on such short notice.

"You were right. Everything's fine. We'll be sealed in a room momentarily."

"Stop trying to convince yourself, and quit worrying. See?" He pointed at the round, lit numbers. "We're here. Unclench, would you?"

"I'm unclenching, I'm unclenching." And privately I thought to myself that I wouldn't be doing this in the future if it were at all possible. Air travel used to be a much more in-and-out event, something that didn't require two hours of lead time on either end. Henceforth, anything farther away than two or three hours by air would have to be broken up into multiple trips.

Adrian wheeled his suitcase out of the elevator ahead of me and looked back to say, "You're thinking about taking shorter flights next time, aren't you?"

"Shut up. You're not my fucking ghoul."

I pushed him aside and used my card to let us inside a blissfully dark and accommodatingly spacious hotel room with blessedly thick curtains and an air conditioner that could blow the red off an apple. I turned it down immediately and dropped my shit on the side of the bed farthest from the window.

"I don't even get a chance to call dibs?"

"Do you burst into flames when sunlight hits you? No? Then you get the side of the bed closer to the curtains."

"I hadn't thought about it that way."

One thing *I* hadn't thought about: sharing a bed with Adrian. It could get weird, or it could not get weird. This was a business trip after all, and it didn't need to go any further than that. Or that was what I told myself as he started peeling off his clothes and yanking the curtains shut.

I was tired, and cranky, and relieved to be indoors, which put the kibosh on any sweet-talking anyway. The sun came up all the way before long, and I settled in for the day, burritoing myself into a light-proof bundle facing the wall. I could feel the morning even though I couldn't see it.

Adrian and I had done a good job of plugging the cracks before full blaze manifested, but I was still grateful for the space between the bed and the wall—where I could roll off to the floor and hide if I had to, in case that jet-powered air conditioner moved the curtains while I was sleeping.

I used to be afraid of killing people in my sleep, but that only ever happened once. My body will sometimes take measures into its own hands (or my own hands, whatever) if I'm out cold during the day and someone pokes at me with a stick . . . or, um, anything else, which put a damper on one or two of my relationships, early in my vampire days. Eventually I learned my lesson and quit chasing pretty mortal boys. Or anybody else.

Come to think of it, this was the first time I was sharing sleeping space with a regular old day-walker in decades.

I was sure it would be fine. Adrian was smart, and he knew the general peril—though I made a point to remind him of it before I dozed off.

"Hey Adrian?"

"Hm?" he replied from his spot by the luggage, where he was unpacking some essential item or another.

"Do me a favor, huh? Remember to give me space while I'm sleeping."

He frowned thoughtfully. "How much space? Should I just take the floor?"

"I don't think that's necessary. But, I don't know. Just don't get snuggly. I don't have a lot of personal control when the sun's up. I'd hate to wake up and find you smeared against the wall or something."

"No personal control. Got it."

I grabbed one of the small, purely ornamental pillows and chucked it at his head. "Don't make it sound dirty. It's not dirty, it's *dangerous*."

"Lots of dirty things are dangerous. All the best ones, I hear."

"Shut *up*. Just . . . don't stick your finger in my nose, and I won't break it off. Does that sound fair?"

"Yes ma'am."

"Don't do that. Don't do that ghoul thing, it skeeves me out."

With a twist of his mouth he changed his voice to sound like the typical lisping Hollywood Igor. "Yes, mistress."

"I will kill you."

"Not if I run outside."

"I'll kill you *later*," I vowed.

Then I rolled over and conked out.

Later, as I dozed in the typical near-catatonia that engulfs me during the day, I slipped in and out of consciousness a tiny bit—rising near the surface, like a diver not quite ready to call it a swim and climb back up to the dock. And while I lurked, or lingered, or bobbed up to the edge of awareness, I sensed something large, warm, and familiar nearby. He was stretched out beside me, his breathing deep and regular, and some tiny part of my mind recognized him.

At some point I dreamed (or maybe I didn't) that I was curled up next to him. His body was warm and firm, even through the blanket burrito in which I'd encased myself, and the softness of his breath in my hair was almost comforting.

It might've been the blood he'd swallowed, or it might've been something less concrete and obvious. He was my friend, and he was beautiful, and he was strong enough that I surely wouldn't take off his head by accident or surprise, particularly since he knew it was a possibility and could plan against it.

(Then why was his arm wrapped around my waist? I remembered the weight of it, the way it cinched me close to his body like a roller coaster's safety bar.)

I'll be the first to confess that the whole thing was utterly strange, but when the sun set and I got up and around, Adrian wasn't there and I was alone in the king-sized bed. And inexplicably, I was disappointed.

While I was still getting myself awake and oriented to being upright, he came back to the room toting more carryout for supper. Or breakfast? I didn't know how long he'd been up.

This time, he didn't bring any for me. I feigned disappointment, but he only chucked a french fry at me and told me to go get my own, since my head wasn't broken anymore.

"You're a lousy ghoul," I accused.

"I'm a hungry date," he corrected me. "Fancy suppers never have good food, and who knows? We might not get to eat. Creed might make a scene, and then where would I be? Starving, that's where."

"Starving isn't a place," I said down into the sink, because I was listening to him justify his failure to provide for me while I was washing my face. "And *I* won't be eating anything at the supper anyway. All the more reason you should've brought me something."

"I've seen you go for weeks without . . . eating."

"I bet *you* could go for days," I speculated as I toweled my cheeks off. "But you wouldn't like it much."

"Yeah, well, I won't get arrested for picking up supper. You might."

"But that's not something that informs my spotty consumption. I'm lazy, that's all."

"And honest, which is something."

"Hey, you brought a tux, right? Let me see it."

He bobbed his head toward a clothing sleeve shaped like a tombstone, and left draped across the large seat that was under the window. "It's over there."

"Get it out. I want to look at it. Got to make sure we won't clash."

"You're anal."

"Very, yes."

"What are *you* wearing?" he asked, and I realized I'd forgotten to play show-and-tell before we left.

"It's hanging up in here." I pointed at the closet. "If I'd had more time, I would've sent it out to be dry cleaned before heading out tonight—"

"I thought you didn't like dry cleaners."

"I don't. The chemicals leave a funny taste in the back of my throat. But with vintage, sometimes it's the only proper care alternative." I dug it out and let him touch it, because that's the kind of giving spirit I am.

He *oohed* and *ahhed* over it like an appreciative girlfriend, feeling the silk gently between two fingers. "It's a shame you didn't bring one in my size."

"Back in the thirties, I'm pretty sure Chanel wasn't designing for . . . people of your height," I finished with mock care. He knows he's a dude. I'm not insulting him by being aware of it.

"More's the pity," he said, and in those three words I heard his drag voice peek through the macho ex-SEAL persona, the barest smidge. "This is from the thirties?"

"Yeah. 'Thirty-one or '32. I don't remember, exactly. It's been a long time."

"But it was new when you bought it?"

"Uh-huh. It was a present to myself. Because sometimes, I deserve presents."

"Damn," he whistled. "What an opportunity."

I went to my rolling case and started fishing around for the appropriate underthings. "What do you mean?"

"I mean, living so long, with so much money. Your closet must be loaded with vintage stuff like this. You can't find a dress like this anymore, not for love or money," he purred.

"Oh, that's not entirely true. Collectors, vintage enthusiasts—they're out there. But it'd cost you an arm and a leg, and that's a fact. Anyway," I said, balling up my delicates and strolling back into the bathroom for the illusion of privacy. I didn't shut the door all the way, so we could still talk.

"Anyway what?"

"It's not like I knew it'd be such a prize item when I first picked it up. Obviously it's a nice dress, and I spent a pretty penny on it. But you never know what'll turn out to be a valuable antique or a hot collector's item. Over more than your average life span, I've been picking up things I liked, just because I liked them. Some of it turns out to be worthless in twenty years, and some of it quadruples in value."

I could see him in the bathroom mirror, through the crack in the door. Technically this meant that if he gazed at the correct angle, he could see me, too—but he was absorbed in the clothing worship that somewhat characterized his alter ego.

"It's a good thing you have such good taste, then."

"Thanks, darling."

"There's no need to be sarcastic," he fussed.

I poked my head around the door as I wrestled myself into a girdle. Okay, so it was Spanx, but the effect is better than the old-school wonder-garments, and even the skinniest supermodel would need a little smoothing underneath the classic Chanel lines. "I'm not being sarcastic," I said as I shimmied into the stretchy, difficult underpants. "I'm happy to be on the receiving end of a professional lady's style admiration."

With a laugh, he set down the corner of fabric with which he'd been toying. "All right, I believe you. And this *is* lovely. One of these days, when we get back—"

He stopped because I bonked my head against the door. It was an accident, brought on by my overconfidence regarding one final hop into the other leg of the damn Spanx.

"You okay?"

"Sure," I said, then strolled into the sleeping area looking like a fashionably swathed mummy. "Sorry, *do* go on."

"You look ridiculous."

"Give me my dress."

Reverently he picked it up and passed it over to me, and before long I was satisfactorily sheathed for a fancy event. My hair was even doing something cute, a little flippy thing that I didn't arrange on purpose, but it looked like I had.

"How do I look?" I asked.

"Adorable, with a dash of deadly. What about your makeup?"

"Makeup? Aw, *shit*."

"No, no. I've got it," he informed me. "Sit down, and I'll tart you up."

"Not *too* tarty. This is black tie, not Neighbors. Not that there's anything wrong with Neighbors, but you know what I mean. San Francisco was costume time. This isn't."

He said, "Don't worry," and was already digging out his makeup bag. "We'll keep it minimalist. You already have great skin; all you need is a touch of polish. Some mascara, some blush. A dab of gloss, and you'll be golden."

"Great," I said, trying not to sound too dubious. It's not that I didn't trust his skills. It was just that I didn't ever wear makeup. It feels weird, all that stuff all over my face.

But he did a good job. When he was finished I looked decidedly "more put together" but not a bit "draggy," as promised, and he hadn't even gotten a speck of powder on my collar.

Ten minutes later he was fully dressed as well, and looking mighty fine, if I might say so as a completely impartial and disinterested observer of a fine male form in a well-tailored suit. I said, "You clean up real nice."

"Thank you. Now if this were only the sort of gig where I could get away with some false eyelashes . . ."

"I bet you were one hell of a prom date."

"Never had a prom," he said. "But it would've been fabulous, yes."

"Really? No prom?" I hadn't had one either, but it wasn't surprising, given when I was last in school. "That's a shame. Feel free to pretend this is the big day, if you like."

"But I didn't bring a corsage."

"Screw the flowers." I picked up my fancy-schmancy purse, a strapped jobbie that was too large to be called a clutch and a little too big to go nicely with what I was wearing. "You brought the eye makeup, which is much more useful."

"True, true. Say, are you carrying *that*?"

"Yes, and hush up about it. I don't have anything smaller and perkier or more appropriate that will hold everything I need to bring tonight. Some things just won't fit in a tiny satin clamshell, okay?"

"I know, but——"

"No buts. I need stuff. This holds stuff. And it's black velvet. It's not like I'm waltzing in with a backpack made of olive drab."

"It's your fashion funeral."

"You don't really care about that. You don't want to be seen with me, that's all."

"I don't want to be seen with that bag," he clarified. "You, I'm happy to have on an arm."

He held out an elbow, and I took it. It felt weird, considering this was the same guy who just gave me bigger, brighter eyes with his travel stash of cosmetics, but oh well.

Downstairs, the doorman hailed us a cab and before long, we were pulling up to the Johnson Space Center, which was lit up like a Kennedy. Though it was closed to tourists or other assorted space buffs, the whole compound glowed with a thousand and one electric lights, including a few spotlights and some banners and flags that were artfully illuminated on the main building's exterior. At first I thought it was overkill for an honorary ceremony, but then we emerged from the taxi into near silence, and I realized that this was just what the place looked like at night.

"Cool," I said.

"Yeah," he said also, and he paid the cabbie out of the leftovers of whatever cash he'd lifted from me earlier in the day. "You ever been here before?" he asked as the cab pulled away, leaving us there to our own devices.

"No. I've been to Cape Canaveral, but that was a long time ago. Have you?"

"No. So I have no idea where we're supposed to go to get inside this thing."

"I do," I told him. I triumphantly held up my somewhat-too-big-bag and pulled out our printed invitation confirmations, and also a small wad of other printings . . . mostly the kind that gave me a good layout of the space center and its surrounding buildings. "I didn't have time to memorize everything, so I brought everything that looked important."

"All of it?"

"There are over a hundred structures here! I had to leave some of it back home, but everything pertinent to the building where we'll be dining—and the half dozen buildings nearest to it—can be found in this-here wad of shit I printed out before leaving Seattle."

"I don't know exactly what's wrong with you, but I bet it's hard to pronounce when you're drunk."

"What's wrong with me is that I'm an old hand at this, and I'm totally smarter than you, and that's why I get paid the big bucks."

"Because you're crazy," he concluded.

"Crazy like a fox. And that's where we're headed." I indicated a big place to the right of where we'd been deposited by cab.

We began walking toward what was known only as "Building 3," or the first employee cafeteria and store. According to the invitations, it'd been freshly remodeled—top to bottom—and this banquet was one way not just of honoring the hilariously named Buck Penny, but also of showing off the new digs.

Building 110 was the one that housed all the security, where nice young men and women in uniform checked badges and invitations, but that building wasn't convenient to where we were headed, so the security guards had come to us. They lined up on either side of a red carpet that looked like it was made of bloody Astroturf and, with cute little flashlights in hand, they noted identification and scanned the bar codes on the announcements with weird tricorder-looking devices.

I experienced a momentary pang of nervousness, or really, I experienced a pang of mistrust wherein I strongly considered the wisdom of taking anything Horace told me as factual, complete, accurate, and capable of withstanding outside scrutiny.

The moment passed as soon as a mustachioed fellow in a beige jumpsuit covered in patches scanned my invitation and the machine spit out an approving *beep*. Adrian was similarly accepted, based on his equally valid (or valid enough) invitation and a fake ID I'd helped him arrange shortly after he'd shown up in Seattle. Everyone needs a good fake ID. Especially people who hang around *me*.

As we approached the "cafeteria" (a spurious place for a black-tie event if ever there was one), more people joined us and we began to feel less alone, visible, and conspicuous. Not many of the banqueteers were arriving via cab; most of them worked in the area or had friends who did, I assume, for most of the attendees were walking from a parking lot around the side of the building.

We got a few sidelong glances, and when I poked around with my none-too-impressive psychic senses, I mostly got the impression that people were trying to figure out what department we worked in. Fair enough. We didn't look familiar, and for very good reason.

I also picked up a few appreciative glances. Mostly for Adrian.

I didn't take it personally. A majority of the guys in attendance looked like the same breed you find in your average basement comic book shop, with the exception of a few astronauts. They stood out from the crowd like rock stars at . . . at . . . well, let's not say a comic book shop. For the sake of variety, let's say a science fiction convention. Even if they hadn't clearly been born of superior genetic stock, the astronauts were easy to pick out.

They were the only ones with tans.

I obviously didn't come from finely engineered astronaut stock, but Adrian looked like he might have. Even in a penguin suit, any idiot could see that he had a body like a Greek statue, and from the neck up he displayed the bone structure of an Armani model. At least one gawker (the wife of a pasty man in thick glasses) wondered if my date was perhaps the sibling of an astronaut . . . a good cover, and something I wished I'd thought of sooner.

That's always the rub. When I have nothing but time to prepare, my outings run smooth as butter on silk. But when I have to do things on the fly, I miss opportunities. It would've been easy as hell to find a few astronauts with siblings of approximately the right age—and then cross-reference that list with people who were comfortably far away, and unlikely to crash the banquet. Anyone floating around the stratosphere in a space station, for example.

Ah, well. I filed it away as something that someday might prove useful (or not) and strolled along the walkway into the reception area—just beyond which waited the banquet hall.

Security guards came and went, chattering into headsets and tiny microphones in code that any idiot could translate, but almost no idiots paid them a lick of attention. I did, naturally, but mostly I smiled coyly (no teeth showing) and pretended to flirt with my date.

"Any sign of her?" he asked me quietly.

"Not yet." I felt around with my mind—and since that was really what he was asking anyway, he didn't bug me about closing my eyes and taking a deep breath. I didn't know what I was "looking" for, exactly, but I opened myself to the possibility of menace, rage, and vengeance. Surely that was something like what she was feeling, if she intended to come to this place and tackle this guy.

Otherwise, why bother?

But no. Nothing. All I got was the swirling mass of hungry people, bored people, nervous people, proud people, curious people, and people who were freaking out a little about the prospect of public speaking. No crazy people—or more to the point, since I knew what to look for better than anyone in the world, I didn't feel anyone's focused, driven, laser-like concentration. So I knew she wasn't here yet. Because when she arrived, that's what it'd be—that's what I'd feel. It wouldn't be wild and mindless, or outrageous and nonsensical.

It'd be precision hatred in motion.

Yeah. I'd know it when I saw it. Felt it. Whatever.

Adrian and I were ushered to a set of seats at a round table with about a dozen other people, none of whom we knew and all of whom we actively sought to avoid from a conversational standpoint. We kept our heads close and acted like newlyweds, talking softly to each other and generally ignoring everyone else—as if no one could *possibly* be as fascinating as our own company.

It was rude, absolutely, but couples in a new relationship are rude beyond belief, and nobody ever throws them out of a banquet for it. Or that was *my* rationale.

The waiters came around asking what wine we wanted, and what our selection from the very narrow menu might be. Adrian put in a request for the prime rib with braised asparagus, and I echoed the request because it wasn't like I gave a damn what food they put in front of me.

I did put in for a glass of their house red, though. It sounded nice. I didn't intend to down a whole serving, given how slowly I process the stuff, but that wouldn't stop me from giving it a taste.

The room was huge, and split into two halves with an aisle in the middle. I got the distinct impression that this was not the usual layout, but it was to be expected when a special event was on deck. Whatever usual folding or otherwise cheap tables were in use, they'd all been put away for the evening and replaced with fancier versions, covered in posh white tablecloths with expensive floral centerpieces and candles that could've brought the whole joint down in under an hour.

Up front there were two long tables separated by a podium— or a "lectern" as Adrian was so gauche as to correct me when I whispered something about it into his ear.

"You have to stand *on* a podium. A lectern is what you stand *behind*."

"You're a douche-canoe."

"Where did you pick *that* one up? It's hilarious."

"Don't you undercut my insult," I joked in a soft breath, this time up against his cheek. "And I don't know. I just heard it somewhere. I like it, don't you? I think I'll bust it out more often."

"It's rich. Alliterative. Disgusting. It's very *you*."

"Thanks," I said, and would've said more but I stopped my-self short and froze, with my head hung low and close to his.

He noted the change and asked, all business, "What is it?"

At the very distant edge of what I could perceive and what I couldn't, I noticed her. Not as a spark, or a flash. Not as a swelling of emotion or maniacal havoc-wreaking, but a presence sharp and true.

"Her," I whispered. "She's here."

"Where?"

"Outside." I looked up.

"Oh for Christ's sake," Adrian swore. "Not another rooftop battle."

"At least it isn't raining. And no, she's not on the roof. She's outside, that way." I cocked my head in the general direction of the stage—but I meant behind it, on the other side of the wall and another dozen yards into the night.

"What if she didn't bring the bones?"

"You can bet she's brought *one*."

"What if she left the rest at home?"

I'd been wondering along similar lines, but now wasn't the time to start backtracking and overthinking things. "I don't plan to kill her," I murmured. "If I have to, I'll drag the location out of her."

"Using your . . ." His eyebrows wiggled, like he was trying to use his face to gesture at his own hair.

I knew what he meant. "Yeah, using those." My psychic pow-ers, that is.

It was mostly untrue. My powers aren't worth a shit, in the grand scheme of useful powers. I'd get a lot more mileage out of telekinesis, or levitation. But *no*. I get coach-class brain waves, and that's it. Better than nothing, but not much.

Not without divine intervention could I have wrested any information out of anybody's head except maybe Adrian's—and only him because he'd taken a swig out of Lake Me. Someday, we were really going to have to test the limits of that communicative ability.

But today was not that day. And I didn't want him thinking maybe I'd smack around a woman nearing sixty, bullying her like an old-fashioned pimp. I'm not saying I've never roughed up a fool in the name of information-gathering, because that'd be a bald-faced lie. But I knew before it even became hypothetically in the cards that I wouldn't do it to Creed . . . and not simply because I didn't think it'd work. Don't ask me why. Just a feeling I had. Maybe I'm psychic or something.

"Ray?"

"I have to get outside."

"I'm coming with you," he said.

I grabbed his hand. "No, I need to take care of this alone. I want to talk to her, crazy-bitch-to-crazy-bitch."

"Are you serious?"

"Yes," I vowed. "Please, I don't want to spook her, and I don't want to hurt her if I don't have to."

"You're being weird about this."

I frowned at him, hard. "Which sets this occasion apart from all others exactly . . . how?"

"You've got me there."

"Thank you. And now, I hope, I've got you *here.* You have your cell?"

"In my pocket." He tapped it with his free hand. I heard the plastic case slide around in his pants, and knock against the seat.

"Good. Put it on vibrate. I'll ping you if I need anything."

"You're just . . . leaving me here? With all these . . . people?"

Some of those people were now looking at us, as the

conversation had gotten barely loud enough to overhear in snippets. And up front, over by the *lectern,* thank you very much Adrian, the show was starting to get under way—thus the sudden lack of background noise that revealed us to be obnoxious chatterers.

A spotlight was aimed at the still-vacant position of honor, but the "important" guests—or the guests who had seats up front with the honoree—were shuffling into position at their labeled place settings. The dull roar of a room full of whisperers dropped precipitously as a tall, thin man stepped up to the microphone and gave it a tap.

A squeal of feedback cut through the remainder of the noise, and only served to underscore the similar peal of energy that was raring itself up outside. Elizabeth Creed was getting closer.

"Adrian, I'm going. If you want to leave too, hit the men's room or something. Just leave this one to me, please?"

"Men's room it is," he grumbled and rose with me. He made some excuses disguised as pleasantries to meet the curious questions in the eyes of our tablemates, then hustled off behind me.

He really was good at this high-society thing. Better than I would've expected, given his blue-collar, fighting-man background. Mostly he just kept his mouth shut, took care not to spill anything, and nodded politely when spoken to. I guess sometimes it really is that simple.

I wondered idly if he'd done any undercover work. It would explain a few things, and it would also get me fantasizing about him busting out James-Bond-like all over the place. I rather liked that thought, but I shelved it for the moment and let him accompany me from the rear, all the way to the back exit where a man in a suit and an earpiece asked if he could help us.

What he really wanted to know was, "Why are you leaving right now, when things are just getting started?"

With feigned embarrassment and in a breathy voice, I asked if he could point me toward the ladies' room. Adrian put one arm protectively at my waist and added, "She isn't feeling well."

"Oh, absolutely," said earpiece man. He indicated a corridor to our left and said, "All the way down, you'll see the signs."

"Thank you," I said, and I meant it. Earpiece man was sending us in the right direction; I could feel the signal getting stronger as I tap-tap-tapped along in my not-too-high heels down the marble-floored hallway. Adrian's footsteps were likewise noisy in my wake, which only served to remind me that he was effectively accompanying me even though I'd told him not to.

Outside the men's room and ladies' room was a pair of plush benches, perfectly primed for impatient husbands and boyfriends who were waiting on someone to touch up her lipstick one last time before deigning to rejoin his presence. I stopped, faced Adrian, took him by the shoulders, and shoved him down onto a seat.

Surprise registered in his eyes. I'd shoved him pretty hard. He needed a reminder that I'm the big strong mean one, and I'm in charge here. This was my job, my commission, and my crazy lady who needed to be addressed.

"You're going to stay here and wait for me."

Applause broke out in the big room behind us, where we should've been sitting at our round table surrounded by strangers.

"Are you sure?"

"I'm positive. This might take a few minutes, so if I were you, I'd go back inside and grab a bite to eat."

"I already had takeout, remember?"

"Yes, but this will be better. And it's *free*," I told him, and I left him sitting there when I began my dash around the corner.

I had no clue if the hallway would eventually lead to an exit of some sort, but it was pointed the right direction, so I took it. I didn't run into anyone coming or going, which was good, because I was really trucking—fast enough to make any passersby wonder *real hard* about that red streak blazing past. Even in the high heels I was making good time.

It's hard to describe the sound of someone else's mind. It's not a frequency, or a cadence, or a colored light. It's all of that and something else, too, both more distinct and less so.

But I heard Elizabeth Creed. I would've known her anywhere, with that demented, dazzling-bright consciousness. Something broken, but still beautiful. I can't explain it any better than that.

I went toward it, feeling the pull of it like a leash, but I stopped when I hit a dead end with two doors. Both were offices, and the one to my right was closer to the direction I wanted, closer to Creed, so I followed her in the straightest line I could. I pushed the appropriate office door open and found it empty, cluttered, and uninteresting except for a window against its far end. Somehow, I'd made it to the exterior edge of the building—which was great, since I didn't really want to punch a hole in a wall to let myself out.

I'm not afraid of taking the direct approach, don't get me wrong. But even for me, making a hole through drywall, studs, and framework takes more time than oh, say, opening a window.

I didn't break it open, though that would've been marginally faster. Instead I felt around its edges for any hint of a security system. Finding that it was wired into the main building's components, I took care to unlock it properly and slide it up without too much speed or urgency. Some of these newfangled systems are very sophisticated; they can tell the difference between a window cracked for the breeze and a window flung open in an escape attempt, so I played it slow and steady. This was NASA, not the Starbucks down the street. They actually had shit in the space center that they didn't want people looking at.

It didn't take me more than ten seconds to suss all this out, formulate a plan, and put it into action, but it sure as hell felt like forever. I needed to be careful this time. Creed had caught me off guard in California, but she wouldn't do it here.

Finally I got the window jacked up enough to let me out. I had to pop out a screen but it wasn't attached to the alarms, thank God, so I bent myself over double—almost folding myself in half—to get outside into the warmish, southeast Texan air.

A breeze kicked up around me and I froze.

It might've been nothing, or it might've been the start of a Creed spell coming down the pike; either way, standing there like a pink flamingo on a lawn wasn't going to help anything, so I roused myself, shook off my nervousness, and followed my ESP as far as it would take me.

It took me over an open field of grass, into which my heels sank like I was drilling for oil. I whipped them off, held them by jamming my wrist through the heels' slingback straps, and carried on—hoping I was moving fast enough that surveillance equipment wouldn't catch me, but knowing that it might regardless. With the swirly logo everywhere, stamped on everything, it was hard to forget I was at a NASA compound, and hey, this place is where they do all the wazzy tech that fires shit up into outer space. I might as well assume they had very good security.

Once I was outside, I found her signal harder to follow. I'm not sure why, but it may have had something to do with the electricity in the air—the now-all-too-familiar tang of ozone rushing up to clutter the atmosphere. And with it came humidity, swirling and lifting; I could feel the hairs on my arms rising, and I even started to sweat, which made me mad. Nobody wants to *sweat* in an eighty-year-old Chanel.

But there was nothing to be done about it now except find the woman who was fiddling with the weather before, heaven help me, it started to rain. My poor dress would never be the same if it got all streaky with watermarks.

There.

I felt her again, a blip on an overwrought radar in my brain.

I spun around, hunting for some sign of her, wondering where she'd gone off to so quickly—and why I'd lost her psychic trail so fast upon exiting the building. But there she was. She'd stopped moving. She had ensconced herself on a set of stairs leading up to a building covered with banners that looked designed to attract children. They announced things like SPACE CAMP and had pictures of stretchy-faced kids screaming with joy on the astronaut training simulators.

I didn't know what number building this was, so even if I'd had time to go fluttering through all my handy-dandy printouts, it wouldn't have done much good.

Regardless, I had her in my sights.

She stood with her feet planted firmly apart, braced on the middle stair in the middle of the way—as if she'd triangulated it that way on purpose. Beside her left foot was a canvas bag (which I prayed held the rest of the bones), and in her right hand something pale and white glowed. And so did her eyes.

Either she hadn't done that before, or I hadn't noticed it last time. Could be, this was a different spell, that's all. What the fuck did I know about magic, anyway? Virtually nothing, that's what.

But I knew that a schizophrenic woman with a whole lotta power was on the verge of bringing down a building (somehow) in which I had (stupidly) left one of my only friends in the world, sitting outside a ladies' room and twiddling his thumbs. And I also knew that last time's strategy of "confront, accuse, and attack" hadn't gone so smashingly, so this time I was going to bring her down like an antelope. It wouldn't be personal, and it'd go down with regret, but I'd do what I had to do, now that I knew what needed to be done.

I couldn't tell if she'd seen me or not. She hadn't acknowledged my presence at all, and she was preoccupied with destroying the space center, so it's probably safe to say she had a lot on her mind and might not have been giving her surroundings her full, undivided attention. I used this to my advantage, sneaking up on her with my best burst of blinding quickness.

I swept up the steps—there were about thirty of them, tiered like a fancy old library. Then, before she'd gotten a good look at me or seen what I was up to, I zoomed up behind her, swiped the bag at her feet, and slung it over my shoulder.

I retreated to the overhang at the top of the stairs, out of her immediate reach though not, I guess, out of range of a tornado or whatever. I didn't feel safe, but I felt like this was as good a defensive position as any. There in the shadows, I unzipped the bag and checked to make sure that yes, all was in order. It was full of penis bones.

I watched her.

At first, she didn't notice that anything had happened. Why should she? She hadn't seen anything, hadn't heard anything, hadn't expected any interruption. A chant was rising in her throat, moving incrementally from a gasp to a growl, to a normal speaking tone, and it could only get worse from there—or that's how I looked at it.

From my position close to the entrance doors, at the very top of the stairs, I called her name. "Elizabeth Creed."

I said it calmly, with as much authority as I could muster. I didn't have to work too hard for it; after all, if all the bones that weren't in her hand were in the bag, all I had to do was keep her from destroying Houston before the sun came up. Don't ask me why, but that didn't feel so daunting. This all sounded so much worse when I had to track her down and find her, too.

She stopped chanting, surprising us both. The glow in her hand waned ever so slightly. She turned to look for me, and then spotted me. She cleared her throat and said, "You again."

"Me again, yes. Please—" I held out a hand to forestall whatever move or proclamation she was about to make. "I only want to talk."

I could tell by the way her eyes narrowed that she didn't buy it, and she knew it for a goddamn fact when she looked down and saw that her satchel was gone. It was slung over my back, so not in her direct line of sight—but the incriminating strap across my chest no doubt told her plenty.

"You want to talk?" she asked, a rhetorical uselessness if ever there was one. "Then tell me why you keep interrupting."

Barefoot, still holding those shoes dangling from my wrist, I descended a couple of stairs—bringing myself closer, but not so close that I looked aggressive. I wasn't trying to threaten her; like an idiot, I was trying to connect with her. "I'm *not* trying to stop you. I was hired to get the bones, that's all."

She absorbed this, considered it, and said, "I can see that you've got them. Mission accomplished?"

"Except for the one you're holding, basically, yeah. It's nothing personal. It's only money."

"It's exactly the opposite of that," she told me—in reference to her own situation, I assume. "Mistakes have to be unmade. I'm unmaking them."

"No, not really. You're just destroying things and places that have made you angry. That doesn't undo them. It just makes a big mess for other people to clean up."

"You're wrong, but I don't give a damn."

"Neither do I, as far as that goes. I realize you see it differently—"

"Because I'm crazy?"

"Well, you said it so I didn't have to. But I'm not judging."

"How refreshing."

"No, you don't understand. I . . . I have *issues,* too. Not the same as yours, but bad enough that I've spent a lifetime—longer than that, really—listening to the same things you have, I bet."

"You don't know anything about me." Calmly spoken—a declaration more than an argument.

I responded in kind. "Yes, I do—but only what I've seen on paper. I only know the dry details, like why you're here—and why you want to wipe Buck Penny off the face of the earth. And let me be clear, I have no problem with that."

Still narrow, her eyes were made sharper as her brows lowered in a frown. "Then . . . what are you doing here? Why are you interrupting if you've taken what you came for and you don't care about me bringing down the house?"

"My friend is inside. Will you do me a favor and let me text him so he can get out? Then I won't interfere, I swear. I'll take these, and you can burn up that baculum, or whatever it's called, and we'll part friendly acquaintances, going our separate ways and nobody ever needs to speak of it again."

Her eyes had relaxed, but somehow that only made them look keener. The madness and magic that made up her psyche . . . it didn't billow around her so much as concentrate on her, like she was standing in the eye of a very tight storm. I couldn't tell what she was thinking, or even feeling. Her aura, if that's what it could be inadequately called, gelled around her like armor.

There on the stairs, she quivered. The night shook behind her, bringing back to mind the bells in California, and I tried not to shudder. But it was there, definitely—she was doing something bad, and something odd . . . occupying not one place, but maybe many. She was here and not here, out of time and out of space.

But right in front of me.

I couldn't penetrate her thoughts, not with my crappy psychic abilities. I strained to read her and failed, but I sensed she was deciding how crucial her plans for the rest of the bones might be—assuming she had such plans—and whether or not she wanted to fight me for them. While we exchanged this weird moment, I tried to shift gears and shoot a message to Adrian. It didn't work. I could feel my projected query die out somewhere between me and the banquet hall, like I'd blown a fuse trying to read the crazy lady.

After an awkward span of seconds, she finally said, "You aren't human."

"I used to be."

"But not anymore. What have you done?"

"I didn't *do* anything, except fall in with the wrong crowd when I was young."

"Are you immortal?"

"I can be killed, but I don't know if I'll ever die of old age."

"That was a strangely straightforward answer, albeit a useless one."

"Thanks."

"And it's only about the money?" she asked.

"I took a retrieval gig, that's all. A friend of mine—or rather the guy who gets me most of my gigs—he wants them. They're worth a fortune, did you know that?"

She snorted. "Of course I knew. And even if I hadn't, I would've figured it out when that lying weasel on the antiques tour tried to bullshit that yokel about them."

"Lying weasel. Yeah, that's Horace. So I'm asking you, would it be all right if I buzzed my friend and told him to get outside before you blow the place down, or knock it down, or whatever you're going to do?"

"It's not the lying weasel, is it?"

"Oh Christ no. Totally different guy, I swear."

She nodded. "All right. Go for it—since you could've just tackled me, bashed my brains in, and gone back inside to finish supper without a second thought. It was good of you not to."

"Thanks," I said, making no mention of my initial plans to bring her down like an antelope. I dug out my phone and started dialing, in case he'd pick up if it buzzed as a ring, not a message.

"But I have to wonder why you didn't."

"Didn't what?"

"Kill me and move along. You could have, couldn't you? This time you had the drop on me."

Adrian didn't answer right away, so I took a different approach. As I fumbled to text on that stupid little keyboard, I replied, "Did I? My attempt to intercept you at the mission didn't go so well, after all."

"I surprised you. And you're surprising me now."

"Back at ya," I told her as I hit SEND. All I'd sent was, "Outside. NOW."

"How so?" she asked.

"I've never met anyone who was schizophrenic before. I didn't know what to expect. But you don't seem too . . ."

"Nuts? You've caught me on a good night," she said with more gravitas than the sentence seemed to call for, but then again, what did I know of her brand of illness? Nothing but what I'd seen on television.

The woman midway down the stairs seemed pretty rational, except for her assertion that she could change the past by demolishing the present with magical dynamite. But I've been accused of worse.

I received a text response from Adrian. It said, "OMW" for "on my way," and I hoped he meant "on my way really fucking *fast*," because Creed's bone-holding hand was starting to glow again.

"He's coming," I related his message. "Can you give him a minute? It's a big building. I want to make sure he's clear."

"Boyfriend?"

"Oh no. He's . . . a partner-in-crime, you could say."

"Nice. It's good to have partners. And don't worry, this takes a minute to work up. I won't bring down any wrath yet. I'm just setting up."

I nodded hard and said, "Okay, thanks. Hey, do you mind if I ask . . . and I'm not trying to be rude, I just honestly want to know: What's the rationale? You're a smart lady; like I said, I've seen your paperwork. How will detonating mystic penis bones change anything about your past?"

She grumbled something under her breath. I heard it, but didn't understand it; it sounded like a swear-word in a foreign language. "If I can kill them hard enough, force them back far enough, they'll die before they meet me and make trouble for me. It's physics. I don't expect you to understand."

"What, like string theory or something?" I didn't know thing one about string theory except that it's something conspiracy nuts use to justify their wacked-out ideas.

"No, nothing like string theory," she said contemptuously, and I feared I'd maybe undone my tentative goodwill. Fortunately, she seemed to assume I was an idiot and not malicious. "It's a quantum thing, but experimental, too. When you work magic into the equation, things change. Things reach farther—farther backward and farther forward, too. It's too complicated to explain to a layperson."

I tried hard not to blurt out, "Yeah, I bet it is," and I

succeeded—barely. Instead I said, "I accept that there's plenty out there that I don't understand."

"That's downright wise of you. Where's your friend?" The object in her palm gleamed ominously, and the air around her body hummed. I could almost see it, as if a thin sheen of black water outlined her.

"Hmm," I said, and sent out a psychic feeler, in case it would work this time.

He responded by asking where I was.

Thrilled by this small success, I tried to tell him, but all I had was a vague direction and a building with some stairs and some banners, so I projected, *Just get the hell away from that building. She's going to bring the whole thing down, and maybe a lot of buildings around it.*

"He's coming," I told her. "Or he's getting out of the way, as instructed. How long will it take you to pull this off?"

"You want to watch?"

"Kind of," I admitted. "The only magic I've ever seen has been the fake kind, or the very minor kind. Disappearing pennies and the like."

"You want to sit here and watch me tear down a building with a tropical storm and its accompanying tornadoes, killing perhaps hundreds of people, just because you've never seen it before?"

"When you put it that way, it sounds callous," I agreed. "But you're the one talking about . . . really? A tropical storm and tornadoes?"

"I need at least *one* tornado, an F3 or better. A tropical storm isn't the most precise way to go about making one, but tornadoes are a natural by-product of such things, and I think I can control one easily enough when I get it here," she informed me matter-of-factly.

"You *think?* That's kind of taking a shotgun to a game of rock, scissors, paper, isn't it?"

"And?"

"And . . ." I didn't want to make her angry. "It seems like it'd be easier to just hire someone to lure him to a secret location, then magic the fuck out of him. It'd save a lot of collateral damage, too."

"I thought you didn't care about the collateral damage."

"Except for my buddy, I don't. Actually, never mind. He's clear." I knew because he picked that moment to shoot me an ESP text message equivalent, telling me so. "I'm just saying. Less trouble, that's all. Less dramatic, sure. But less effort."

She was actually thinking about this, which I didn't expect. "You might have a point, but it's too late for that now. You've taken the rest of the bones, so this is my last shot. And I don't have the money to pay someone to call him out for me."

"You couldn't save the bone for later? Lay a trap? Psych him out?"

"Not now. The bone is charged, and the storm will come when I call it. Once it's ready, and it's been given a command, it can't be uncommanded. It must fulfill its spell, or else it just loses all its power, like a battery drained of life."

"I did not know that." I was about to ask her something else, but a new sound at the edge of my hearing—my actual hearing, not my pitiful ESP—distracted me and I asked her instead, "Do you hear that?"

"Hear what?" She frowned, like she thought I was messing with her.

I held up a finger. "That . . . it's . . ."

"It's *what?*"

"Electricity," I concluded.

"A storm's coming. Of course there's electricity."

"Not *that* kind," I insisted. "The kind that comes from walkie-talkies, radios, cameras, and the like. Ms. Creed, I think they're on to you."

"Ridiculous," she said, and the glower on her face went all the way to her skull.

"No, I'm not fucking with you—they're coming. If you're going to whip up a storm, you need to do it now. And I mean *right* now, not *later* now, because they're on the way."

"Where?"

"Coming toward us. We have to get out of here."

"*No.*"

"Do you have a tornado up your sleeve, right this second?"

"No," she replied. "It'll be another minute or two. *Someone* interrupted me."

"Can you summon one on the fly?"

"I don't see why not. The storm is nearly here." She looked up at the sky.

So did I. And as was becoming common when dealing with Elizabeth Creed, there were no stars at all. The wind was picking up from the south, or I thought it must be the south. Wasn't that where the Gulf was? South, and a little to the east? The wind smelled like brine and very old things, wafting off the ocean. It also smelled like magic—a scent I was learning to separate from the ozone, gasoline, exhaust, smoke, and other odors that billow on any given current in the civilized world.

She was right. The storm *was* nearly here.

But so was security from Building 110.

Small cars and a pair of golf carts with flashing green lights came homing in on the bannered building with the stairs tiered like a birthday cake. Elizabeth had to have seen them; the spinning lights were shortly joined by bursts of a whining, whirring alarm. But she did nothing to indicate she noticed them, or cared about them. She raised her arms again and restarted the chant she'd been spinning when I'd wandered up to steal her bones.

"Elizabeth, we have to go." Her name almost stuck in my mouth. I couldn't decide whether to call her "Ms. Creed," or "Doctor," or "ma'am." Simply "Elizabeth" felt too informal for a woman who, frankly, sort of awed me. But what else was there? We were pressed for time.

Her answer came in the form of an unbroken chant, a glowing bone in her hand, and a surge to the storm that was coming on shore. She had no intention of moving, running, or otherwise leaving. Slowly, she began to rise off the stairs. Not far. Only an inch or two. But she did it effortlessly, or that's how it looked, and the shimmering darkness vibrated around her. With fleeting curiosity I wondered if my impressions hadn't been right—if she wasn't both here and not-here, on these steps but on some other steps, too, somewhere else.

I wondered if she could turn her head, or break the bone, or say the right string of words and simply vanish into the other place she straddled with her magic and madness.

But her storm wasn't fast enough to outpace the security people.

One by one, like popcorn kernels, they bounced out of their cars and carts with guns brandished—or being whipped out of holsters in preparation for brandishing. These were real guns, not neutered security-guard billy clubs or Tasers.

"Elizabeth, you said you could do this on the fly."

She nodded, but didn't insert so much as a comma into the string of words that spilled out of her mouth.

"Good. Because we have to fly."

The two guards who were fleetest of foot were getting near enough to fire off a shot or two, if they really wanted. And with Creed's hands and eyes glowing LED-style, she made a tempting target. Would they shoot an apparently unarmed woman just for standing on the stairs and glowing? Maybe. They didn't know she was holding a bone and not a weapon. I mean, it *was* a weapon, but no rational, right-thinking person would've assumed as much if he or she could see it clearly.

Over the rising weather, I heard the clicks of guns cocking and the shouts of men and women in uniforms, telling Elizabeth Creed to stand down, put her hands up, and step down quietly. None of that was going to happen.

Time stretched—an effect of the dangerous situation or per-haps the magic that filled the air, making it dense and heavy, very much like high humidity.

No one had seen me yet. I was beneath the overhang, standing in shadows. They would have had to come as close as the mania-cal sorceress to detect me, and none of them were overly eager to approach her. More commands were shouted. Precious seconds ticked past—only a few of them—while I wrestled with myself over what I knew I was about to do.

It was a terrible idea. A stupid idea beyond stupid ideas. But that'd never stopped me before, and it wouldn't this time, either.

"Fuck it," I said.

I snapped the heels off my shoes and jammed the now-flats back on my feet, then unzipped the bag of bones and tossed my purse inside it. The purse was bigger than a clutch, yes—but not heavy enough to break anything, or so I prayed. There was no time to play gently and I figured, hey—if one or two went bust, it wouldn't be the end of the world. Right? Oh God, I hoped not.

I adjusted the bag's strap, tightening it across my chest so as to hopefully keep it from bouncing around while I ran. Because baby, I was about to run.

Adrian? Where are you?

Parking lot behind the banquet building.

Lots of cars there?

Duh, Ray.

Start one for me. I don't care how, but get one moving. We're about to need a getaway car.

I'll pick something snazzy.

I didn't care if he picked a '72 Gremlin, so long as it ran. Well, that's not true. I didn't really want a Gremlin, but I'd settle for one—so long as it'd hold three people, one of whom might be joining us against her will.

I screwed my courage to the sticking place, took a ceremonial deep breath, and right as the security people were getting ready to open fire . . . I dashed down the stairs at my very top speed.

Because I am aware that getting grabbed at such a blinding run could hypothetically hurt someone (or at least mightily stun and confuse someone), I braced myself to nab Elizabeth Creed with as much support as possible. This meant that I threw my right arm behind her knees—all the better to sweep her off her feet—and my left arm behind her shoulders, so I effectively picked her up like a child in a big squeezy bear hug.

Her breath caught in her throat, and the incantation stumbled as I stumbled, too, but I crushed her against my chest and kept running. Thirty seconds earlier, I'd had time to change my mind and head in the other direction. Now people were shooting at me.

Holding her felt like holding a really high-powered sex toy cranked up to eleven. She was solid in my arms, but the darkness moved with her, and it tickled at me—sending little jolts of energy up and down my body. Panic made me contemplate my own existence. Was I in the real world? Was I somewhere else? Was I in two places at once, just like her?

This was no time for philosophy.

Bullets banged against buildings and ricocheted off the sidewalks at my feet. I took it off road, leaving the sidewalks and the brightly lit oases of NASA buildings for the quieter, darker, soft-shoed progress of the lawns. Just once I felt the sting and ping of a round snapping into the turf nearby—casting up grass, dirt, and pebbles. I wasn't worried about any near-misses, though. If they had a trained sniper watching from wherever, that was all right with me. Let him waste his ammo. I'd be well out of his range shortly after I was out of his sight.

(Look at me, assuming masculine pronouns. I'm a shitty feminist, it's true. But surely the sheer statistical majority of snipers are men? Does this let me off the hook?)

To her everlasting credit, Creed didn't actually stop chanting. Her words snagged when I hit bumps, and her cadence became forced more than the easy, steady stream of syllables she'd spewed out before. Of course, she was being carried at something close to the speed of sound, so power to her for not losing her place, or however it goes when you've clearly memorized hundreds (thousands?) of words on a very destructive, sensitive subject like "assassinating people via hurricane."

On and on she spoke, breathlessly, fiercely, practically in my ear.

On and on I ran, not fully certain of where I was headed, apart from "back toward the building this lady is trying to blow up, and then behind it."

I crossed my fingers and prayed that Adrian had found a suitable getaway vehicle, and decided to assume the best, since he hadn't offered any objection when I gave him the assignment in the first place.

Above us the sky was moving in a big black block, broken up by the shadows and outlines of clouds bigger than mountains, sailing in dark and monstrous from the Gulf. Lightning cracked among them, lacing them with light that was smothered almost instantly, as if it'd drowned in oil.

I tried not to look.

It was hard not to look, or it was hard until the rain started—and then it was hard to hold up my face because the droplets were huge, jabbing down from the hideous, plague-sick night clouds like vengeful thumbs. I blinked against them, but running as fast as I was, they only hit me harder and smacked me to the point of stinging—and to the point of wondering if one could be flayed alive by raindrops.

I clutched Elizabeth against me tightly, trying to shield her by holding her head and torso inside the hollow of my neck, and up against my breasts—taking the brunt of it if I could. In retrospect, it was *her* damn storm; I should've let her get smacked around by it for a while, but I didn't. Even though she was larger than me, taller by a couple inches and heavier by twenty or thirty pounds, she felt fragile in my arms.

At the edge of the parking lot I stopped, stunning us both—but not stunning her so badly that she ceased her susurrus whispers, even as I set her on her feet and she swayed there, then leaned on me, then stood upright without me. Upon letting her go, I shook my hands like they'd fallen asleep, for they were racked with pins and needles. Then I stood there, shivering and clutching myself while her power gathered and her bone glowed like the moon.

After a moment, the pattern of her mumblings drew to a close and she bent forward to rest her hands on top of her knees. Her head hung down. She breathed like she was fighting the air for every lungful. I could see that she'd finished something. I could tell it from the cracking shock of light that cut the sky from horizon to horizon, and the way the wind screamed in waves that came steadier and steadier, until the whole world was a wall of billowing air that couldn't be fought, cajoled, or reasoned with. I could see it in the way the undulating aura dissipated, and left her concretely before me without any of the distortion she'd carried with her thus far.

"Elizabeth?" I asked her, putting a hand on her shoulder.

Before she answered, a squeal of tires somewhere far away—no, somewhere very close—made a valiant effort against the buffeting wind and the persistent noise. I craned my neck and looked around, hunting for the source and hoping like hell it was Adrian, because if we hadn't lost those security people, they could well be coming up on us. Or the cameras. Shit, there were cameras everywhere. If they had any kind of central authority, someone in Building 110 was watching every camera in every zone. They'd spot us eventually.

This wasn't that.

My first guess was the right one: It was Adrian, screeching around a line of parked vehicles in a big-ass Hummer. "I thought they quit making those," I said to no one, and the storm ate my observation. Who cared if it was old, new, or vintage? It was exactly the kind of vehicle someone might need to move through a hurricane, and fuck me but we needed something to move us through a hurricane.

Had Elizabeth thought that far ahead? Had she ever planned to leave in one piece, or was she expecting to sit down and die in the place where she used to work? But there I went again, trying to rationally analyze an irrational situation. Besides, I had her. I could ask her later, when we were someplace dry and unassailed by meteorological mayhem.

At the edge of the chaos, I heard people's voices. I looked behind us, worried about more gunshots and thinking that I sure was glad some earth-hating redneck fascist had bought a war vehicle in which to tootle around southeast Texas.

No worries. Well, not the worries I expected. The security people were out there, yes—but they'd either lost interest in us, or they hadn't figured out we were the people they'd been chasing earlier.

They were distracted by other things at the moment, namely the crowd that was leaking out of the banquet building via every door that would allow an exit. The overdressed guests were shouting to be heard over the weather commotion, and some were saying, "Bugger all this for a lark," and heading toward the parking lot. Bowed against the wind, ducking wind-tossed debris, and in some cases holding menus over their heads for the world's most inadequate rain protection . . . they pooled around the building like a bunch of morons. Who the hell leaves the shelter of a big, secure structure when a sudden storm comes galloping onshore?

But maybe they weren't total morons. I want to think they sensed that something wasn't right, or that they needed to escape the venue rather than hide inside it. They couldn't have known it was the right thing to do, not on any conscious level, but instinct is funny sometimes.

So are cell phones, and iPhones, and the kinds of devices that might have told them they were being subjected to a very *personal* form of attack. Everyone who'd subscribed to severe weather alerts would've gotten a text message that something messed-up was under way.

And, I had to conclude, no one could've guessed how quickly it would come. I'm sure some of them assumed they could outrun it and wanted to head home to beat the rain. Even so, it all felt counterintuitive to me. Maybe that's because I don't know dick about hurricanes. Perhaps there's some protocol with which I'm unfamiliar, but I doubt it. I think it was just people being people. Being clueless, and inadvertently self-destructive.

Adrian squeezed the Hummer between two cars with cheerful abandon—the kind of cheerful abandon that creates a great rending of steel and leaves paint chips and broken light covers everywhere. It put him right in front of us, though—stuck in his headlights.

Through the windshield, I could see his face. It was contorting into something like surprise, confusion, suspicion, and outright disbelief. Fair enough. I hadn't told him I was bringing company.

No time to fight with him about it.

I dragged Elizabeth to the back passenger's-side door, wrapped my chilly hand around the rain-soaked latch, and gave a yank that almost pulled the door off, but didn't. It opened, and I bodily tossed my companion inside.

She didn't put up even the slightest token of resistance. From looking at her, I assumed this was due to the fact that she was exhausted. We both appeared half drowned and run ragged, but I hadn't been hanging around summoning the elements all evening, so between the two of us I was in better shape.

As I climbed into the passenger's seat and whipped the door shut, I heard her say, "Ah. There it is. In time, I hope." Then she put her head down on the seat, and exhaled with a smile that signified a job well done—or vengeance well achieved. Or that unicorns were bringing her diamond cough drops, I don't know.

She wasn't dead, but she was out cold.

I knew it immediately. The presence of her psyche disappeared from mine, as neatly and suddenly as if someone had flipped a switch—meaning, of course, that her aforementioned plans of controlling twisters were out the window, unless she'd somehow programmed them before passing out.

"What the hell have you done?" Adrian all but shouted at me.

"Don't yell. I'm right here. And you—get us *out of here*."

With a draw of his elbow he threw the Hummer into gear, but not without complaining. "You brought her along for the ride? Have you completely lost your mind this time?"

"I couldn't leave her," I countered. "People were shooting at her. And she seemed nice."

"Nice?" He hit the gas and the wheels spun, then caught and shot us forward. The windshield wipers were banging back and forth full tilt, doing virtually nothing to clear the view but giving it the ol' college try.

"Nice enough. I wanted to help."

"You're deranged."

It was rude of him, yes, but I didn't press it. I grabbed the seat belt instead and strapped myself down. I'd never been inside a Hummer before, so the buckles, braces, and *Oh-Shit* bars were in an unfamiliar formation. Struggling with the buckle, I got myself fastened into position just in time for Adrian to hop the curb and take us bouncing across the flooding prairies of neatly mowed grass that lay in strips among the compound's structures.

"Where are we going?" he asked me. "And what did she mean?"

"As far away from here as we can get. Inland, whichever direction *that* is. And what do you mean, what did she mean?"

"Inland? That's the best you've got?"

Conveniently enough, there was a compass built in a bubble on the dash. It said we were going south, which wasn't good. "North, then. North or west. Look." I poked the bubble, and the small globe within it swayed. "Turn around."

"*Ha.*"

Behind us, the fastest of the vehicle-owning engineers had made it to their chariots, and the parking lot was clotting with a honking knot of fender-benders. "We need a detour. And just before she conked out back there, she said *It's here, and in time,* or something like that. *What's* here?"

I craned around to see into the back. Adrian took a sharp left turn and Elizabeth Creed rolled off the seat, down onto the floorboards.

My bad. I should've strapped her in, but at the time it hadn't seemed like the most efficient use of those scrambling moments. She was probably better off down there anyway. She didn't have as much room to toss about and get herself hurt. But she wasn't really the focus of my attention now. After making note of her position, the only thing I could see was the back windshield.

Or that's not quite what I mean. I looked toward the windshield and saw nothing but a sheet of black. At first I thought it was a ludicrous tint job, the kind that douchebags sometimes get when they want to pretend like they're drug dealers. But no, it was not a tint. Just the sky, which was falling down.

"*Adrian . . .*"

"I'm going as fast as I can!"

The Hummer scuttled over the curbs and over the grass at a speed so uncomfortable that every bump felt like someone punching me in the tailbone.

"Get us away from the banquet hall. Or the cafeteria—whatever that was."

"I'm. Working. On. It." He informed me through gritted teeth.

Something huge and round smacked loudly against the front windshield, breaking off one of the wipers in a violent, smashing twist. Lightning told me it was a stop sign. The brief blip of illumination also told me that it'd cracked the windshield, but the structural integrity held.

We weren't driving anymore; we were wading through the fiercely blowing litter of the entire NASA compound, all of it being hurled via winds traveling so fast I shuddered to speculate. Rocks, leaves, a bicycle, and a single cell phone kamikazed the Hummer en masse. We bullied onward, despite the fact that we couldn't see where we were headed, and if it weren't for the bumbling bubble compass, we would've no doubt driven around in circles.

"Shit," Adrian declared. "Shit shit shit shit *shit*."

"I heard you the first time."

"This place is a goddamn maze!"

"I have maps!" I remembered.

"Fat lot of good they're doing in your bag, there."

"Give me a second, would you?"

I unzipped the sodden duffel and retrieved my bag, which was not quite soaked through. That damn duffel was "water-resistant" at best.

It dawned on me that I should pray I hadn't broken any of the bones, but right then and there it seemed like a minor hypothetical calamity compared with being trapped in a space compound while a hurricane and all its attendant twisters came barreling toward us.

"Got 'em," I announced, and I flipped through the damp sheets in a frantic hunt for the pertinent schematics. "We need a point of reference." Gaining one was easier said than done, since water cascaded over every window, and on the other side of the water was nothing but mobile darkness incoming. "Forgive me, but I think I have to roll down a window."

"No."

"Yes. Can't see anything with it up. My apologies, but here I go." I pressed my first two fingers down on the window button like I was taking its pulse. The sheet of tempered glass went skootching jerkily down until I was on the receiving end of a downright *biblical* facial.

I squinted against the water and leaned my head out as far as I could—then unbuckled my seat belt so I could climb up on the window and sit on it Dukes-of-Hazzard-style because, son of a bitch, if we didn't find our way out of this rat trap soon we were all going to fucking drown . . . or possibly be picked up and chucked into a wall by that giant tornado behind us.

It was my turn to say, "Shit. Shit shit shit shit *shit*!"

"Do you see anything to guide us?"

"Yes!" I screamed back inside the cabin. "A tornado! A big black one!"

"And that's going to guide us *how*?"

"We're going to get as far away from it as we can, as fast as we can!" I wiped a sopping curtain of hair out of my face and threw my head left and right, hunting for anything of use. But it was so hard to see, even for a monster like me, and it was so hard to look away from the tornado.

It's not like she hadn't warned me.

The woman said she was bringing a tornado, and by God, she'd brought a tornado. Say what you will about her mind or her methods, but hot damn. That's follow-through.

Off in the distance I saw a huge banner waving—the kind of vinyl sheet that's easily the size of a house, flapping from one corner and being on the very verge of ripping loose. A lightning strike landed way too close, causing Adrian to jerk the wheel and nearly fling me out of the open window . . . but it also gave me the short clarity to see that the banner advertised a new exhibit in the space museum. Something about the progression of flight suits from the sixties to the present.

Okay. Space museum.

I lunged back inside the Hummer and sat wetly on my maps, which were now absolutely dripping. That didn't stop me. They were still readable. I pulled them out from under my butt and ran a finger along the pages until I found the museum building—only to learn that it wasn't one structure, but several. Regardless, they were close enough together to give me an idea where we were. This idea, combined with the tempest-tossed compass, sufficed to show me the way.

I force-rolled the window back up—an exercise in futility tantamount to closing the barn door after the barn has burned down.

"We're about to hit a cross street," I said, pointing pointlessly up ahead, as if he could see what I was trying to indicate. "Take a right, and the road ought to go straight for a few blocks."

Adrian discovered this cross street by virtue of plowing over the YIELD sign. Its red-and-white design mocked us from the windshield until it slid slowly off the side and stuck corner-down into the street. It didn't stay there long. The wind grabbed it and threw it like a discus, surely beheading or otherwise belimbing anyone unfortunate enough to get in its way.

"Yes," I said, gesticulating wildly. "This way! Now at the next . . . it's not an intersection, I don't think. It's a roundabout. Take it far enough around so that you're going straight."

"That doesn't make any sense!"

"Yes it does! Just pretend it's not a roundabout, and you're going straight! Or shit, just do what I tell you!"

"You'd like that, wouldn't you?"

I growled, "You're the one who wants to play ghoul. Here! Yes! Go right—go around to the right, I mean."

He did, and I looked behind us only to see that the tornado had not gotten any farther away, and if anything it looked bigger, meaner, and closer. That might've been my imagination, but I didn't think so.

"Here," I said, punching him in the right arm. "Here, right here. Now veer off to the right again—see? It's like there was no circle in the middle and you just went straight."

"Roundabouts are fucking retarded."

"No doubt."

"Now where?" he asked, straining to see through the insufficiently cleared glass.

"Straight, until the road dead-ends in a T," I said, consulting my notes. I consulted them fast. They were falling apart in my hands. "Then go left, and we ought to be home free."

"Ought to be?"

"Let it never be said that I made promises I can't keep."

"Sometimes I hate you. A little."

"Back at you, gorgeous," I said, giving up on the maps. I wadded up what was left and chucked the clumps of disintegrating paper into the backseat before I remembered Creed was there. Upon checking her status and noting that it was unchanged, I decided that it didn't matter if she played host to some enormous map spitballs. This was all her fault anyway.

The Hummer heaved and jumped one more curve—a big one, and I had no idea if it'd been on the map or not—but suddenly we were on something that drove like a regular road. Beneath the tires, regular asphalt crunched, not the poured cement of driveways and compound paths; and within the sheets of water slicing down through the headlights I could see streaks of yellow.

Adrian saw them, too. He said, "Lane markers."

"Is this the interstate?"

"No, we haven't gone that far. But I'll take it."

"I don't see any other cars," I said with the first wisps of optimism I'd felt in an hour.

"Me either. It might just be a service road, or a local route. Who cares? It's empty, it's straight, and it's pointing us away from the tornado. Right? I don't see it." He sat up to look into the rearview mirror.

I turned around and said, "I see it, but it's not getting any closer. I think we're leaving it behind."

"Jesus be praised," he said under his breath.

"I wouldn't go that far. I think it stopped on top of the cafeteria. That's why it's not coming toward us anymore. It's busy tearing shit up back there."

"Just doing its job," he said, and gave the Hummer more gas than was probably safe—given that we were headed top speed down a two-lane road, in the dark, in the absolutely-not-fucking-around rain, with only one working windshield wiper. But we rolled like hell now that we weren't scaling curbs, medians, and signs at every turn.

Every tick of every yellow stripe took us farther away from the Johnson Space Center, and away from the storm.

11

Via the world's most circuitous route, we returned to the hotel about an hour before dawn. I had to carry Elizabeth up into the room, partly because she was still unconscious, and partly because Adrian refused to help me.

"Oh no. She's *your* pet project. You deal with her."

"If you're my ghoul, then she's *your*—"

"Forget it. This ghoul shit can go out the window."

"Not if you want to pass in Atlanta, it won't. We should practice. This would be good practice; here, take her arm."

"No."

So I was the one who wrangled her up the elevator and to the relative safety of our hotel room. I dropped Elizabeth on the bed just before remembering we were both still kind of wet from our adventures, so

I swooped her up again and deposited her on the love-seat-type settee up against the window. It'd probably wind up being her bed anyway. Might as well let her get comfortable, or get out of my way as the case may be.

Then I set to peeling off my own wet garb and simultaneously digging round in my rolly case for something clean and dry.

Adrian did likewise over on his side of the room, trying to pretend that he wasn't so mad that he could barely stand to look at me. He's not a very good pretender. He blew it when he asked, "Tell me again what the fuck we're going to do with this woman?"

"For starters, we're going to let her rest."

"And then what? Am I in charge of her while you're asleep? Is that the cunning plan?"

"It'd be nice if you keep her off me while I'm napping. I don't want to make a mega-mess for housekeeping in our wake—certainly not the kind of thing that might prompt them to contact the authorities. So yeah, do me a favor and mind her while I'm out."

"I swear to God, I can't imagine what you were thinking . . ."

I threw my hands up. "I was thinking, *Shit, this lady is really powerful and kind of fucked-up, but maybe she needs a little help and not a violent take-down.*"

"I don't believe you for a second. I think you've got some weird mommy-complex going on."

"You take that back!"

"I won't," he declared, breaking eye contact long enough to pull his tuxedo shirt off and throw it at the curtains for no apparent reason. "It's obvious—you've met this woman who's old enough to be your . . . well, she *looks* old enough to be your mother, and she's as crazy as you are. Maybe even crazier! And you think, *Hey, I have to help her because we're, we're, I don't know. From the same planet or something.*"

He's an asshole when he's being smart, but he's hard to argue with. "Okay, I don't see it like that," I partially lied, because I could totally see the sense in what he was saying. "But even if every word were true, who cares? I grabbed her, I brought her here, and more important, I scored the bones."

"You scored *her* and the bones. One of these things you can sell. One of these things you might be stuck with for a while!"

"So goddamn shortsighted," I accused as I turned away from him, unfastened my bra, and peeled it off my chest. It made a slurping sound as it unstuck from my boobs. While I still had my back to him, I yanked a T-shirt on over my head. "We can sell the bones, yes. I'll call Horace and let him know I have them, first thing tomorrow night. But Ms. Creed over there . . . she can stay with us, or head off on her own. She might be a little unbalanced, but she's an adult. All I did was rescue her from the NASA security goons. I didn't *adopt* her. I'm not going to get her spayed and find her a good home."

"You ever tell yourself that about Pepper and Domino?"

"All the time, but that's different. These days, I kind of *need* them. Or Ian does."

"*These days,* yeah. Whatever lets you sleep at night."

"I sleep like a stoner, and it's no business of yours whom I rescue, adopt, or kick to the curb. You're not even really my ghoul, anyway. If you were, you might be in some place to criticize—but of course, if you were really my ghoul, you wouldn't dare. You'd have too much sense for that."

"Maybe we should put this whole 'ghoul' thing to bed right now—it's not going to work."

"I couldn't agree with you more," I said. I held the absolutely trashed Chanel in my hands and tried not to cry. It was a stupid thing to cry over, but I'd bought it new, when I was young. And I wondered if I could save it, because I'm a sentimental loony. "So *obviously,*" I said, feeling spiteful at the world and aiming it at him, "you can't come with me to Atlanta."

"Say what now?"

"You heard me. If you can't pass as my ghoul, you won't survive the Barrington Household. So forget it. You're headed back to Seattle tomorrow."

"Like hell I am." He did a 180. "I'll fake it so good, you'll give me an Oscar when we get home."

"You haven't done much to demonstrate it yet. Don't you understand? Ghouls are deferential, they're quiet, and they're useful. You aren't any of those things. Ever."

"I learned on the fly in San Francisco."

"That was for the span of half an hour. And you weren't *great,* even for that long. Look, I know you think I'm laying this on thick because I want a lackey, but that's not the case. I've never had a lackey before, I don't like lackeys, and I particularly don't like *ghouls,* if you'll recall. Ergo, the fact that you're the world's worst ghoul is a huge point in your favor from a personal standpoint, but it'll get you killed in the kind of scenario I'm looking at in Georgia."

"Obviously, I'll fake it *better* in Georgia. I'm much better at kissing ass when my life is on the line."

"Not good enough," I countered. "I can handle the trip myself, and if you can't convince me otherwise by next nightfall, you're going home."

He looked like he wanted to call me names—creative names, names that I'd write down and use again for how awful and brilliant they were—but he swallowed them down and only glared. Then he said, "You're im-fucking-*possible.*"

"I am also exhausted and to paraphrase the bard—here comes the sun." I drew the curtains shut and fastened them with the binder clips I'd picked up on a whim a few days previously. They're perfect for the job—cheap, portable, and efficient. "So if you don't mind, I'm going to burrito myself up in the comforter and call it a day. If you want to prove to me what an awesome ghoul you're capable of being, perhaps you'll consider helping Ms. Creed get her shit together while I'm not looking."

I kicked my mutilated shoes under the bed, grabbed the comforter, and swathed myself therein—pulling the covers up over my head until I couldn't see a thing, including the thing I least wanted to see. (Read: The expression on Adrian's face, which no doubt could've killed dandelions.)

Much to my surprise, he didn't say anything.

I kept waiting for it, lying there wondering when the retort would come. But it didn't. And before long I fell asleep.

I awakened however-many-number-of-hours later to the soft sound of voices, and I was somewhat confused. Was it the television? Not unless Adrian was on TV, which felt unlikely. Then who the hell was he talking to?

Oh yeah.

Her.

I extricated myself from the blankets with about as much grace and speed as you'd expect, then rubbed at my eyes to clear them—revealing Adrian and Elizabeth sitting on either side of a small table they'd pulled away from the wall to sit between them. Upon this table was a game of what appeared to be gin rummy.

The rustling of my unfurling drew their attention. Elizabeth folded her cards down onto her lap and said, "Good evening," like this was the most normal thing in the whole world, sitting in a room with an off-duty drag queen and a vampire, playing cards.

"Back at you," I mumbled. "Who's winning?"

Adrian responded, "This round, she is. I won the last one. We've just been killing time."

"Waiting for me to wake up? How thoughtful."

"Waiting for Elizabeth's flight. She's heading out in another two hours. Had to get her a red-eye; it was all I could arrange on short notice."

"On the Internet?" I assumed.

"With your credit card," he nodded. "Also, we went shopping."

"I'm sure you exercised restraint." I was sure he hadn't, just to get back at me.

"Absolutely," he lied. "She needed some clothes. I needed some retail therapy."

"Perfectly understandable. I hope everyone had a marvelous time on my dime." I stood up and stretched, and cracked my back. Everything ached, but no worse than the night before—which was a step in the right direction as far as I was concerned. *No worse* was becoming equivalent to "good times."

I eyed my roommates with suspicion. They were getting along, successfully playing leisure games. They'd gone shopping. Elizabeth had showered and brushed her silvering hair, and was wearing something tasteful but simple—a white classic button-up and khaki slacks with brown Eastlands. Adrian was wearing new jeans (dark wash, boot cut) and an oatmeal-colored Henley. They looked civilized and innocent, so clearly I must have been missing something.

At the end of my visual appraisal, it occurred to me to ask, "Wait. Plane ticket to where?" Even as I suspected the answer.

"Seattle, of course." Adrian said it lightly, casually. Almost coldly, but you had to know what to listen for.

Elizabeth said, "He told me about your home, the building in Seattle where the homeless children live, and your blind friend."

"Ah." I almost started yelling at Adrian that he shouldn't tell people about Ian like that, but what was it going to hurt? "What else did he tell you? Anything interesting?"

"He said you're a vampire, but I'm okay with that. And I want to thank you for your generous offer to keep me there for a while. I'm not sure what I did to deserve it, but I could use a place to lie low. I'm not saying that the cops were right on my tail or anything, but a simple scry told me that people were beginning to question the coincidence."

I said, "Right. Yes. Well. You're welcome, of course. Adrian lives in Seattle, too, you know. I'm glad you two get along. I expect you'll be seeing a lot of him."

She laughed. "That's funny. A lot of him, yes."

"What?"

"I told her about Neighbors, and the drag show. You'll have to bring her, one of these nights."

"One of these nights, sure. I don't suppose you told her the address, or anything? So she knows where to go when she gets into town?"

"I've arranged for a car service to pick her up under the name of Meredith Hand. And I've already called Ian and given him the heads-up."

"How . . . *efficient* of you."

I'd be lying if I said I was utterly shocked that Adrian had made these arrangements. I wasn't shocked; I was only somewhat surprised. He'd certainly done a thorough job of it, to give him due credit. And, I mean, come on. It's not like his vindictiveness came as a huge, heart-stopping betrayal or anything.

Besides, the longer I stood there like a dummy, the more I was actually okay with it. Was it a bad idea? Yes. A terrible one. But wasn't it what I wanted, in a warped way? Kind of. My feelings on the matter were too complicated to focus into an Official Position.

I went out on a limb and asked a silly question. "Just *one* plane ticket to Seattle?"

"Yeah, just the one. I figured maybe I'd tag along with you to Atlanta. Our flight leaves an hour after hers."

If I was going to pick a fight with him, this was the moment.

But I let it pass. I sighed, sat down on Adrian's side of the bed (it had a better view of the television), and picked up the remote. "Two hours to departure, huh?"

Elizabeth answered. "That's right. We thought we'd leave as soon as you got up. I don't think I have anything that'll get me stopped by security, and I have my own ID under . . . not the name you know. I like to leave myself plenty of wiggle room."

"That's fine," I said. Then I broached the money thing, because it'd better come up sooner rather than later. "Now about those bones—"

She said, "Clearly they're yours now. You stole them from me fair and square, and it's not as if I don't owe you for the hospitality."

"About that . . ." I tapped my fingers on the duffel bag I held beside my lap and did some very hasty thinking. I unzipped the bag and asked, before I could start counting, "How many bones are left?"

She answered fast. "Thirteen."

"An auspicious number," I mused, noting that she wasn't lying. They were all there, bundled together. "But I suspect Horace can be convinced you've burned through a few of them. I don't have to give him the whole batch."

"Horace?"

"The lying weasel, as previously discussed."

"When?"

"Last night," I said, slightly perturbed by her failure to recall—but I didn't call attention to it. It might not've been a mental illness thing. It might've just been a side effect of a crazy night and a whole lot of magic floating around. "He's the guy who tried to buy the bones on the antique parade thing, but don't worry about him. I'll take care of him."

"You're selling him the bones?"

"Let's say instead that I'm passing them along for a very healthy commission."

She pondered this, and said, "Millions. That's what you could get for thirteen bones."

To which I replied, "Yes, and he can still get millions for fewer than that. Say, eight or nine of them. We'll just tell Horace that you blew a handful of them practicing your spells."

Adrian shot me a confused look, then his face lightened. He knew me so well, it surely had nothing to do with the blood link. "You want to save a few?"

"To sell them on the side?" Elizabeth asked quizzically, since she didn't know me as well as my faux-ghoul did.

He told her, "No, no. She wants to save them as insurance."

"Against what?"

"Against future trouble."

"But I don't intend to make any trouble for you," she objected. "I got Buck Penny, and I undid my marriage."

"I'm sorry . . . you did what?"

"Penny's dead, I'm sure. And the marriage never happened."

Adrian frowned, but didn't contradict her. Our gazes met and we fired a whole silent conversation back and forth between us, transmitted via eyebrow wiggles, mostly amounting to, "She's nuts, right?" "Yeah, I think so." "Can you undo the past?" "I have no idea." "Let her think what she wants." "Okay."

Moving right along without arguing, I clarified. "We're on our own up there in Seattle; we don't have a House to protect us." She was about to ask me what a House had to do with anything, but I headed her off at the pass. "Not a house like what you live in; vampire Houses are organizational structures, and they can be useful. They can be much worse than useful if you don't belong to one. That's the short version of what I'm getting at."

"I think I see," she said slowly. "You want . . . to keep these bones . . . so that I can use them? To protect you and your friends?"

"Well, if you're going to be hanging around, you might as well make yourself useful. Are you willing to use them for vengeance-free purposes? For that matter, are you *capable* of doing so? Or is some dramatic motive required to make them work?"

"I'm capable, don't worry about that. But doesn't it require a certain measure of trust on your part? What if . . . I hate to say it, but what if I have . . . you know. An episode? Tonight I feel good. I've had my medication for the first time in a few weeks so I feel fuzzy, but mostly secure."

"We stopped to refill it," Adrian chimed in.

I considered this a very worthy use of funds, but to say so might've come off wrong, so I only nodded. "I know how it goes," I said, because I did. "We'll work something out. Let me think about it, and we'll discuss it when I get home. For now, I'll keep the bones with me."

"I understand." It was funny. When her eyes weren't glowing and she wasn't chanting, she seemed almost normal. Not quite, but almost. She still had a tense, feral posture that said she antici- pated trouble—maybe from within—at all times. And every now and again, her eyes would twitch or her head would cock, like she was looking for something or listening for something that wasn't there. But all things being equal, she didn't come off any nuttier than somebody's favorite aunt with a bunch of cats.

I thought of Pita and realized I was heading down that road myself. I might only have one cat, but I sure was amassing a col- lection of other strays.

"So that's settled," I announced. "You'll head back to my

place, and Ian and Domino will help you get settled in to some corner of the flat or another. They'll bring you up to speed on the ground rules, not that there are very many of those. Meanwhile, me and Adrian will head for Atlanta, where everything will go smoothly and no one will get hurt, and everyone will have a productive time learning a great many useful things."

Elizabeth scooped her cards up into her palm and set them on the table with the rest of the pile. She gave me a funny look. "Right. I know sarcasm when I hear it, but I hope things go half that well, at least."

"It's not sarcasm so much as desperate optimism. And mostly for the second half of what I just said. Actually, I'm pretty sure you'll be fine in Seattle, assuming your trip is uneventful and the car is there waiting. And I'm still holding on to the bones."

She said, "I can make plenty of trouble without them, you know." And it didn't sound like she was bragging.

I hesitated. "Is that a threat?"

"It's full disclosure."

"Okay. Good to know."

Adrian was beaming at me with triumph, smugness, and something else—a faint mirroring of my hopeful desperation, I think. He knew just how hard we were bullshitting here, after all.

But the first half of my cheery prediction went down without any aggravation. In another hour, we'd bundled up Elizabeth with her duffel bag stuffed with toiletries and what few personal items she'd had on her when I'd nabbed her. Then drove her to the airport in Adrian's rental.

Again, in his quest to prove he could be a useful ghoul-type assistant, Adrian had snuck out and dumped the Hummer a couple miles away—in the kind of neighborhood where it'd be stripped down to the frame within hours, or that was the plan. I didn't have any serious fears that it'd be tracked back to us; we were on the guest list under pseudonyms, and according to the local news, the Johnson Space Center was flattened and crawling with chaos.

At least twenty people had died in Hurricane Elizabeth, as I'd come to think of it. Another hundred had been hurt, dozens of cars had been destroyed, several buildings had been ground down to sea level, and many others had been so badly damaged that they would be covered in scaffolding for months to come.

Something told me no one would be making too many hard-hitting inquiries into one missing vehicle. For all anyone knew, it might've been blown to the top of the museum roof. It sounds batty, but that's where they found Buck Penny's Mercedes.

Speaking of the target himself, I didn't know if Elizabeth had actually gotten him or not. The newspeople weren't naming the dead until all families could be notified, and the Internet didn't seem to know . . . so either the situation was messier than it sounded (making it truly epic), or someone was being very careful to keep the particulars quiet.

I couldn't help but wonder if Elizabeth hadn't inadvertently damaged some national-secret-type thing that the feebs were looking to cap. If she *had* done so, it almost certainly hadn't been deliberate, but that wouldn't change anything.

As I'd learned the hard way over the last year, there's no reason to underestimate (a) money, or (b) the government's capacity for persistence and secrecy.

So whatever mayhem had occurred over on the other side of Houston, it wasn't my problem and I couldn't see myself getting too worked up about it. Privately, I thought it was an egregious case of overkill and lunacy, but somehow that didn't bother me.

Although when I thought about it too hard—and I eventually think about everything too hard—I wondered if it was a good idea to send this unstable woman into a household of people who frankly weren't in the world's best position to defend themselves if things were to go wacky. If Elizabeth had another "episode," would they be able to manage her? Or in lieu of that, defend themselves?

Dear God, what if she decided she wanted to "undo" them, or whatever? Maybe she undid her marriage, and maybe she's got quantum magic scrambling her brain, I don't know—but I was shipping her home to camp out with the kids.

But shit, life is full of risks. As it turns out, so is the afterlife.

Anyway, the kids already lived with two vampires, including one with a nasty case of post-traumatic stress disorder and an inability to see where he was throwing things. It's not like they were living in Nerf City. One more homicidal maniac shouldn't make much difference, or that's what I told myself as I waved at Elizabeth from the send-off spot outside the security checkpoint.

Soon she was gone, slipped through the scanner without a hitch, and headed toward the terminal where she'd catch her flight back to my place. My stomach felt sour, and the farther away from us she got, the less confident I became.

I smiled at Adrian anyway.

"What are you grinning about?" he asked, sensing that I was full of shit.

"One thing down, one to go. We got the bones. Now we just have to get in and out of Atlanta alive, because tomorrow's our last night to do so. The convocation goes down the night after that."

We already had our tickets, though our flight left an hour later—so we had time to kill before it was worth submitting ourselves to the TSA tickle.

"I knew you'd cave," he said to me.

"Cave on what?"

"Your vow that I wouldn't come with you to Georgia."

"Don't get too self-righteous. I knew if I dangled that carrot over your head, you'd take care of my incidentals and do a decent job of it. Really, I just wanted you to get Elizabeth squared away and ditch the getaway car."

"I bet. You just magically planted those ideas in my brain."

"I didn't say that," I argued. "Those things needed to be done, and I couldn't do them while I was out cold for the day. But you would've half-assed them or ignored them without some positive reinforcement."

I expected it to piss him off, but he only shrugged. "Doesn't matter. It wasn't that big a deal, and now you have to bring me along. Totally worth it."

"I don't *have* to do anything."

"Yeah you do. *Now* you do, anyway."

"Whatever. What I'm saying is, don't get too full of yourself. I could jettison you tomorrow and get a lot more work done."

"Not during the daytime."

"Fuck you."

"Yes ma'am," he said happily.

We spent the rest of our downtime plotting in a wine bar I found, sorting out our story—nailing down our cover until he could recite everything blindfolded, backward underwater, and drunk. It was the equivalent of drilling a name, rank, and serial number into his brain, so it worked admirably.

The tutoring (which continued all throughout our subsequent flight) might have been helped by our psychic link, which we played with a little bit—testing its abilities and limitations. We didn't learn anything we didn't already know, but I considered it a useful exercise all the same. In Atlanta, we'd need to feign the ability to communicate cleanly without speaking to one another; and in truth, we'd only sort of figured out the particulars of how it actually worked.

It was rather like that old adage about a watched pot never

boiling. The harder we tried, the less it worked. But on a lark, as a sudden "shout" or a thoughtless jab, it came through loud and clear.

I strongly considered pestering him to see if I could get him interested in drinking more of my blood. Likewise, he was strongly considering asking me if I'd provide some. In the end, neither of us brought it up, having independently decided that it was more trouble than we wanted.

All in all, he did quite well.

I taught him everything I could remember about House rules and regulations, about the behavior expected of ghouls, and about how we'd be expected to treat each other. I also told him everything I knew about the Barringtons, which didn't take long, because I didn't know volumes upon volumes when it came to the House. Mostly I'd heard stories about that weird, violent, insular crew, and secondhand information is better than no information at all—but not much. Even so, I threw in every scrap of gossip I'd ever heard, on the off chance any of it proved to be true or useful. He absorbed it like an expensive paper towel.

By the time we'd landed at Hartsfield in Georgia, he was even in the habit of cringing when I glared at him the right way.

It unnerved me, though not in a pile-on-some-fear way. He was doing a good job—exactly what I asked of him—but it was turning him into someone else . . . someone I didn't like much. Someone I didn't have any respect for.

This made him a good actor, and it shouldn't have surprised me. But it did. And hearing him call me "mistress" gave me a warm, unwelcome indigestion feeling in my throat. I pretended that all of this was fine and we were unlikely to get killed within the next forty-eight hours.

We made our hotel without much time to spare, settling into a suite that Adrian had reserved for us the night before in the big

Marriott Marquis, which looks sort of like the inside of a UFO as designed in the eighties.

(It is true that I used to have a secondary safe house in Atlanta, but I lost it when I lost my last identity. That's one of the drawbacks of doing a nuclear reset on your personhood—some of your possessions get claimed by the state, since you seem to have died and not left a will.)

Before I was really ready to settle in, dawn was creeping up outside, flushing the far side of the curtains. I could feel it approaching, like the footsteps of someone unpleasant coming up the stairs.

That day, my dreams were strange and unsettling.

I didn't remember them well when I awoke; they just stuck with me in the form of a groggy sense of nausea, and the irrational certainty that I was forgetting something important. But when sundown came a dozen hours later, it was time to get moving, dream-sickness or no.

I got up, got myself dressed, and braced myself for the night to come.

Adrian was ready to go by the time I was ready to open the curtains, but as I've mentioned before, that's easy when you don't have to sleep all day. I don't know if I was supposed to be proud of him or what, but it's not like it's tough to outfox me when I'm out cold.

Still, I didn't like this tension between us. A few days before we'd been chatty and friendly as the evening got under way. Now we weren't talking. We weren't even making a lot of eye contact. Neither one of us was happy, and both of us were nervous. But if we could survive this together, everything could get back to normal.

Right?

Just this one last hurdle.

Well, one last hurdle and then the obvious, looming hurdle of what to do about Ian and the San Francisco gang, but I couldn't think about that yet. One horrible thing at a time, thanks.

My partner-in-crime fussed for "breakfast," but I urged him to stay close to the hotel. We'd picked up a rental at the airport—a 2009 Lexus; don't ask me why Adrian had to go all high-end on us all of a sudden—but it'd been parked downstairs in the garage, and the hassle of moving it didn't feel appealing. Five minutes on the Internet told him there was a twenty-four-hour diner three blocks away, so he hoofed it and I stayed put, wrapping up the last of those last-minute details like the obsessive nutter I am.

I had email from Ian. If the note could be believed, he was still in Seattle. I didn't think he'd lie, but the deeper I went down this rabbit hole, the more I learned about how little I knew—so there was always the possibility that he was humoring me, and he'd stuck out his thumb and headed down to California.

I refused to assume the worst.

Or rather, I quietly assumed the worst, but ignored it—focusing instead on convincing myself that everything was running According To Plan. God was in his heaven, my Ian was in Washington, and all was right with the world. All I had to do to keep it that way was stroll into the lion's den, solve a murder, and stroll back out again without getting me or my not-a-ghoul killed.

Easy-peasy.

Rather than dial up Ian and run the risk of him not answering (because he was dead in a ditch someplace, or he was avoiding me, or his brother was busy burning him down to ashes), I made a phone call to Maximilian in San Francisco. Max confirmed that he'd emailed the documents to give me seneschal proxy, and they'd been accepted and acknowledged by the Barringtons. This meant they were expecting me—a prospect that should have been a relief, but wasn't.

This was my first and last night on the case. If I couldn't provide results, Ian would be screwed. Even if I *could* provide results, he might still be screwed—but if I could make Atlanta look bad enough, the Barringtons would back off long enough to give Max some breathing room . . . and me time to think of a more permanent way to get Max off Ian's case.

At my request, Max forwarded me a copy of his email with the document attached, and after we hung up, I logged on to take a peek at it. How incongruous it felt, with its semi-archaic language and formality. Once upon a time, hundreds of years ago, such things would've been handwritten on parchment, sealed with wax and the ring of somebody important, and delivered in person.

My, how things have changed.

> I, Maximilian Arnold Renner, do hereby present Raylene Pendle (who may present herself as Emily Benton)—and she shall temporarily serve as seneschal on behalf of the Renner Household in San Francisco, California. This proxy appointment is valid in the entirety of Georgia, with particular interest to the Barrington Household in Atlanta, where she should be received with hospitality and treated as a representative of the San Francisco House in all regards.

Jesus. And that was just the beginning. I was amused to note both that his middle name was "Arnold" and that he'd looked me up by my new fake identity, Emily Benton. I hadn't told him what it was, so he was obviously showing off. No big whoop. Having a public face that's relatively easy to find is part of what a disposable identity is all about.

I wasn't worried that he'd track down my homestead and thereby his wayward brother, though. I didn't own the building as Emily Benton. I owned it as the estate of someone named David Peterson, who had died ten years previously. In theory, David has a son named Gerald who operates the estate's affairs. It's a little complicated and utterly untraceable back to me—which is exactly how I like it.

While I was hanging around wrapping up loose ends, I also called Horace.

He answered on the first ring. "Tell me you got them *this time*."

"They're sitting right here beside me," I fibbed.

"Excellent! How many did that deranged bitch burn up?"

"I don't know. You never said how many she started with. But there are nine unmolested, so to speak."

"Nine?" he shouted in my ear.

Innocently I asked, "What? Were you expecting more than that?"

"There should've been at least fifteen or sixteen. How . . . how the hell? What the fuck was she doing to burn through so many of them?"

"I have no idea. Practicing?"

"Practicing?" He shut up, but only for a conversational beat. "Hypothetically possible, but I doubt it. You don't just *fiddle* with those things. They require an expert hand, and people who aren't experts tend to blow themselves up in the learning process."

"That sounds counterproductive. From a Darwinian standpoint, I mean. How do you get to be an expert if studying to become an expert is fatal?"

"It's not *always* fatal. But it's a messy enough learning process that not everyone survives it, that's all I'm saying. Maybe she was up to some mayhem off the grid," he pondered.

I let him go right on pondering. "It's not like we were watching her every move. Chasing her down with credit card receipts is like playing connect-the-dots. There's a lot of blank space in between."

"True, true. But fuck me, only nine of them left?"

"Sorry."

"Hm. Well, it's still a lot of money."

"And there's no sense crying over spilled . . . what? Millions?"

"It depends on which ones she used. Can you look through them and tell me?"

"Seriously? You just now asked me to identify penis bones for you?"

He sighed heavily. "Raylene, they were *marked*, remember? Little dick-tags? You can read, I'm pretty sure."

"Oh, yeah. I forgot about that. Hang on."

I went to the edge of the bed and dug out the bones. I unrolled them from their bubble strip as if they were makeup tools in a pouch, and I squinted at the tiny handwritten labels that had been Scotch-taped to the ends.

"Holy shit, whoever wrote these things had terrible handwriting. Um, I see two lycanthropes, a djinn—seriously? A genie weenie?—a centaur, a . . ." I sounded out the word, "cockatrice? I don't even know what that is."

"Chicken–lizard hybrid."

I almost accused him of shitting me, but restrained myself. "Right. One chicken–lizard hybrid, plus, let me see," I muttered. "One gnome, or I *think* that's what it says. One . . . I can't tell what this one says." I turned it over in my hand, attempting to guess the size of whatever creature once sported it in a dangling fashion.

"Spell it."

"S . . . e . . . s . . . q . . . u . . . a . . . c."

He thought about it momentarily, then said, "Bigfoot."

"Bullshit."

"No bullshit, Bigfoot. That's the old Indian word for them."

"I guess it kind of looks like *Sasquatch*."

"No coincidence, there," he told me. "Now. Go on. What else?"

"Bunyip?" I confessed, "I don't know what *that* is, either."

"Australian beastie. It's a lake monster that looks like a walrus crossed with a horse."

"Now you're just making things up."

"No, I'm not. And what's the last one?"

"Last one?" For a minute, I almost contradicted him like a dumbass, having forgotten I was holding a few of these things in reserve. I chose one at random. "Incubus."

"Incubus?" His voice pitched higher. "Oh good, that's a good one. Those boners get lots of use, so they store up massive amounts of magic."

"That's so Freudian, I barely know where to begin."

"Then don't bother. I'm writing these down, you know," he informed me.

I had a split second of panic, trying to remember what I'd said. Quickly I retrieved the rattling bones and stuck the promised items aside, leaving whatever remained in the duffel bag for Elizabeth's future use. I hoped I'd left her some good ones, but I had no way of knowing—and I briefly considered kicking myself for not asking her about them before I'd sent her on her way.

Nothing to be done about it now.

Horace was quiet, but not for long. "I wonder which ones she used."

I told him the truth. "I have no idea."

"You are *useless* to me," he sulked.

"I love you too, dickhead."

"Fuck off, darling. At least you got most of them." Another diva sigh. "It'll still be enough, one way or another."

"Enough to what? Buy your own private island?"

"Don't think it hasn't occurred to me. But no, it ought to be enough to add a row of zeros to my bank account; that's the goal here. Keep your eye on the prize, Ray."

I shuddered to consider the sheer stores of wealth the greedy bastard must be hoarding like a dragon in a cave. "I'm glad I could be of service," I told him. "How do you want to get these, anyway? I can't remember what we decided."

"If you drop those things into the mail, I will come to your house and kill you myself. Same goes for UPS or FedEx, I swear to God. You sit on them, and I'll come get them. Or you can bring them out to me, whichever you like best—I don't care."

"Sit on them. Got it."

"You know what I mean."

"Of course I do. And I'll keep them safe between now and such a time as you can get your sticky little paws on them, don't worry."

"Excellent. Where are you now?"

"Atlanta. It's a long story. Don't worry about it."

"Ah!" he said happily. "That's not too far at all. I can hop a flight tomorrow night, and pick them up from you then."

"No."

"Don't tell me that," he commanded.

"I'm here on business, Horace. Business of a different and personal nature. I won't be around much, and I can't promise you I'll be available to nurture your every whim."

"When you put it that way, it sounds unreasonable."

"I'll call you when I get back to Seattle, and we'll work something out, okay?"

He hung up on me.

I shut the cell, then leaned back against the bed, suddenly so tired I could hardly see straight.

You think vampires don't get jet lag? Think again. Just because the sun shuts us down doesn't mean that the shifting time zones don't screw with us big time. I'm not always ready to sleep when the sun comes up, particularly if I've been in the northern latitudes and I'm on a steady schedule. And then, naturally enough, I don't always want to wake up as soon as the sun sets.

Not that it matters. When half your day is potentially fatal, you have to make hay while the sun shines. Or the opposite of that.

Adrian came back within half an hour. By then, I'd had a shower and dried my hair, and was mostly dressed. Usually it doesn't take me even that long, but this was different. I was visiting the Barringtons, on behalf of a big important House, and I wanted to look more presentable than usual.

By which I *don't* mean that I wander around looking like roadkill. In my opinion, I usually look awesome. Effortlessly so, if I do say so myself.

Yet somehow I felt confounded by the prospect of the Atlanta House. I'd heard a hundred years of stories about the place—how crazy it was, how dangerous it could be, and how easy it was to commit a grievous faux pas without realizing it.

Southern hospitality *my ass.*

Perhaps it isn't fair for me to put it like that, because by all reports, the Barringtons aren't local by origin. They're carpetbaggers from Philadelphia—an offshoot of a House that had grown too big to govern. Or more to the point, it'd grown too big for everyone to successfully get along without a whole lot of murdering going on.

It happens like that, sometimes. A House gets so huge that it can't sustain itself in peace, so a few of the more difficult family members are kicked out to start their own party. Or to take over someone else's.

A hundred years ago, Atlanta was mostly rebuilt from Sherman's firebug drive-by, but the vampire population hadn't returned in force. Any serious diaspora is hard on the undead, since the patterns required for our survival can require weeks or months to establish with any real security. It took me years to carve out my little safe zone in Seattle, with all my attendant identities, bank accounts, and property holdings. I don't know if it was harder or easier to get a setup established back before computers and telephones and security cameras, but it couldn't have been easy to return and rebuild after a fire of that magnitude. Whoever had held the House before the war could hardly be blamed for abandoning the place in its wake.

Any survivors had surely started new communities elsewhere, or joined others. Organizing a move home was probably more trouble than it was worth.

Enter the Barringtons.

They came, they saw, they conquered the chaos with yet more chaos, and they were demented enough that no one ever challenged them on it. Their reputation was one of capriciousness and cunning, ruthlessness and violence.

But no one ever accused them of being dumb.

"You nervous?" Adrian asked me. He may as well have asked if I'd been to the beach lately.

"Yeah. Are you?"

"Yeah."

I settled on black. Head-to-toe. It's classic, it all matches, and it's a power color. Seneschals used to wear white, back in ye olden days, but these weren't those days and I didn't have a stitch of white to my name anyway, with the possible exception of a crisp dress shirt or two.

"Dramatic," Adrian observed. He was dressed like a dude. Dark jeans, gray sweater, and black motorcycle boots. Dudes always have it easy when it comes to wardrobe. So do ghouls, I guess—unless there was some dress code of which I was unaware. With the Barringtons, one never knew.

"Well," I said when I was done.

"Well," he said back.

"Let's do this."

He jingled the keys at me. Together we headed downstairs for the parking garage. The valet nabbed the car, and Adrian drove. Ghouls chauffeur.

I didn't ride in the back, though. It would've felt too weird, so I sat beside him in the passenger's seat, breathing deeply and steadily, like I was in labor. Anything to soothe my nerves, because my nerves were rubbing off on Adrian, and if both of us were nervous, we'd never get anywhere.

I closed my eyes as we headed out toward the Buckhead neighborhood.

In my brain, I replayed the voice-mail message to which I'd awakened, informing me that Elizabeth had arrived safely and was settling into her new accommodations. Ian and Domino had helped her into the floor immediately below our living quarters, since it was mostly finished and we were out of bedrooms in the main area. It was for the best. It'd give her some privacy, and it'd give them a buffer between our safe space and her episodes, should she have any before I got back.

She was already asking about the bones, wanting to know when she'd get the ones I'd promised she could keep. I tried not to fixate on that. I tried not to wonder if this had been a bad call, and if I shouldn't have maybe put my foot down before Adrian had started buying plane tickets.

Oh wait. He did that while I was asleep.

Well, I was the idiot who'd agreed to it upon awakening. But if there was a piper to be paid, he'd have to take an IOU because *one bad thing at a time.* Just one. And Atlanta was pretty damn bad.

"Everything will be fine, you know," I said out loud.

Adrian glanced at me. The streetlights cut bars of white and gold across his face as we drove, and he mustered a smile. "I'm sure you're right."

"The thing is, we have to stay cool."

"I am all about staying cool."

"Just remember that we have a right to be there, and we don't even have any lies to remember—except that you're a ghoul. Beyond that, this is on the up-and-up."

"And except for how I'm going to look for Isabelle, or some trace of her. And you're trying to prove that they're horrible, deranged murderers."

"And except for those things, yes. But there's nothing on the books to keep you from asking around while you're there—and no law or rule against it. As long as you remain discreet, and don't get yourself into any trouble while we're guests of their House—"

"I know, I know. And don't worry. I won't get myself killed."

"It's hard not to worry. If you do anything to get yourself killed, they'll be after me right behind you."

"It warms my heart to hear you express such concern for my well-being."

"Nothing but love for ya, baby. And in all seriousness, maybe that's the best way to think of it. We're guests in their House, and that gives us both rights and obligations. Be a good guest, and we'll be all right."

"Stop worrying," he ordered me.

"I can't. It's what I do."

By the time we pulled up to the new-money mansion that served as Barrington headquarters, I was vibrating with tension.

"This is the place?" he asked dubiously.

The engine idled. We were sitting at a gate with a call box.

"This is the place," I confirmed, my voice both drier and weaker than I would've liked.

And what a place it was. A McMansion in the most ridiculous sense, in a neighborhood full of them. Buckhead is the place where all the football and basketball players have their residences, and although some of the homes are older, most of them are circa 1990 or later, with all the design sense and charm of post-modern architecture, if one may be permitted to use a term loosely.

The Barrington mansion sprawled on a lawn perhaps two acres big, and surrounded by a stone fence that was maybe ten feet high, by my best guess. I could've predicted broken glass cemented into the top, since it's less conspicuous than barbed wire and more difficult to simply clip one's way past. Though it was nighttime, obviously, I could pick out that the mansion was painted the eggshell beige with white trim that seems to be the industry standard for such homes. It would probably be uncharitable to call the look "neoclassical Georgian plus IBM taupe and gingerbread revival meeting in a dark alley for fisticuffs and insults." But there I go anyway.

It wasn't my kind of joint. I shall leave it at that.

Suddenly I was glad we had a Lexus. If I'd showed up in one of my throwaway beaters, I would've felt ridiculous. Never mind that I can afford to buy something much nicer; that's not the point. Inconspicuousness is the point, though I could assume it would be lost on the Barringtons.

But I had to admit, they fit in with the rest of the block.

Therefore, it may be that inconspicuousness is in the eye of the beholder . . . or in the zoning laws, as the case may be.

Adrian rolled down the window and leaned out to press the red call button. I tried to shake the idea that it was summoning dogs, or activating a trapdoor that would swallow us and the Lexus whole, but that was easier said than done. The place was a brick-and-mortar caricature of Mr. Burns's mansion from *The Simpsons*.

A tinny voice came through the call box. "How can I help you?"

Adrian cleared his throat and said, "I have Raylene Pendle, seneschal from the San Francisco House. We're expected."

The box didn't answer right away. When it did, the voice said, "Yes, please come inside. Follow the driveway up to the house, and then around back. You'll find a small lot where you can park."

Then the gates buzzed, but they didn't swing slowly open like I'd expected. They retracted to the left and right of the entrance, coming to a stop behind the wall.

The smell of electricity wafted in through Adrian's open window, and it wasn't just the call box. Up on the stone walls, I could see cameras tracking our every move, and there were no doubt cameras I couldn't see lurking in other spots. Either birds or bats flapped up and into the night as the gates rolled back into position.

My money was on bats. Little blingy ones, carrying tiny Louis Vuitton clutches.

Slowly Adrian drove us up the long, gently curving driveway that led up to the house and then around it. Much to my personal amusement, the path was lined with solar-powered lawn lights— one every few yards, on both sides. That had to count as irony in some universe, right?

Behind the house, the place was blessedly well lit from a vampiric standpoint. Lights were installed behind bushes and from overhangs, all of them diffuse enough to give the yard a glow without blinding anyone who pulled up to park. I could tell someone had put a lot of thought into it.

Like I said, crazy—not dumb.

The Lexus stopped in a logical place, alongside a BMW and another fucking Hummer, both of them so highly polished and meticulously detailed that they gleamed like ghosts. Adrian cut the engine and turned in the seat to face me.

"We can do this. And it will be fine."

"What you said."

He brandished the knuckles of his right hand, calling for a fist-bump. I gave him one and said, "Let's go, ghoul." And I prayed that he remembered Rule Number One above all.

Rule Number One: We aren't friends.

And this sucked a lot, because I wanted nothing more than to approach this house with a really good friend to back me up. Even though I had one, the employer–employee façade was going to take the edge off my fragile feelings of security. But that's the nature of the beast.

We exited the Lexus and closed our doors in sync, smacking the evening silence with one loud bang that made us both jump, even though we were the ones making the noise. But we pulled ourselves together, tossed each other the nod of a cohort, and made for the big back porch—where a large set of double doors with glass panes were illuminated by a helpful, handy-dandy spotlight . . . in case visitors had any questions about where they were expected to go.

"Me first," I whispered without moving my lips. "Don't forget."

"I'm not," he replied in kind.

Up the prettily cherry-stained deck steps I went, with him close behind, and before I could reach the doors to knock or search for a doorbell, a dark silhouette appeared on the other side of the glass. It was not a large shadow. It implied someone approximately my own size and shape. The lights from the house's interior backlit this woman so that her features were all but indistinguishable until her hand was on the latch to let us inside.

The swaying open of that door on its hinges was no creaking of a cemetery gate, but it felt no less sinister for the smooth arc that opened the home.

Her hand remaining on the latch, the woman said, "Welcome to the Barrington House, Ms. Pendle. I am Sheriden."

Sheriden was a pixie-faced frosted blonde in her thirties, wearing simple clothes but a diamond that could've choked a Doberman. I suppose marking one's ghouls with tattoos is seen as tacky these days. Jewelry certainly has more holding power. I hear you can get rid of a tattoo, but it'd be tough to part with a rock like that.

"Hello, Sheriden." I nodded politely. The one-name introduction and her obvious mortality told me she was probably the head ghoul of the household. So far as slaves went, it was a pretty good gig. Rather like being a high-end butler, but with more bodily fluids involved—unless being a butler is much weirder than it looks on *Masterpiece Theatre.* "I thank you for your welcome. I've brought an assistant, as you can see. This is Adrian, and he answers to me."

"Excellent. Won't you both come inside? The family has assembled to meet you in the main living area downstairs."

Awesome, I thought. What I said was, "Certainly."

Adrian didn't say a word because no one had spoken to him. So far, so good.

Sheriden stood aside as we stepped into what looked like a rear parlor or some other kind of sitting room, and off to our right was a dining area. I mean, a *regular people's* dining area. Vampires don't need a hardwood table and seating for eight, but I suppose it's nice to preserve the illusion.

Something unpleasant about this niggled around in the back of my head, and as Sheriden closed the door behind us, shutting us inside the Barrington compound proper, I remembered something.

Southerners don't typically receive people at the back door. And when they do, it's considered an insult.

12

As we followed the narrow, retreating back of Sheriden the ghoul, I made a hearty effort to observe and memorize absolutely everything. The first observation had to do with their security system: It was extensive, and part of it was new. *Very* new. It still had the smell of wires unused to warming, and in the corners I heard the digital clicks of unworn lenses shifting to watch us. At the windows I spied the telltale signals of electrical monitors, no doubt routed through some call center in which the Barringtons had the sort of friends who understood discretion in a vampire emergency; and just over the threshold, as the door had shut behind us, I'd felt the almost imperceptible give and shift of a pressure plate. Disabled, I assume. Or else, if I were feeling particularly paranoid (and I was), I'd guess that it was gathering vitals about us newcomers—our weight, maybe height or some other indicator that would set us apart from the regular family members.

I try to keep up on the newest security technology but it moves fast, and there are always private enterprises making exciting new prototypes . . . the likes of which a wealthy family might pick up on a lark.

This mix of the usual stuff and exciting add-ons told me that they'd recently made some major and expensive upgrades. What had previously been satisfactory had failed them, or else some new threat looked meaty enough to warrant the trouble.

I was willing to bet it had something to do with William Renner's untimely demise . . . or possibly Isabelle, if she was still hanging around making trouble. If she was anything like her brother, I wouldn't put it past her.

Deeper into the house we went, passing by the indoor entrance to the garage. It was wide open, and someone was inside, doing something noisy to a vintage Bentley. Two other cars were parked in there—one red and shiny, one black and shiny. We buzzed past too quickly for me to pin down makes or models.

The home's interior was posh and leaning in the direction of a televangelist's favorite set, but again, this might be an attempt to fit in with the neighbors. The carpet was pale, silvery, and plush enough to eat my pointy black boots; the hall mirrors were surrounded with baroque gilt and the occasional sconce. The walls were done in decorator colors—muted wines, grays, and golds. It hinted at someone somewhere with taste—but whoever this someone was, he or she was given too limited a rein to make a dent in the overall Dolly Parton feng shui.

The Barrington clan had assembled in the living room— a spacious, vaulted spot immediately to the left of the front door with its two-story portico. Again I considered the insult of showing us through the back, and I wondered if the pressure plate hadn't been the goal, rather than a subtle nod to their own perceived superiority.

I didn't yet have enough information to form a conclusion, so I let it go.

If Adrian had made note of the slight, he said nothing. I wanted to glance back at him, to exchange a look or just see how he was taking this, but I didn't dare. And I could smell him, anyway—tension, but restraint. Fear tempered with curiosity.

Though I obsessed over it, I didn't think his pheromones would set off anyone's alarm bells. His physiological reaction was perfectly normal, in my estimation. Maybe a more seasoned ghoul wouldn't have felt so ill at ease; but we'd worked his newness into our backstory.

The Barrington family, or those who felt like being present, lounged about the oversized room. They were scattered across a curved, elongated couch and its matching separates, and all the furniture in this particular area was the same bone-pale shade of white, which made some sort of statement, I assume.

Sheriden bobbed her head at the room in general—with a specific flinch of eye contact directed toward a man standing by a fireplace. What the hell he needed with a fireplace in Atlanta I'll never know, but he stood beside it like Vanna White awaiting a vowel call.

My initial instinct was that this was the man in charge. My second instinct was to override that, and suspect that he was the ghoul's master or lover. This second instinct gained traction when a woman at the crux of the couch's arc spoke first.

"You must be Raylene Pendle, or is it Emily Benton? Max's note was not especially clear on that point."

"It's Pendle," I informed her, not wishing to have them thinking of me on a first-name basis. It's hard to demand respect, but I could ride on the formality. "Emily Benton is a public identity and a false one. I wouldn't be so rude to your House as to insist upon it."

This drew nods of approval, so it must've been the right answer.

The same woman said, without getting up, "Welcome to our home. Won't you join us?" She gestured at a plush white seat next to the fireplace. The obsessive-compulsive in me wondered how they kept from getting ash all over it, and then remembered that this was Georgia, and it surely didn't see a lot of use.

"Certainly." Now I had a chance to look toward Adrian. He looked good, and not half so queasy as I felt. "However, you can see that I've brought an assistant."

"Sheriden will see to your ghoul. He'll be established downstairs, where we have a fully finished basement. It serves nicely as temporary housing, or space for guests of a certain stripe."

"Understood. Thank you, Adrian, that will be all then."

I shouldn't have said it out loud; I should've just projected it, or made the attempt. Too late. And probably, not too big of a deal. For all the Barringtons knew, I was only trying to be polite and not "whisper" in front of them.

Somehow, watching Adrian leave this time was harder than the first time, in San Francisco. It wasn't any great mystery. There, he only had to play along. Here, he intended to play along and investigate his sister's . . . disappearance. Here, the risk was greater.

I refused to think about it and concentrated hard on the matter at hand as I took my seat in what did, in fact, turn out to be a man-eating chair of the cushy persuasion. It was virtually impossible to sit with any dignity in that thing; there was no support, only the velveteen pillowing of foam. I did my best, and tried not to feel any resentment at what was likely a deliberate—if admirably subtle—power play.

I do not think it was irrational of me to suspect it. The entering via back door, the cushy and undignified chair . . . I could call it a coincidence, but all I needed was a third strike to go straight to conspiracy. These people liked to make sure visitors knew their place, and I suppose it's their House and that's their prerogative, but that didn't mean I had to like it.

"My name is Theresa Barrington," the woman in charge said to me. "My husband Paul and I"— she indicated the fireplace lurker—"are chief in this House."

As if I couldn't have guessed.

They were dressed to match—something I didn't notice until I'd had a chance to stare at them from my triangulated position. Not identical-clothes-matchy. More like prom-dates-matchy. She wore a blue dress that cost more than the Lexus we'd parked outside, and he wore a gray pin-striped suit with blue accents.

They didn't sit together, like one might expect. Several others lingered between them, and beside them.

"Theresa, Paul," I acknowledged in greeting. "And this is the rest of the House?"

"The important members," Paul said bluntly. I took an instant dislike to him—not for his bluntness but for something else, some other weird, vague malice. Everything about him screamed bland and cruel. There was nothing good or even useful about him, I could sense it.

Theresa gave his declaration a smear of propriety by introducing the rest. She went around the room, starting with the young man to her left. "These are our children, Gibson, Raleigh, and Marie." Gibson, at least, was no biological relation to either one of those slick brunette weirdos. He had a Nordic look to him that was so severe it almost made him appear albino. The other two shared a cornfed similarity that could've been family resemblance, but might've only been regional.

I turned my attention pointedly toward a short, heavyset man who had parked himself by the foyer entrance. "And you?" I asked, making it clear that I did not intend to speak through Theresa at any length.

He answered for himself, and I appreciated it. "Clifford O'Donnell," he said. And since he did not specify any family relationship, I assumed he was merely an affiliate, not a relation.

Theresa cleared it up by saying, "Clifford is an associate from Macon. He often serves as our seneschal, particularly when we feel the need to send someone out of town."

"Or when out-of-town trouble comes knocking?"

"Then too," he said without taking his eyes off me, or even blinking. "They called me here to see about William Renner when he died, and likewise they've summoned me now—due to your appearance. I assume you intend to investigate the matter."

"They dragged you all the way back here from Macon on my account?"

"I came back of my own accord."

Paul Barrington chose this moment to interject, by way of shifting the subject or simply annoying everyone. "He's a helpful man, our Odo is. He's the one who mailed William Renner's ashes. It's a good thing, too. Heaven only knows when one of us would've gotten around to it."

I ignored the casual rudeness inherent in his statement, and latched instead onto the nickname. It seemed safer. "Odo?"

Clifford made a face that stopped just short of an eye roll. "A ridiculous contraction, but that's beside the point. I come when I'm needed, and I leave when I'm not." He drew a breath like a sigh in reverse, let it out, and told me, "I try to keep the peace—something easier said than done in a climate such as this."

He blinked, and I knew I liked him—for a relative value of liking anyone. He was telling the veiled and toothless truth, but telling it at the Barringtons' expense, and right under their noses.

"Fair enough," I said, trying not to smile at him. His small insubordination made me a little bold. "I, too, am interested in peacekeeping of all sorts. However, I am here to discuss a violent matter and I hope we can discuss it openly, without delays, evasions, or games."

The blond wonder said sharply, "Is that what you think we do here? Play games and evade questions?"

"I have no idea how you comport your House," I lied diplomatically. "This is my first visit to your fair city, and my interest is purely on behalf of another party. If this is a situation that will require a light touch, and some ambassadorial understanding, I hope we can come to an arrangement. I have no wish whatsoever to create any conflict or confusion, so I hope you'll agree that we should be open with one another to the fullest extent possible."

Odo coughed. It would've been a better cover for a snort if vampires were more frequently congested.

Marie, who was more of a girl than a woman yet, or had been at her death, sat forward in a display of earnestness. "We're absolutely prepared to cooperate," she said—prematurely, as it turned out.

Her father did not bother to hide *his* snort. He said, "Cooperation implies that we've done something wrong, and need to account for ourselves. This is no such case. Watch what you offer, Marie."

"I have nothing to hide," she said stubbornly.

"*Everyone* has something to hide," her mother murmured. "But my child's impulsive statement of good intent will stand. Ask us anything you like, and we will attempt to be helpful. We wish no ill blood between Georgia and California, certainly not on the eve of the convocation. We only wish to help our West Coast friends.

Though perhaps I could ask *you* something first."

"Go ahead," I told her, not that I wanted to leave her in the interrogator's seat, but I was willing to give a little before I started taking.

"You aren't *part* of the San Francisco House, are you, dear? Something about your accent . . . I don't know, but it doesn't say 'California' to me."

"And yours doesn't say 'Georgia peach' to me, but we make our homes where we find them." Never lie when you can misdirect. Or, um, only lie when you're reasonably certain no one will call you on it. Take it on a case-by-case basis, that's my advice. "Regardless of my hometown, I am here with full authority of the Renner Household, and that ought to be enough to place me in fair standing. If you've found some problem with the paperwork or the permissions—"

"All was in order," Clifford—Odo, whoever—said quickly, like he was cutting off a more incriminating response, should anything blurt forth again from one of the children. "You are well within your rights to ask anyone in this House anything about Mr. Renner, whose passing came as a most unexpected and unfortunate event. We have extended our deepest condolences and regrets on the matter."

I decided to give him the benefit of the doubt, and assume that he didn't know such condolences and regrets had been submitted via email. "Thank you for the confirmation, Mr. O'Donnell," I said, giving him a "mister" whereas I'd called the rest by their first names.

It could be written off as a civilized nod between family lackeys, or so I supposed. Just like coming in through the back door and being assigned a man-eating chair could be written off as incidental.

I wished he'd step inside the room and quit hanging about

by the exit, as if he'd like to scram at the first possible opportunity. If I was going to meet any real cooperation in that joint,
it'd almost certainly come from him—I could deduce that much
already. But he stayed where he was, casually leaning his stocky
self against the doorway.

"Honestly." Theresa frowned and shook her head. "I wish I
knew what all this fuss was about. There was nothing we could
have done; William was a grown man in every respect, and what
he did was his own decision."

"Are you suggesting that Mr. Renner committed suicide?"
I tried to keep the astonishment out of my voice. It was a bold
fabrication on her part, if she intended to stick by it as a story.

"I'm not suggesting it. I'm telling you outright, the man offed
himself from our roof. It was embarrassing for everyone, and if
anyone should feel any modicum of obligation or uncertainty, it
should be the San Francisco people who allowed him to travel so
far without assistance. The poor man was clearly in an unrested
state of mind."

"Unrested?" What a stupid word. I could've sworn she'd
made it up on the spot.

"You know what I mean." She gave a lazy hand-flap. "He
wasn't himself the entire time he visited, and when we found what
was left of him on the roof one night, it'd be an exaggeration to say
that anyone was surprised."

"Surely you aren't suggesting that the San Francisco head of
House came all this way merely to 'off himself' on your premises?
If he was feeling that fragile, he could've done an easier job at
home—and he wouldn't have left his son in a fraction of his
present turmoil."

Paul said drolly, "Suicide is selfish."

"So I've heard," I said, struggling to keep my disbelief in
check. "It also feels . . ." I started to say "unlikely," but checked

myself before I wrecked myself, as the kids are putting it these days.

"It feels sudden, I imagine." So said Raleigh, I believe.

He was a smallish man with cold eyes and a pinched shape to his face that would've implied nearsightedness if he'd been alive. As it was, he just looked like the kind of guy who'd shoplift for kicks.

I seized the word. "Sudden, yes. There was no indication in San Francisco that he was unwell in any manner, much less—" I stopped. I was about to ask if anyone else heard what I was hearing—a thin, high-pitched beep coming from deeper within the house.

I didn't have to ask it. Everyone sat up straight at the first chime, rigid with varying states of alarm and discomfort. Odo immediately vanished, with Raleigh and Gibson dashing off in different directions—all but bouncing off each other in their haste to vacate the premises.

Marie cringed and clutched at her "mother." "Not again," she gasped. "Mother, do something!"

Theresa's response was swift and direct. She rose up off the couch and backhanded the girl hard enough to have broken the neck of an ordinary mortal.

Marie grasped at her face in shock. Blood oozed from between her fingers, via a crushed nose or busted lips, I assumed. To my surprise, her eyes hardened above those bloody hands, and in an instant she was on her feet and lunging at Theresa—who shoved her back onto the couch. Honestly, I wouldn't have thought the little milquetoast thing had it in her.

"You're too fucking *weak*, dearest. Get in the safe room if all you're going to do is cry!"

"I won't!" she burbled, and when she removed her hands I could see that yes, her nose was tweaked in a bad direction and there was blood on her teeth. "I won't hide with you, not anymore!"

Theresa bent forward and hit her again, hard enough to engage the girl's rage or defensive mechanisms—and within the batting of an eye, they were tumbling together on the floor, wrestling and biting like kindergartners, flinging blood all over the weird white furnishings. Paul finally left the fireplace, where he'd been standing with one foot on the slate frontispiece like it was first base, dove into the spinning pile, and kicked them apart. "Not now, you dumb bitches! Get up—get moving! And you." He directed one long, waxy finger at me. "Do your fucking job."

"My . . . my fucking job?" Pleasantries at an end already?

"Seneschals keep the peace, and you're here under our auspices. Go keep some goddamn peace." He swung out a leg to clip his wife but she caught it and threw him—hard—right up against a window on the other side of the room. He crashed into the curtain-covered portal. It didn't smash, but it crunched strangely.

Shatterproof glass, as I could've predicted.

"Keep the peace?" I damn near shouted at all the melee's participants. "I don't even know what's breaking it!"

"You're an investigator. *Investigate,*" Theresa sneered, and now there was blood all over her face, too, and on her hands. It was also all over the couch and the carpet, and since this brawl didn't look like it was excessively out of the ordinary, I shuddered to consider their cleaning bills.

Paul crawled out of the curtains in time to chase the two women from the room, leaving me alone and very confused about what had just happened. The tweeting, pinging chime of the alarm still dinged through the premises undaunted by the scattering of all the occupants. I didn't know what had tripped it, and I didn't know where to turn it off.

Adrian? I sent it as hard as I could. *Adrian?*

What's going on?

No idea. Can you get back up here?

His answer was a garbled negative, and no matter how hard I listened or pushed, I couldn't get anything more. I told myself that he'd sounded fine—concerned, but not threatened—and I should leave him wherever he was, in Ghoultown downstairs. Whatever wanted inside (assuming something *was* attempting to get inside) was trying it at night. This meant that it (a) was willing to take on real, live, awake, and pissed-off vampires, so therefore it (b) probably didn't have much interest in the staff.

Why was he/she/it trying to get inside now, anyway? I wondered it in a flash, and then jumped to a conclusion that was not at all reassuring, but somewhat logical: The intruder had seen us come in, and welcomed us as convenient distractions.

Well, I had to tell myself something. Otherwise I'd barge downstairs (providing I could find it) and rip the doors off the hinges to get Adrian out, while swearing about how this was all a preposterously bad idea in the first place and vowing never to let him out of my sight again.

Hey, the Barringtons wanted to act crazy?

I would give them crazy.

But not yet. I tried to be logical and treat this like any other case of me being inside a place with an alarm going off.

Mind you, it's not often that I'm sloppy enough to set off any alarms during my acquisitive activities. It's happened a few times, I confess, but only a few. And there are protocols in place, things you do to minimize the damage and regain control over the situation.

First things first. An alarm was going off. Something or someone had set it off. What or who? Couldn't say.

No sign of any assault on the grounds, not yet. I mean, no firebombs were going off and no windows were breaking. If anything, the place was eerily dead except for that beep, beep, beeping of the distant alarm.

So, all right. The alarm.

Where was it coming from, and how did I shut it off?

Both of these questions could likely be answered if I could track my way to a central control room. There had to be one. Anyplace as huge and guarded as this most assuredly had some command central deep in the house, likely in—or close by—this "safe room" . . . into which I had not been invited, not that I was crying about it.

Frankly, I'd rather be running free with an alarm going off and someone trying to get inside than trapped in a room with that loopy bunch. Again I felt a pang of concern for Adrian, but I talked myself off that ledge by recalling that the ghouls were bunked elsewhere, segregated as a class.

No self-respecting vampire in his or her right mind would hide with a bunch of ghouls. They're worthless, except during the daytime when there's nobody else to watch you. At night, we're better off watching our own backs. Only the most desperate and feeble of vampires would use ghouls as pawns or cannon fodder.

And just like that, I was back to being worried sick.

But it wouldn't do me any good. Finding a control room, that would do me some good. It might even have cameras showing me what was going on in the basement's Ghoultown, if I was lucky. All I had to do was find it.

Unaware if I was now effectively all by myself in this ludicrous McMansion's tacky corridors, I dashed through them with all my wimpy psychic sensors thrown open like a net, trawling the place for signs of previously undisclosed inhabitants. I didn't find any. I found overturned tables and chairs that had been knocked askew; I saw a kitchen with gleaming steel pots and pans hanging from a center rack, and these pans were swaying gently like they'd been recently touched. I found two spare bedrooms that were furnished as lightly as a hotel room, and I breezed past a home gymnasium proving that yes, these people would do anything to look like regular . . . um, *people*.

Then I snared the sense that someone was close, up ahead, to the right.

I veered that way and nearly collided with Clifford O'Donnell, whom I was determined not to call "Odo" anymore. His wide, square face was set in grim lines, but he didn't look particularly frightened. It was something else I saw in him, and something else I felt radiating off him. Not fear, and not protectiveness. Not even a grudging awareness that self-defense might be called for at any moment.

No.

When I drew up short to keep from face-planting into his collarbone, I saw his face very clearly, very closely, and I realized that it was *contempt*. Not for me, I didn't think—for his expression changed when he realized I was the one who'd nearly smacked into him.

"Ms. Pendle," he said. "They abandoned you up here with me, did they?"

"Up here? Their safe room is underground?"

"It's more of a safe compound, really."

"What about my ghoul?" I asked, not even caring if it gave too much away for me to be so concerned.

"Oh, they don't stay with the ghouls. Their hideaway is underneath the backyard, all the way back to the pool."

"Wait. There's a pool?"

"Behind the freestanding garage."

"Jesus Christ," I muttered.

"I've never seen any of them swim in it, that's for damn sure," he said.

The beeping went on patiently, persistently . . . more loudly, now that I was closer to the home's dense center. It called unceasingly from somewhere nearby.

I asked Clifford, "They must have a control room—someplace where the security cameras, feeds, and sensors converge."

"Yes, it's this way." I got the impression he had just come from it, and this impression was verified when he said, "I was trying to figure out how to turn it off, but they've changed so much since the last time I was here . . . I have no idea how it works. I need a goddamn tutorial, I swear."

"No you don't. You just need *me*," I said with a forced smile.

The room felt claustrophobic and rounded, stuffed as it was with control panels, keyboards, screens, wires, and buttons, but not a window in sight. It was the size of a huge closet or a small bedroom, take your pick, and its lights and signs were going bananas.

"You know how to deal with this kind of thing? Because I won't lie, it's well above my pay grade."

"Oddly enough, it falls right within mine. At least, my *usual* pay grade."

"San Francisco checkbooks must be more generous than Atlanta ones."

I scanned the equipment, looking for the master panel and finding it. "I'm not a seneschal by trade, only for travel purposes."

"And for your usual gig . . . ?" He let the question hang as he watched me flip switches, press buttons, and turn things on, up, and off.

"I do something else."

The system was an epic mess in every direction—a Frankensteined work of artlessness combining at least four different security systems without a central mainframe. Whoever installed it ought to be dragged into the street and shot. I had a feeling the Barringtons thought they were being clever when they hired four different companies to do the installation.

It wasn't clever. It was certifiably retarded.

"What are you doing?" Clifford asked, now genuinely interested.

"See those split screens over there?"

"The ones that go into four quadrants, or two?"

"Four," I specified. "Something tripped the system that watches those areas—I can't really tell what it was. I can see in the dark, but you need better infrared than this if you want to guard property without good exterior lights."

He squinted at the monitor. "That's the northern edge of the lawn." He poked at one square. "That's the southern edge, and these two are the property behind the garage. Did you park at the small lot by the back door?"

"Yeah."

"Then if you tilted the camera a bit, you'd be able to see your car in this square."

"That's useful to know, thanks. You don't see anything there now, do you?" I asked, my fingers still flying over the controls like they were Braille and I was reading the ever-living shit out of them. It sounds like hyperbole, I know—but I was very close to flying blind. I know what these systems look like and how they work, sure. However, that doesn't mean I can magically parse a clusterfuck such as this without taking some time to get to know it first.

"No, I don't see anything. Whatever set it off is gone now."

Over to my left, something lit up with a squeal. A green light flashed. I swatted it like a Whac-A-Mole. "Gone, but not far. What's this monitor showing?" I pointed at a split-screen with one side lit up, and one side in near darkness. Who the hell puts a camera in the dark when it doesn't have infrared? Idiots, that's who.

These people weren't crazy, they were morons. There's strength in madness—I knew that better than anyone, and I was pretty sure my new tenant Elizabeth Creed would agree with me there. But this . . . this feigned insanity? It was a paper mask, a fragile thing worn for show.

But it didn't fool *me*. Not anymore, now that I'd seen it up close.

Clifford indicated the dark half of the screen. "That's the yard by the gate. And the front yard outside it, where the street is."

"Got it."

"What does that mean?"

I said, "Someone's checking the perimeter—moving back to front, skirting the edges."

"Dammit, I think you're right. Look, there!" he said, jamming his finger at a screen so hard he nearly cracked it. "Did you see that?"

"No, but I'll take your word for it."

"A fast-moving sucker won't show up for shit on these things."

I grinned. "Oh, I know. Keep your eyes on them anyway, will you? All the monitors you can watch at once, just . . . watch. And don't blink. We need to know how many intruders we're dealing with."

"I've only seen the one blip so far, but that might not mean anything. If only these stupid screens were closer together."

"I know, right? Wait, hang on." I examined the farthest screen, realized it wasn't hooked up to anything that couldn't be unhooked for the purpose of moving it, and yanked it off the wall. "Here," I said. "Prop it up there, for easier watching."

The connecting lines now ran across the panel, but that was okay. I was getting the hang of this.

"Okay," I declared, and I began to narrate. "I was confused at first because the screens and the sensors aren't lined up with their controls, but I think I've got it now. This screen here is connected to that panel there; those screens answer to these keys; that screen ties to this section."

"It's like this was designed by monkeys."

"No shit. This slate over here handles the windows, I think—they're on an electric current system, a little old-fashioned but perfectly serviceable. This same section of buttons and levers probably also handles the doors, and . . . and . . . *this*." I found the newest slab of electro-tech, which had an LED readout but not a black-and-white screen. "This is for the pressure pad in front of the back door. I'd bet money on it."

"There's a what-now?"

"A pressure-sensitive sensor. It—"

He cut me off. "I know what it is, I'm sorry. That's not what I meant. I had no idea they'd put one in, that's all. How did *you* know about it?"

"I felt it when we came inside."

"You must have very sensitive feet."

"Outrageously so, yes."

"Or," he said drily, "you have a very interesting primary career back there on the West Coast."

"That, too. But don't jump to conclusions just because I know what to look for." Though for real, his conclusion-jumping was on base as likely as not. I'm not sure why I bothered to attempt a disclaimer, but with that, I flipped the switch to silence the beeping. The immediate quiet startled us both, even though I, for one, knew it was coming.

"Now . . ." His eyes were locked on the screens, now conveniently positioned more or less in front of him.

I withdrew from the console and went to stand beside him so I could watch, too. "Now *what*?"

"Now we see what our visitor is getting up to. Can you tell if he's breached the house itself yet?"

I checked the panel and saw that the circuits were still unbroken. "Not yet. So far, he's staying outside. Maybe he's just looking."

"Like hell he is. He's back, and God knows what for this time."

"Back?"

"Yes, *back*. For you. Me. Them. I don't know. But this same thing—all this scoping, swooping around, and sneaking—it happened the night William Renner died, too."

"Were you here that night?"

"Yes. They were nervous about him. They didn't want him here, but stood to lose a lot of face if they didn't extend the hospitality. They were so damn desperate to keep anything from interfering with their Chicago merger that they had to put up the show. But they invited me to help keep an eye on him." He delivered the last sentence with a dash of ironic disgust.

"And I guess we all know how *that* worked out." Then I caught myself with a mouthful of foot, and said, "Not that I'm saying you had anything to do with it. Just that whatever happened—"

He shook his head and waved a hand at me. "No, it's all right. It wasn't my job to protect him. It was my job to protect *them*. Still, it's hard not to feel a little egg on my face."

Together we scanned the screens, and I kept one eye on the console lights. We were waiting, anxious because we didn't know what we were waiting for. But it was out there, and it was coming, and we both knew it.

I noted, "You said he got himself killed."

"As if you bought the line about his suicide."

"No, you're right. That was a bullshit pizza, and any idiot could smell it a mile away. How did he really die?"

"I'm not positive, but I can guess." He hesitated.

"But you're not supposed to tell me, I get it. All that stuff about transparency, cooperation, yada yada yada—we all knew it was just for show. I understand if you're tied up with them, or tied to them, whatever. You've got lots to lose if you go against their wishes."

"I suppose."

Something about his tone made me not quite believe him. "Look, I don't know what your arrangement is, so I can't hold it against you if you don't want to share. But it's worth pointing out that I'm here with the specific intent of preventing something really bad from escalating up to the level of international incident."

"International?"

"'International' sounds more dramatic than 'interstate,' don't you think?"

"I do."

After a long moment wherein we both pretended to dedicate our full attention to the screens, he finally spoke. "Let me ask you a question first, and if you answer it honestly, I'll respond likewise. Deal?"

"Deal."

"How powerful is the Renner House? Strong enough to knock down the Barringtons, should it turn out to be worth their time?"

"That's hard to say without knowing more about the Barringtons. How many others are there—inner-circle-wise?"

"Not many. Two or three not-quite-children who have been orphaned from other places. It's strange, how the Barringtons have chosen their kind for the last . . . I don't know how long. As long as I've been acquainted with them, so let's say forty years or so."

"What do you mean by that?" I asked.

"Theresa got this idea that the line had become inbred, which wasn't a far cry from the truth. She wanted to bring in new blood, reinvigorate the House with new people."

"A worthy goal."

"Yes, but the way she went about it . . . that's the odd part. She was obsessed with the idea that her children weren't devoted enough—that they'd leave her, or overthrow her one of these days. And Paul wasn't too far behind her. He's more arrogant than she is, and even happier about the prospect of control. She wanted it because she's insecure; he wanted it to feed his ego."

"But how do you guarantee loyalty?" I wanted to know. "Money won't always do it, and money is the glue that holds civilization together. Makes the world go 'round, or that's how I hear it."

"I heard it was love, but maybe we listen to different radio stations. You're right, though. Money wouldn't do it. She didn't want people on her payroll. She wanted addicts to be controlled. So she hooked up with this chemist from the east side, about twenty years ago. Between them, they developed a drug they could use to keep the newbies close to home. Nothing's hard to escape like a bad habit, right? She tried it on a handful of kids but it didn't work like the charm she'd hoped. There were too many side effects, like rage and paranoia. And besides that, the resentment ate them alive, until they either ran away or she killed them."

I said "Hmm" because it lined up neatly with what I knew of Adrian's sister—a young vampire in peculiarly poor health, begging for help, escaping her House and being left to her own devices . . . oh yes. The pieces fit nicely. Or horribly, as Adrian would probably see it.

"But you didn't answer my question," Clifford noted.

Drat his perceptiveness.

"I'm sorry. I got sidetracked." And as I pondered how much to tell him, another blip went dashing across the screen—right to left, in front of the gate and around the inner edge of the wall. "Did you see that?"

"I did. He's headed back to the east side. I think he's covered the whole perimeter now. There's nothing left for him to do but make a play to get inside. But I still want an answer to that question."

Fine. "The answer is yes. Honestly, I think the Renner House could wipe this place off the map. I wouldn't have thought so until tonight, but meeting these maniacs has sealed it for me."

"Does San Francisco know this?"

"No," I admitted.

"Do you plan to tell them?"

"I haven't decided yet. But I probably will."

He was no longer looking at the monitors, but looking at me. "You don't give a shit about the San Fran House. What are you really doing here?"

"I believe that's more questions than I agreed to answer."

"Answer anyway."

"No," I told him. "Not until you tell me what *you're* really doing here. You aren't like the Barringtons, and it's obvious enough that you don't care for them. They drive you nuts, and they treat you like something they found on the bottom of their shoes. I didn't know Macon even *had* a House. Are you really part of their family?"

"Sort of. The Macon House isn't much to speak of. There are only three of us, and we keep to ourselves."

"I see. So if you want any authority or muscle, you have to keep yourself allied with these yahoos."

"That about sums it up. Now what about you?"

"I'm not sure you'd believe me if I told you." And I had no intention of telling him that I was here because my favorite blind vampire was in hot water, and my not-a-ghoul had lost a sister. "But it boils down to San Francisco wanting to know what the hell happened here, before Atlanta and Chicago come down on it and install a pet judge to drive California crazy. Maximilian sent me here in case I could turn up something that would derail—or at least delay—Atlanta's efforts to mount a hostile takeover."

"But you're not one of the California people."

"Look, buddy—I'm trying to help some friends, okay?"

I might've gone on, but right at that moment something landed hard on the roof.

If we hadn't been vampires, we wouldn't have heard it. It only reached us as a dull thump—something that could've been mistaken for the shutting of a door or the dropping of a heavy book. But we did hear it, and we both jerked our eyes up to the ceiling like a couple of dumb-asses—since neither one of us had X-ray vision.

Then we looked quickly at each other.

"He could be doing anything up there—setting the place on fire, cutting a hole in the roof . . ."

"Hanging out, disabling cameras," I said, noting that the second screen with four quadrants had just lost the feed from the top of the chimney. "Were those new?"

"I don't know."

"How should we play this?" I asked him. "Do we go up there and try to take him down? We don't even know if he's alone."

"I haven't seen anything to indicate anyone else, have you?"

"No, but that might only mean that they're really, really good."

"Shit," he cursed. "You're right." He leaned out of the small room, looking back and forth down the halls. Seeing no one, he said, "Between you and me, I'm tempted to say, 'Let him have it.' Maybe it's time this dynasty rolled over and died. It's been badly, stupidly run for decades. The Barringtons are coasting on their reputation, getting by because they stay so insular nobody knows how weak they've grown. Christ, the big fucking babies all bolted for their ironclad closet the moment that alarm went off!"

"They *do* seem a bit skittish."

"I'm not saying they're fragile. I'm saying they're dumb, and they were given power without responsibility. They took it, and they wrung it dry."

"And now you want it, don't you?" I asked him levelly, even as I tried to track the sound of footsteps above—and I watched one more camera feed go dark. "You want to move in and take over."

"I'd do a better job."

"I bet you're right," I said, and I meant it. "But are you seriously proposing a coup d'état to a woman you just met half an hour ago?"

"No, I'm proposing that you go back to San Francisco and tell the Renners the truth—that this place is a sham, and that the Barringtons let a burglar kill their father one night in the back bedroom."

"That's how he died?"

"That's where I found all the blood. They moved his body up onto the roof to cook it when the sun came up. But he didn't smoke himself to ashes. He bled out in the guest room after someone broke in. *This* someone, I bet."

The third camera went down. One tiny square was left, wobbling on the roof—up at the edge of some gable or rain gutter. Whoever it was, he was knocking down dominoes and getting ready to come inside to play. But he didn't want to be seen, or recorded at any rate.

I met Clifford's eyes and didn't blink. "What are you saying, Mr. O'Donnell?"

"I'm saying, let's get out of here while the getting is good. You and I go our separate ways, you deliver your message to San Francisco, and you have a new ally when the Barringtons fall. I don't know who *that* is upstairs, and I don't want to know. Whoever it is, I'm sure his grievance is legitimate, and I don't feel like standing between him and some righteous retribution."

"Neither do I," I admitted.

"Then let's go." He was pleading now, so desperate to get away and to get out from under the political thumb . . . for how long? Hadn't he said he'd known them for forty years?

As they say down there, bless his heart.

I said, "I'd love to, and maybe I *will*. But I'm not leaving without my ghoul."

"Well," he said, shaking his head, "that's your call. But I'm going to hit the road—and get out while I can. It's been nice chatting with a rational person for a few minutes."

"Likewise," I told him.

He turned to run but stopped himself and faced me again. "One last thing. You really *will* send in the Renners?"

"Like the fist of God." Something brilliant dawned on me, and I added, "If I can ask you for a little favor in return."

"How little?"

"Very little," I assured him. "I'll give you a call about it later."

"It's a deal. And it's time for me to take advantage of some vacation time."

"Good luck," I said with a wave.

"You too."

He disappeared with a bang—the sound of him striking off down the tiled floor—then I heard nothing at all. His departure was swift, smooth, and utterly seamless. I didn't even hear any doors open and close, but the alarm for the front door made a little chime and its blue light began to blink.

Just like that, Clifford O'Donnell was gone, and with him my sole ally of any supernatural power.

As I shut down the security systems one grid at a time, I considered my strange new . . . friendly acquaintance. Older than he looked, certainly. Confident and strong, and tired of being in the background—second fiddle to a pack of weaker creatures. I sensed a whiff of *eau de old cop* about him, like maybe he'd been a real investigator, back in the day. It sure parlayed nicely into a seneschal position—even a position that was only part time and odious.

I flipped the last switch to deaden the final alert, leaving the house utterly undefended from a security point of view. And I wondered if that wasn't why I'd taken such an instant liking to the guy—that *eau de old cop*. He dimly reminded me of my dad.

"There," I said to the control room.

It didn't say anything back. Not a blip or a beep, or a tiny flickering light. I'd disabled the whole damn thing, or so I was reasonably confident.

Grimly, it occurred to me that should I encounter this intruder, I wouldn't have much time to explain my helpfulness, but that would have to be okay. If his grudge was with the House, it might not be with me. Maybe we could do that whole "my enemy's enemy" thing and skip off into the night, holding hands.

Or maybe I'd just do my damndest to avoid the fellow, get my ghoul, and get out of Dodge.

I heard scrabbling up above—not nearby, but on the other side of the house. Someone was slipping down off the roof and hunting for a window to kick in. Unfortunately for that someone, all the windows were the same shatterproof (bulletproof?) design as the ones in the living room. He was meeting with difficulty.

Not a pro, then. A pro would have a cutter or, in a pinch, a little C-4.

Good to know. Definitely somebody with a grudge, not a hired gun.

Since the Barringtons were still AWOL and I wasn't sure how to find my way to the basement, I wasted a few minutes fluttering back and forth between hallways, looking for stairs. I found a set going up, but nothing going down. I wished I'd thought to ask O'Donnell where the entrance was, but I hadn't, and now he was gone, so screw it. And then I remembered an old place of mine, years ago, and how the stairs to the basement area had been just off the kitchen.

It's an old architectural hang-up, left over from the days when people stored food in their cellars. Or if you asked me in a pop quiz, that'd be my guess.

Back to the kitchen I ran, and sure enough, I'd gone right past the door several times without seeing it or realizing its purpose.

I got it now, though. I grabbed the knob and yanked, and met a lot of resistance. The thing was barricaded like a motherfucker from inside, and I noted when I began to beat upon it that it was steel-reinforced. It probably had a bracing bar on the other side— the kind you need a goddamn blowtorch to cut around if you ever expect to open it.

More often than not, the simple precautions are the most difficult to bypass.

(I, for one, have always fantasized about the day I can have a moat.)

Adrian! Adrian, can you hear me?

Is that you upstairs?

Yes, come open the fucking door.

I'll try . . .

"Do or do not, there is no *try*," I muttered.

I heard motion on the other side, and an argument, and what sounded like close-quarters fisticuffs . . . and then a grating slide of something metal being moved out of the way.

Adrian burst backward into the kitchen and crashed against an island's countertop. He was holding a metal crossbar, and brandishing it at someone on the top of the stairs.

Sheriden bulleted through after him, holding—I swear to God—a sword, and swinging it like maybe she knew how to use it. It was the fancy kind, like Renaissance faire freaks hang up over a fireplace mantel but never actually use. Even so, it looked sharp enough to do some damage.

She didn't see me, so she was easy to catch. I nabbed her from behind, took her sword away in a flash, and shoved her headlong back down the stairs with prejudice. Adrian heaved himself forward and slammed the steel door shut, then leaned against it for good measure—and jammed the crossbar through the latch to keep it fastened. Nicks, swipes, and a fairly deep cut blossomed red through his sweater and along his forearms. There, where he'd held up his arms to defend himself, the wounds were deepest.

"Jesus, Adrian!" I took one of his hands, attempting to better assess his damage.

He yanked it away from me and said, "It's not as bad as it looks."

"Good to hear, you fucking liar. What the hell was *that*?"

"*That* was a crazy bitch with a sword."

"I gathered that much," I told him. "Is there anyone else down there?"

"No one who'll do any damage. I had to kill one and beat the shit out of the other one to get them off me. They *knew*, Ray. They knew I wasn't a ghoul, and they didn't like it."

"Shit, man. I'm sorry. And I let the Barringtons just . . . lock you down there with them."

"I'm the one who insisted on coming. And there's nothing to be done about it now," he added under his breath. He reached for a dish towel and wrapped his right forearm. "And I didn't learn anything about my sister, so all these stitches in my future are for nothing. Hey, where is everyone?" he asked mildly.

Oh yeah. He didn't know.

"I guess you couldn't hear it down there, but there's been some excitement up here. An alarm went off. Someone's trying to break in."

He stopped his makeshift swaddling and eyed me. "What? Like, right now?"

"I assume. I disabled the security system, but it took me a few minutes. Maybe it'll help the guy."

"Why did you do that?"

"Let's get out of here and I'll tell you all about it on the way home."

"Where are the Barringtons?"

"Hiding behind their pool, I think. That's where they went, and I haven't seen them since. I assume they're still there, ostriching themselves and eating paint chips, or whatever it is they do in their spare time. I don't know. Actually . . . I have an idea."

"Oh no."

"No, it's a *good* idea."

"I don't believe you," he said.

Despite the fact that he was clearly injured, having him back at my side made me bolder. After all, I now had free rein of the McMansion (so far as I knew) and a hot tip on a crime scene. Also, I didn't hear any more ruckus from the would-be intruder.

"Do you hear that?" I asked Adrian.

"What? No."

"Me either. Maybe the burglar gave up."

"And maybe I'm your dear aunt Rose."

"Well, you *kind of* are."

"You know what I mean."

"We're still leaving, don't worry," I assured him. "But we're going to take a little detour first. Stick close."

"What are we looking for?"

"A bedroom with a lot of blood in it."

"Whose?"

"William Renner's," I said. "And they'll have tried to clean it up, but I'll still smell it if I find it."

"Not a suicide?" he asked, falling into step behind me. He was clearly in pain, so I kept up a pretty good clip as I went down halls, opening doors.

"Not a suicide," I said, reaching the bottom of the stairs and starting to climb them. "He died in one of the extra bedrooms."

"There could be a dozen in a place like this."

"I bet there aren't more than six or seven, and I've already breezed past a couple of them with nothing to hide. Up here, I bet." I climbed the steps two at a time because no, I didn't seriously believe the intruder had given up and moseyed on home, and I likewise didn't really think that the Barringtons would stay conveniently holed up all night.

Adrian lagged behind.

"Stay close!" I commanded.

"I can't—you're going too—"

"Fast, yeah, sorry. Then stay there. I'm just going to do a dash, okay?"

"Fine," he said. It told me he was tired, from fighting downstairs I assumed, more from the loss of blood. Though over my shoulder I saw him in a flash, just before I snapped around the corner, and his right arm was absolutely crimson.

I was glad I'd pushed pixie-faced Sheriden down the stairs. I hoped she'd broken her little pixie neck.

"I'll be right back," I said. I was already out of his line of sight.

"Hurry, Ray," he called behind me. "I don't like this."

I said, "Me either." But I said it quietly enough that he wouldn't hear it.

Okay, so I'd been wrong about the McMansion having only six or seven bedrooms. I counted at least nine in total, and there were five just on the second floor landing, where I shoved open doors and took a deep breath inside each space.

Room number three stopped me in my tracks.

I threw open the door—or rather, I bashed it open with my shoulder—and right as I was about to take a big ol' sniff . . . I realized I wasn't alone.

Somehow without me hearing it, the intruder had come inside. He'd done so by literally disassembling the window—with the big crowbar in his hand, I could only assume. So *that* was the scuffling noise we'd heard. I was amazed that he'd kept it so quiet.

An iron lever combined with a vampire's strength equals serious brute force. See? It's the simple things.

Another simple thing I halfway saw coming—the intruder wasn't a "he."

She was wearing black in the finest old-school tradition of such things, and a ski mask too—though why, I couldn't say.

I knew immediately who she was. So would anyone else from that household; they would've recognized her movement, her body, her scent. They would've known her as one of their own, or that's how they would've thought of her.

As for me, I thought of her in a possessive sense, too, though we'd never met before and shouldn't be meeting now.

Not like this.

Not with her hands frozen over a dresser with a huge vanity mirror that doubled the whole room. Three of the drawers had already been pulled out, searched, and thrown down in disgust. Three more remained, and I was interrupting her.

All four of us—me, and her, and our reflections in the big square mirror—held the pose and held the moment, neither one of us sure what would happen next.

Our eyes grappled and locked, and hers flinched away. I saw what she was thinking; it was all over her, in her posture, her shaking hands, her shallow breaths. She didn't know me. I was an unknown quantity. I might be a problem. She might be better served to try again another day.

Before she could act on it or look away from me, I blurted out quickly—while she could still see my mouth moving, before she either jumped me or ran: "Isabelle, you didn't come here to kill them, did you? You set off the alarms to lure them away from the house. What are you looking for?"

And I prayed that she could read lips.

"You know my name," she whispered back. The words were imperfect, dulled around their edges, but I understood them without difficulty. "How?"

"I know your brother."

She didn't react, except to tense even tighter, her whole body as rigid as rebar.

"He came here for you, wanting to know what happened."

"You're lying. He can't be dead. He can't be one of us!" Her refusal to believe ended on a shrill note.

"I'm not lying, but you're right: Adrian's not one of us. He's my friend."

"People like us, we have no friends."

"Please, what are you looking for?" I moved slowly into the

room, releasing the door and tiptoeing toward her. "I can help you look. I've turned off all the alarms. The Barringtons are hiding behind their pool."

But now she was uncertain. She let go of the drawer's glass knob. "Adrian is . . . here?"

"Downstairs. Look." I extended a hand. I had some of his blood on my fingers. "He's hurt. We need to get him out of here. Me and you, okay? We'll get Adrian someplace safe. You can smell him on me, I know you can. You can smell him, and you know it's him—just like I smelled that the two of you were kin."

The poor kid had no idea what to do, and that made a pair of us.

"They kept my grandmother's ring," she said, in case it explained something. "Theresa kept it, and wouldn't give it back. I saw her wearing it—she wore it to Chicago. There was a picture . . . and the ring was on her hand."

"Don't worry about that now," I begged, desperate to not chase her away, not when I'd have to explain myself to Adrian. "Come with me, please! I can get us out of here. You can tell me all about it. I'm a thief, Isabelle. I'll come back for it. I'll get it for you." I would've promised her anything at all to get her out of that room.

"Raylene!" Adrian shouted from downstairs.

"See?" I said to Isabelle, forgetting that she couldn't hear. "That's him!" Then out into the hall I asked loudly, "What?"

"We gotta go!"

I heard the sound of preternaturally strong fists banging something, and at first I thought of Sheriden, but no. The sound was coming from the house's back, at the garage's door to the interior, or so my ears suggested.

The Barringtons.

They were tired of burying their heads in the sand, and they wanted back inside their house. Had the door locked down behind them? A crash told me no, that it had only stuck or only locked, and whoever pushed behind it was really impatient to get some ass-whooping under way.

"Ray!" he all but screamed, and that was all it took.

I whirled out of the room and left Isabelle, not willing to beg her to stay if it meant letting Adrian get murdered downstairs. I was on him in a flash, a split instant before Paul Barrington could reach him.

I punched Paul in the throat—hard, since I had the weight of my full descending velocity to back it up. He choked and flew backward into the hall, where he made a very big dent in the far wall.

Theresa was right behind him. She came at us like a harpy, all wild hair and long fingernails and a face full of hate. Adrian pushed something into my hand. Sheriden's sword.

Now that I had it in my hands, I knew I was right—it was a cheap replica—but it'd have to do. I swung it at Theresa's throat and only winged her; she grabbed my wrist and tried to wrench the weapon free, but Adrian bent over and charged her, catching her in the side and throwing her off me, only to land on top of her. He wasn't stronger than the vampire woman, but he was heavier, and for that moment, weight was the more important advantage.

I grabbed him by the back of his sweater and jerked him back to my side. I pushed him in front of me and said, "Run! I'm right behind you!"

He didn't ask where I expected him to run to. There was only one way out for us because the Barringtons were blocking the way to the back door. We had to make for the nearby front door and run around the house, back to our car—assuming we could get it past the front gate. I was fully prepared to make a whole ency-clopedia of assumptions, as long as it got us out of that hall as fast as possible, and preferably *faster*.

I brandished the sword, expecting any of the children to pounce at any minute, and I wasn't disappointed.

Raleigh flew around the corner and into view. He didn't slow down, he just charged—making a whole bunch of his own assumptions about his personal prowess, considering that I was armed and he wasn't. I caught him through the upper torso without even meaning to; it was that fast, that's all—he was over there, and then he was right here on top of us.

The wound wasn't mortal but it was a serious inconvenience for both of us. For him, because hey, sword in the chest. For me, because he spun away from me and took the sword with him.

I said, "Uh-oh."

Adrian heard me. "Uh-oh?"

"Nothing, keep going. Here, here—go left." I pushed him around and into the foyer, where the front door loomed like the devil's tombstone. It was locked eight ways from Sunday. You could see the locks doubled and tripled, and set in metal plates.

Adrian saw them and had a perfectly rational thought. He reached for the narrow hall table and picked it up like he could throw it through one of the skinny windows on either side of the door.

"Won't work," I told him with a hand on his arm. "They're shatterproof, the lot of them."

With that I went to work on the locks. And damn the whole Barrington clan forever and ever amen, because only about half of them were actually, you know, *locked*. And to think, my instinct to just run down the line and flip them all as fast as possible had looked so good on paper. I swore loudly and copiously, and Adrian said, "Hurry up!" like I was hanging around giving myself a manicure or something.

At least his shout gave me a heads-up about Marie, who was barreling in our direction. She let out a scream like a very small hawk and went after Adrian, who had nothing but the narrow end table with which to defend himself. It was too bulky to work, or do anything more useful than hold her out of reach for a second or two.

Thank heaven, the second or two was enough for me to crack the last dead bolt and throw open the door. Once it was ajar, I whipped the table out of Adrian's grasp. It was hardwood, oak maybe, and heavier than I expected. But that only meant it made an unexpectedly satisfying crunch when I swung it upside Marie's skull.

Adrian didn't need micromanaging; by the time I had dropped the table and returned my attention to the gaping door, he was already on the front lawn and heading around to the left.

Onto the freshly mowed grass I ran, playing catch-up and playing it well. I was beside him in the span of a few heartbeats, encouraging him along and eyeing the house warily, knowing that I hadn't actually killed any of them and there was still at least one Barrington we hadn't seen yet.

I threw a last look up at the bedroom where I'd found Isabelle, and I was truly impressed by the speed, scope, and silence of her work. She'd literally pried the entire window frame out of the building, thereby bypassing the need to smash or cut her way through the reinforced glass.

I didn't see her. I didn't see even a shadow, slipping across the wall.

Had she followed behind me? Had she believed me?

"Shit," I mumbled.

"What?" Adrian panted.

"Where the fuck is the car?"

"I know, right? How big is this place anyway? Wait—there's the garage. We're close."

"Hell yeah," I said as our rental Lexus came into view.

It was a premature "hell yeah." No sooner had we reached the car and Adrian was fighting to find the right key than the yard was brilliantly, suddenly, completely awash in columns of blinding white light.

"What the—?"

"Floodlights!" I squinted and wanted to howl. My eyes felt like they were boiling in my skull. "They're back in the control room!"

"What does that mean?"

"They're re-arming the property. Let's go, now!"

"I'm working on it," he insisted, and then he had the door open, and then he'd popped the locks.

I leaped into the leather seat and slapped the door shut. Then, because I couldn't stop myself, I pressed the button to lock the doors, as if that would stop anybody who was chasing us. The engine turned over immediately, like a good luxury car should, and Adrian nearly blew out our back tires peeling off the lot and onto the driveway.

Then it was Adrian's turn to say, "Oh *shit*. What about the gate?"

"We'll ram it if we have to."

"I don't think we can ram our way through it," he said dubiously.

"We have a better shot of ramming through the gate than ramming through a stone wall," I said, reminding him that the entire property was surrounded by one. "Just drive!"

The car skidded down the driveway and beelined for the gate. I was afraid he was right, but what could we do?

I leaned over and buckled him into his seat belt, then did my own. And I prayed for air bags, because I had a feeling this was not going to go very smoothly at all, goddamn it.

The big black gate was rolled into position, hulking there and blocking the way to freedom. Adrian slammed on the gas and the tires screeched, but I hollered, "Wait!" and grabbed at his thigh. He took his foot off the gas and hit the brakes instead, so the car fishtailed on the concrete, losing a wheel over the edge and into the grass before righting and getting the traction to go straight again.

"Look!" I said, flailing toward a black-clad figure beside the gate. It was bent over the chain mechanism that drew the gate forward and backward, and it was doing something useful, I just *knew* it.

He didn't ask any questions. He applied the gas again, more reasonably this time, lest we smash through a gate that was actually being opened for us, slowly but surely.

Isabelle was using every ounce of strength she had to pull the thing aside. Impossible under normal circumstances (I was sure the Barringtons had seen to that), she'd first snapped the chain and now had only the weight of the gate to fight her. She shoved it along the track until it was open enough to squeak-birth a Lexus, and she waved us through as if we had any other plans at the moment.

"Who the hell?" Adrian asked, craning his neck to get a better look at the still-masked woman.

She was looking back at him, too.

The way the gate had unspooled, she was on my side of the car—but she gazed in through the window, past me, and stared at his face so hard I thought she'd crack it. It would've been a touching moment were it not for the shadow that reared up behind her.

Gibson.

I recognized his shape before I could see his face, so backlit by the industrial power spotlights.

I tried to warn her but she wasn't looking at me. She was looking at her brother. And of course, she couldn't hear Gibson sneaking up behind her.

The Barrington seized her. Her eyes went big as nickels and she wrestled him, using her weight to pitch both of them forward, into the car. Her face pressed against my window, then smeared away from it in a smudge of cheap ski mask yarn as they tussled within arm's reach.

Adrian was paralyzed, unsure of whether to gas it and go or help our mysterious benefactor.

I spared him the agony of a decision by unbuckling myself and throwing my fist through the Lexus's window. The glass shattered into a billion shards of blue-green safety coating and razor-sharp edges. I shoved myself to my feet, forcing my upper body out the window and grabbing Isabelle by the neck.

Undignified and potentially painful? Yes. But it was the only thing I could get a grip on, and she didn't hold it against me.

Forcibly I sat myself down, towing her with me and into my lap—and smacking Gibson's face against the door frame hard enough to dent both his forehead and the car. Stunned, he released her. It gave me the leverage to draw her all the way inside in an ungainly move that ended with us both covered in safety glass pebbles—and with her head smashed against Adrian's right thigh.

"Go!" I yelled, and he didn't hesitate anymore.

He punched the pedal.

The car swerved, its driver-side mirror stuck on the gate. It snapped off with a pop and a scrape, and without an inch to spare, the car cleared the opening and leaped out into the relative safety of Buckhead's suburban dream-land.

Isabelle pulled herself off my lap and slithered into the back-seat, where she picked the tinted glass off her clothes.

The funny thing was, Adrian *knew*—even before she'd pulled off the mask. He knew while she was lying in the back of the Lexus, panting and looking back out the window in case they were coming after us. They weren't. We all knew it. I think she just needed a reason to look away, because when a moment is a long time coming, sometimes it can wait a little longer. Sometimes it needs to, when the anticipation has been so much that the buildup becomes a barrier of sorts, and it needs those extra moments to dissolve and defuse.

When she turned around and pulled the mask off over her face, her hair came tumbling out in a dark, wavy ponytail she'd twisted up under the covering. Her face was stricken—not with terror or confusion, but with a gut-twisting nervousness that maybe this was not how it ought to be. Her eyes darted to the car door's handle; I saw it in an instant and knew she was considering just . . . jumping for it. Getting out now, before anyone had to talk—before there were explanations or questions, or potential recriminations and shouts.

But none of that happened.

What happened was that their eyes met in the rearview mirror, Adrian driving and looking back at her, for he'd been staring with certainty and relief even before she'd admitted her identity by removing the mask.

He didn't know what to say any more than she did, but I could feel some of the pent-up *wanting* in his chest, radiating toward my psychic senses with all the subtlety of an electric oven. He wanted to say that she looked exactly the same as she had ten years ago, but better now—not quite the sickly monster who'd hid in his closet while he was home on leave. He wanted to tell her how hard he'd looked for her, and how long, and how much it had almost cost him—but he couldn't tell her anything to make her feel guilty. Despite the fact that he was driving and he could not watch her as hard as he wished, already he could see that it'd take little more than a word to send her flying away from him.

I was on the verge of turning on the radio, just to have

something to fill the pressure-cooking silence of the car, when Adrian said, "I thought you were dead."

But she couldn't hear him and she couldn't see his mouth moving, so she did not know what he'd told her.

Isabelle couldn't hear anything, for almost exactly the same reason that Ian couldn't see anything. Both of them had been part of the same god-awful experiment, intended to restore sensory ability to one god-awful ghoul who'd been stripped of it all in punishment for some heinous but unknown crime.

Someday, I intended to find him. And I intended to take away everything he'd managed to retrieve. As far as I was concerned, he deserved everything that had ever come to him and much, much worse—for what was done to my friends, before they were my friends . . . and for how he'd tried to do it all over again.

I didn't know how I'd go about it. I had only the vaguest idea where he was, and he was surrounded by money and technology and well-paid minions who'd serve him better than ghouls. But one day, one way or another, he was going to pay for what he'd done to Ian and Isabelle.

13

Those first few hours together were strange and wonderful, I guess.

Strange for me. Wonderful for Adrian. Sweet but awkward for Isabelle.

She read lips quite well, and as long as we spoke within her line of sight, she understood everything we both said without any real difficulty. This was good, because although at first no one had known what to say, by the time we were back in the hotel they were ready to try.

It was like watching two people reach out to each other over a gulf of ten years, clasping hands, pulling hard, and drawing the chasm to a close. Or if not a close, then something more narrow and more easily bridged.

In an attempt at discretion, I left them alone

and wandered the city by myself for a while while they got reac-
quainted. I poked around Five Points, moseying in and out of the
bars and clubs that remained open, and sitting around a park with
my eyes half closed, waiting for the sun to rise enough for me to
head back and crash.

I halfway hoped someone would try to mug me so I could get
a guilt-free meal for my troubles, but no. No one bothered me, and
a homeless woman gave me some peanuts to feed to the squirrels.
There weren't any squirrels at such an hour; all sensible squirrels
had holed up in their trees, burrows, and apartment building walls
like decent, civilized creatures. But I felt like it would've been
rude to refuse.

From my position in the very dark park, mostly alone except
for a few snoozing pigeons and the feral cats who hunt them, I
pulled out my cell phone and called home.

Ian answered on the second ring, and I almost imploded
with relief. He was there. He was alive. He hadn't gone back to
California.

"Hello, Raylene."

"Hey sweetheart. How's it going there at the homestead?"

"All's well. Or all's typical, at any rate. The kitten has decided
that your pillow belongs to him."

"Awesome. I'll correct him on that point when I return."

"You might want to wash it," he said.

"I'll do that."

After a moment of quiet, Ian asked, "When might that be?
You returning, I mean. I . . . I haven't heard anything further from
Maximilian, and I don't know what's going on. I'm in the dark
here. More than usual, that is."

"Soon. Very soon. Tomorrow night, I hope—depending on
what airplane ticket bounty the Internet is able to provide me.
We're all done out here. All done, and then some."

I could hear him frown. "What does that mean?"

"Long story."

"You say that a lot."

"Well, lots of things are long stories. I always tell them eventually, don't I? Don't go to California, Ian. Don't let Max talk you into it, if you reach him again. There won't be a convocation, and I know who killed your father. Also, I know how we're going to get Max off your case for good."

"You still think you can fix this? Time is running out, Ray. It might have run out already."

"No. You're still alive, so I'm still ahead. And once I get back, I'll explain everything. You'll see. You'll believe me. Hey," I said, trying to divert the topic before I felt the need to wibble and beg. "How's Elizabeth settling in?"

"Well enough. She's an odd bird, but an intelligent woman. Schizophrenia, isn't that right?"

"Unfortunately."

"Sometimes she seems perfectly normal. Sometimes she lectures Pepper in quantum theory and how magic can change the past. Every now and again, she calls Domino 'George.'"

"Who's George?"

"I haven't the foggiest. Either she doesn't know either, or she doesn't feel like telling us. Raylene?"

"Yes, darling?"

"She doesn't have anywhere else to go, does she?"

"You looking to get rid of her already?" I asked.

"I'm only wondering," he said, which didn't answer the question. "You're accumulating new household members at a steady clip, that's all. We may need to renovate the next floor down in its entirety."

"Does Pita need his own room?"

"Pita does not need his own room. He already has his own floor."

"Next you'll tell me I shouldn't buy him a bed, because he already has the queen-sized Posturepedic in my room."

"Now you're getting the picture."

"I think you're right. We *will* need to remodel. Maybe the whole place—top-to-bottom, all four floors."

"Are you thinking of opening a halfway house for strays?" he asked, approximately half joking and half worried.

"Not exactly. But I may as well tell you now, I'm bringing yet another new one home with me."

"A new . . . person?"

"A new vampire. I don't know if she'll stay with us at first—in fact, I suspect she won't. She'll stay with Adrian."

I could hear him breathing on the other end of the line. "You found Isabelle?"

"Almost by accident, but not quite. I knew she was around, I just wasn't expecting to find her so quickly."

"Is she . . . ?"

"Deaf? Yes. I think she hears roughly as well as you can see."

"The poor dear."

"Oh, I wouldn't feel too sorry for her. She's tougher than she looks. It's my favorite thing about her, so far. That's one of my favorite things about you, too."

"Why thank you. But now you're buttering me up."

"Not at all," I insisted. "I miss you, and I'm relieved to be talking to you. You're alive, and you're home. It's all I wanted."

"I miss you, too," he admitted, and then a moment of silence hung between us, occupying the line with nothing except the companionable knowledge that we were only a couple thousand miles apart, and we wouldn't be for very much longer. "Tell me about

San Francisco. Maximilian wants me to meet him in Chicago tomorrow night."

"I told you already, there won't be a convocation—in Chicago or anywhere else. And Maximilian can go jump in a fucking lake."

"I suspect he will not."

"His loss. A nice swim can be good for the soul."

"Raylene? Stop beating around the bush."

"Who's beating around anything? I have a plan."

"Oh *no*."

I sighed. "Why does everyone always say that, every time I say I have a plan?"

"Because your plans are—"

"It was a rhetorical question, okay? I have a plan. I think you'll like it."

"If you really thought I'd like it, you'd have told it to me by now."

"Untrue, my dear. I'm only withholding because I have a few minor details to iron out."

"Oh no."

"Stop that, would you? They are *minor* details—details of convenience, not details of necessity. And they aren't worth going into, not over the phone."

"You're not going to kill me, are you?"

"Not exactly."

"Oh no."

"Oh *yes*," I pressed, and the evil smile that stretched across my face felt really fucking good. "But there's both more and less to it than that. Things are going to change around here, Ian."

"Around Atlanta?"

"Well, around Atlanta, too, yes. But you know what I mean. In Seattle. Things are going to change."

"For the better, I hope."

"For *our* better, yes. Yours, and mine, and the kids. And Elizabeth, Isabelle, and Adrian. Shit, better for Pita, too—what the hell. No reason to leave him out of the fun."

"You may reconsider your charitable attitude when you see your pillow."

"Oh Christ."

"Raylene?"

"Yes, Ian?"

"Come home soon."

"I will. And when I do, I'm going to fix *everything*."

We hung up, and I folded the cell phone back into my pocket. Then I rolled down the edges of the brown-paper bag that held my gifted peanuts, and I left it open on the park bench before I headed back to the hotel.

14

I was right, and Isabelle wanted to stay with Adrian. But first she was willing to swing by the homestead with her brother, where she met Ian. They had lots to talk about . . . but didn't seem to know what to do with one another.

One of the easier topics of conversation was her escape and subsequent life of freedom after escaping the island compound at Jordan Roe. She, Ian, and a handful of other preternaturals had been held there for experimentation by the military. But when a storm tore the compound open, those who had not died, fled.

Isabelle had tried to swim to the Florida mainland, but was washed out into the Gulf of Mexico. By sheer luck, she was picked up before dawn by a yacht called the *Saraphina*. *Saraphina* was owned by a woman named Samantha Carey . . . a woman who was dying of breast cancer—though no one else knew it at the time. It was her secret, and the reason she'd bought the boat: for one last great cruise, taken on her own terms.

Fishing a young vampire out of the ocean changed things.

Isabelle and Samantha became friends, then lovers (despite the age difference), then parent and child when Isabelle bit Samantha—taking away the cancer for good.

Their union hadn't lasted long, but it ended on good terms. Samantha's new lease on life led to a desire for world travel, and she didn't really have room for a partner, but she gave Isabelle enough money to live on, and they stayed in regular touch.

Otherwise, the girl vampire had been essentially on her own for the better part of a decade.

She knew that Adrian had disappeared, too, and she'd worried—but not known what to do. She knew that the Barringtons still ruled Atlanta, but she also knew that they were not as strong a House as everyone assumed.

"Theresa had kept Grandmother's ring," she explained with a glance at Adrian that said he knew which grandmother and which ring she spoke of.

"The diamond?"

"Yes, the one Mother brought from Cuba when they left. I wanted it back. They could keep everything else I'd left—just clothes, and some CDs, and nothing, really. Nothing worth looking for. But the ring . . . it was the only thing of value I ever owned, and Theresa was wearing it. I saw a picture of her with Robert Croft, from some party they attended. It was in a newspaper, and people were talking about Atlanta and Chicago forming an alliance—and that sounded awful, but I didn't care about it any more than Theresa cared about the ring. She's so stupid, she probably thought it was fake."

"Wouldn't surprise me," I said. "She didn't strike me as the type to know coal from cubic zirconium."

"It made me mad, so I went back to the house while they were still away in Illinois, before they came home. I broke inside and looked everywhere in their room, but I couldn't find it. That's when I realized she must've put it somewhere else."

"She could've still been wearing it."

Isabelle shrugged. "True, but I didn't want to take it off her hand if I could help it. I didn't want to see her, or talk to her. I didn't want anything to do with her after the things she made me drink. All I wanted was the ring."

"Did you ever find it?"

"No. Someone came in and almost caught me, so I had to come back later. When I came back the *next* time, they'd added some security. I set it off when I got inside one of the bedrooms—the window, when I opened it. It was very close to dawn, but I was willing to take the risk. The alarm went off. I disturbed a man who was staying there. He was settling in for the day, but he saw me, and he attacked me."

"A man who was staying there? In that extra bedroom where I found you?"

"Yes. He was an old vampire, older than me. Older than you, I think. He was very strong, but I was lucky—we struggled, and the mirror over the dresser broke. I picked up a big piece of glass and threw it. It almost took his head off. Before he could kill me, I killed him the rest of the way," she said, which was one way to put it.

"Father," Ian murmured.

"Who?" she asked.

I filled in, "The man you killed. His name was William Renner. Ian knew him, but they were no longer part of the same House."

"I'm sorry," she said. "I didn't go there to kill him. I only did it in self-defense."

Ian said, "And he attacked you for the same reason, I bet. You surprised him. He thought you were there to kill him, and it's hard to blame him. He was under the Barringtons' roof. I'm sure every one of them looked like a potential murderer."

"It was a misunderstanding," she said, nodding. "I wish he hadn't been there. I only wanted the ring. Now I'll never find it. If I go back now, the House will be locked down like Alcatraz. I'll never get inside."

"You may not have to," I told her brightly.

Adrian, who was sitting in front of the television with Pita on his lap, asked, "Why's that? Are you going to go back there and get it for her? I don't know if she told you or not," he said to his sister, "but Raylene is pretty good at getting in and out of places."

"If I have to, I'll totally sneak in and swipe it for you. Frankly, I'd do it for giggles—and for the chance to put my fist through Theresa's face. But I suspect it won't come down to that. Give it another few weeks, and I can probably collect it with a phone call."

The room got quiet, primarily because the kids weren't present to start asking questions. They were out, as was their custom at three AM on a weeknight. Hey, it's like I said—I'm not their mom, and I don't monitor their comings and goings. Very much. Actually, I knew where they were . . . or at least, I knew what they were doing. I'd sent them on an errand.

Ian prodded me first. "Raylene, you said you had a plan and I said 'oh no.' Is this the part where you tell us exactly how much 'oh no' we ought to be feeling? This situation." He waved toward where he knew Isabelle was sitting, cross-legged on the floor beside her brother. "It could get very tricky, politically. She killed the head of a House . . ."

"By accident," I interjected.

"Regardless, it's been pinned on the Atlanta House—"

"As it rightly should've been, since Isabelle is technically still a member of the Barrington clan. And it happened on their watch, under their roof."

Elizabeth piped up, startling the whole room. "I've hidden the bones." She'd been downstairs when we'd begun the conversation. I hadn't heard her come up. Damn, that woman was spooky when she wanted to be.

Isabelle saw us all turn to look at Ms. Creed, so she looked, too.

Elizabeth entered the room and took the free seat next to Ian on the short couch. She moved a little slowly, as if she'd only just awakened. It takes time to adjust to a vampire's schedule. Or a drag queen's.

"Good evening," Ian told her.

She smiled at him. "Good evening to you all, too."

"Elizabeth, I'm glad you're here," I told her.

"And why is that?"

"General principle?" I tried.

"Ha."

"Okay, I'm glad you're here because now this makes everyone. All the grown-ups, anyway. And the time has come to unveil my nefarious plan—the plan that's going to keep Ian from turning into dust at the hands of his brother, and prevent his brother from going on the warpath after us. This is the plan that is going to keep us all safe and secure for the foreseeable future."

"This sounds like a big plan," Ian said.

Adrian said, "Tell me about it. I've been trying to drag it out of her since Georgia."

"All right—let's hear it," Elizabeth said. "I'll like it best if I don't have to use any of the bones. They wear me out, and I still have plans for at least two of them."

"Two of them?" Did I really want to know?

"Two more things to be undone."

"Is there any rush?" I asked nervously.

She glanced down at her wrist, which did not have a watch on it—or a calendar, or anything else to tell her anything. But upon checking that patch of skin, she concluded, "Yes and no. One of them, I'll need to start soon. One can wait."

"Will you be blowing up anything in Seattle?"

Elizabeth considered this question. She stretched out and relaxed, a move that caught the attention of the resident cat. Pita abandoned Adrian's lap and sauntered over to Elizabeth, who patted her thigh in an invitation. The kitten took it, purred, kneaded his claws around into her leg, and conked out again.

Finally, she said, "Not at this time."

I'd take what I could get. "Fine. Here goes." I cleared my throat for dramatic emphasis. I made sure Isabelle was watching me, and could see my lips move. Since this once, for these few precious seconds, I had everyone's attention . . . I laid it all out.

"As you're all aware, the ranks of this household have begun to um . . . swell. Last year at this time I was living by myself, and I had lived by myself for a really long time. I've been staying in Seattle because it didn't have a House, and the vampire population is very low. Outside of this room, I know of maybe three or four of us who live within the city limits, and we all go out of our way to avoid one another.

"I've always assumed that the original House—if the city ever had one—went up in smoke during the 1889 fire, much like the original Atlanta House during the Civil War. But this is neither here nor there. The city is big enough, and there are now enough of us hanging around, that we need to work out some kind of formal arrangement for our own protection."

"Holy shit, Raylene," Ian exclaimed—making the first time

I'd ever heard him swear. From sheer surprise, I stopped talking long enough for him to ask, "Are you suggesting that we form a House?"

"Yes. That is exactly what I'm suggesting. We don't have to do it all formal-like, with titles and ranks and other assorted forms of bullshit, but we do need to have the structure in place. We need it because if we don't form it, someone else will. It won't be much longer—there just aren't any cities this size anymore that lack a House. It's only a matter of time before one of the big boys decides to unload a few of its more problematic members on King County. My money's on Chicago, since Atlanta is looking like a shitty bet these days—but it could just as easily be LA or San Francisco. Eventually, someone will notice that Seattle is unoccupied from an official standpoint. And then, my friends, we are going to be in trouble."

Isabelle nodded gravely. "Unless we do it first."

"That's right. We don't have to be the biggest or baddest House to work as a deterrent to would-be squatters. If we're openly present, we have to be challenged by anyone who wants to come in and start up a franchise."

Ian wasn't on board yet, but he had his pensive face on. "And that doesn't happen often. Not anymore. It's too costly, for everyone."

"Precisely. Best of all, in order to claim a House, all you need are three vampires willing to sit in a room together without killing one another." I pointed to myself. "One." And then to Ian. "Two." And to Isabelle. "Three."

Elizabeth frowned thoughtfully. "Then what about Adrian and me? What part do we have in this, or do we have one at all?"

"Good question. I bet you didn't know this—for that matter, not many vampires know it—but there's nothing on the books that says only vampires can be part of a vampire House." I saw Ian open his mouth to make an objection, but I prattled onward before he could interrupt. "Granted, it's usually *understood*. But who gives a damn? I say anyone who's capable of holding their own in such a House is welcome to be part of it. Some Houses might get the idea that we're disorganized and weak, but fuck 'em if they're that shortsighted. We're more like pirates than high society over here. Why would we turn away anyone with power or talent, purely because they don't match the undead criteria?"

No one argued. Everyone sat there looking at me. I had no idea what to do with so much undivided attention. It came along so rarely, after all.

"You guys *know* I'm right."

No one said anything. So I went ahead and opened the floor to questions.

"Anyone have anything they'd like to say? Any objections? Anyone not game? All you have to do is say so. I won't bully anyone to playing House with me. If everyone isn't on board, then it won't work. But I think it *can* work. I think we can finish the bottom three floors, beef up the building's security, and have ourselves something far cooler than a Buckhead McMansion."

Isabelle giggled. "I like this place better, yes," she said. "I like all the brick."

"Me too. I'm keen on brick. It's simple but effective."

Again I thought about a moat. Briefly, I pondered the particulars, and then sadly I discarded the idea.

"What do you say? Adrian? I've seen your apartment. It's tiny. You don't have room for yourself, much less yourself and Isabelle—but you two could have half the downstairs once we split it up and fix all the electrics. Elizabeth, these days you're on some of the same Most Wanted lists as me. I can help you set up a new identity, something solid that'll pass a closer inspection than mere airport security. And Ian—" I stopped there.

"Yes. Then Ian," he referred to himself in third person. "I'm your problem, Ray—not your solution. Remember? San Francisco wants to call me home to kill me, and if Maximilian finds out you're harboring me, your fledgling House will be over before it has a chance to stand on its own two feet."

"You're right. But now we get to the truly brilliant part of my brilliant plan."

In perfect time, Adrian and Ian both said, "Oh *no*."

"Knock it off, you two," I commanded. Behind me, I heard the service elevator clatter shut and begin its humming ascent. "Oh good, the kids are home."

Momentarily, Domino and Pepper appeared. Pepper drew back the gate, because Domino was carrying a puffed-up garbage bag.

The boy said, "Ray, that is without a doubt the most disgusting thing you've ever asked us to do."

"For free room and board? I think it's the *least* you can do. And no one's even been assigned the permanent role of litter box cleaner, so don't make any grand declarations just yet."

"Not it!" Pepper declared.

"You don't get to do that!" her brother immediately told her. "I carried a trash bag full of cigarette ashes all over Capitol Hill—"

"And I emptied out the containers!"

"Kids! You've both done disgusting things on my behalf tonight, and I thank you. I didn't mean to bring up the litter box. I'm sure we'll come to some fair arrangement later on. It'll wait for now, though. Get in here."

"They've been doing . . . what now?" Ian asked.

"Emptying public ashtrays," Pepper grumbled. "Raylene, I think I need a tetanus shot."

"You don't even know what tetanus is."

"Do you get it from fooling around with dirty metal things?"

"Very well. Vaccinations for everyone!" I announced with excessive glee.

"No! That's not what I meant! I was only kidding."

"Good," I said, though now she'd gotten me wondering. I looked at Pita, who didn't so much as crack an eye open to look back at me. Pets need vaccinations, don't they? Surely children do as well. Maybe it was the kind of thing I ought to look into.

Domino stomped into the room and dropped the garbage bag on the floor. It settled with a soft poofing gray cloud, but at least he'd thought to tie off the top.

Adrian wanted to know, "Why on earth were they cleaning out ashtrays?"

Ian caught on fast. He answered before I could.

"Because they're going to kill me."

15

Isabelle put the finishing touches on the box.

It was a nice box, roughly the size of an overnight case—the kind ladies used to carry, back before rolling carry-ons became the rage. Made of mahogany and polished to a pretty shine, it had a plaque screwed to the top. The plaque read:

Ian Stott
2011

Inside the box we'd stashed a plastic bag full of ashes, and in the process we'd gotten a dusting of the damn substance all over the place—thus Isabelle's final ministrations.

The corpse himself said from the foot of my bed, "This will never work."

"It'll totally work," I assured him.

"They'll never believe you."

"That's not the same thing." I was sitting at my computer desk where, yes, like an old-fashioned relic of a person I have a desktop computer. It's a nice one, with a slick flat-screen monitor. "They don't need to believe you're dead. They just need to know that you're not alive anymore. This is very simple, Ian."

"The best plans usually are."

"See, that's why I like you."

"Read it to me," he urged. "I want to hear it."

"Your own death notice?"

"Yes. I want to know what it says."

"It's a little long."

He said, "I don't care. I want to know what you're telling him."

Isabelle finished her polishing and came to stand behind me, so she could read over my shoulder.

I took a deep breath, and began to read.

To Maximilian Renner, Head of House,
San Francisco, California

I regret to inform you of the passing of your brother, Ian Stott Renner. Rather than return to your city and debate or duel with you for control of the House, he chose instead to immolate himself on the roof of a warehouse in downtown Seattle. This was witnessed by myself and one other, a representative of the O'Donnell House in Macon by the name of Clifford O'Donnell. With this correspondence we return his remains to you, to bury or store as you see fit.

In accordance with the old laws and statutes of which you are so fond, we must all consider this matter closed. I trust that you will henceforth leave Seattle and its new House to its own devices, without influence or interference.

However, I do not wish to close our correspondence without providing you a report of my findings while serving as your seneschal in Atlanta. You were kind enough to grant me the position, and I do not wish to seem rude or ungrateful. I have fulfilled my obligation by learning the truth about your father's death, and the role of the Barrington House therein.

In short, your father was killed by an intruder who'd come to settle a score with the House. Both the intruder and your father caught each other by surprise, and it is my best estimation that his murder was an accident of shock and self-defense. But this murder occurred within the Barringtons' home, and under their auspices. They went to great lengths to cover up the matter, including—as you know—making the claim of suicide, which was a low blow indeed.

Unless they've burned down the home or abandoned it, you should find the evidence you require in an upstairs bedroom of the Buckhead house. They've replaced the carpet and repainted the walls, but your father's blood still stains the place. It is a strike against their honor, and a nasty bit of subterfuge that—in my estimation—should not be allowed to stand.

And now for something that may prove a greater surprise than the Barrington treachery: The House is much weaker than is widely known. It has shrunk to a small family—the alpha pair and three children, plus a handful of assorted others. In my estimation, you are fully capable of extending your influence in their direction, in a violent, forceful manner that would absolutely prove successful with a minimum of effort on your part.

(In addition to your brother's remains, I am including a printout of the Barringtons' security system—current as of last week, but it may not remain so. I recommend you act quickly, if you do intend to act.)

If you would like confirmation or further details with regard to the family's status and standing, you should contact the Macon House and ask after my new friend (and fellow signer of this missive) Clifford O'Donnell, who moonlights as the Atlanta seneschal. It should tell you something that the Barringtons do not have one of their own, and Clifford is interested in relinquishing the position. He could prove a valuable ally.

I hope this concludes our professional obligations to each other, though if you have any questions or concerns, feel free to contact me at any time. You can reach me through the website on the letterhead.

Signed, Seattle Head of House Raylene Pendle
Witnessed: Clifford O'Donnell, Macon Head of House

"Well, what do you think?" I asked them both.

"Sounds very official," Ian said. "And O'Donnell agreed to sign this?"

"Just this evening. I'm going to email him a copy, he'll print it out and sign it, and scan it—then send it back."

"Sounds very roundabout."

"He's too busy to fly out here, and more's the pity. I think you'd like him."

"Because you do?"

"Because he's likable," I insisted. "And anyway, I swear, Ian. You worry too much."

"I worry just the right amount. *You're* the one prone to worrying too much."

I refreshed my email to see if Clifford had returned the letter yet. Nope. "I've got to tell you, I'm feeling pretty good about this. We've announced ourselves and staked our claim, and I'm checking my last P's and Q's regarding your new identity. All our bases are covered, baby. Now all we have to do is find your son and invite him on board—and maybe track down Jeffery Sykes for a little hellfire and brimstone."

Ian rolled his eyes. "Oh, is *that* all?"

I reached down to pat Pita's head and indulged an evil grin that went from ear to ear. "Trust me! This is going to be a piece of cake."

ABOUT THE AUTHOR

CHERIE PRIEST is the author of ten novels, including *Bloodshot* and the steampunk pulp adventures in the Clockwork Century series. Her 2009 book *Boneshaker* was nominated for both the Hugo Award and the Nebula Award; it was a PNBA Award winner and winner of the Locus Award for Best Science Fiction Novel. Cherie also wrote *Fathom* and the Eden Moore series from Tor (Macmillan), and three novellas published by Subterranean Press. In addition to all of the above, she is a newly minted member of the Wild Cards Consortium—and her first foray into George R. R. Martin's superhero universe, *Fort Freak* (for which she wrote the frame story), debuted in the summer of 2011. Cherie's short stories and nonfiction articles have appeared in such fine publications as *Weird Tales, Subterranean Magazine, Publishers Weekly*, and the Stoker-nominated anthology *Aegri Somnia* from Apex. Though she spent most of her life in the southeast, she presently lives in Seattle, Washington, with her husband and a fat black cat.

COMING SOON FROM CHERIE PRIEST:

THE EDEN MOORE SERIES
Eden Moore can see and communicate with ghosts. Knowing
that a dark secret lurks in her family history, she is determined
to find out the truth about her origins, no matter the cost.

Four and Twenty Blackbirds
Wings to the Kingdom
Not Flesh Nor Feathers

"Southern Gothic at its best. An absorbing
mystery told with humour and bite."
—Kelley Armstrong,
bestselling author of the *Women of the Otherworld* series

"Spooky and engrossing, this revenge play is as sticky as a
salmagundi made from blood and swamp dirt. Priest can
write scenes that are jump-out-of-your-skin scary."
— Cory Doctorow, author of *Makers*

"A creepy modern-day Southern gothic that doesn't rely
on cliché but delivers an emotionally powerful tale of self-
discovery and the supernatural." —*San Francisco Chronicle*

"The classic Southern gothic gets an edgy modern makeover …
Eden is a heroine for the aging Buffy crowd." — *Publishers Weekly*

Available in 2012.

WWW.TITANBOOKS.COM

AVAILABLE NOW:

BLOODSHOT:
THE FIRST CHESHIRE RED ADVENTURE!
By Cherie Priest

Raylene Pendle (AKA Cheshire Red), a vampire and world-renowned thief, doesn't usually hang with her own kind. She's too busy stealing priceless art and rare jewels. But when the infuriatingly charming Ian Stott asks for help, Raylene finds him impossible to resist—even though Ian doesn't want precious artifacts. He wants her to retrieve missing government files—documents that deal with the secret biological experiments that left Ian blind. What Raylene doesn't bargain for is a case that takes her from the wilds of Minneapolis to the mean streets of Atlanta. And with a psychotic, power-hungry scientist on her trail, a kick-ass drag queen on her side, and Men in Black popping up at the most inconvenient moments, the case proves to be one hell of a ride.

MORE FANTASTIC FICTION
FROM TITAN BOOKS:

ANGEL OF VENGEANCE:
The Story Which Inspired the TV Show "Moonlight"
By Trevor Munson

LA-based P.I. and vampire Mick Angel has been hired by a
beautiful red-headed burlesque dancer to find her missing sister.
But the apparently simple case of a teenage runaway is soon
complicated by drug dealers, persistent cops, murder and Mick's
own past. Mick must learn the hard way what every vampire should
know - nothing stays buried forever, especially not the past.

AVAILABLE NOW!

WWW.TITANBOOKS.COM